I0524099

Mario 7

Aftershock

Mario 7
Aftershock

by

George Hatcher

Warning
Adult matter

This book is intended for adults. Violence and sexual antics are not intended for minors, sensitive readers, or people living in the real world where there are sexually transmitted diseases which are incurable. Mario is a work of fiction. The people in the book lived and died only in my imagination. Any resemblance to actual people will be only in your imagination. The story is purely a product of long plane flights, random flights of fantasy, the wild goose-chasing of ideas like what if this (or that) happened on top of my experience in wrongful death cases. Like Mario, I am no lawyer. I do not employ nubile sex groupies, or toss people out of high rise buildings when they get on my nerves.

This is a work of fiction. All of the characters, organizations and events portrayed in this novel are either products of the author's imagination or used fictitiously. Any resemblance to actual events, to persons living or dead, is purely coincidental.

This book can be purchased at over 39,000 bookstores and libraries including brick and mortar stores, and online, in print and digital, including Apple, Kindle and Audible formats. Casa Hatcher Press books are available at special quantity discounts for bulk purchases, for sales promotions, premiums, educational use or fund raising.

Casa Hatcher Press is an imprint of
Pretty Face, Inc.
225 South Lake Avenue Suite 300
Pasadena, CA 91101

For details, contact:

Casa Hatcher Press.
http://casahatcherpress.com
(818) 519-2976
Mario 7: Aftershock

Copyright © 2019 by George Hatcher

All rights reserved.
Printed in Pasadena, CA, United States of America.
No part of this book may be used in any manner except in the case of brief quotations in critical articles or reviews.

Book and Cover Designed by Casa Hatcher Press
Cover photos
© revleha /Adobe Stock
© 2mmedia /Adobe Stock
©ZoomTeam/Adobe Stock
© George Hatcher
Interior photos
© George Hatcher

Mario 7: Aftershock by George J. Hatcher
First Edition July 2019
Library of Congress Control Number: 2019944243
ISBN: 978-0-9983762-8-8 (Hardback)
ISBN: 978-0-9983762-9-5 (Paperback)
ISBN: 978-1-7332351-0-5 (E-book)
R: 20190717

George and Molly 1968

To my one and only.
My inspiration.
My past.
My present.
My future.
My Molly.

Acknowledgements

If it were up to my editor, Allie Bates, this book would still be in edits. I had to pry it out of her grip while she was still marking up. Every pass makes it a little better, she says. Just let me proofread it one more time, she says.

Works by George Hatcher

Ambulance Chaser Series
Mario 1: Woman in Jeopardy
Mario 2: Coming of Age
Mario 3: Risky Business
Mario 4: Free Fall
Mario 5: Afire
Mario 6: Marked
Mario 7: Aftershock

Coming Soon
Mario 8
Arabe
Gabi
One Wilshire (revised)

Prologue
Pasadena January 1987
Mario

On January tenth, Olga and Camila arrived at the Rome house and contacted me. After that, nothing. The girls and I were back in Pasadena, dark and sad over Pepe's death. The funeral had left me exhausted. Pixie left for Mexico City to prepare for a tour in South America. I missed her by three days. In the weeks that followed, I tried calling Olga twice, but she didn't answer. It felt strange not to be anticipating Pepe's next phone call.

Seventeen days later, Olga finally called. "Pack your bags mi Amor," Olga said. "We have plans to make. You're coming to Milan."

Chapter 1
Pasadena January 28, 1987
Letty

"I don't know why we can't go. What could be so secret?" I was pissed.

Across from me at the big table in Casa Luna's conference room, Tangles uncrossed her legs, nudged me with her tennis shoe, and flopped her feet down on the highly polished surface. The staff keeps the house spotless. I could smell the lemon oil coming off of the furniture and knocked her feet off the tabletop. She stuck her tongue out at me. We were on the speakerphone with Pixie, who is our third sister from another mother, even though she's a diva now, and flies around the US and Spanish-speaking countries making her voice famous.

"Oh, relax, bitch," Pixie said. "He's probably coming right back. You're with him twenty-four hours, Monday thru Sunday. You're so greedy."

She's right. I am always with him when he's in town. I attend his every need, even before he asks. I have it covered. He's the center of my life.

"Something is going on," Tangles said. "Olga and Camila were out of touch for more than two weeks, then Olga snaps her fingers, and he orders his plane to be ready in four hours. Destination? Milan."

Pixie laughed. I pictured her sitting cross-legged in her hotel suite in Cancun, or where ever the hell her concert was. "You sound jealous, both of you. You have your own apartments and that great big palace of a house to live the life of Riley in. You have free rein in my house across the street. What else do you want already?"

"I want to be like you," Tangles said.

"Who doesn't?" I asked, as Tangles closed her eyes dreamingly. I gave her a shove, knocking her kicks off the table again, and her eyes popped open.

"The cost of fame is a whole bunch of loneliness. I'm alone on tour all the time. I miss you guys," Pixie said.

"Just you and a couple thousand people every night. You love it," I laughed even though my heart twisted a little inside. She is alone out there, and I miss her too.

"Yeah, you love it," Tangles agreed with a giggle of her own.

"I do love it." Pixie laughed until we all chimed in. "But I still miss you two."

"Dial Lainie's cell," I said to Tangles after we hung up. "She's two hours ahead of us."

Pixie's daughter, Lainie, had earned fame of her own with her pop songs. Like her mother, she can play any instrument she's handed. Their record company RIALTO pushed Pixie more in Central and South America, and Lainie more in the United States. Seems like they spend all of their time on the road now.

Pixie and Lainie are more than musicians and singers in Spanish and English. They are both performance wizards. They make magic. Lainie's music videos are gobbled up by fans everywhere. Lainie's new handle Bebé caught on quickly. Lainie digs the name. Me, I just wonder why they didn't use her real name, Elena, after Boss's mom.

Milan January 28, 1987
Mario

I sat next to Olga in the family room on the first floor of the grand Milan villa and ravished her with kisses while Camila looked on, smiling and clapping. I did not say it aloud, but the Milan house brings back memories of Pepe and his girl Caprice, and how they had hosted me here twice.

"You should have brought the girls," Camila said, referring to Letty and Tangles. The girls are members of my team and usually go everywhere I do.

"On the way to Italy, I wished Letty and Tangles were with me at least fifty times. It's a long flight alone. I will bring them next time," I said. I especially missed Letty. "You wanted me here pronto, so I'm here."

"We want you to take over the leasing company," Olga said.

I wasn't sure I heard right. I sat there with a Tommie Lee Mötley Crüe drumroll thundering in my chest unable to breathe. To use one of Sami's words because it's the only one that captures the feeling, I was gobsmacked.

"I'm flattered, but I know zero about running a plane leasing company. I am still learning how to find planes for Pepe…for GAL[1] to buy."

"I knew you'd say that," Olga said. "What you don't know, you'll pick up along the way. Who else would we trust for this but you?"

"When Pepe bought the small airline in Colombia, he didn't know anything about running an airline, but in two years, he took over three other operators and went international. Pepe didn't know a damn thing about leasing planes at first either, but he leased all the planes from his airline and then some in a short period of time," Camila said.

"Should we have some wine?" I asked. My heart was still racing.

"Lots of wine, but later," Olga said.

"Fuck," I said. I hopped up, walked a lap around the elegantly furnished room, and sat down.

---

[1] Global Aircraft Leasing

"We're going to get to that, too," Olga said with a laugh.

"We have two people, Jules and Andrea, at work for the leasing company," Camila said. "They know the ins-and-outs of aircraft leasing. Pepe's headhunter snatched them from two major leasing companies. Though he would never have admitted it, Pepe bounced everything he did off these two before he made any final decisions. I know...I knew my brother. He learned from the best. He fed on their expertise."

Olga nudged me. "Pepe used to say that you are the same way," she said. "You reminded him of himself."

Camila laughed. "He said you reminded him of himself, but that as smart as you are, he was smarter."

Olga and I joined in Camila's laughter.

"He was absolutely correct," I said. "He was a lot smarter than me."

"Amor, running this company will be the same as when you purchase an asset for LAI.² You make purchasing decisions, then use company money to close the deal. You will just be buying assets with wings."

I hadn't accepted or refused the offer, but I could feel my face frozen in shock.

Camila's eyes narrowed at me. "What's the difference? Is it the responsibility you are worried about?"

"I wouldn't call it worry. I don't know the business."

I felt a pressure on my arm and turned to Olga.

"Amor," Olga said. "We love you no matter your decision. Come with us to the office. Look around. Talk to the people we have working there. Meet Jules and Andrea."

"Of course, I'll do that, hands down."

Olga and Camila exchanged a smile.

"Let's eat," Olga got up, and affixed herself to my left side. "Wait till you see what was prepared for my Prince."

---

² Latin American Investments

I felt a pinch on my butt. Camila gave me a look that was anything but innocent and took my free arm.

It was cold in Milan but not inside. At ten at night, Camila, Olga, and I swam some hard laps in the indoor pool, then slowed. Their mood had lightened, leaving the somberness behind in Paris where we all had been waiting for Pepe when we got the call that he had died, and in Bogota in the family crypt where Pepe had been laid to rest. We played around, floated on our backs, treaded water, and splashed around. The indoor swimming pool was too warm for my taste but wonderful. We wore robes to the sauna, then to the wine room where Camila lit a joint. Temperature-wise, it was pretty cool adjoining the wine cellar in one of the older parts of the house, in a basement that might have been hundreds of years old. We'd baked long enough in the sauna that we welcomed the chill. Olga asked for one of my favorite reds, an Argentinian wine. With three bottles in hand, a houseman emerged through a couple of heavy wooden doors. He put one red on the table, and opened the other, filling Olga's glass and my own. He poured champagne for Camila and went upstairs to fetch a tray of cheeses. For me, the atmosphere of the huge old property was tinged with the mystery of all its unexplored rooms and long history, nowhere more evident than here at this scarred table and well-worn wood and stone.

Camila raised her glass. The three of us clicked and drank and smoked.

"What did you do all those days I couldn't reach you? Was it your way to mourn?" Those seventeen days with no word from either of them had been hard on me. Maybe they'd been overcome with grief. "If it's too personal, don't answer."

"We plotted our future without Pepe," Olga said. "We made some decisions."

"We made the decision that you were the person to head the leasing company. That will be a huge moneymaker for all of us," Camila said.

"We needed to be away from everything." Olga took a long sip of wine.

Milan January 28, 1987
Olga

I cried for Pepe but only when Camila was stupid enough to cry for the bastard. Mourn? Mario, if you only knew what a prick he was. You wouldn't be talking so nice about him. I hope the explosion didn't take him out too quickly. I hope he suffered. He deserved it.

During the past few weeks, I bared the entire financial picture of Camacho assets for Camila—hundreds of bank accounts in several hundred banks worldwide. Only I know the details. Pepe had known how much money came in and from where, but he never questioned where I parked the cash. Smart as they are, they both needed me then. Camila needs me even more now.

Milan January 28, 1987
Mario

Olga's face had a strange expression.

"Baby, are you okay?"

"Let me have another hit of that joint," Olga said, sitting up. "I'm fine. Amor, are you getting tired? Want to hit the bedroom?"

"I'm good. I slept on the plane." There's nine hours difference between Milan and Pasadena, but I wasn't feeling it.

We raised our glasses and clicked again.

I was feeling mellow. I love the ambiance of the tasting room. The weed and wine hit me, and I was mesmerized by the ancient red brick floor patterned with two kinds of brick that formed rectangles in squares in rectangles, with the inner bricks all at an angle, and varnished to a high sheen. Candles were lit behind me, torches on the table, and the electric chandelier had candle-shaped bulbs that seemed very bright. The pot smoke overwhelmed the scent of burning wax. I was sinking deep in a soft chair at the head of the table, facing the cellar doors, getting higher, spellbound by the room. Olga and Camila were at either side of me, facing each other, in padded dining room chairs that had extra cushions, and checked cloths looped over the headrests.

On the table, the houseman left a board of cheeses and other goodies for us to nibble. Solid oak table, stained to match the tones of the floor, well varnished, decades or maybe even centuries old. Not that big, but it was about as big as the room could comfortably hold. I drank more wine. I used the square paper napkins as coasters and got lost in counting thirty-four bricks going up to the center of the ceiling, thirty-four going down the other wall. The chill of the room made its way into my loopy head, and I stifled a yawn. It wasn't jet lag, but I was reeling from the wine and pot.

Olga noticed.

"Let's go to bed, Amor. You're drifting."

"Amor, wait," Camila stopped us. "Andrea is on her way over. Let her meet our prince before you to bed."

I laughed at the mention of prince again and pretended to adjust a crown on my head.

"I didn't know she was coming over," Olga said.

"I don't want to sleep alone tonight," Camila said, hugging the cushion that had been on her chair.

I expect Camila and Olga had been sharing a bed until my arrival, no big deal for them or for me.

We did not get up. A houseman led Andrea down to join us. He offered Olga and me refills of Argentinian red, but we both declined. He poured Andrea some. Andrea was about my age. She had a Roman nose, and was heavily made up as was the trend, but she would have been pretty without it. She shook my hand firmly. We did the European air-kiss thing, both cheeks. She smelled of grapes, but maybe it was the room.

"You are the plane finder."

"You are the leasing whiz," I said. "And way too young and pretty to be a leasing whiz."

"Also, I am not a boy."

I laughed at that. "You are definitely not a boy."

"Ah, you see, in Italy, Andrea is a boy's name. But I am named for my

American grandmother who is also not a boy."

"Lucky for us," Camila said.

Andrea turned to face me. "You are the best. Pepe loved you."

"And I loved him."

There it was again. Every conversation led to Pepe. Camila interrupted what was about to turn sad.

"Andrea, they were just going to bed, but we wanted Mario to meet you. We are planning for you and Mario and Jules to have a long discussion about the company tomorrow."

"Looking forward to that," Andrea said with a big smile.

Camila put her arm around Andrea's waist and a full wine glass in Andrea's hand.

"We will see you in the morning," she said.

Olga and I held hands all the way to our suite, showered off the pool, sauna, and wine room, and slid between the sheets. I had my hands full with Olga alone, but my mind was full of Camila and Andrea with us. I knew that somewhere in the villa, Camila and Andrea would not be sleeping.

Andrea was hot.

Milan January 29, 1987
Olga

He's controlling how much of his weight is against my body, so I am not crushed. I want to be crushed. It's been too long. Why do we let so much time come between us?

"Amor, put that big body of yours on top of me. Crush me. Hurry, Amor, hurry."

I've known many men who are as big as he is down there, but none of them come close to going as long, or as many times as my Mario. He's a sex freak. I'm always sex starved. The more I get, the more I want.

Everyone fucks. Swinging is in even with AIDS rearing its head. The people I know still fuck all they want. I don't care who he fucks as long as he doesn't flip out for the pussy that spreads her legs for him. I don't fuck anyone that will think of it as serious. I expect him to do the same.

I'm usually on top, but he knows exactly how I like it when he's on top. His hands cup my ass, squeezing as he pushes deep. He slowly pulls out, almost out, but not all the way, just enough so that when he pushes in, I feel the length and thickness all the way in.

My hands are all over his muscular body. His washboard abs rub my stomach.

"I adore you, Amor," I speak into his mouth as his body moves against mine.

"I love you, Olga."

"Amor, I'm going to come. Say my name, again, and again. Tell me you love me, Amor...."

Pasadena January 29, 1987
Letty

My uncle is Mario's chef at Casa Luna. When Mario is away, there is very little for Uncle Miguel to do, so he reads and works out and takes it easy. I have a room in the main house. He lives in the personnel quarters at the back of the property with the rest of the help. Sunny and the two couples there cook for themselves, so Miguel has no one to cook for other than himself and me. When he cooks just for us, it's a family thing, not a chef thing.

Mario's kitchen is the biggest ever. Walk-in refrigerator. Walk-in freezer. More refrigerators and freezers, like you expect to see in a hotel or restaurant or something. We cozy up and eat at the island, thirty square feet of granite that serves as a prep place for pasta or pastries, and you will never prove it is more than a single piece of rock. Uncle Miguel says I'm a great cook, but it's baking pastries that I love to get into, especially when he isn't hovering over my shoulder and guarding 'his' kitchen.

"Fuck me." Tangles walked in the kitchen. "You're making the damn chunky cookies."

"Right, you don't have to eat any and yeah, I'll fuck you." I was breaking Hershey almond bars into a stainless bowl. The secret of chunky cookies is the chocolate. Nothing works better than almond Hershey bars. Hand broken, big chunks.

"You don't have a dick, bitch. How would you fuck me?"

"You know how," I yelled over the MTV blasting from the TV hanging from the ceiling.

"You are so nasty," Tangles said, laughing, taking a seat on a stool across from me.

"Stop egging me on with sex. You'll get me horny, bitch."

"You sound like Pixie."

"I want to sound like Pixie," I said.

"I'm going to have some of your cookies, but we need to do a double work out."

"Deal," I said.

"We are wasting our lives," Tangles said. We were still in the kitchen, cookie tray between us, empty milk glasses.

"Speak for yourself. I love being here," I said.

"I know you do, and so do I. But."

"But what? You always start up with this shit. If you're unhappy, split. You have money in the bank. You own your car. You have an apartment. Go find your knight in a shiny suit or whatever the fuck you are looking for."

"Fuck. Listen to you. You get so rattled."

A refill of milk and a cookie later, Tangles moved around the counter to sit by me.

"You want me to lick the chocolate from you?"

Tangles nodded, crushed a broken cookie, rubbed her lips with the dust, and presented me a crumbly smile.

"Dig it. You do me. I do you."

We kissed. I sucked the cookie from her lips.

"If anyone saw us, they'd say we were dykes," Tangles said, lips on mine.

"Who the fuck cares who says what? What would you do about it?"

"I would kick their motherfucking ass!" Tangles said.

She had made it to her first black belt. I was working on my third. Pixie was holding steady at five.

We separated, did a high five, and jumped off the stools to head to the lower floor, where we started off with weights. Then we put on our dojo t-shirts and baggy pants. Mine says 'Bringing my mojo to the dojo' on the front and 'Ninja Trainee' on the back. Hers says 'Heading for black, don't look back.' We switched to karate for an hour or so. I am proficient in karate and taekwondo. Tangles likes taekwondo and is getting good.

Milan January 29, 1987
Mario

The GAL office building is at least a hundred years old and beautiful. The leasing company office is at the top of the eight-story building, like the jewel in the crown. I got a tour of the floor, far too much space for the small staff of eleven. The interior reminds me of Oscar's plush space in the Crocker Bank tower in downtown Los Angeles.[3]

"Plenty of room to grow," Jules said. He and Andrea had spent five minutes individually reviewing their resumes for me. Olga, Camila, and Andrea took me on rounds of the place before our joint meeting in the conference room. Olga and Camila betrayed no emotion when they opened a door to Pepe's office. Andrea got a little weepy but remained in control. The conference room reminds me of conference rooms found in a typical lawyer's office. Not bad, but not in the same league as the conference room in my home. We sat at one end of the table, Camila at the head, Olga on her right, me on her left. Jules sat by Olga facing Andrea who was next to me. I fired off my questions.

"Have you leased any planes yet using the bank consortium?"

The consortium had agreed to pick up fifty or sixty percent on leases

---

[3] Oscar was a lawyer whose big firm handled aviation cases that I took to him. RIP, Oscar. He'd been shot getting out of his car. His bodyguard managed to kill the shooters. The case went unsolved. The police were convinced paid assassins had been involved.

that Pepe didn't want to finance out of his own deep pockets. Pepe had told me that once the leasing company was going full barrel and the consortium was in place, unlimited financing would be available.

"Not yet," Jules said. "Every lease we have on the books was financed entirely by GAL. I was not instructed how to use consortium funds."

"I have an operator interested in three new Boeing 727s. Pepe said it was one for the consortium," Andrea said. "I'm in the same boat as Jules. No instructions on consortium financing."

"Not a problem," Olga said. "We'll cross that bridge when we come to it."

"Let's say you lease a used Australian plane to an operator in Buenos Aires. Who does the paperwork?"

Jules said, "We do it here. A law firm in Milan looks over what we prepare and makes changes when needed, and that's it."

"What country's law are you using in the paperwork?" I asked.

"Good question, Mr. Luna," Andrea said. "The lawyers tell us what law is best to use. If we use Italian law, the operator travels here to sign the lease. If the law is Argentinian, as in your example, we send the paperwork for signature before a notary public there."

"How many planes do you have ready to lease right now?"

"We only have six planes not in use. Their leases are currently in negotiation. They will soon be gone."

"Where are you keeping the planes when you have inventory?"

"A small airport here in Milan," Andrea said. "They have a certified maintenance company that has been working well for us, and we keep our inventory there."

"How do you get customers?"

"We advertise in a number of global airline magazines. Very little advertising. Pepe was already known for his airline. Potential lessees would call to see if he had a plane to lease out. I think that's how he got started with it.

Word of mouth. We get calls all the time," Jules said.

"Our fixed overhead is small. Right now, we have sixty-one leases. I believe if we had more used planes, we could lease them out," Andrea said.

"The leases bring in a hundred percent or more in profit," Jules said.

The return on my apartments was nothing close. I was getting a nice monthly payment on my own plane that I had leased out, thanks to Pepe.

"The leasing company I worked with only handled used planes," Andrea said. "In my opinion, that's where the money is. With new planes, you sometimes have to wait a long time for delivery. And in the meantime, a chunk of money tied up. The risk is greater than with a used plane."

"Where I came from, we did used aircraft, but we also did new planes," Jules countered. "Mostly planes made in France. Big returns." He gestured with his hands wide apart. "Big."

Jules didn't have the numbers handy to support his big returns comment. He wanted to show me he knew more than Andrea. I knew from his initial introduction that he had more years in the business.

"Do we still have a deal with the consortium?" I asked.

"I'm not privy to that," Jules said.

"Nor I," Andrea said.

Olga said, "I'll fly to Portugal next week and meet with Felipe Carrera."

That must be Riana Vas's father, the banker who'd put the consortium together for Pepe.

"Do what you must to keep him happy," Camila said.

"Of course," Olga agreed.

Jules did a good job of being temporarily hard of hearing.

"Did he show for the funeral?" I asked.

"He called a number of times," Olga said. "I told him not to worry about it. Riana was there on his behalf."

Riana Vas was Olga's travel companion. They flew to places where Olga did business on behalf of LAI. Only she and Camila knew everything she had going worldwide. Riana was just along for the ride. She didn't know anything about the business. Olga was happy to have her along.

"If Riana's father backs out because Pepe is no longer in charge, what is the ceiling? How many more planes can we buy and lease out?" I asked, looking from Camila to Olga.

"He won't kill the deal," Olga said. "It's a sweet deal."

"Pepe had a great idea when he came up with that," I said. "It's like me putting up half the money on a lease GAL wants to do, then we split the income from lease payment."

"Exactly," said Camila. "Don't worry about money. *Al Diablo con*[4] Riana's father if he backs out. I'm not my brother. We have the money to continue doing it alone."

"He won't back out," Olga insisted.

Milan January 29, 1987
Olga

I first met Riana's father in Portugal. He was sixty something, a sharp dresser, well-mannered, a banker right off the high society page. I had already transferred money by wire to open two bank accounts. I had millions more in cash to deposit. I just wanted to drop off large sums of cash into the two accounts monthly, or more often if he'd let me get away with it. I met him in a huge suite.

Hotels do not impress me. I have seen them all. His suite was a penthouse apartment in Portugal with a bedroom fit for a queen. Our first meeting, I was with him two hours. That old warrior had a bat between his legs that still worked. I closed my eyes and let him do it. The next week I dropped off ten million dollars in suitcases to his bank office. Had another penthouse meeting with him overnight. Soon after, I met his daughter Riana who was in a troubled marriage. In a short time, she and I became friends.

Pepe had the idea to go into aircraft leasing. After we'd done a lot of cash business with Felipe Carrera's bank, Carrera agreed to put a consortium

---

[4] To the devil with

together to finance a portion of the aviation leases. He never made another at-tempt to get me to bed, perhaps because I became such good friends with Riana, or perhaps because Riana was totally off cocaine when she was with me. He encouraged Riana to accompany me. After she started traveling with me, she filed for a divorce. Early on, I confessed to Riana that I had had sex with her father and why.

Riana laughed and asked me if he was any good.

"You'd be proud of your daddy," I told her. "Don't be offended. Not sure why I told you."

"Oh, please. I know my dad. If I wasn't his daughter, he'd hit me up for sure."

It's a small world. Her story reminded me of Camila's. Riana's father was a dog but not as bad as Camila's father. Camila's mother caught her father in the act of molesting Camila. That same night, Camila's mom killed her father. That's when Pepe took over the business.

Old history.

Milan January 29, 1987
Mario

"If I come in, who will hunt for planes?" I asked. "Kinko?"[5]

Olga nodded. "Amor, it's up to you who hunts for planes or what planes you buy. You can hop around the globe looking for planes, too."

"The office will run under your direction, but you have Jules and Andrea to assist," Camila said.

"Is this the plan? To have Mr. Luna come in?" Jules asked.

"He hasn't committed yet," Camila said for me.

Jules looked as if he had just left the conversation. I didn't know him well enough to measure his reaction. I wondered if he'd expected to step into Pepe's shoes. I wanted to see more of his responses.

---

[5] Kinko owned or leased a thousand acres in the high desert near Los Angeles where planes were stored temporarily, or as used parts, and for sale. An aviation bone yard. He had hangers there for mainte-nance and plane restoration. He was a fabulous asset to me in finding airplanes for GAL to lease out.

"Jules, running an operation like this is way above my head. If I take this on, GAL will need you, and I will need you. The first thing I'll do is review your employment package and see how much room I have to give you an increase in compensation." I looked at Andrea. "Same goes for you. Is there a reason why GAL has to be headquartered here in Milan?" I asked.

Jules and Andrea looked blank. Both of them glanced over at Camila.

"No reason," Camila said.

"Pepe opened the office here because he loved his house here, and the people. He was comfortable in Italy. He loved Milan," Olga said.

"How much is the rent for this big space?" I asked.

"Amor, Pepe bought the building years ago," Camila said.

Why was I not surprised?

"We have no vacancies," Olga said.

Dinner that night was Mexican food in the wine-tasting room.

"Amor, we know you love Mexican," Olga said.

"We do too," Camila said, munching away at a soft beef taco.

"What did you think?" Olga asked for the third time since we left the office.

I took a bite of my carne asada smothered with pico de gallo and considered her words.

"If I do this, what's in it for me?"

"What do you want to be in it for you?" Camila asked.

"Six hundred thousand for the first year against ten percent of the net profit. If our net profit is ten million the first year, you get one million minus the six hundred thousand you were already paid," Olga said, getting the negotiations rolling.

I didn't stop eating, but I did look up from my taco for a few seconds.

"No way. You gotta to be dreaming. I make that kind of money on one big plane crash. I make double that and more buying assets for you in the US, and that's not including what you pay me to find used planes."

"Amor, so what do you want?" Olga asked.

My tacos were gone. I looked at the two ladies who were trying to screw me with this proposal.

"You really want to know what I want?"

"Yes," Camila said.

Olga nodded.

"I want to fuck both of you."

Camila has a way of screaming with glee. She squealed, took the napkin from her lap, and placed it on the table. "Si, Amor, count me in."

Olga ignored Camila. "Amor, we just ate," she said. "We want you, too. After."

"After what?" I was teasing now, still in my seat, watching Camila who looked ready to spring out of her chair, charge up the stairs, and get busy.

"After we make a deal. We want you to start right away, Amor. This is serious."

"Tell me about the ten percent," I said.

Olga looked happy at my response. "If we lease a plane for one hundred thousand a month and the costs are twenty-five thousand, you get ten percent of seventy-five thousand."

"Amor, do the math. You will make a lot of money," Camila joined in.

"What about the planes that are already leased out?" I asked.

"Amor, you want a piece of what we have on the books?" Camila asked.

"Of course. If I'm in, I will have those accounts on my plate. I'm making a good chunk of change buying planes. Under the agreement, I make ten percent of what we buy the plane for and five percent if the cost is a million or more. What happens to that?"

"Amor, you're making fifty thousand a month base pay no matter what. It's going to be more because the ten percent will add up."

"All my life, I have done what I want when I want to do it. I'm going to lose the ability. Between aviation cases, hunting planes for you, and acquiring assets for GAL, I already make more money than you are offering me."

"Amor, I promise, you don't have to punch a time clock." Olga laughed. So did Camila.

"I have another problem. I must know what I'm making. Simple math. The cost you apply to each lease to get the net amount will govern how much my ten percent is. That will never work."

"Eight percent of the gross amount that comes in on each lease." Camila said.

"So, the net is out?" I asked.

"Yes, out."

"That's on top of the six hundred thousand a year, right? The six hundred thousand cannot be a draw against a percentage. The six hundred is my base pay."

The silence stretched on for a minute.

"Okay, you got it," Camila said. "You have the percentage on top of the base pay, and that includes the leases already on the books."

Olga smiled. We are going to get married someday, but I couldn't read her. Was she happy for me?

"I'll give it everything I have," I said. "But I must warn you, my commitment at this rate is for one year."

"Two years," Camila said, still negotiating. "We can review the deal in two years. I promise you will be happy with what comes next."

I hesitated. The deal would be good for me as long as I could lease a bunch of planes. I had so much to learn about this business.

"Okay," I said. "What happens when I want to take on an airline crash?"

"Amor, you don't need that anymore." Camila looked surprised that I would bring up the topic.

"I have a handshake deal with the attorney who is getting my cases. If he figures out that I'm not sending him any more business, what will happen to his incentive on the cases I have pending with him? I can never enforce a handshake deal because I'm not a lawyer, but I'm not sure I'm ready to give it up."

Olga knows about my deal. "When a case settles, he gets thirty percent of whatever the lawyer gets in attorney fees," she explained to Camila.

"*Muy Bueno*. Why would he not live up to his agreement?" she asked. "He has the cases. It's not like you're married for life."

We finished eating, deferred dessert, and drank more wine.

"I'm going to be busy handling the business Pepe used to take care of. Olga will be very busy. You are a natural fit here," Camila said. "We need to know that the leasing company will be taken care of. If not, we keep the leases we have and phase out the business. Planes are a bigger investment than anything we've done in the past, even if the banks finance a portion. A plane costs five, ten or more million."

"Amor, no pressure. It's not like we are going to lose anything already invested. Jules says the leases we have are good. If you opt out, we just won't get any more planes after we lease the six that we have sitting," Olga said.

This was no bluff. They were ready to walk. If they walked, I would lose the income from buying planes. Who knew if they would want me to continue buying businesses property for LAI?

"What happens if I recommend that we move the operation to the United States?"

"The bankers may not like that," Olga said.

"We don't even know if the bankers are still in the deal," Camila said in rapid Spanish. "Olga and I already discussed that if you accept the deal, you may want to have the business at home in Pasadena. We are okay with that. This business can be anywhere. We have taxes to pay here or there. Location doesn't matter to us."

Olga stood, and I along with her.

"Amor, try it here in Milan for a while," Olga said. She hugged me from behind and kissed my neck. "Bring the girls to work with you. Live in this house."

"Consider it your home away from home," Camila said. "We won't be here."

They had homes of their own all over the world. This one had been Pepe's.

"If you are here in Milan, I will see you more often because it is closer to where I travel the most. You can fly to Pasadena whenever you want, just as I do," Olga said.

"As the CEO of GAL, you will have no more plane expenses. Fly in one of our planes or your own, and GAL foots the bill," Camila said.

I loved that fringe benefit. Considering how much time I spent in the air, the savings could add up to more than my base pay. Camachos sure know how to bait a hook.

"There is something else," I said. "When we review in two years, we negotiate how much twenty-five percent of the company will cost me. That goes in the contract."

"We will look at the company value and come up with a figure. I won't commit to twenty-five percent," Camila said, rubbing her chin.

I frowned. Said nothing.

"We never have partners, but you are family. I will look out for you, I promise, Amor," Camila said.

"Amor," Olga said, grimacing, pretending pain. "Roll with what we have agreed on so far. There is plenty of time to buy in."

"One more thing, Amor," Camila interrupted. "Find us two new planes a little bigger than your Falcon. Jules says Dassault has a bigger model."

"I've been telling Olga to do that forever," I said. "It never made sense to me, you two flying around in those huge airliners. I'll find you two Falcons, heavier, with a longer range than mine, and room for big beds like you like. Why the change?"

"With my brother out of the picture, we may not need the big planes. It's not for sure, but look around for us," Camila said.

Camila didn't say which of Pepe's activities she was abandoning. For that matter, she wasn't saying what she was taking over either. It wasn't the right time to ask. Her explanation would have to do. Fuck, my imagination just doesn't stop. I had long suspected Pepe was packing their planes with cocaine, not that I ever saw anything of the kind. My random opinion did not mean the walls and niches were or weren't packed with the stuff. One day, I'm just going to ask them, but in the middle of wrestling out our agreement is not the right time for nosy questions.

"Do we have a deal, Amor?" Olga nuzzled me from behind, nibbling at my ear.

"I may have missed a thing or two," I kidded. With Olga's lips busy on me, I was perfectly aware I was being 'handled,' but I consider it a fringe benefit. "I'd say we have a deal."

"We're going to be so rich," Olga said in my ear, not in a whisper.

"You're already rich," I said.

"Amor, let's celebrate like Americans. You can have Olga and me, or I can call Andrea to come over, and the four of us can have a party."

"That's how Americans celebrate?" I laughed aloud.

"You want that girl?" Olga's lips on my ear tickled.

"Do you?" I asked.

"I've never been with her, but there's a first time for everything."

"She's wonderful," Camila said.

I called my used plane dealer, Kinko, to tell him about my taking over the leasing company.

"I trust you, Kinko. I know you're busy running your own business, but

I need to count on you. I need a steady source of used planes."

Kinko laughed. "I love your type of currency. I can use it. Count me in."

He meant green cash. Unless something changed with Pepe's death, the Camachos had countless supplies of green. I had intended to call home to speak to Letty but waited another day because I still had decisions to make. Did I want to bring Letty and Tangles to Milan? Betty? Would we be safer in Milan or at home? Was someone still after me? The safety of my team is my biggest worry. As for me, if my stalker can take me down, I deserve to die. I have reason to worry about those I love. I lost Tanis because someone was gunning for me. I can't let it happen again.

February 1, 1987

Three days later, I was on my plane headed home with no plan to dismiss any of my employees that worked at the house, including the overkill security. Everyone is family to me.

Pasadena February 2, 1987

Letty and Tangles were at Van Nuys Airport when I landed. As soon as the stairs were pushed up to my jet, one of the pilots opened the door, and I was out of there. Both girls ran up to hug and kiss me and make a fuss. I felt their love, Letty's especially. I was like someone who was dying from thirst, suddenly able to drink deeply. I hadn't even known I was thirsty. Tangles was pretty, but the February sun kissed Letty's face like a halo. Her hair smelled like spring. Her scent moved me. I hadn't realized until I saw her how hungry I'd been for just a glimpse of her face.

I've had drivers, but now I don't. Letty was my driver at one time. Raul is Pixie's driver. He lives at her house across the street from me. I have a Rolls. Pixie has a bigger Rolls. When I need a driver, and Pixie is out of town, Raul drives me.

"I asked him to drive us so we could fuck the daylight out of you on the way home, Boss," Letty said.

I could think of quite a few times we'd done just that when Johnson was driving. Johnson had been my friend and Melina's chauffeur, gunned down in a parking lot. Melina had just barely survived the attack. Water under the bridge.

I shook hands with Raul. He wore a military looking uniform, very severe, something he'd started after Pixie started getting famous, and crowds started gathering at the gates. He always looks important, and like he means business. His greeting was formal and serious. He gave a crisp little bow, shut the door, and put my luggage in the trunk. In a few moments, we were on our way. The window between Raul and our compartment was up, so we had our privacy, or at least the illusion of it.

"Are we going to do it?" Tangles asked, unknotting my tie.

Black silk tie, something I'd picked up in Milan. No color, but a subtle pattern was embroidered on it. The slick fabric rasped against my cheek, and I heard more than felt it. I needed a shave. The back seat was nice and warm, and I was feeling cozy nestled between them. I touched the side of Letty's face. Silk purer than the damn tie. I had to shave before we got frisky.

"Babies, hang on till we get home," I said, putting my arms around them. They were bundled up in bulky jackets, boots over leggings. "You have too many clothes on."

"And the drive is too short," Tangles said, leaving my tie loose.

"Then let's smooch," Letty said. She turned toward me and put her hand to my cheek, mimicking my gesture. "Mm. Scruffy is sexy."

"Let me in, bitch," Tangles said, turning me to face her.

"You're the bitch."

Milan has a lot of women, but I cannot live there without Letty.

My present masseuse, Betty, once turned her clients over to Tangles and came to work for me. After a while, she said she couldn't handle the anguish of meeting with families of victims who died in airline crashes. She returned to massages, and Tangles joined my team to replace Betty. In a relatively short time, Tangles has grown on me.

Here is the team history: Jo was my original case hunting assistant. Then Pixie, my childhood girlfriend, joined us. After her sister died, Niley joined us, and when I hired Miguel to cook, Letty came aboard. Miguel and Letty were a package deal. Jo and Niley quit case hunting, opened their own management firm, and took over managing my apartment rentals, now over fifteen hundred units. When my fiancée arranged an audition that opened the door to fulfilling Pixie's lifelong dream of becoming a rock star, Pixie left the team. Her fame started in Mexico and now was crossing borders, not just in the United States but all over Central and South America. Losing Pixie to the world of music took the team down to Tangles, Letty, and me.

Raul pulled up to the front of my home. The tall iron gates opened. Letty lowered the window, and I leaned over to say hello to Quito, the guard on duty who had seen us on the video monitor and electronically opened the gates. Raul drove the last hundred feet to my front door.

It is always good to be home.

Casa Luna is my new four-story house that fits well among stately Pasadena mansions. The original house had been torched by persons still un-known. It took the architect a year to come up with the plans, a year to get the building permits, and a year of construction, but it was worth it. The house I had just come from in Milan is a bigger house, and while its location and age make it precious, my house is my own private paradise. On the ground level, I have a spa to die for: steam bath, sauna, ice-cold and steaming hot Jacuzzis, four showers, and five granite massage tables; a gym and workout room, wine room, a disco, an arcade, and an indoor swimming pool; on the second level is the entry, kitchen, dining room, breakfast room, eating niches, den, living room, library, sunroom and some rooms that have no name; on the third floor, nine guest rooms with en suite bathrooms; on the fourth floor, my home office and my master suite, a sitting room, his and her bathrooms, and a bedroom with a custom made bed equal to two California king beds, not to mention the beveled mirror on the ceiling overlooking the bed.

For years, Letty has rented one of my apartments, but she lives at my house. Tangles also rents an apartment from my management company. She lives in her apartment when she can get away from my house. Letty's and Tangles's workspace at my house is the large conference room in my office. We still have one teletype that bangs away news dealing with air crashes. If news comes in of a small crash in which the victim's family has a chance to recover damages, my private investigator, Tricia, digs up details of the victim and their family. No one is contacted right away. If there are deaths, Letty and Tangles wait a month or more after the funeral takes place before they make contact. If the heir of the victim happens to be a male, the girls have a good chance of at least getting a meeting. Once they have an appointment, they take my plane. Deferring contact to a later date is crucial to show respect for the families, although it increases the chance that another lawyer may get the case.

As I started for the stairs, Miguel came out of the kitchen.

"Boss, so good to see you. What should I prepare for you?"

I gave him a hug. "A porterhouse, two baked potatoes, mac and cheese, and biscuits."

"You got it, boss. What time you want to eat?"

"Ask the girls. I'm going to shower."

"Miguel, don't rush it. We have some business with Boss, first," Tangles said.

"Ring me."

"Don't hold your breath, Tio. It may be a while."

I started up the stairs.

"Boss, the elevator. Come on."

"Elevator is for sissies," I said, taking the stairs two at a time.

The girls followed me, but Letty stopped for a moment to unstrap a pair of high heels before she came racing after us. Both of them are fit like deadly weapons. Letty is a sharpshooter with something like fifteen different firearms. Tangles is still getting there, but I've seen her shoot a forty-five as though it was a small handgun. Pixie has five belts. One time when she left my house to go to her house across the street, a crazed fan got out of his car, and before he could get his hands on her, she had him on the ground. The cops took him away.

I had a shower and close shave. We had a quick but passionate reunion just to take the edge off, followed by dinner in the master bedroom at the table where I often eat breakfast. The fireplace had a big fire going for ambiance, though the forced air heating had the house comfortable. Letty had at least a dozen candles burning. It was good to be sitting down to one of Miguel's delicious meals.

Letty directed Caro when she brought up the steaks, sorting out what got put where, the whole deal—tablecloth, napkins, wine, condiments, silverware. She had Caro carry away the big silver cloches that had been keeping the dishes warm.

"No need to come clear," Letty told Caro. "I'll put our dishes in the dumbwaiter when we're finished."

Letty was like a wife to me only without the arguments.

"I missed you," I said.

I said it to them both, but it was Letty I truly missed. Even with all the pussy in Milan, I missed her. It's not just sex with her. She's my gem. As much as I love Olga, I often wonder if it should be Letty who should be wearing my special ring—the engagement ring that my dear departed Sami gave to me on her death bed—that I gave Olga.

"We missed you, too, Boss. We hardly talked on the phone," Letty said. "We missed your calls."

"Let me tell you what's going on."

They dug into their salad and steaks as I launched into the story. Without getting up, Letty topped off our glasses of wine. Tangles buttered a roll for me and one for herself. I had planned to avoid the word 'move,' but it was a move. I explained the deal that required me relocating to Milan. I *was* moving to Milan. I would be like Pixie who kept an entire staff at home, with only the head of household missing. Pixie was always on tour or doing something to promote a record.

"The good thing is it is not a full-time desk job. I'm going to travel around searching for planes to buy."

"Fuck-me," Letty said, between bites. "Are you in for this?"

"Fuck-me, too, Boss." Tangles polished off her glass of red wine.

Letty filled Tangles glass again. I put my hand over mine and Letty returned the decanter to the middle of the table.

"I just did both of you," I reminded them. "Here's the other thing. If you want, you can come with me. Home base will be the Milan house. With Pepe gone, it will be home for us. You know how big that place is, big enough to get lost in. Camila and Olga will be living at their own houses, probably Bogota, so it will just be us."

All the silverware hit the table with a clatter followed by ten seconds of excited silence. I kept eating my steak and felt their eyes on me.

"No pressure," I said. "Whatever you choose, you still have a job. I'm not quitting finding crash cases, but it might come to that. You can still look for the small stuff. Goner will always take those cases. You can stay here and work the cases, or you can work them over there and fly over if you get a hit here."

Tangles took up her fork and knife, and finished up what remained on her plate, then buttered another roll.

"Have you told Melina?" Letty asked.

I thought of my precious Melina. For years, I'd believed she would become my wife.

"I didn't call her, and she hasn't called me. I will call her tomorrow." I looked from Letty to Tangles. "What do you want to do?"

"We can look for small aircraft cases over there," Letty said.

"Do you need help at the leasing company?" Tangles asked. Her plate was empty, but she poured the remainder of the salad on her plate. She gestured to Letty, who handed over half of her unfinished baked potato. Tangles slathered butter, chives, and salsa on everything, and finished it off.

"I don't know the business yet, but there will probably be something you can do, if that's what you want." I told them about our in-house experts Jules and Andrea.

"Sounds like you don't need us," Tangles said.

"How can I know exactly what you'd be doing when I don't know the business yet? You can always file or make cold calls. Point is that I want you to come along."

"Boss, it's your call. I can stay here, work on small aircraft cases and continue running the house, or I can be there with you. I'm yours. You tell me," Letty said, putting her hand in mine.

"The way you put that makes me feel guilty. I don't own you."

"Boss, you don't own me. What I said is 'I'm yours.'"

Tangles looked us impatiently. "You two." She shook her head. "It's still hard for me to believe Pepe is dead, and we'd be living in his house. Seems like yesterday Pepe and me were hanging out."

She was wearing the six-carat pear-shaped diamond that Pepe had given her after she'd had a party a weekend alone with him in Milan.

Letty took her hand from mine and patted Tangles on the back sympathetically.

"Don't tear yourself up. Such a drama queen," she said. "Do you want to stay here or come with?"

Tangles showed us her teeth. "I want to stick close to your pussy and the boss's big *verga*[6]. Does that answer your question?"

"Yeah, you just got me wet," Letty said.

---

[6] Penis

"You two so nasty." I hammed it up and pretended disgust.

"Don't you know it, Boss."

Nasty giggled. They got that giggle from Pixie.

When Letty had first come to work for me, her ears were virgin. No more. Pixie was a real swear-master. She used profanity the way other people use exclamation points, mostly to make us laugh. She'd been raised in a cathouse, after all. She'd been the heart of my team before she got discovered, and her language rubbed off on everyone.

Tangles pushed her chair away from the table and leaned against the headrest. She looked uncomfortable. I had already finished. Letty grabbed the dishes, carted them off to the dumbwaiter, and returned to the table.

"We're in, Boss," Letty said. "Can we go to bed now?" Letty hopped out of her chair and gave the tabletop a quick wipe with the one remaining paper napkin.

"I'm so full," Tangles said, watching Letty finish up.

"Cool, you stay put," Letty said. "Boss and me, we will hit the bed."

"Bitch, no way."

I didn't run to bed right away. I took another shower, then called Olga.

"Letty and Tangles are coming with me. They can handle teletype there like they do here, and if a case looks good, they can fly and get it."

"If that makes you happy, Amor, I'm happy."

"Baby, thanks for that. I love you."

"*Y yo te adoro.*"[7]

---

[7] And I adore you

Chapter 2
Pasadena February 2, 1987 (Late Monday night))
Letty

When I tell him, he snores, he denies it. I would record him right now, but when he found out about it, it would make him self-conscious. Tangles is sleeping like a baby. She's so quiet, I have to move up close to make sure she's breathing. I'm a worrier. I want to be excited about Milan. It's kickass to be going there with him, but there's Olga to worry about. Sure, lately, she's nice. In Colombia, we got tight. I got good vibes from her. She hasn't always been that way. It's water under the bridge now, but once I aborted Mario's baby. Olga would have done something terrible if she'd found out I was carrying his child. The baby would be two now. I'll never be careless like that again. I probably wouldn't be a very good mom, anyway.

I'm not afraid of Olga or the round-the-clock army of security people around her, but Olga is a problem. I can defend myself to the fullest, but that could get messy for both of us. Thank God for karate so that I can defend myself. I'm more worried about her plotting than her guards. You can't see her coming. Look at how she's weeded out Melina and Pixie. I don't know who will be next.

Pasadena February 3, 1987
Mario

During lunch with Jack Fino[8] at Pacific Dining Car in downtown Los Angeles, I brought him up to date about the plane leasing deal.

"I'm going to miss you."

He reached across the table and tapped the top of my left hand. "It's a good move."

"Jack, it's not a life sentence. I'm not moving to Milan permanently."

Fino's laugh is hearty and rough, like he is gargling rocks. He doesn't hold back.

"I'm serious," I said. "If things go well, I'll move the company here."

"Mario, if things go well, why do anything that could mess things up?"

"Moving here won't mess up anything."

The laugh again. He picked up his fork and went for more steak.

I don't know the entire story, but my Aunt Carmen raised me from birth. I love my aunt and have never questioned her too much since it seems to bring up bad memories for her. I know that my mom Elena was my aunt's little sister, and that she died right after I was born. Before I was born, like her mother, my aunt was a mid-wife in Nogales; later in New York City, she got into some government program and became a nurse. She moved from New York to Los Angeles with my stepfather who everyone called Mooney because of his last name, Luna. I vaguely remember him, a big, warm man who laughed a whole lot, and worshipped the ground my aunt walked on. When he died, we moved to East Los Angeles, and she became the local midwife in the Spanish-speaking community where we lived. She also worked as an accountant until hippies in California got into home births, then she gave up the office job and taught birthing classes in the house in Monterey Park that I bought for her. I've

---

[8] Jack Fino is a rich criminal lawyer who heads a financial company that loans money to attorneys across the United States. When lawyers max out at their bank, they turn to Fino to finance their cases. The interest rates are two percent on the unpaid balance payable monthly. A life insurance policy insures the borrower for the amount of the credit line. If the borrower dies, the beneficiary is Fino.

never gotten a straight answer about my father, but he's never been in the picture. I figure he must be dead by now. My aunt still lives in Monterey Park, about fifteen minutes from my house. As close as our houses are, except for the occasional holiday dinner, I don't see her very much, but I do stay in touch by telephone. I tried to get away with a phone call telling her I was going to Milan for an extended period of time. She wanted me to present myself in person at her house. Aunt Carmen is the only living relative I have, and she never lets me forget it.

"Amor, forget about the planes for Olga and me," Camila told me on the phone. "We're going to keep what we have."

"Sure, no problem," I said. What else could I say? If they wanted to continue blowing through the buckets of money needed to run DC9s, there was nothing for me to say.

"Gracias, Amor. How are you doing?"

"I'm winding things down. Tomorrow I meet with Kinko."

"Te Amo, querido," Camila said.

"I love you, too, baby."

Milan February 3, 1987
Camila

I could have had him. He was infatuated with me from the first day we met in Rome when Pepe invited him to spend a few days in our home. Right after I was introduced to him, Pepe told him that if he fucked me, he had to marry me. Well, we fucked and fucked, and it's Olga who's going to marry him.

"I told him we're keeping our planes," I told Olga.

"What did he say?"

"He said no problem."

"That's all he said?"

"That's all. Why?"

"For a while there, he'd ask 'Why the big plane? Too expensive to fly around in.'"

"Don't ever tell him why."

"I would never tell him."

"I know, Amorcito. A few more years and we're out. I've met with them; they all agree that I will fill Pepe's shoes from now on, but it's over in three years."

"I'm counting on that."

With Pepe gone, I thought our five main connections would call it quits, but I was wrong. In the movies, characters in this business go around shooting each other for turf or in revenge. Not so in real life. My father supplied cocaine to countries no one in Colombia serviced. Between him and the product were walls of insulation. He and my mother were so confident of their safety that they lived in a mansion. Instead of hiding their assets like other cartel families, my parents entertained and showed off their wealth, and hosted high ranking politicians, including presidents. When Pepe took over, he introduced an entirely new business. He let the competition keep the drug business his father had controlled for so many years.

With Pepe gone, it is just me. I will always look after Olga. Without her, we'd still have warehouses filled with cash we couldn't use instead of money in banks across the globe. I make it worth her while. Olga must have tens of millions in the bank by now. Three years from now when we shut down the business, she'll have a whole lot more.

Milan February 3, 1987
Olga

I had hoped that with his death, Pepe's clients—the five cartel families—would terminate our relationship. It didn't go that way. Camila came out of her meeting with them with an agreement to continue to take care of their money. Camila didn't want out. After the meets she had, she was elated that business would continue as before. I believe she believes when she says we will get out in three years, but I don't see her turning her back on business. The income generated by what we do for the five families is an immense amount of money. Camila doesn't need more money and for that matter, neither do I.

We're much alike. We want more. Before, only Pepe had contact. For the first time, Camila will have direct contact with the families. The problem is that with Pepe dead, Camila is more exposed. If Camila is more exposed, so am I.

Pasadena February 3,1987
Jack Fino

I spend my quality time unwinding deep in my leather chair in my den at home, drinking Louis XIII with the scarlet, Bogart, and the blue, Cleo. There are perches for them in most rooms where I spend time. As I sit, my macaws are bobbing on a perch right next to me. Sometimes Cleo climbs down from the perch to park himself on my shoulder and softly bump my neck with his head as though to get my attention, to comfort me if I feel angry, anxious, or depressed. I trust my birds and they trust me.

With the grip strength of a macaw beak, there would be nothing left of my carotid artery if the bird bit me instead of softly bumping my neck.

Pasadena February 4, 1987
Mario

"Pack light. It gives us one more reason to come home to Pasadena more often."

"Milan has stores," Tangles said. "Thanks to you, I got so much money in the bank. Hellfire, I'm going to shop and shop."

Pixie called from Lima, Peru, a stop on her tour.

"I hope you have an extra bed in Milan. I'm going to be flying there a fucking bunch. Without you waiting across the street, I'm not ever going to want to return to Pasadena."

"Baby, I'm not staying in Milan for life."

"But it's about the now."

It sounded like she was crying.

"I love you, baby," I said. "Come to Milan."

"Bet your ass. I'll be on your doorstep in Milan the day I finish the tour."

Even Lainie called, also on tour.

"Uncle Boss, I can jump over and see you when I'm in London."

I am her honorary uncle. When Lainie was born, Pixie was living in Aunt Carmen's house. Lainie calls my aunt *Abuelita*.[9]

Before we left, Letty went over the monthly house bills with Jo and Niley and gave them access to the payroll service that takes care of the household staff. I told them to bill me for their services, but they wouldn't have it.

"They make plenty managing your apartments," Letty said. "They can handle this little bit of work."

"Who asked you?" Niley kidded.

Jo only smiled. We were all still family. When Letty first joined my household, Jo had tutored Letty all the way to a GED diploma. She'd done the same thing for Pixie.

Pasadena February 4, 1987
Letty

There was nothing in my apartment to pack, but it was a different story for Tangles. Unlike me, she lived in her apartment. I helped her pick out what to bring. When we were done, we grabbed two Coca-Colas from her refrigerator, sat at her little dinette table and clicked bottles.

Her kitchen is clean but plain. It's just the standard apartment kitchen, nothing fancy. Hardly anything in the way of cookware, and only paper plates. Low ceilings, small rooms, standard white paint. It seems tiny to me after living so long in Mario's grand spaces. Tangles doesn't spend anything on decorations. No curtain anywhere, just plain blinds at the windows. No pictures on the walls. No plants. The freezer is usually full of tv dinners, but she told her cleaner to take all that stuff home.

"Milan here we come," I said.

"Sweet."

We kissed.

"I'm glad you decided to come with us."

A drink of Coke. A lick of her lips.

---

[9] Grandmother

"I told you, I'm sticking to your pussy and his dick." She grinned.

"Tangles, I love the smell of your pussy." It was my turn to lick my lips.

"We got time to do something here before we go," I said.

"I got toys."

"Nah, I want to give you head."

"You can even call me Pixie when you're doing it."

"I told you I was sorry. It's just that Pixie and me, we were a thing. We did it a lot."

"No sweat. Now she's famous and gone all the time."

"Tangles, let me show you how much I care."

"I care about you too," Tangles said. "You do me, and I do you. Deal?"

We headed into the bedroom.

Pasadena February 5, 1987
Melina

I tell him I'm seeing a liquor salesperson and that turns him off? He spends his nights in bed having sex with his team, all at once or one at a time. What happened to me? I miss our Sundays together.

He can't leave without at least calling me or coming by. I don't believe it.

No one has ever made love to me like he does. No one fucks me as good as Mario Luna.

I love you, Mario. Can you hear me? How can you leave for Italy and not call?

If not for my own stupidity, we'd be married now. Being ten years older than him, that was my reason to keep backing out. I just couldn't bear to grow old under his nose. When he got engaged to the bitch, I thought it would end fast. I was wrong. The cunt waves six million under my nose, and I sell her my house like a chump. I never should have given in. She didn't want me across the street from him. It was too close. Now, I'm ten minutes away. Still too close for Olga. Now she's got him moving out of the country. Thanks to Letty, at least I know he's leaving for Italy.

I get Betty on the line.

"Sorry haven't called you. Can you do a massage for me? I'm at the Hacienda Heights market."

Betty says, "If you can wait till tonight when you get home, I'll bring what you like, and fuck you for hours. Do we have a deal?"

I agree. Betty is the only one I trust like that. I hang up. I don't wait. My fingers find the spot. I'm already wet. Orgasm is tremendous. My guy Ronnie is the nicest guy in the world, but once he gets off, it's done. He's no Mario.

Pasadena February 5, 1987
Mario

I don't like good-byes. I left Miguel in charge of the house. Jo and Niley will handle the bills since Letty is coming with me.

As Raul was driving us to the airport, I called Betty from the car. Letty and Tangles were listening as best they could to my end of the conversation.

"I know you'll miss the money with us gone," I told Betty, "but listen, I left an envelope with Miguel to tide you over. Please go by and pick it up."

"Oh, Boss, you didn't have to do that."

"Of course, I did. You're family. You've got to come see us in Milan. Camila was asking about you."

"She was, really?"

"I wouldn't lie."

"Say hi to her. Let me know when you want me to come over. Hell yes, I'll be there. Thank you."

"Betty, if you do Janice, and she mentions my name, let me know right away." Janice, Oscar's widow, has been a bitter drunk ever since Oscar died. I'd bailed her out financially more than once. She blames her current state of near-poverty on me, and I half-suspected her of plotting against me. It's not as paranoid as it sounds.

"Oh, I will. She hasn't called. I told her if she didn't have the bread for the massage that I'd do it on the house, no sweat. She was wasted out of her gourd and hung up on me."

"Work her. I'll make it worth your while. Don't trust her."

"You know I will, Boss. I'm going to massage Melina tonight. I'm on the way there now. It's been a long time since she had me come over. Does she know you're leaving?"

"No, I didn't call her."

I saw Letty pointing at herself holding her hand up to her ear like a phone and mouthed 'Melina.'

"Letty called and told her," I said.

Letty nodded and gave me a thumbs up and a huge smile.

I told Betty, "Please tell Melina that I'll be in touch."

Melina has a boyfriend now and his name is Ronnie. I have no face to put to the name. Olga was cool about all the women in the world except Melina. Melina I'd had to give up.

"I will, Boss. Safe travels."

"Love you, Betty."

I heard her sniff. "Oh, Boss, I miss you already."

Letty gestured wildly, so I gave her the phone. She talked and a few minutes later, Tangles took the line. When I got the phone back, it was dead. I handed it to Letty.

"Please charge it on the plane. Make sure all the phones get charged."

"Of course," Letty said, her eyes on mine.

"My phone still has some juice. Want me to get her back?" Tangles asked.

"We were already done."

Raul took the turnoff to the airport. In under an hour, we were airborne. I was excited about the changes in my life and felt like the prince that Olga and Camila had recently started calling me.

Fuck, I had it made.

I am a long way from the east Los Angeles barrio where I grew up.

Somewhere over North America, in the sitting room of the plane, we dined on food catered by the Pacific Dining Car. Their steaks for takeout were never the same as eating them at the restaurant. We ate on an extended table that fit between two seats on each side.

"Great dinner, Boss," Tangles said. "At this rate, I'll end up getting fat."

"Not a chance," Letty said with a wicked grin. "Soon as we get to Italy and dump the jet lag, I'll work it off of you. Every day."

They high-fived.

I lifted my glass of wine, and we clicked.

We had a layover in New York City for fuel and sleep. The crew would then be fresh to fly us nonstop over the ocean to Milan the following day.

"We're staying at the Waldorf. I didn't go crazy. Just a one-bedroom suite. Hope it's okay, Boss," Letty said.

"It's fine. We're in and out anyway," I said.

"Yummy. We get to snuggle up in one bed," Tangles said.

As soon as we were in the hired car that was waiting for us at JFK, Letty's phone rang.

"It's Jo, Boss."

I checked my watch—one in the morning in New York, ten at home.

"Jo, what's up?"

"Boss," Jo said. Her voice sounded strained. "Something terrible happened. A helicopter dropped Molotov cocktails on the house. The sound of the helicopter brought the help outside. They saw it happen."

"Saw what happen?" I shouted so loud the driver slammed his brakes.

"Boss, what?" Letty asked.

Tangles had been watching the road, but now both girls' eyes were on me, their mouths open. I could hear Jo talking. Could not believe my ears. It was déjà vu.

"Jo, tell me I heard you wrong. Tell me you did not just say someone torched my house again."

Letty and Tangles both shrieked. Letty put both hands over her mouth, like it took both of her own hands to silence herself. Tangles got quiet, but her face contorted in shock. I was feeling pretty shocked myself. I tried listening to Jo, but it was like words in a nightmare.

"Boss, it's not a total loss like before, but there is damage. The arsonists caught the house on fire, but they lit the helicopter they were in, too. It crashed between the main house and the quarters."

"Is everyone okay? Where are you calling from?"

She laughed shakily. "Everyone made it out. No one got burned. I'm outside with the guards. The fire department is here. Fire is out. The yard is filled with cops, and the front yard is full of neighbors. No one was in the main house. They had shut down early and were in their quarters when it happened. The fireman wrangled everyone into the front yard for a while, but there was no damage to the quarters."

"What about the guards?"

"They are fine. They've been helping the firemen and keeping everyone calm. The main damage is to your office on the top floor. TJ scoped it from down here the best he could. We can't go in yet. I'm so sorry, Boss. Miguel called me right away, and I drove over here with TJ. Niley got here a few minutes ago. She's here with me."

I could hear the commotion on the phone line. Voices, sirens. I realized that Jo was still on the line, her voice entreating. "Boss are you there?"

"Yes, yes, I'm here. We're in New York on the way to the Hilton, No, I mean the Waldorf. The flight crew must sleep. I'll cancel our flight to Milan, and we'll be in Pasadena tomorrow."

"Boss, this is Niley. You should go on to Milan. We can report to you what is going on. TJ can work out whatever is needed to put the house together."

"I got to think this out. Thank you for being there with Jo. Please thank TJ and give my workers a hug for me."

There was dead silence in the car, a silent bubble streaking through the chaos that is New York City. We walked through the motions of the hotel check-in like a bunch of zombies. I could not believe the house was targeted again.

New York February 5, 1987
Letty

He looks devastated. His color is gone. He must be so pissed. We are being quiet as can. If I knew who is doing this to him, I would not hesitate to take them out. I would shoot to kill. Oh God, I never pray, but if you really can hear me, please stop all these bad things that happen to him. If you really know everything, then you know how I love him. His hurt is my hurt.

New York February 5, 1987
Mario

"Boss, what can I get for you?" Tangles asked.

The room wasn't anything special. It was nice enough, and just big enough for the three of us, with two king sized beds in the suite. We pushed them together to make a single bed and lay on it crossways with the crack at our waists instead of with me in the middle, falling between the beds.

"Order something to eat. You must be starved," I said, staring up at the pebbled ceiling.

"Not starved," Letty said.

"Listen, what happened at home, happened. Nothing we can do to change it. You need to eat."

Letty talked to Miguel. He was fine, but she said he was crying. She gave me Miguel's description of the fire as he saw it from outside the quarters. He saw the helicopter light up, and spiral down till it crashed and burst into flames.

"I'll order you a hamburger, Boss."

I felt like crap.

"Order me two hamburgers, double meat, the works."

"Any booze?" Tangles asked.

"Not for me but go for it."

"We're cool," Letty said.

Newspapers would have the details in the morning. We picked at the burgers room service delivered. All the mobile phones were on chargers. I needed to be one hundred percent in the morning. I accepted a sleeping pill that Tangles offered me and passed out.

New York February 5, 1987
Letty

I got up and walked around the bed careful not to wake him. I slipped in by Tangles and spooned her like he spoons me. I whispered in her ear.

"You better not be taking any pills. I will kick your ass."

Tangles turned to face me. It was pitch black in the hotel room. The room smelled strange, and the noises were strange. I could hear the central heating system go off and on, the buzz of the hall lights, and the elevator opening and closing. When Tangles whispered to me, I smelled her toothpaste. Colgate.

"I am not taking any drugs. You should know I couldn't work out the way I do with you if I was high, bitch."

I whispered, "I saw your pill stash when you gave him the sleeper. You got a pharmacy in there."

I felt her lips move on mine as she whispered back.

"I always come prepared. Stop with the interrogation. Our poor baby needed to sleep."

That moment he let out a huge comic snore. It broke the tension. I wanted to giggle.

"He says he never snores."

Tangles laughed.

"You'll wake him, dummy."

"He's out for six hours at the least."

"We better get some shut eye."

I slipped into bed so that he was between us. He snored again, launching Tangles into shaking the bed with her stifled giggles. He must have felt me move behind him because he leaned against me and pulled my arm tight around his chest. The snoring stopped.

Pasadena February 5, 1987
Melina

Jo called to tell me about his house getting torched. I wanted to go over there but she persuaded me otherwise. I cried when I heard. I was not happy that he actually left for Italy without calling me. He didn't call me from New York like he always did when something big happened to him. I tried calling him. I tried Letty's cell first, then Tangles's. No answer. Jo told me that they stayed the night in New York.

When I got home, Betty was waiting for me in my media room, watching television. We had touched base on cell. She knew I was aware of the fire, and I knew she had talked to Jo and Niley who were at Mario's.

"Tricia was there, too, with her boyfriend, the retired F.B.I. guy," Betty said.

"Who could be doing this to him?"

Betty shrugged. "Come on, it's massage time. I can set up in the bedroom unless you want it in the spa?"

"Bedroom is perfect."

Betty waited for me to shower then helped me dry off.

"You're beautiful, Melina. How old did you say you are?"

"I didn't say, brat."

When I get off work, sometimes Ronnie meets me and sleeps over or stays late. I hope I can teach him a thing or two about sex. Betty used to be over every night for a massage, but this was the first time she's done me at home since I'd been seeing Ronnie. Lately she's been bringing her portable table to whichever of my markets I am working in. She turned off the bedroom lights. The fireplace was giving off good heat, and candles set the ambience. On the massage table, I lay face down and had a heavenly hour of bliss.

"I needed that. Thank you, Betty."

"Are we done, or do you still want the other?"

"Did you buy a new one? I don't want one that you used on anyone else."

"Melina, you know better than that. I have three, and they are yours. No one gets this treatment but you."

I got in bed as she walked toward the bathroom. "Wake me when you come out of the shower." I didn't sleep. I waited for her. I was lying on my side. I felt the bed lean in from her weight, and she moved close to me from behind. I reached behind me and found what was attached to the strap on she wore. I thought of Mario as I touched it. He was so big.

Betty whispered something, wanted to know if this one was okay.

"It's perfect," I whispered.

Her hands cupped my breasts. I felt the hardness slide inside of me and shut my eyes.

New York February 6, 1987
Mario

I can count the times I have voluntarily taken a sleeping pill. The day after hits me worse than a hangover. Remarkably, when I awoke in New York at eight, I felt good after about five hours of sleep. Letty and Tangles were still in dreamland.

I walked on eggshells getting to the parlor and managed not to wake them up. The phones—my three plus the girls' phones—were all on chargers. New York is three hours ahead, but I had to call Jo.

TJ, her husband, picked up. He's my contractor. He has rebuilt my house once already. Looks like he is going to do it again.

"It may be a number of days before we can go inside," TJ said. "From what I can tell so far, the fourth floor took the lion's share of the damage. The Molotov cocktails struck the roof. The fire captain said that I can get a better look this morning from the staff building. Even if the fire was limited to the top floor, we will have to deal with smoke and water damage. You got insurance. Shouldn't be a problem."

He made it sound so simple.

"TJ, I am glad that you know the house, and you know me, and you will be handling it. I only wish it was that easy for me to accept that this happened again."

There was silence on his end.

"Sorry, TJ. I'm twisted up wondering who the fuck did this to me? Again."

"I can only imagine how you feel, Boss. It will be okay."

I heard the creak of a door, and the girls walked in. Tangles was in a pink babydoll nightie, and Letty in a t shirt that hugged her damp skin. Tangles hair was tousled, her eyes were at half-mast, and she was carrying the full coffee decanter that resided in the bathroom. I caught a whiff of toothpaste and shampoo. Letty's hair was plastered to her head, and I could see comb lines running through it. Her skin was moist and fragrant.

"Hold on TJ. One second."

"Morning," I said to the two sleepyheads. "Letty, call the Senior Officer. Tell him to stay put at the airport and delay our departure. Explain I have an issue in Los Angeles. Not sure where we're going."

"Right away, Boss."

She returned to the bedroom. I could hear her dialing the hotel phone.

"Coffee?" Tangles asked. I nodded. She picked up one of the four white mugs on the dinette, filled it and handed it to me.

"Order room service," I said. I took another sip and returned to TJ. "Do you need me on the construction part?"

"Not if we're going to return it to what it was."

"Yes, I just want it like it was," I agreed. "What did the cops say about the damn arsonists?"

"We were there when the coroner came and took what was left of them. Crispy critters. My words, not the coroner's. They sure as hell won't be torching anyone else. Here's Jo."

"Should I come back now or later?" I asked her.

"Boss, there's nothing here for you but stress. Nothing to see or do right now." I thought about my cash in the safes. The safes were fire and water proof. I trusted the cash would be there.

"What about the staff?"

"They can clean up the areas that are habitable. We won't know the extent of the damage until the fire department lets us back in the main house, and the cops release the house to us. I'm going to be there as long as I'm needed. I got it."

"Jo, you remain a trooper. I love you."

"I love you more, Boss."

Olga was in Rio.

"I got your back, no matter what you decide," she said.

"It's just a fucking house," I said. The black hotel brew left a bitter taste in my mouth. Room service had delivered breakfast. We were now seated at the dining room table. The girls were silently eating omelets. I poked at a pancake heavy with syrup. My stomach wasn't interested.

"I know, Amor. We just lost Pepe and now this. It's haunting."

"Does Camila know?" I asked.

"Niley called Pixie, and Pixie called us. I tried calling you, but you didn't answer."

"We burned the batteries last night," I said.

When I called Quito, the guard in charge of security at my house, he was upset. Unlike the rest of the staff, security did not live on the property.

"Boss, we never planned against a hit from the air. I'm terribly sorry."

"No one is hurt, and that's what's important."

"The crew dormitory is intact. The house is taped off all around. The help can come and go through the rear exit, but otherwise have to stay in their quarters. Don't worry, Boss."

"Any word on who the attackers were?"

"The LA Times quotes..." I heard newspaper rustle, then he read aloud

"...a source says that the information retrievable from the charred remains of the two occupants is quite limited..." Paper rustled again, presumably when Quito put it down. "...whatever that means. I looked at the wreckage of the helicopter from the back building. It's just rubble. There is nothing left."

I was fuming, but my brain was working. Anger was not going to do a damn thing. "Quito, thanks for the update. Call me if you hear anything at all, if you need anything at all."

"Yes, sir."

This was not the first time a helicopter had flown over my house to cause havoc. One night an armed intruder— Luca Rossi, the biker who had plagued me for years—had been dropped on the roof of my house. In the middle of the night, he crept through a balcony and into the master bedroom. He had taken me by surprise, but Letty and I could handle ourselves. Letty shot him in the feet, and I threw him off the balcony. He had landed in the koi pond below my bedroom. By the time we made it downstairs, he had escaped in a helicopter. When the police found him in the park, he was dead but not from the fall. He'd been shot between the eyes.

My next call was to Melina. She was a workaholic, and I know she'd be on the way to one of her grocery stores by six, so she would be awake.

"Sorry to call so early," I said.

"Cuz, where the fuck you been? I called you a hundred times last night."

"I took a sleeping pill and turned off the phones to charge. I'm sitting here at the Waldorf in New York wondering if I should go home or continue to Milan."

"If it wasn't for Letty and Pixie, I'd know nothing about your current life."

"I'm sorry, baby. You must know how important you are to me."

"That's a story for another day. What are you going to do?"

"On to Milan, I think. TJ and Jo have everything in hand. If I'm needed,

I'll hop on a plane. Quito and TJ tell me the house is a crime scene. You know how that goes."

"Go to Milan," she said firmly. That's the way she was.

"I'm sorry for not staying in touch."

"It's not the end of the world," she said.

"I'll stay in touch now," I said. "I will, I promise. Baby, one favor. When you get to work, call Fino and bring him up to date. Tell him I will be in touch. He knows about Milan, but not the house."

"I'll do that, Cuz, but trust me, he knows it happened. You made the front page of the L. A. Times. I think the headline is 'Pasadena Mansion soaked with flames from a helicopter.'"

"Quito read me a line or two. If it's in the news, I better call Aunt Carmen. Thanks, baby. Love you."

"I love you a whole lot more, Cuz." She'd been calling me Cuz for a long time, ever since back in 1972 after we first met, I got into her hospital room by saying I was her cousin.

Letty had room service clear out, and Tangles was out of the shower and waiting for orders.

"We're going to Milan. Call the plane and let them know, airborne in two hours if they can manage that."

Letty gave me a thumbs up.

Tangles stood in the bedroom doorway; her eyes red from crying. "You are one strong dude, Boss. If I was you, I'd be pissed off."

On the way to the airport, Letty got a call that confirmed catering had been delivered to the plane.

"We are all stocked up. All sorts of snacks and goodies to prove to the crew that we're not good-health freaks, and we got a couple of restaurant meals to look forward to."

In the cab, my mobile rang. It was Kinko. "Are you all right?" he asked. "I saw your house on the front page. I get the Times."

"Yeah, headed for Italy as planned. My house is a mess, but no one was hurt."

"There's aerial views on channel five going on right now. This is like a mafia hit."

"Kinko, give me a break."

It rang again as soon as I hung up. Tangles reached across my lap and turned off my phone. I glared at her and turned it on.

"It could be important," I said. "The cops with news, maybe."

"Sorry Boss," she said. "But it's going to be nosy neighbors and shit, now that you're on the tube."

"What did Kinko say?" Letty asked.

"Said it's on TV, and it's like a mafia hit."

"He watches too many movies." Tangles laughed.

"It's not a Mafia hit," I said. It wasn't professional enough to be a mafia hit. Two dumbasses blew themselves up. I started to laugh. I laughed so hard, I had to run to the restroom to pee.

"It's not that funny, Boss," Letty said. "If it was a hit, maybe their bosses didn't want them to survive either. Anyway, they deserved to die. If I had been there, I would have used them for target practice. I would have shot them down, for sure," Letty said. "I have an elephant rifle that would have brought it down."

"Fasten your seat belt, Calamity," Tangles said.

The girls started debating about which movie to watch first on the big screen. They narrowed their choices down to Ferris Bueller's Day Off, Top Gun, Highlander, and Big Trouble in Little China, all released last year.

The screen flickered to life, and the girls were quickly absorbed, and listening through their headsets.

In the silence, my thinking got serious. Whoever was doing this to me was not only burning up my property, they were tearing into my privacy, putting me front dead center in the media when I'm buying up buildings and planes for a foreign company using cash. That's all I need is for the news to put a focus on my great big house. Inevitably, people will wonder who the fuck I am. The cops who will investigate this attack on my property will also wonder. I file my tax returns religiously and pay my taxes, everything I have is rooted and there is a trail where I showed the income to the internal revenue service and the state of California. But who the fuck needs that kind of attention? I sure don't.

Milan Feb 6, 1987

A line of uniformed staff that worked at the Milan villa—some that I knew, others that I didn't recognize—were waiting outside the house. When the car came to a stop, Monjo, the butler opened the door.

Monjo did a little bow.

"Don Mario, Senorita Letty, Senorita Tangles, allow me to present to you the staff."

For the moment, I forgot about my torched house. It was like something out of a movie. I shook hands with twenty-six servants.

When we went inside, Monjo was leading the way. Letty was just behind me, Tangles on her right. I heard Letty say to Tangles, "No shit, I just came. Can you believe the reception we just got?"

I could have said something, but I didn't. This is who we are. Monjo and the others who greeted us would get used to it. Besides, this had been Pepe's staff, and they knew Camila and Olga. No telling what they'd heard here before us.

I guess someone had told the Camachos we'd arrived. Within minutes of our walking through the door, Camila and Olga called the house phone. Monjo put the conference call on the speaker in the den, which is where we were when it rang. We hadn't even gotten to our rooms yet.

"Amores, welcome home," Camila said.

"Si, Amores, welcome," Olga said. "I love all of you."

"We love you, too," I said.

"I love you," Letty said, followed by Tangles.

"Thank you for having us. It so generous of you."

"Nonsense," Camila said. "We love you. I am terribly sorry about your house. In time, you will learn who is responsible. We will help you."

"Mysteries don't have to last long," Olga said. "We will learn who did this, just as we will learn who ordered Pepe's tragedy."

"Damage to my house is no comparison to the loss of Pepe," I said.

"Thank you," Camila said, "I love you, Amor."

"I adore you, Amor," Olga reminded me.

"You can have any bedroom you wish, Mr. Mario," Monjo said, and gave us a quick tour.

Pepe had used one of several dens as his bedroom. I stayed away from there, and chose one of the three master bedrooms, the same one I had stayed in before. The girls picked rooms close by. Olga and Camila's regular rooms were in a newer wing of the house.

"I love this room, Monjo." I patted his back. "Monjo, call me Mario. Really."

Monjo grinned. "Of course. Thank you, Mr. Mario."

I'd never had trouble communicating with the help on any of my earlier visits. I had never noticed before that Monjo's English was nearly perfect. They were Italian, but English was used in this house. Jet lag hit. It took two days for me to get accustomed to the time change. It usually wasn't so long, but I was upset over the mess at home. I talked to everyone, and reassured my staff who were worried about their jobs.

There was still no access to the house.

Olga had arranged a driver for me. I refused him, and instead drove myself in Pepe's Ferrari. Olga told me that Pepe would have loved for me to have it. I told the driver Lombardi to chauffeur the girls.

"I don't need security," I told Olga.

"Okay, but the girls will have someone with them when they go out." Camila said.

The first day at the office, I felt awkward, especially sitting at Pepe's desk. The drawers were empty, the desk cleared of all personal things except for a bust of Pepe and a beautifully framed picture of Olga and Camila on the credenza. They looked like sisters. Maybe they really were half-sisters. Who knew such things? It was a family of secrets. I must love the intrigue, or why the hell else would I be a part of their lives? I had a meeting with the office staff. Their biggest jobs were accounting, collecting, and banking monthly lease payments from operators on the planes they were leasing. Andrea's job had been to oversee. Now that Pepe was gone, she handled calls from operators interested in new leases. Jules spoke six languages, an all-around person.

Pasadena February 6, 1987
Jack Fino

I said to Cleo, "Melina called to tell me Mario would be in touch when he settled down in Milan and to let me know that his house was torched again. Stupid woman. She must think I don't read or watch the news."

"Who gives a shit!" Cleo squawked.

Bogart whacked Cleo. "Shit bad word!"

"Shut up! I don't want to hear any arguments!"

"Shut up!" Cleo echoed.

"Who gives a shit!" Bogart sang out.

"I'm going to make a call. I'll throw you out if you say another word!"

"Who gives a shit!" Bogart said.

I heaved the newspaper at them. They were in the air fast, headed to another room.

I wanted companionship from something without feathers. I dialed the phone and readjusted the perch as the phone rang. It took six rings for her to pick up.

"Janice, it's me. Did you hear about the house being firebombed?"

"I did. Serves him right, fucking asshole that he is."

She was loud, angry, and slurring her words. I recognized that tone in her voice and was ready to hang up. I was better off with the birds.

"You're drunk," I said, hearing the disgust in my own voice. I didn't care if she heard it too.

"I'm not drunk. You're the drunk."

I looked at my empty shot glass and filled it. Took the shot, neat.

Long silence. I could hear the television playing on her side of the line.

"I should visit you soon," I said.

"If you come over, bring cash. I'm in the dumps over here."

"How long till you're sober?" I asked.

"Fuckin fool. I'm sick of you."

I heard a click. She was gone. No great loss. She'd been a different person when her husband had been alive.

I looked at the empty perch.

"Cleo, Bogart, get in here, now," I yelled. My shot glass was empty again. I should go get the snifter, but it wasn't in its usual spot. The shot glass would do. Any port in a storm, they say.

I poured from the Louis XIII bottle. Best brandy in the world.

I yelled out for Alessandro, my assistant, my butler, my sometime driver. He came running.

"Bring me a treat, Alessandro. Blonde this time."

"One hour," he said, heading for the door.

"Alessandro, wait. Cleo and Bogart. Find them and get them back here."

"Right away." He took another step toward the door.

"Alessandro."

He halted.

I emptied the glass and looked over at my friend. I've known him my whole life.

"Have China prepare a nice dinner. We can have something to eat first."

"I will speak to China to get her people in the kitchen."

I gave him a satisfied smile.

"Alessandro."

He stopped and turned around again.

"Thank you," I said.

"My pleasure."

Milan February 20, 1987
Mario

In the first two weeks that we were in Milan, the planes on hand were leased out. I reviewed the contracts that Jules and Andrea had put together with the local law firm that occupied an office on the second floor, a tenant of LAI.

The authorities in Pasadena released their block on my house. TJ reported back that the damage was bad but not terrible. He was looking at estimates of the insurance adjusters. The investigation had been taken over by the ATF and FBI because of the use of a helicopter. The lead officer talked to me by phone as did Pasadena's arson investigations commander-in-chief.

The helicopter had been stolen from Channel 14 the night before it burned up in my yard. The bodies of the arsonists were so badly charred that positive identification going to be a challenge. The Fed introduced himself as Seth Ludgood.

Do you want me to fly in? I can do that."

"Not necessary. At least we don't need you right now."

He said he would notify me when he got the results from Washington. He warned it might take a long time if the only thing they had to work with were dental records.

"I am puzzled that your house has been hit twice with Molotov cocktails. I understand the first time; it was a total loss. Any idea where this is coming from?"

"No clue," I said, trying very hard not to wisecrack over his being puzzled. The last thing I wanted was for him to get curious.

I talked to Melina three times, maybe four times in the two-week period.

"If you need me to speak with the investigators, I'll be happy to," she said, each time we spoke. "If you have any trouble with the insurance company, I can handle that, too." She was a lawyer who had never practiced law. For years, she handled my affairs that needed legal counsel. She always came off like she had the law right there to backup whatever argument she was making on my behalf.

"Love you, baby," I said.

"How's Milan?"

"I've been so busy I haven't had a chance to roam around. I know the city pretty well."

"I remember when you took off for six months. You spent a good amount of time there living with two Chiquitas or was it three?"

"Two. I wonder if they are still around."

On my third day at the office, I had Letty and Tangles accompany me. They spent all day with Andrea. The plan was that they would look for small aircraft crashes just as they did at home. Instead of the telex machine, Letty signed with a service that would send everything by fax, a quieter way to get the information that used to be transmitted by telex.

"Makes more sense since you have the dedicated fax in the office," Letty said, after being in the office for a week. "I'd rather work at the office than at the house, unless you have a problem with that."

"No problem at all. We have plenty of vacant offices."

"Cool," Tangles agreed. "I like working at the office. I dig leasing."

"If I don't get out there and start finding planes, there won't be any new business."

I had a list of eight used planes that we could probably make a deal on. I called Kinko every day for updates.

I had once bought seven planes from an operator in Australia that had lost routes. I'd met him through Kinko. It was the kind of deal Pepe had loved because the operator accepted cash for the planes. It was a good deal for Pepe, and the operator told me it was a great deal for him. Chuck Morrison had flown to Los Angeles and stayed at my house where we made the deal, then returned for the cash when we took possession of the planes.

Kinko told me Chuck was back. Chuck wanted to sell the rest of his planes. He thought he'd get a better deal piecing it out rather than trying to sell his airline intact. He had fourteen planes to sell. Kinko faxed me the inventory, and I went over it with Jules and Andrea.

I would have traveled to Australia, but when Chuck found out I was interested, he agreed to fly to Milan to meet in person. I promised Kinko his commission even if I made the deal direct as before.

This time he couldn't take cash because he would have trouble banking it. He owed too much money to banks secured by the planes. It took two days for us to reach an agreement on price. Kinko, as always, was a valuable asset to guide me on the market value of the planes. He didn't have physical possession of them, but he had videos and pictures and maintenance records on each just as I did.

Neither Camila nor Olga came to Milan to discuss the big purchase. I had committed to millions of dollars. All of it needed to come from a bank, and not cash. Fourteen planes had to be flown from Australia to Milan, a costly task. The day before Olga was to wire the money, Andrea came into my office, and handed me a list of pilots she had lined up to fly the planes to Milan. She stood there waiting for me to approve the list.

I didn't add it up, but the cost of fourteen flight crews was substantial not to mention the fuel needed to fly from Australia to Milan.

I dialed Chuck.

"One small favor," I said.

"Shoot, son."

"My associates are pissed that I didn't make the deal conditional on your delivering the planes to Milan."

"Will that delay payment?"

"Not at all. I trust you. It's my associates who are unhappy."

"Tell you what. I'll get the planes to you," Chuck said.

"You get the planes over here ASAP. I'll get that wire to you tomorrow."

"You got a deal, son."

Andrea heard the pitch to the seller. Her eyes got bigger as I went along.

"How clever of you," she said with a big smile. "He went for it. What a nice savings for us."

"Not sure how admirable it is, but it will save us a chunk of bread."

"Bread?" Andrea asked.

"Dough. Funds. Greenbacks. Pesos. Hard Cash Money."

"Oh, of course." Andrea nodded.

Jules was happy that he had fourteen planes to find a home for.

I told Kinko, "I can wire you the commission, or I can give you the green when I hit LA. Not sure when that will be."

"For green, I can wait. I'm searching for planes everywhere."

"Bring them on," I said with gusto. "Too bad you don't have a place here in Italy. Out local air field is going to make some bucks going through these planes for us."

"Rents are way too fucking much."

"You're used to the desert," I said. Kinko has a vast collection of planes he warehouses in the desert.

"Believe it. Italy is to vacation in, not to live and do business."

"One day, I'm coming home with the company," I said.

Chapter 3
Milan February 20, 1987
Tangles

My parents were janitors employed by an agency that had contracts to clean banks in Los Angeles. They both worked nights, and they worked together. I had a stepbrother on my dad's side that lived with his mother. I hardly knew him.

Going back as far as I could remember, we lived in a small rented house in the San Fernando Valley. My mother always said that if my father would stop getting a new car every three years, they could have bought a house long ago. My dad argued that wasn't true because the bank was financing the cars. It wasn't like he was paying cash.

I had my own bedroom and a collection of dolls, gifts from my parents on birthdays, Christmas, and Easter. I was always careful when I played with my dolls and always put them back on their stand except for the doll I selected to sleep with. I never had a male doll, and as I grew older, I realized that I was sleeping with a girl. I wondered what it would be like to sleep with a boy, like mom did. When I asked my mom about a boy doll, she said girl dolls were more fun.

Until I was ten, our neighbor Jannah came over to stay with me until my parents got home at three in the morning. Jannah was a tall, pretty Caucasian from Austria. She didn't have a husband or kids, but she did have a whole lot of boyfriends. If I was still up, she'd introduce me. I'd go to bed and they would watch television in the living room.

One night I came out of my room going to the kitchen, and through an open door, I saw her boyfriend behind her, his pants around his feet, his bottom staring at me. I shut the door. Next time, it was another boyfriend. The second time, I was more curious, and managed to see an erect penis for the first time.

After my tenth birthday, my mom said we could save money if Jannah only stayed until I was asleep then went back next door.

I did okay in school, but after the tenth grade I squeezed by. My male teachers liked my looks and flirtations and gave me good grades. I got C's and D's from my female teachers. My hair was sexy, long, and it curled naturally. That's where I got the handle Tangles.

My parents wanted me to go work with them cleaning banks. I did it in the summer but working nights sucked. My counselor was a fortyish guy who insisted everyone call him Munoz and not mister, and everyone went along. I told Munoz how my parents wanted me to go to work with them, but I didn't want to.

He handed me a career assessment aptitude test. It started off with off the wall questions, like which did I like better, going to the office or research. At the end of it, he suggested, "Become a therapist. Learn massage. Someday it will be good business."

Massage school tuition was five hundred dollars.

My father was a hundred percent against it.

"Read the newspaper," my father told me. "They are shutting down the massage parlors on Western and Vermont Avenue for prostitution. Masseuses are whores."

"That doesn't mean I will be a whore."

My dad was a madman when he was pissed off. He didn't use his fists but taking a hit from his mouth was as bad as a body blow. I love my mother, but she always agrees with my father.

"Why would you want to work that hard for a living?" my friend Rachel asked when I told her I wanted to go to massage school. "If you want to make men and women feel good with your hands, be a hooker."

We laughed it off.

Right after graduation, I went to work with my parents and continued to live at home. I saved every nickel. I dated but never went Dutch. It took months to save up five hundred dollars. I hung on till I had eight hundred. My parents had a fit when I quit working with them and started massage school. The arguments became so bad that I moved out of the house and into Rachel's small studio apartment. She advertised in a free paper in Hollywood where her apartment was located.

Her two-line ad was this: Come relax with me, I guarantee results. The second line was her phone number. I took the bus to school and looked for a part time job that wouldn't interfere with my school schedule. I had a massage buddy at school. Her name was Betty, and we would practice on each other. She had a nicer apartment because she used to be a secretary or receptionist for a law firm, or something like that. We practiced at school and at her place. I didn't bring her home to Rachel's.

The studio apartment was nothing fancy, but it was tidy, and it had a kitchenette and bathroom. The bed was a murphy bed where we both slept. A guy who answered Rachel's ad could have a hand job for ten dollars on the bed; a hand job and they could touch Rachel while she did it for fifteen dollars; a blow job for thirty dollars. Rachel had rules. The guy had to be clean, not too young, not too old, and he could not come in her mouth. If he didn't have the full amount she was charging, Rachel might accept what the traffic could bear.

My share of the rent was twenty a week. I ran out of money. Five hundred went to the school. The remaining three hundred didn't go very far. I was no virgin. I had given that up in high school.

"Should I put up my own ad?" I asked Rachel.

That wasn't going to work because I would need another phone. What Rachel did was give me the business she didn't want to handle, especially if she went out on a date.

Two weeks later, in the same building, I rented a studio. I paid an extra five a week for the landlord put in some old furniture. The bed was just a bed, not a murphy so I didn't have the luxury of a living room like Rachel. I got my phone and put in my own ad: Quickie available for a song, after 7pm.

After I graduated from massage school, I went to three different massage places looking for a job. Everything was on commission. If I did no massages, I got nothing. I was paid ten dollars if I gave a massage. Since I got that much giving someone a hand job, I didn't take those jobs.

I couldn't get any steady clients. I had three regular clients, but they were not what I would call steady. I waited to be called when one of them wanted me over. Things were so rough I struggled to get enough for food. I had to choose between feeding gas to my old clunker or a fast food taco to me.

The free rag where I had gotten my business was shut down by the cops. There were other papers that cropped up. More ads. Some massage places were shut down, and new ones cropped up. I would pick up work for a little while, but the source would get shut down.

If a repeat customer called, I never said no. I needed the bread. I was desperate.

Out of the clear blue, my mother, who had never called me since I gave her my phone number, called to say they were moving up north to work for the same maintenance company. I still wasn't sure if they were pissed at me for becoming a massage therapist or for moving out of their house. It's not like they knew of my newspaper ads and the things I did to keep money in my pocket. I left all my dolls behind. There was no room. My mother also gave me a message. Betty had called my parent's house and left her number. I returned her call right away.

"How are you doing?" she asked

I didn't give her much of an answer, not wanting to admit how bad things are.

"I have an offer for you," Betty said. "I have nine steady customers, plus one customer that lives in a mansion where sometimes I do more than five people. I want to turn over the clients to you."

I didn't jump in right away. "What's the catch?"

"There's no catch," Betty said. "I was offered a different position by the guy with the mansion. I don't want to leave my customers high and dry. I know you're good because we practiced on each other for long time in school. And you look good. And they will love you."

"Betty, I don't get it."

"Let's meet. Let's have lunch at the Pantry. My treat."

I couldn't turn down that offer.

We got a corner booth. Hungry as I was, I was almost too excited to eat, but I managed to get some food down. They have huge portions, and I had my eye on a doggy bag. Meanwhile, Betty told me she was moving up in the world. Mario Luna, the guy with the mansion, was putting her on his team. She didn't go into her job much, just that it had something to do with getting cases for lawyers. She already called Mario Boss. I knew she was serious when she paid for my lunch. She pulled out a wad of cash—three hundred dollars—and handed it right over to me. I took home the doggy bag, plus I hit Micky D's on the way home. I was a happy camper.

So, I took on her clients, determined to make them happy. I splurged and got a portable massage table secondhand, and took my massages to them, the way Betty did. Betty was right. Not only did I feel her clients liked me, I liked them. I gave Mario a massage at his unbelievable house, Casa Luna, plus I worked on his whole team, a crazy bunch. I got so busy I ran into myself coming and going. I walked into a salon and came out of there looking like a boy. I took my hair home in a plastic bag. There were a whole lot of years of growing and grooming in that hair just to have them throw it away. I still get cat calls and stares. Maybe I didn't need the long curls after all. Then again, it might be my beat-up car that is getting the attention.

I started seeing dollars building up in my purse. I saw Betty regularly because she was always at the Boss's house. He had me calling him Boss too.

"Are you sure I can't do something for you?" I kept asking her. "Head? A full body tongue massage?" She was as happy with her new job as I was overjoyed with my clients. I felt reborn. Fucking wonderful is how I felt.

Other than at Casa Luna, my clients got no sex. Well, Melina, wasn't actually part of his team, but she was a close friend of the Boss, so I think of her as being part of his team. Only she's her own woman. She owns a bunch of supermarkets and doesn't fly off with the Boss on his client-gathering trips. When I worked on Melina, she'd sometimes move my hand to an erotic part of her body, but that was nothing. I learned to love that lady. Her big tips had nothing to do with it. If I massaged her at one of her markets, she always insisted I do some grocery shopping and she'd call from her office upstairs and tell the floor manager to bag it up for me at no charge. The first time she did that, I had no food at home at all, and had barely eaten for days.

Betty had done me a great justice.

My life changed. One day I was practically starving. The next, I was living the high life. But then it all came to a crashing stop.

One day, as abruptly as Betty had turned her clients over to me, she was there to take them back.

She had shadows under her eyes and looked like she hadn't slept in weeks.

"There's too much death. I can't handle working with the families of victims who died in plane crashes. I've tried hard, but I can't do it. The money is great, but I can not deal with the grief. In Europe they show the pictures of the corpses. Did you know that? They never show that stuff here in the states. Those pictures keep me up nights. And all the sadness of the families." She turned haunted-looking eyes in my direction.

I felt bad for her, and worse for myself. I saw my better life evaporating before my eyes. I missed what Betty was saying.

"... since Boss and the team like you."

I was confused. "What is that again?"

"Boss said you could take my place on the team. I'm returning to massage."

Once again, I offered Betty anything from me.

"I'll be your slave, just tell me what I can do for you."

She laughed it off.

I had already made friends with the team, so I was delighted with the arrangement. Duh. Before I knew it, Boss offered me my choice of one of his apartments for half price, only one twenty-five for a two bedroom. I was paying more than that for my studio! I was able to leave the dump I was living in. He bought me a new car. Of course, I have to pay him back, but he wasn't even charging me interest. It is a brand-new VW Bug!

My clunker was so bad, I couldn't give it away. I called Hollenbeck Towing and told them if they picked it up, I'd give them the pink slip. When the driver looked at the car, he said no. I grabbed him by his shirt. He turned around.

I smiled up at the big guy. He shook off the sweat beading on his forehead, smiled back, and said, "No," again.

I grabbed his khaki crotch and squeezed till he was in a happy place.

"Yes," he said.

When I walk into Casa Luna, not as a masseuse but to work up on the fourth floor alongside Boss and Letty, I feel like the luckiest person in the world. I have a salary and bonuses for every case the team signs on any aircraft case, big or small.

I had my old phone disconnected, a parting of the ways. Repeat clients would no longer be able to reach me. I gave up my studio apartment and gave most of my knickknacks to Rachel. Rachel was so stoned when I said goodbye that she probably didn't realize I was leaving. I hugged and kissed her and promised myself I would help her clean up when I am on my feet enough to do so.

I hope it won't be too late.

I sort of know the ropes of this business since I have been working it since May of 1985. It has taken a while to learn, but Letty is a good teacher. It's like having a sister, except I can't imagine being this close even to a sister. Maybe I'm in love with her, except that I know that she's in love with someone else.

In Milan, Letty and me always go out to lunch. Guys hit on us all the time—you know Italian guys. The guard that Olga insisted had to be our shadow kept his distance. Letty gets hit on as much as me, but she swats them away like flies. She has no interest at all. I know she loves Pixie, but I think she's in love with Boss. She won't admit it though. I've asked her. She says she loves him but not like *that*. I love the Boss, too, but I'll give up some booty to a hot Italian if he turns me on.

I get so much sex already, sex from Boss, sex from Letty, sex from Olga, sometimes sex from all of them. I have come so far from where I was buried in Hollywood. As tight as I am with Letty, I've never told her about the struggles I had in Hollywood before Betty threw me the life preserver. Betty only knew that I was hurting financially but had no idea I was soliciting in a newspaper, scrounging tens and twenties for turning tricks. I admire Pixie for being so open about her past.

I called Betty in the states.

"I miss you," I said to her. "Every time I think about my life today, I remember that I owe it all to you. If you only knew how bad off I was when you opened the door for me."

"You owe me nothing. I love you, Tangles."

"I wish you knew how much I love you," I said.

I'm thinking of the booty I gave up to Pepe in Milan, three nights that I slept with him. I thought about the hand jobs I sold for whatever the traffic would bear. I feel bad about Pepe being dead. I remember when Pepe gave me this six-carat pear-shaped diamond mounted as a pendant on the coolest chain. When he gave it to me, I went ape shit. That ain't never going to happen again. Pepe is dead, and ain't nobody around is that crazy for me. Maybe I'll luck into somebody like Jason, the rich London dude who loves Pixie and Lainie both.

I'm living one day at a time. I'm having a blast in Milan in a mansion bigger than anything I've ever seen in the movies and surrounded by servants falling all over themselves doing every little thing for me. Olga and Camila take them for granted. I never could. My life is not the shit pile it has always been. Life has embraced me. I love my life. I owe Betty for everything good that has happened to me. I owe Mario Luna for everything that has happened since I walked through his door. There is nothing I would not do for him.

Milan February 20, 1987
Mario

Someone torched my house over four years ago and got away with it. That they got away with it still amazes me. This latest fire left two whole dead guys on my lawn, but the cops are still clueless. The feds are clueless. They say the fire had burned all the evidence that could have helped identify them.

"It's not over till it's over," Seth Ludgood told me on the phone. "It's possible that the decedents acted alone and were not hired to burn the house."

"Detective, yes, that's possible, but with my history, do you believe that?"

"It's not over. Give it time. Secrets have a way of coming out eventually."

The fire partially burned the fourth floor that houses my office and master bedroom. Structurally the house was sound, but it would take six to eight months to restore what needed restoring, rebuild what needed rebuilding, and replace what needed replacing, including my custom-built bed.

"The smoke damage is throughout," TJ said. "Water damage isn't good either."

I asked TJ to get a crane and move my three safes to the ground floor where he originally wanted to put them. I had Jo check the contents and she reported everything was dry and my million plus dollars was intact. I had no Camacho money in the safes as I had in the past.

Lainie aka Bebé came by and spent a weekend with us. We settled in the Milan wine room for wine and cheese. Olga was in a plane thousands of miles away, and Camila was in Bolivia.

"When you getting married?" I asked, taking a sip of my favorite red.

"I'm having so much fun the way things are, I don't know about getting married."

"What does Jason say?" Letty asked.

"He's fine as long as I'm around as much as possible."

"You so lucky," Tangles said, "I'm so happy for you." She reached for the engagement ring on Lainie's finger.

"I told him that if we didn't get married for any reason, I keep the ring."

"What did he say?" I asked.

"He asked if I wanted it in writing. I handed him a pen and paper." Lainie laughed.

The girls did a fist punch, then a high five.

On Sunday night, Lainie was in Jason's plane headed to London where he was waiting for her.

February 28, 1987
Lainie

I'm flying at thirty thousand feet, my eyes closed, the main cabin lights dimmed. Maybe I'm asleep in on my bed in the Monterey Park apartment. No, I'm here, and this is real. I can barely believe the crowds that came to see me sing in Mexico City last week. It's outlandish. Jason's incredible generosity continues. He told me on the phone he has a surprise for me. No doubt another expensive gift.

If I was a good person, a good daughter to my mother, I'd tell him to fuck off. He would get interested in mom again. It's confusing. I offer him my body, and he turns me down. I sat on his face one night, my pussy right on his mouth, and he gagged. I should have walked out. Instead, I worked his dick for thirty minutes to get him hard, and nothing.

When we watch X-rated movies, he wants me to fondle him. He gets hard when he sees the guy stroking himself or having an orgasm. Took a while for me to catch on, but now I understand.

"Jason, between us, if you like boyos, no one will ever know it from me, I swear."

Jason shook his head. "Don't be ridiculous." He even sounded offended. "If I liked guys, why would I want you?"

"Good question," I said, then I cuddled him. "Listen to me, Jason. Bring a guy to bed with us and I'll watch. Whatever turns you on."

Jason got instantly hard.

"Yes," Jason agreed. "I would like a guy in bed with us, but I want to watch, not the other way around. You don't need that career," Jason said. "When you marry me, you will have more money than you ever dreamed of."

I stayed cuddled in the dark, my hand on his dick, trying to get it hard again. The movie was over, and so was Jason's excitement. Jason kissed me. He does that very well.

"I want both," I said. "I want my stardom, and I want you."

He said, "If you want both, both you will have. I love you."

"I love you, too, but are we ever going to make love?"

"Give me time," he said. "I can find trustworthy boyos. Are you willing?"

"Yes, I'm willing. You're responsible though."

"Let me take care of it," Jason said.

I wonder what would happen if something leaked out to the press. It could ruin me, and I'm barely getting started. Every time I think of splitting up with him, I take a look at the stone on my engagement ring. I just can't do it. I'm too greedy.

Milan March 2, 1987
Mario

Jules was terrific with operators inquiring about leasing. One time he had an operator who wanted six used 737s.

"What did you tell him?" I asked.

"I told him the plane was in high demand, and I wasn't sure I could let him lease what I have in inventory."

"Jules, we have no inventory."

"I know that, you know that. Why does he have to know it?"

We both laughed.

"He'll come back, and by the time he does, I'll have the planes he wants."

I let Kinko know to be on the lookout for six used 737s.

Andrea cold-called operators across the globe looking for planes they may want to sell. Letty and Tangles sat with Andrea for days, observing as Andrea talked on the phone.

Two clerks put together a list of airline operators, their phone numbers, fleet operations departments and headquarter numbers, department heads. Andrea pushed the calls to operators, instead of relying on aviation dealers. Dealers are across the globe with planes to sell, but the inventory of air-worthy airliners with these outlets is limited. Prices are out of proportion.

Andrea came into my office with coffee and a fresh idea.

"I know you have it under control," she said, "But I have a suggestion that may help you expedite checking out the planes you want to buy."

I said, "Good morning."

When she smiled, she was quite pretty. "I'm sorry, good morning."

"Sit down and tell me."

"I can see you rely on your friend Kinko in California to give you advice."

"Yes, I do.

"It doesn't look like he can fly out to inspect planes we are lining up to buy."

"It's a problem. He has made do with films of the planes, and records."

"I worked with a plane expert named Dante Russo," Andrea said. "As you know, the company I where I used to work dealt only with used aircraft. Dante headed the department of acquisitions. There is nothing he doesn't know about planes."

"Tell me about him."

"He's in his early sixties. His wife passed away. He's alone. I've already asked if he will relocate, and he says yes. He wants to sell his house and get away from the memories."

I had a feeling that Dante was going to be the answer I had been looking for. I smiled at my assistant.

"If this works out, I'm going to give you a bonus that will make you very happy."

There was that smile of hers again, the one that lit her up like a candle.

"No need." She got up.

"No need, but you'll accept it?"

Our eyes met. "Of course."

Two days later, when Dante flew in, I hired him.

Milan March 4, 1987

Dante arrived ready to work.

"We have a possible buy of eight 737s in Morocco. I know you need to go home and clear up your affairs, but I would consider it a big favor if you went over there to check on the planes and their paperwork."

Dante spent nine days in Morocco. He faxed over what he felt each plane should be purchased for.

"I already love you," I told Dante on the phone after reading his report. He had expedited the purchase. I could not have been any happier.

"Go home, settle your affairs then head here soon as you can."

Milan March 16, 1987

"Andrea, you did great bringing us Dante. Let's prepare an offer, or I can ask Jules to do it?"

"It will make Jules feel good if you ask him to do it. He has a copy of Dante's report."

"Tell him for me, please."

Andrea got up. "I can do that, but I think the request coming from you will add to his feeling good. This is a big purchase."

"I'll handle it. By the way, your bonus."

I opened a desk drawer and pulled out an envelope with ten thousand US dollars. Everyone loves dollars in Italy. I came around my desk and handed her the bucks. I got the smile. I kissed one cheek, then the other and then she repositioned herself. I leaned in and kissed her lips.

"Thank you, Jefe."

"You earned every dollar," I said.

Andrea was looking up at me, a hooded glance.

"Do I appeal to you?" she asked, betraying no emotion. It was a straight question.

"From the first day I saw you," I said.

I had the feeling that Andrea and I were on the verge of something, but with impeccable timing, Letty and Tangles walked in. Of course, they didn't knock, not that Andrea and I were doing anything to hide.

"Thank you, Mario."

"Did she dig the bonus?" Letty asked.

"She didn't open the envelope, but she should like it."

"She has it coming," Tangles said. "That dude Dante is one smart mother."

"Would you fuck him?" Letty asked.

"We're talking business, not fucking," Tangles said.

I could hear them going at it, but my mind was on Andrea. Maybe a roll in bed, just the two of us. When the girls left my office and I was alone, my intercom rang. I picked up the phone.

"Do you do anal?" Andrea said, point-blank. No hello, no intro, nada. Caught me off guard.

It was probably a lame reply, but I said, "Do you?"

"Whenever you're in the mood, let me know and I'll show you," she said. "It's tight like you won't believe."

I knew Andrea was no saint. Out of the blue, she'd given me a mouth full that punched my thing to life. It wasn't the thought of doing anal. It was how she asked me.

Milan April 14, 1987

Less than thirty days from when I gave Andrea the bonus, the planes we purchased were flown directly to the operator in Madrid, Spain. Jules flew there with the paperwork. The planes were leased for thirty-six months, certificates of airworthiness were in play, the condition of each, as is.

I had the in-house accountant give Jules a check in Italian lira equal to five thousand US dollars as a bonus. "I can't give you a bonus every time we lease a plane or planes," I said to a very happy Jules, but I'm going to do my best to keep you happy."

Jules gave me a hug and when he pulled away his eyes were slightly watery. I seriously doubt that it was the money that moved him. I wished I had given him a bigger bonus. Not that it was my money I was giving out—it belonged to GAL, the leasing company that I had no stake in. Yet.

When Camila was in New York, and Olga in Mexico City, we had a conference call. "I haven't used the consortium because the return on our investments so far has been too good to give up to a partner."

"Amor, you need to throw them a bone from time to time," Camila said.

"Riana's father called me yesterday and asked if everything was okay because they had not gotten any leases from you," Olga said.

"I have one right now, three new Boeings. I'll let Jules know that he should alert them that it's in the works."

"What kind of planes?"

"747s."

Olga and Camila laughed, miles apart but very much in sync on how they reacted to good news.

We were in the dining room of the Milan house—not the actual dining room, which is huge and ridiculous for three people, but a small den that had a card table in it. The card table was just the right size, plus the room was close to the kitchen. Most nights we found ourselves eating in this cozy spot. It was a simple meal: pasta, salad, ice cream. Say what you will about Italians—they do know how to make pasta and bread and wine.

"What makes Milan such an attractive place to do business for the Camachos?" Letty asked.

"I think that was Pepe's doing," I said. "One day, I expect to take the company to the states."

"Pepe told me he loved the house." Tangles said. "No matter where he went, he found that he missed it and kept coming back."

"I thought all you did was fuck for those three nights you were with him," Letty said.

"Pepe was not like Boss. I mean, he couldn't just go and go." Tangles laughed.

"I see," Letty teased. "So, you took talk breaks."

"Exactly," Tangles said. "Talk breaks, pot breaks, and once a temper break."

"Enough about Pepe. Let him rest in peace," I said. "I can understand how the house would draw him or anyone for that matter. I never asked who sold it to him. It would be interesting to know how much he paid for it and when. It wouldn't mean much to me though. I don't know Italian property value the way I know Pasadena. It's a big property."

"I still get lost here," Tangles said.

"So do I." Giggles from Letty.

High fives between them.

Camila and Olga were in touch every day, but it had been over thirty days since either of them had shown themselves. Olga handled the wire to pay for the planes from wherever she was at the time. No hesitation or questions, at all, or from Camila.

"Amor, I will see you soon," Olga promised. "I'm crazy busy."

When Camila checked in, she always says something like, "See you in no time at all," in Spanish. The Milan mansion residents were Letty, Tangles, me, and the staff. I was getting used to it. I stopped calling TJ daily to get the status of the rebuild of my house.

I think the reason Andrea called me on the intercom was to avoid running into Letty and Tangles who mess with her brain. She always talks in a low voice as though she fears being heard.

"You must not be attracted to me," she said. "It doesn't have to be what I suggested before."

"I'd love to try it," I said. "When?"

"I will go out first. You follow five minutes later. My apartment is close by."

I was so hard, I had to wait to be G-rated enough to get through reception without drawing the attention of the two gals who handle incoming calls.

Letty and Tangles were in the office they shared, both on the phone, no doubt with airline operators. I walked out the building entrance and saw Andrea across the street. We took the short walk to her place.

"Three bedrooms, an office, kitchen, living room and dining room," I said. It was a boss place, a lot of space for one person.

"It comes with my job. I can't take credit for it, but I love it. It came with the furniture," she said. "Sit. Let me get you some wine. I know what you like."

I knew she had fringe benefits but not what they were. "You live alone?"

"I don't even have a dog or cat."

We talked for a while, then she said something about getting comfortable, and hit the shower.

I made myself comfortable in her stark modern living room watching a channel like MTV at home. The decor was very different from what I had in Pasadena, and here in Milan. Not much fabric, no wood, mostly angular hard furnishings, and nothing on the walls to personalize the place. It made me think that she hadn't had time to make the space her own, or maybe she just wasn't into decorating.

She came and got me and led me into her bedroom. I sat on the bed propped up by pillows and reached for her.

She got on top of me, but not before kissing me, deeply. Then she let me in. We did it the traditional way. I'm not complaining. We parted for a minute, shared a couple glasses of wine and I had a question.

"What happened to the other position you inquired about."

She laughed. I seldom heard her laugh.

"I don't think you're an ass man," she said.

"How do you know if you don't try?" I said. I slid down flat on the bed.

"Okay, you asked for it, Mario Luna."

She got off me, rolled on her back and beckoned me to mount her. As I did, she positioned her legs on my shoulders.

"*Fallo Papacito*" she said.[10]

At nine that evening, I walked the few blocks to the office to get the Ferrari. I drove to the house where my team awaited my arrival. They had held

---

[10] Do it Papacito (Italian)

dinner an hour or so waiting for me. Not that long, because dinner in Italy is late anyway.

"Boss, I was ready to call Olga. What the fuck? You disappeared," Letty said.

"Did you have fun, Boss?" Tangles asked.

"I was working," I said. "What fun?"

Tangles rolled her eyes. "I wouldn't cop to it either."

Letty laughed, but only a little.

"Boss let's hit the wine room. Dinner's been ready."

"I need fifteen minutes to shower. I'll be right in."

I came down in a robe over swimming trunks.

Dinner was Italian beef, which is some kind of stewed beef that is shredded and served on Italian bread with pepperoncini peppers and cheese. I waited a bit, then we all swam some laps. I'd had the staff lower the temperature a little. It was still warmer than my pool at home, but I think the girls liked it warm this way, at least while the weather was still cooler.

Milan April 14, 1987
Andrea

No wonder Letty and Tangles are so possessive. He's delicious. If I didn't have to work, I'd stay home tomorrow to recover. I hope I can walk. I better use flats. I had not been fucked like that in how long. He's big but gentle. Very different from Pepe. Pepe was not so big but left me with bruises. He loved it like that. He was vicious. With him, it was scary to do it, but even scarier to think of saying no.

Milan April 14, 1987
Letty

He came in smelling like that bitch Andrea. I know her fragrance. When we went to the wine room, Boss said he needed to shower. When he was back, the fragrance of his afternoon was gone. She thinks she's cool, sneaking out with the Boss in the afternoon. If she has AIDS, we're all fucked.

After swimming, we showered together and went to bed.

Boss was at one side of the bed, Tangles and I at the other.

"You better be careful who you fuck. Don't want to catch anything we can't cure. Got it?" I said to Tangles.

"I'm not fucking anyone yet, bitch."

She moaned softly when I touched her there.

"Tell me how to be careful, know it all. What the fuck is AIDS? What the fuck is careful?"

I pinched her, not hard. She's right, which is frustrating. How do you fight an unknown enemy?

"Tell Boss to be careful. I dare you. Who knows who that slut sleeps with besides Camila?"

"And who else does Camila sleep with?"

Suddenly, I'm jealous.

I can never be jealous. I have no right to be jealous. So what if I am? I just have to keep it to myself.

Then he kisses me it's like I'm the only person in his life. When he's inside me and he kisses me, it's like he's discovered that it's me he really loves. That's how it feels. He says "I love you," and my heart hears "I love only you."

Milan April 15, 1987
Mario

Letty came in my office, excited. It was afternoon, the blinds half drawn to block out the fierce Italian sun.

"Boss, I have an operator in Peru that is folding. They have twenty-one planes."

I got a jolt of adrenalin. My heart pounded. I was excited.

"How did you get the lead?"

"Cold call. Fuck-me!"

"Come over here."

She ended up on my lap, arms around me.

"Proud of you, baby," I said. I could tell her heart was racing too. The excitement was in her voice, and her pulse was beating a rapid tattoo against my cheek.

"I should get an inventory by fax by tomorrow."

"You're learning the job, baby. Good for you."

Letty sniffed. Her nose traveled around my neck and face.

"Hey, what's that for?"

"Just checking, Boss."

"Checking what?"

She didn't say. I checked my pits, but that seemed okay. I let it pass.

Getting small aircraft crash information in Europe was the same as at home. Acting on it proved a problem. Letty or Tangles getting the families of victims or the victims to talk on the phone was a different story due to the language barrier. When we normally flew in to European crashes and used the hotel strategy, it worked differently. When we are there in person, for days, weeks, or longer, we had translators with us, had events, shared spaces, got familiar. It was a slow process. A cold call didn't have that advantage, and the language barrier was insurmountable.

"You don't need to work the plane crashes like at home. I'd rather you work with me with the leasing," I told Tangles.

She nodded.

"Keep working with Letty. You got the hang of the calls Letty makes looking for planes to purchase."

"I do, Boss."

"Okay, then drop the effort on the plane crashes."

"Thanks, Boss."

The conversation was done, and I returned to looking at some reports on planes we were considering purchasing. After a moment, I realized Tangles was still standing there. I looked at her for a full minute before she said what was on her mind.

"Boss, I have a date with a guy I met at lunch the other day. Is it okay?"

"Baby, of course it's okay. It's your life, sweetheart. Make the best of it."

"I love you, Boss."

"I love you, too."

"What about Marty Lombardi?"

Marty drove Letty and Tangles to and from the office and shadowed them when they left the office for any reason during the day. For their protection.

"Baby, I assume you aren't double dating with Letty?"

"No, Boss, just me."

"Marty stays with you. I'll take Letty home when I leave."

"Boss, come on. I don't need him on a date."

"You do, baby. I feel better if you have someone with you. It's not like he's going to be right next to you."

Too much had happened for me not to be protective. We were still new in Milan, there was much to learn, and my unknown enemy was out there somewhere.

"You must know that I'm good enough to kick my bodyguard's ass, so what good is he?"

"It never hurts for someone to have your back."

She stuck her tongue out, made a funny face, bent over, pulled her skirt up and mooned me.

"Smartass," I said. But I was laughing when I said it.

On the drive home with Letty, I had to ask. "Tangles wants to date. How come you don't date?"

"No one wants me."

"Liar."

Letty giggled. "You want me to date? I never did in Pasadena."

"I want you to be happy."

She touched my right arm. "I am happy, Boss."

I changed the subject. "What do you say we go on our own date."

"Fun!"

We had a wonderful dinner at one of the local spots and shared a small bottle of wine. I wanted more, but I was driving. When we arrived home, Olga was there. I wasted no time lifting her off her feet to where our lips leveled up.

"We stopped to eat. You should have told me you were coming in. We could have come straight home, baby."

"I just arrived fifteen minutes ago."

I set her down, and Olga hugged Letty.

"Where is Tangles?"

"On a date," I said.

"Does she have security?"

Letty answered for me. "Yes, Marty."

"Good. Why aren't you on a date?" she asked Letty.

"No one wants me."

"Not true," Olga said, her arm around Letty. "Let's have a drink."

Milan April 15, 1987
Olga

Marty tells me Letty and Tangles draw male attention every day, everywhere they go. He calls them eye candy. If Letty is not out on a date, it's by choice. She only wants to be with Mario. I know that's what it is. The question is if she really wants Mario to be only with her. Except when I see her around Tangles or Betty or Pixie, she seems just as happy with girls as with Mario.

April 16, 1987
Mario

Olga and I were in bed, enjoying the ambience Letty had choreographed for us but left us alone to enjoy. Candles were lit, flowers, here, there, everywhere. The colors flickered in the candlelight, and long shadows somehow made the large room feel cozy. We were on our sides, facing each other. When we spoke, our lips bumped.

Olga was telling me that the consortium of banks had finally voted and were on board to participate in any lease we wanted to partner out with them.

"Baby, fabulous. You are a genius." I kissed her with gusto, though it was her time of the month, and she was cradling a heating pad.

"It was teamwork. I didn't do it alone. Riana pushed her father, and her father pushed his friends to stick to the agreement signed when Pepe was alive."

"Should I ask what you did for Riana's father?"

"A lot less than what you do in one night with Letty and Tangles."

"Ouch, baby. You're a big grump."

"It's not sex like you are imagining."

She thumped my chest with her fists, but we were so close she couldn't get any swing.

"I'm sorry, Amor."

"Olga, Sorry for what? We do what we do. Everyone around us is sleeping with each other."

I had not been picturing anything, but now that she'd mentioned it, I had a wall to wall technicolor mental image of this old guy on top of her. Do older guys lie on their back and let the woman do the work? I wasn't going to ask.

"Is Riana going to fly around with you like before?" I asked. I could feel Olga breathing against my nose.

"I dropped her off before I took off for Bogota. She doesn't care for Colombia."

I wanted to say I didn't either, but I remained silent.

"When I leave here, I'm going to Barcelona to get her. She calls me every day. Why you ask?"

"You are grumpy."

"Amor, no I'm not. I adore you."

Andrea came in my office first thing the next day.

As she came in, I had a quick flashback of us in her apartment. I wondered why she had not called to suggest an encore.

"Mario, I suggest we stick to used aircraft for now. We're going to be hit from all over for new airplanes. The math is better leasing used than new."

"I assume you know the banks voted to stay in the deal?"

"Yes, Camila called me last night."

"As I see it, the problem is getting used inventory that's worth a damn."

"Inventory is out there, Boss. I mean Mario."

Tangles got two hits in a row. One operator had three airliners to sell in Venezuela and another had two in New Zealand. I squeezed her tightly when I congratulated her. These finds kept Dante busy. Once we had a lead, he checked out the planes. He was proving to be as valuable as we'd expected.

I called Olga on her cell but couldn't reach her. She'd left early in the morning. It had been a short visit. No doubt she was still up in the sky.

I was in bed lying in the dark when we finally connected. The light were out, Tangles was asleep in her room, and Letty was curled up against me, half-asleep. I had just pulled the covers up over us and got a little hug in response when the house phone rang. I spoke in a low voice but did not whisper. I brought up new planes to Olga.

"Baby, when you get time, do the math on leasing new versus used like we're doing."

"I did it for Camila when you two visited Boeing. It's too difficult to figure out unless I see a deal on the table. There are too many variables involved to be able to generalize. Everything depends on the details. The model plane, cost, lease term, etc. If you get a taker for new planes, do it. If it doesn't work, we will know soon."

"Are we going to use consortium money for new?"

"It's up to you, Amor. You're running the company. Ask Andrea to run numbers when you have a deal in front of you. Compare the cost to give part of the lease to the consortium against the costs of doing it ourselves."

"Thanks for the confidence," I said. We're talking millions of dollars. She was sounding less grumpy. "How are you feeling, Olga?"

She gave a little noise. "You say my name like that, and I am all better."

Chapter 4
Milan August 20, 1987
Mario

TJ reported that my house was one hundred percent again.

I called Melina, and she concurred. Casa Luna had returned to perfection, with no indication that a fire had burned the fourth floor and caused drastic smoke and water damage throughout. Repairs had cost the insurance company over two million dollars. I was still furious with the unknown author of the arson. The cops, fire department, even the feds had no clue who was responsible, beyond the two unidentified arsonists who burned themselves up.

When I first got to Milan, I expected to make plans to fly to Pasadena to check the house when it was done. I loved that house. It had been built, and now rebuilt, to my very exacting specifications. But now that I was busy with work, Pasadena and the house I loved seemed very far away. Maybe I would have felt differently if Oscar or Jake were still alive and waiting for me to come home. But they were six feet under.

At least plane-leasing was booming.

One day toward the end of August, Olga called, catching me during a meeting. I pushed everyone out of my office and shut the door so we could be alone.

"Amor, Riana and I were in the neighborhood, so we are here."

"What neighborhood? Are you here?"

"Yes, here. Not in Milan," she said. "Here in Pasadena. I had to see Pixie, so I am sitting behind your new desk. Everything looks wonderful. Can I make myself at home?"

I matched her laughter.

"Baby, you are at home. If it is mine, it is yours. If I knew you were going to be there long enough, I'd fly over."

"Get on a plane and fly over, Amor. I'll wait for you."

I was tempted, but I had piles of reports in front of me. It is amazing how much paperwork went into every deal.

"I'm so busy. I have four deals on my desk."

"It's your call," she said, "But I'm of the opinion you and your two assistants should book a flight and come see."

I passed.

Maybe it was safer for us and my house if I wasn't there. Maybe I am being too dramatic. I was in no hurry to go home, maybe because the house was attacked twice by helicopter. First there had been Luca Rossi, the biker who lost his life after going after me and Letty. The decision to helicopter on to my balcony was the beginning of the end of his life. At least the house was fixed, in spite of the dead duo who dropped Molotov cocktails on my home. I hated the men who did it. What good was that? They were dead. The job they did on my house cost them their lives.

I told Letty and Tangles that Olga was in Pasadena and that I had passed on meeting her there.

"We know, Boss. Pixie told us," Letty said.

"If you want to take off for a while and go home, no problem."

"Not unless you want me gone. I love it here," Tangles said.

"That's a ditto from me, Boss."

"Both of you are doing good. Proud of you. Do you miss doing plane crashes?"

"Not even," said Tangles.

"I can do either, Boss."

Since we'd been in Milan, there had been two airline crashes that I didn't pursue. Goner bitched and complained when I let the first one go. He had Fino call me when I let the second one go.

"I'm on to something here with the leasing," I told Jack Fino. "I'm not dropping Goner. He owes me on several cases. Money has nothing to do with me not taking off chasing a plane crash."

"Let the girls go," Fino had said. "You had them doing small craft crashes in the states. They can handle an airliner."

I knew they could handle it, but I had asked the girls if they wanted to handle the first plane crash. The second one was in Ecuador and not worth pursuing without me along for the ride. Ecuador was notoriously sexist.

"If you want us to go, we'll do it," Letty had said. "I don't think two women is enough to bring in the clients."

"We could dress up to look older, more experienced," Tangles said. "I'm in for whatever, Boss."

I didn't send them.

We looked at new angles on getting the word out that GAL purchased airliners and leased used and new airliners and executive jets. Letty and Tangles worked with an ad agency in New York that put our ads in aviation magazines. I don't know how much business we actually got from the ads, but they generated a lot of phone calls. Andrea had helped set it up, and the girls had been getting to know her. Letty was impressed by the ads. She had the original art framed, and it hung in the front office, where clients could recognize it if they happened to come in. She had the ads themselves enlarged and framed and put on her office wall too.

Letty and Tangles had joined me in my office. Letty had brought a few copies of the just-published aviation magazine that had full-page ads. I looked them over.

"Andrea did a good job," Letty told me.

"But Boss do be careful where you put your pecker," Tangles said. "I don't want to catch anything incurable. Who knows who she's been with?"

I should have gotten pissed, but I loved her too much.

"I'll be careful," I promised.

"Boss, Tangles is fucking this dude named Andy," Letty said, "She claims it's okay because he uses rubbers. You think that's protection?"

"Oh stop," Tangles said. "I only fucked him once, and it was a quickie at best."

"Oh right," Letty said sarcastically. "Quickies don't count. What's that? Five second rule for sex?"

"What's the five second rule?"

"Urban myth. If you drop food, and it hits the ground, it's ok to eat if it is only on the ground for five seconds or less."

"Sounds like the five second rule would depend on what floor the food fell on. And I have no clue if rubbers offer that kind of protection. They aren't a hundred percent at preventing babies, so how could they be a hundred percent at preventing disease?" I hated to think of using rubbers when I fucked. I never had. What a turn off.

Letty remained seated.

Tangles walked behind me to look over my shoulder at the magazine layout. I expected her to comment on the advertisement.

"Boss, I douche really good. Don't be afraid of my privates. I'm clean."

I laughed, and my laugh coaxed a giggle out of Letty.

"It's true," Tangles said looking at Letty. "Isn't it true?"

"As far as it goes," Letty nodded. The giggle was gone. "After Andy and a douche, you're probably as clean as Andrea after Pepe and a douche, and Olga after that banker dude. Let's go take your condom and douche idea to the American Medical Association and see if they will give us a bucket of money for coming up with something that prevents AIDS."

"Made your point, Letty," I said. "Enough already."

New plane leases were different from used ones. I would have been dead lost without Jules handling it. The engines, the seats, navigation, all the options were elected early in the process by the operator leasing the plane. Most of our used planes were leased out as is, though we had cherried up a couple of private business jets on the lease-holder's dime. These were the first two leases I handled using money fed to GAL from some other source. Olga handled the money transfers. The two leases were going to be a great investment for us, providing of course, the operator made their monthly payments and didn't go bust.

"We can always repossess the plane and lease it out," Jules said, indifferent to the risk.

Camila and Olga shared the same attitude. "Don't be afraid, Amor."

I thanked them for their confidence. I wondered if things had changed since Pepe. Was the fortune in assets that LAI, GAL and the Camachos had now just Camila's?

Olga always talked about how much money she was making, but she never mentioned owning a piece of the assets. I asked her outright. It was late one night, and we had talked each other into orgasms on the phone, a strange consequence of this jet-setting lifestyle. We were at the phase of the night that would —in a movie—showing a couple of people smoking in the afterglow. Of course, my afterglow was in Milan, and Olga's was in Bolivia, but at least it was simultaneous.

"Do you own a piece of LAI or GAL or any Camacho assets?"

"Nope, Camila owns it all. Amor, I have enough for you and me and a dozen kids to live in luxury for at least ten lifetimes."

"Hey, wait," I said joking but not joking. "I'm not exactly broke."

My plane wasn't getting much use. On September seventeenth, I told

Jules to lease it out. Pepe had persuaded me to lease out my first plane to an executive. That lease was due to run for another year. That monthly payment coming in on the investment was a nice perk. I expected my current plane—the Falcon Olga had given me—would bring in a great return.

"I can pay you for the plane," I told Olga. "I feel bad that I have it on the market."

"Don't feel bad, Amor. It's a good move. If you need to fly somewhere, we have planes sitting around like the Lear that Camila keeps in New York to fly around in the states, or the DC9 in Mexico City that we use as a back-up if our planes go out of service, or the nice 737 in Cali. You can keep any of these yourself, or check with Camila if you should put them out for lease."

When I asked Camila about the 737, she said, "I forget we have that sitting. By all means, lease it out."

"Jules and Andrea will lease your Falcon in record time. It's primo," Letty said. "Boss, when you do that, we'll have no plane."

Milan September 18, 1987

After she told me she'd leased my plane out to the wealthy CEO of a London corporation, we were in my office, alone. I gave Andrea a bear hug, lifted her off her feet, and kissed her on the lips.

"You've never called me again on intercom to meet," I said.

When I put her down, she straightened her skirt.

"I dare you to do it right now."

"Five minutes from now across the street," I said, watching her shapely ass move toward my office door.

Olga's call woke me up Saturday morning, the next day. I was in my own bed and took the call on the house phone.

"I don't think you should be having afternoon flings with her, Amor."

"You mean Letty and Tangles?" I knew she didn't mean them, although they were on the leasing company payroll now and not my payroll. I wondered how the gossip flew so quickly to Bolivia. Olga *would* have people in her own company to keep her informed. No surprise.

While I was sitting there, Letty brought in a tray with cappuccino and Italian bread. I had given up asking for black coffee. The Milan house had its own barista who prided himself on the quality of his coffee. This morning the foam was an elaborate weaved pattern that could have been on the wall of one of the many local museums. I nodded my thanks to Letty and took a sip. I didn't watch her leave, caught up in my conversation with Olga.

"I mean Andrea."

"Camila sleeps with her."

"It's done at the house. Andrea comes over there. No one in the office knows. That's the difference. Amor. It looks bad."

"So, what you're saying is if I want to fuck her, I should ask her to come to the house?"

Silence. I could tell I'd struck a nerve.

"If you want her that bad, yes," she said. "I told you before, I'm not jealous."

That was only partly true. She was totally jealous of Melina. And she could say she wasn't, but she was jealous now. I heard it in her voice.

"I'm sorry, baby. I won't be so fucking obvious. I'm a dumbass."

"Yes, you are," she agreed.

"Ouch, that hurt," I said.

"Save some for your fiancée. And do be careful with this epidemic we're in, AIDS and all."

"I had this talk yesterday from Letty. When you figure out what careful means, please let me know," I said. "And you do the same, Olga. Careful who you lay as well."

"Ouch," she said. "That one hurt."

"We should get married and just fuck each other," I said.

"Amor, I think I can do it, but I don't think you can."

"Hey," I protested, but not too much.

Milan September 21, 1987
Letty

You'd think that it would be easier for me with these airline operators I'm calling since I'm not trying to sell them anything. I'm looking to buy inventory they've got sitting around. Fuck-me. I work so hard to get them on the phone. If I was traveling around visiting them face to face, would they shut the door on me, or would we dialogue? I wondered if they'd be more willing face to face. Most of them are men. I asked Boss.

"If you get a serious guy on the phone who thinks there might be something they want to sell, tell him you'll fly over and talk in person."

"Are you serious?"

"This is a business, Letty," Boss explained. "If you score and get a plane, we can lease out, we make money."

"Awesome, Boss."

He gave me that smile that can make me cum.

"Get Tangles in here, and let me tell her about this."

"We could work as a team," I said.

"Face to face is an advantage. You two are fucking gorgeous. You're a team. If Tangles finds an interested seller, or you find someone, both of you go over there. Double-team the bastard. He'll be putty in your hands."

"I just stopped short of coming, Boss. Really."

He gave me that smile again. "What makes you so excited? The travel?"

"Not just travel. It's the challenge, same as when we were running to get retainers signed. We worked hard with the families before we got a signature, and many times we got no signature."

"I totally understand."

I went off to fetch Tangles.

Milan September 21, 1987 (Monday)
Mario

I was in my office with Andrea, and it was almost closing time. She wasn't taking kindly to moving our meet-up to the Milan house.

"I'm telling you, it's okay."

"What's wrong with my apartment?"

"It's like I told you, it is best we do it like Olga suggested or not at all."

"That's rather rude, Mario."

"When I tell you something you need to believe me," I said. "She's my fiancée, and a principal in this business. We're not going to embarrass her."

"Yes, I believe you."

I was going straight home. The girls were going to dine out on what both insisted was not that kind of date, just dinner. I certainly don't blame them. Milan has a cornucopia of wonderful restaurants to experience. Most anywhere in the city, tapas would be out at seven except they call it 'antipasti.' Then there will be first and second courses, *primi piatti,* and second *piatti.* There's more, but I only know enough about this kind of stuff to keep from embarrassing myself in public. It's the kind of thing that Melina was so good at learning. I know she'd had a roommate in college who came from money and taught her all that social shit. Manners, and decorating, and furniture, and how the upper-class lives. But the truth is that Melina and I were pretenders. We picked up on the whole lifestyle, but if you unravel us to see what we're made of, we're really just cut out of plain old East Los Angeles cloth. Anyway, they won't have me to worry about tonight. Marty will be with them.

"Come over about eight if you decide. Okay, baby." I moved close and kissed Andrea on the cheek. I loved the fragrance she wore. It was always the same.

"I'll be there."

When I got home, I tracked down Camila. I told her about my conversation with Olga about Andrea.

"Amorcito, I agree. Keep it secret, as I do. What happens at home stays there. Have fun."

When Letty and Tangles arrived at the house, Andrea and I were in the wine room chowing down on bits from several small platters of different tapas, chasing it with some great red Italian wine.

Andrea blushed a little as the girls kissed her.

"Can we join you or want to be alone?" Tangles asked.

I looked at Andrea, who nodded.

"Join us, of course," I said.

Ricardo the houseboy poured the girls a glass. The girls called him Little Ricky. He did look a little like Ricky Ricardo.

We clicked glasses and drank up.

"Are you into group sex?" Letty asked, looking at Andrea.

"I've done it," she admitted, then glanced at me.

"You like girls and boys, right?" Letty asked.

"I go either way," Andrea said. "Nothing is as good as deep penetration by a man."

"Fuck-Me, Andrea. Say that again, and I'll come right here and now."

The girls laughed.

I had not planned it to go down like this.

"Enough of the third degree," I said with pretended annoyance. I wasn't really annoyed. Fortunately, Andrea didn't look swayed or annoyed at all, not really a surprise because I knew she'd been screwing around with Camila already. But I wanted Andrea to myself tonight. "We'll do the group thing another time," I said to the girls.

"I'm tired anyway," Letty said, getting up from the table, glass in hand.

"Me, too," Tangles said.

I got a kiss from both, and so did Andrea.

"I would have done it." Andrea said after the girls had left.

"And we will if you want to, but not tonight."

At one time, my friend Jason worked for a defense firm that represented insurance carriers in London with focus on aviation crashes. I didn't know for many years that he was a don of wealth. I learned his paychecks from the firm he was with were donated to charity.

"I look at my life like this," he would say. "I went to school to become a lawyer. I don't want to have my own firm. My only choice is not to practice or to work for someone."

Around the time Jason retired, he was enamored with Pixie. She egged him on to buy an executive jet and to start living it up. He followed her advice. Later, he became enamored with Pixie's daughter Lainie. For months now it was no longer a secret that they were engaged. Pixie pretended not to give a damn, but she was pissed. I'm not sure if she was more pissed at her daughter or at Jason.

Even though Jason was retired, he was still well-connected with the insurance carriers he once represented. We seldom talked on the phone anymore. I was a little surprised when he called me at the office. We chatted a bit. He was calling from London. He didn't mention anything about Pixie or Lainie.

"I heard something. Thought I'd pass it along to you. Needless to say, please keep it under wraps."

"No worries."

"I'm not worried, I have always trusted you, Mario."

"Thank you," I said.

"The insurance consortium that handles the paper for Pepe's jet is questioning if Pepe was on board the plane."

"You got to be kidding. I figured by now they would have paid the claim. I don't handle that for his sister Camila."

"They paid the claim months later. Doesn't mean they can't investigate."

"I don't understand," I said. "What difference does it make if he was killed in the plane or not? The claim was property damage only, not life insurance, right?"

"The property damage was paid, and another group paid a life insurance payment of thirty million dollars to his sister, Camila."

"With the kind of money he had, why would he have a life insurance policy? For him, that's chump change."

"Thirty million is not chump change, no matter what you're worth. It's also tax free to the heir."

I found myself hopping up from my desk, and pacing. The long cord of the office phone let me pace the full length of my office.

"I'm on my feet, too anxious to sit down. If there's more, tell me. Jason, tell me the rest."

"When the payment was delayed, Camila got Fino on it. The carrier paid the claim. Now they are saying they are not convinced that the charred body found on the plane was in fact Pepe."

"I can't imagine that Pepe would fake his own death and certainly not to get the thirty million."

"Double indemnity for accidental death. I'm not so sure that a terrorist attack would fall in the accidental death category, but I'm not a life insurance expert. It was sixty."

"Even sixty million is not nearly enough for Pepe to fake his death so that his sister can collect the money, tax free or not," I said.

"Just needed to let you know what I heard."

"I love you, Jason, and I miss you. Got to see you one day soon."

"Milan is only a two-hour flight to London. Get on a plane and come over. Use the penthouse any time you want. You know you are always welcome."

"Thank you," I said.

"I don't want this to touch you. I understand you are engaged to one of his sisters. For that reason, I will bleed my source for anything and everything."

"I went to Pepe's funeral," I said, "He's dead."

I parked myself facing the window and opened the blinds. The sun in Italy can be blinding. I looked out over the bright city, but I was remembering the grim scene of Pepe's January funeral, all too fresh in my mind. In spite of the sunshine, my day felt suddenly overcast.

"Had to be a closed casket, Mario."

"Is this law enforcement investigating?"

"Not law enforcement. These are investigators working directly for the insurance carriers."

After I hung up, I shook my head to dispel the feeing of unreality. There was no way that Jason would expect me not to tell my fiancée about this. Camila had to know already because she was the beneficiary of the policy.

Damn Camachos and their secrets, Olga included. She wasn't a blood Camacho, but she was one of them, nevertheless.

I called Olga on her cell and got no answer. I called Letty in.

"Get hold of Olga. I already tried her cell."

At least I reached Camila.

"Baby, where are you?"

"Amorcito, how about a hello?" She laughed.

She was in Guatemala but on the way to Bogota.

"I need to speak with you and Olga in person."

Camila didn't ask why. "Olga will be in Bogota on the day after tomorrow when I'm there."

"I can fly there," I said. "I leased my plane. Bad timing."

"Use the DC9."

"My plane would have been a lot more reasonable on fuel."

"Amorcito, your plane is leased. Let the company worry about the fuel cost."

Why did I keep worrying about costs? No one listened anyway.

"If take it to Bogota, I may not want to give it back," I warned.

"Keep it as a company plane. Use it when you need a plane. It was just sitting anyway."

I told Jules and Andrea that I was going to meet Camila and Olga, and that I'd return as soon as possible.

I left them in charge.

At home, Letty and Tangles wanted to know why they couldn't go along.

"It's personal, more for them than me. Don't ask me questions. Got it?"

I got a salute from Letty. Tangles noticed and aped the salute.

I wanted to be able to laugh, but I was far from it. I was worried about the domino effect. I believe in the domino effect. I have killed more than one man in my life, in self defense. Everything has consequences. My life is a line of escalating dominos with each subsequent fall being worse than the one before. The attempts on my life, the burned house, just one more domino going down.

I hope that Olga was totally in the clear, that Camila was in the clear, that they were safe from being just another domino going down. I hoped that Pepe was dead or so well hidden no one would ever prove he was alive.

Andrea arranged for the crew that would fly the plane, three pilots and a flight attendant. For my small plane that was leased out now, Letty had called a service to rent the crew, and the plane was always under maintenance care at the Van Nuys airport where I kept it. A no brainer. All you needed was a check book. A big DC9 was a different story. Letty was watching everything Andrea did. She got a copy of the checklist Andrea used for preparation and studied it.

The girls came aboard to see me off. The interior was similar to Olga's plane. I might have flown in this plane before with Olga or Camila. Rita was my flight attendant. She was curvy with a dynamite personality and blatantly Italian, though her English was flawless.

"Take care of the Boss," Letty told her.

"Or else," Tangles said.

Letty said, "Leave some for us." In Italian, no less.

Rita glanced over where I was already belted in. She smiled.

"Prometto di non consumarlo completament."[11]

Rita had energy galore. Several hours later I was in bed getting hands-on proof that Rita was a terrific masseuse. She came prepared with a choice of oils. It was the longest massage I can remember. There is something different about getting a massage in a bed flying at five hundred plus miles per hour at over 30,000 feet. I loved it.

The plane landed at the military airport I had been to before. A big four door black Lincoln awaited me. I learned from the driver that it was fully armored. Behind us, a car followed with a number of security people, none of whom I recognized. I was delivered to Olga's house. We had stayed at Camila's house when we arrived for Pepe's funeral, but I had never seen Olga's home. The entry gates to the property were as tall as the gates at Casa Luna. The guardhouse was not hidden. It was in front of the gates. A visitor was going nowhere if not cleared by the two guards. The gates opened inward where another a guard was posted at either side, both carrying automatic rifles or machine guns.

Olga and Camila were at the foot of the stairs waiting outside for me. Olga flung herself at me, bathed me in kisses and hugs, then Camila. I walked inside between them. A servant had already carried my suitcase in.

"I love the house," I said when we sat down to eat.

"You will love it more when I give you the tour," Olga said, beaming. "It's not as big as Camila's. I love it though."

Olga had met Jason in Mexico City when he accompanied Pixie, but Camila couldn't remember meeting him. Olga had also seen him in London when he hosted Pixie and her at the penthouse that once belonged to Sami. In confidence, I told them what he had shared with me.

"If we don't keep this between us and Jason's source finds out that there

---

[11] I promise not to consume him entirely

is a leak, Jason will lose that source. I don't need to tell you how important it may be to keep this source feeding information to Jason."

"Pepe is not alive," Olga said.

Camila laughed. "Absurd. Why do they think that?"

"Your guess is as good as mine. Jason has no idea."

"There is nothing for them to find," Camila said. "I didn't even know he had that stupid life insurance policy until they contacted me to tell me I was a beneficiary."

"Jason is correct. Camila asked Fino to push them about the double indemnity clause and whatever he did, they paid double the thirty million policy."

"I deposited the money in a New York bank, "Camila said. "The entire amount is still there. It was tax free."

We agreed that we would never discuss this on the telephone, and that they would not share this information with anyone else. I would not tell my team about it either.

"Amor, don't lose any sleep about this," Camila said. "Pepe died in that plane."

"He did," Olga confirmed. "Frankly, we don't need Jason to tell us any more."

I thought that was rude, but let it pass.

Camila left for her house late in the afternoon. She said she had a date. It was a bouncy, high-spirited Camila without a worry in the world who said good bye. It was odd to see her so carefree when the news I delivered was so bad. Olga and I made it to the bedroom without delay. We made up for lost time, but the topic came up during a break in the sex.

"Is it possible that Pepe staged his own death, not for the insurance money but for some other reason?"

"Pepe is dead," Olga said.

"I think so, too."

"Dead and hopefully burning in hell." Her head was on my chest, my arm around her. The room was dark, and I could not see her face. I wanted to turn on the light and see her expression. Instead, I did nothing. I got very still.

"What are you saying?" My pulse kicked up a notch.

"He raped me so many times. He slapped me around. He beat me so badly that it took weeks for me to heal. My stomach was blue from his boot print. Once I bled so much a doctor had to come to the house to stitch the bloody fissures in my anus to get me through it. He deserved what he got. I regret I didn't shoot him myself or launch with my own hands that rocket that blew him up."

I left the bed. I found myself in the bathroom vomiting till my stomach was empty, and all I could do was dry heave. I felt like someone had hit my head with a bat. Anger filled me till tears seeped out of my eyes. I didn't even notice when Olga came in until she touched me. She was sitting on the floor behind me, and I was still perched over the toilet fighting the heaves.

"Amor, it's fine now. He had an ugly death. He paid."

I got up and gave her my hand. She stood.

"The last kick cost him millions. I skimmed from deposits. It's too bad he's dead. He'll never know I fucked him where I know it would hurt him."

We returned to bed, lying on our sides. In the morning, we woke in the same position. I felt a closeness with Olga I had never felt before. I realized maybe for the first time how much she trusts me. She had not had the life I had expected. Not a life filled with riches and happiness with no bumps or heart aches. I guess money does not buy happiness.

In the morning, I was ready to talk. I wanted to do something. I don't know what. Do something that would somehow make changes, make things better. Before I could say a word, she cut me off.

"I do not want to discuss what I told you, not today or in the future. Promise me, Amor."

"I want to know one thing," I said. "Does Camila know about this?'

"She knows. There's something else. Something I should not mention. Camila was also a victim of his abuse. Their father had molested her. Her brother did the same."

I would not think such a wave of shock and disgust could crash over me twice, but that's what happened. When I opened my eyes, her face was two inches from me.

"It's your secret, Olga. I hurt that you went through the abuse. It's a good thing he's dead. If the insurance company is right and he's not dead, he will be if I ever meet up with him."

"He's dead, Amor." She said this with finality.

I got the tour of her house. Two stories, half the size of Camila's. It would fit in one corner of the Camacho mansion which had, incidentally, a cemetery on the grounds where Pepe and his parents were resting forever.

Bogota September 30,1987

Olga was supposed to leave that day for New York. I was ready to get to Milan.

"Let's play hooky for another day. Let me show you my Bogota. You never got a look when you were here for the funeral." I would have preferred to stay in bed with her all day.

I had not noticed the helipad, but I did now when a helicopter landed on it.

"Reminds me when we ran away from the Bahamas," I said jokingly.

"Amor, we didn't run away from the Bahamas."

We certainly had fled from the Bahamas, but I didn't argue.

In the Bahamas, two guys were shot dead at the Camacho residence. I walked in and saw the aftermath. I never knew learned who killed who, but there were definitely two guys who had walked in expecting to make a deal who left rolled up in a carpet. Minutes after it happened, Olga had Camila and me and herself on a helicopter headed to the airport.

Again, Olga and I were getting on a helicopter, this time in Bogota. This helicopter was a four-seater, two spots in the front where the pilot and a passenger sat, and two seats behind.

We got in.

"Where's the pilot going?" I said, pointing at the guy who landed the aircraft.

"I'm the pilot, Amor."

"No way," I said.

She handed me a helmet and put her finger to her lips indicating for me to hush. I put the helmet on and talked into the microphone.

"Baby, get the pilot back here."

"Buckle up, Amor," she said into her microphone. "I don't want you flying out."

She looked different from the Olga I knew. She fiddled with the dashboard of gadgets. The engine roared. The blades turned. Her smile in my direction was supposed to be reassuring.

I knew I had to fuck her while she wore that helmet.

We were up, up, and away in less than a minute.

"What other secrets do you have?"

"One at a time, Amor. We'll have fun today, I promise."

In minutes we were flying over the Camacho mansion, normally occupied only by maintenance staff. The Milan house had twenty-six people working there, not counting security. I wondered how many worked in this place that was at least three times larger.

We didn't land. Five minutes later, we flew over Camila's house. Not very far over, either. We were close enough that I could have jumped out and landed on my feet.

"Do we need to be this close to the ground?" I said.

"Amor, trust me already."

I thought Camila would come out of her house and wave, but that didn't happen.

"Where is Camila?"

"She left this morning. Let's head to the city center now."

Olga kept her head and piloted that bubble.

Why did this make me think about the assholes who had approached my house with nefarious intent via helicopter? One dropped Luca Rossi on my balcony, and the other dropped fire bombs.

"How long you been doing this?"

"I got a license almost ten years ago."

"You were just a kid ten years ago." I said this for her benefit. We're close to the same age. Ten years ago, she would have been in her thirties.

I heard her laugh over the noise.

"I'm still a kid, Amor."

"I love you, Olga."

She still faced forward, but her eyes flicked at me for just an instant.

"Behave. We could crash if I start coming. You know how I get when you call me by my name."

I looked where she was looking. We had flown over a congested area of the city. Big metropolis.

"All those buildings."

Flying over a city in a helicopter gives you a unique perspective of its personality. Bogota felt very different from Pasadena, and very different from Milan.

"City Center, Amor. That is the tallest building over there. Not that tall."

"Uh oh," I said. I saw a police helicopter also in the air.

"What?"

I pointed at the police helicopter.

Olga was all business.

The pilot was seated on the right like Olga.

She changed direction and headed toward him.

She changed channels. She gave her call sign, and the Colombian cop gave his.

"Jaime, how are you?" she said in Spanish, "Been long time."

"¿Qué cuentas?"[12] he said. "Olga, good to see you."

"Same here, Jaime. Say hi to everyone."

He gave her a thumbs up. She did the same. She also blew him a kiss.

After about an hour in the air, she radioed the 'big house.' She told the chief of staff that we would be there in thirty minutes, and we were starving.

I was still unused to the idea that Olga could fly a helicopter. It seemed very exciting to me. As she circled the big house and readied for landing, I had visions of doing something myself that would be just as exciting. Maybe piloting my own plane.

I wasn't so good at math. Never had been. Maybe math has nothing to do with becoming a pilot.

Olga was full of surprises. Next, she'd be showing me she can pilot her big plane.

I was alone on my way to Milan. I drank more wine than I normally do, probably because I didn't get hours of massage. A friendly flight attendant was there, but she was only so friendly. It wasn't like she was going to have a drink with me.

I was troubled by the recent revelations about Pepe. I shudder to think of Pepe doing what he did to Olga and to his own sister, Camila. I have always thought I was good at reading people, but he had definitely flown in under my radar. I had not read him like I always thought I was good at doing.

The truth is that I'd never spent much time with him. We'd met when he'd given me a ride from Venezuela when I'd been kidnapped. Oscar brought him in because Pepe had lots of underground contacts in the part of the world

---

[12] "What's been going on?"

where I'd been secreted away. Most of our contact had been by phone, an occasional plane flight, and a couple of visits at one of his villas. That he was a total prick was a complete surprise to me. It bothered me to think he had spent three nights with Tangles. She had come through that unharmed, though. I would have seen the bruises if he had abused her. By her own admission, the sex they had was consensual, and she got a diamond out of it. The first time I had an opportunity, I would return to the big house, and piss on his grave.

Olga was certain that he was dead. I wondered if his coffin had been empty. If they had recovered remains. If there were remains.

"I promise you, he's dead," she had said. It was chilling.

We had met in Paris for Christmas, gathered waiting for Pepe's arrival. I remember with great clarity the call from Bogota that had announced Pepe's death, Camila crumbling to the floor, Olga beside her, both of them appearing emotionally distraught. Was that real or had it been drama? Camila had cried. Olga had cried. How could Olga have cried as she did? She should have celebrated that he was killed. Both of them should have celebrated. Had they been acting? And if they were, was it for the benefit of witnesses? That was Pixie, Letty, Tangles, Betty, Riana, me? No way.

The more I thought of it, the more I believed that the tears and emotion had been real. That gave me a sense of relief, because they were too torn up by his death to be responsible for it. I was able to assure myself that they did not kill him.

Olga piloting a helicopter with the ease of driving a car had taken me by surprise. Bottom line, nothing either of these two did should be a surprise to me.

Homecoming to Milan felt like homecoming. I used to feel the same way returning to Casa Luna. After a trip, Letty always made it perfect, and Tangles was her shadow. I loved them both. Maybe it wasn't the address I was coming home to, but my team.

Living in this house that didn't belong to me had not been hard to get used to. Being away from California didn't hurt. The truth is that I have spent a lot of time living out of a suitcase, especially when chasing cases for months at a time, in foreign countries. When it came right down to it, I didn't have much going outside my home.

I missed my aunt and especially Melina, and Betty, too. I missed Pixie too, but she wasn't tethered to a place, now that she spent so many months touring. I was confident that I'd see them eventually. Melina had a boyfriend now, so it would never be the same.

Or would it?

Milan October 2, 1987

Lunch with Letty and Tangles was great Mexican food served in the room we used as a dining room. Flour tortillas stuffed with grilled rib-eye steak, quesadillas, refried beans smothered with cotija cheese. The chef here was good, but not up to Miguel's standards.

"If I believed we were going to keep the leasing company headquartered in Milan, I would buy a house here."

"You got this huge house. Why would you want to buy?" Tangles asked.

"This is not his house," Letty said.

"Letty's right," I said, without interrupting my chewing.

Letty looked over at my plate and rang a little bell that sat in the middle of the table. Ricky must have been standing just outside the room we were in, because the ring of the bell was still in the air when he ran in. He was a small young man, dark haired, and slim, probably in his late teens or early twenties and he favored Desi Arnaz. I could see why Tangles and Letty had started calling him Little Ricky.

"We could use some more guac," Letty said, glancing over the table. "Also, more salsa, cotija, and maybe some crema, you know, sour cream, crème fraîche." She thought for a minute, then said, "Panna da cucina."

"Mastering Italian?" I asked.

She shrugged. "We gotta eat."

Tangles laughed. "Queen of Berlitz."

Ricky returned with dishes of condiments, and left us to our conversation again.

"I don't understand why you want to buy," Tangles said, "You're going to marry Olga, so it's your house."

"Olga says she has no ownership in any Camacho assets. This house belongs to Camila or maybe the business. I don't really know what entity holds the title. My living here is written into my contract with running the leasing company."

"You got to love the deal, Boss," Tangles said.

Before I could agree, Letty did it for me. "He made the deal. Of course, he loves this house. It's just not his."

I could not have said it better myself. I glanced down at my plate and saw my guac and sour cream were gone. I grinned at Letty, and got some from the dishes Ricky had brought in.

Barcelona October 2, 1987
Olga

Riana and I were in her new Barcelona apartment, the one that her father had purchased for her after she broke up with her husband. I had just gotten the grand tour of the place. It had been professionally decorated, and it was modern and nice, but it wasn't personalized. It wasn't like Riana had spent much time here. Low ceilings, lots of windows overlooking Barcelona. There was a lot of empty space. I don't know if it was the decorator's deliberate intention, or that way so Riana could make it her own. It was bright and cold, but at least the place had a nice big bed, though it was weirdly set in the center of the bedroom, almost like a stage. The plan was to play a little that night and take off to Chicago in the morning. I had to call Camila to touch base.

On the phone with Camila. I took a deep breath and jumped in. I had to tell her.

"I told him what Pepe did to me."

I heard a quick intake of breath, even over the phone. I could feel her shock through the airwaves.

"Why would you do that?"

"I did not plan to."

"It's not like you to be so careless."

"It just happened. Too late to take it back. Look, I had to do something. He was mourning Pepe. He talks about him like he's a martyr on a fucking cross. I had to crush that pipedream. I am sick to death of hearing what a loss it is for us. He's your brother, but you and I know we are much better off with Pepe out of the picture. I mentioned you but didn't give him details. I didn't tell him about Santiago and Mateo either."

"Stupid, stupid, stupid."

I heard a click on her end, then Camila was gone. She hung up on me.

If I hadn't been at Riana's, I would have called her to talk it out. Riana did not give me time to brood, or even think about what had just happened. It's probably a good thing. Camila would cool off and see the wisdom of telling Mario the truth, or at least some of the truth.

"You took way too long to come get me," Riana said. "I was dying to be with you. I came this close to going out to buy coke." She used her index finger and thumb to show how close.

We ended up in bed, that bed that sat in the middle of a big empty room with nothing in it but a stark floor lamp. There were no curtains on floor-to-ceiling window to the balcony. Barcelona glittered below us like some landscape caught in a snow-globe.

I kissed my friend. Maybe I felt like I was like an Alcoholics Anonymous sponsor, but sometimes it seems like Riana has replaced her coke addiction by an addiction to me. Not that I'm complaining.

"I'm here now. You can stay with me as long as you like."

Riana brightened.

"I love traveling with you," she whispered.

We cuddled, close as two bodies can get. It was almost like the emptiness of the room brought us closer together.

"*Me encanta estar contigo.*"[13]

"Do you think I made a mistake telling him about Pepe?" I didn't have to say who I was talking about. Riana knew.

"You should have told him before. Then Mario would have killed him and not you."

I sat up. I kicked off the covers and got out of bed, the uncarpeted floor cold underfoot. It was granite or marble. Some kind of stone.

"Don't ever say that again," I said sharper than I intended to, but I meant it. "Don't even think it."

"Olga, don't be mad. Come down here." She patted the bed beside her. "I was joking. I'm sorry."

I lay down close to her.

"No more jokes. Not about that, anyway."

In minutes, Riana was asleep. My escape was not so easy. I turned away from her and stretched out. I was tired. We would be leaving early in the morning.

Riana had only been a distraction. Camila's hang-up was still bugging me.

I sat on the edge of the bed. The only light source was Barcelona through the glass. Naked, I walked across that cold floor into the den and looked at the phone. That room was dark also, lit only by a parallel vision of the city through the window.

The phone's numbers lit up when I lifted the receiver. I dialed.

She picked up. Even though she said nothing right away, I felt a little comforted knowing she was there. At least she had picked up, and not ignored

---

[13] I love being with you.

me.

"I can't go to sleep knowing you are mad at me."

Camila didn't respond right away.

"Amorcito, what is done, is done."

"Thank you, *Hermanita.*"[14]

"After I hung up, I remembered that when I first met Mario, I told him about my father molesting me," Camila said. "I told him how when my mother caught him on top of me, she killed him that night, then killed herself."

"I should have not said anything about you. I had no right. Your secrets are your own. Just...it was killing me how Mario kept Pepe on a pedestal."

"My brother is dead and buried. Between us, his reputation doesn't matter. You know how sorry I am that he treated you the way he did. And Santiago and Mateo—"

I cut her off. I did not want to think about Santiago and Mateo. "I know. *Hermanita, te quiero con todo mi corazón.*"[15]

"*Yo también te quiero, Amor.*"[16]

"I feel better. I can sleep now," I said.

Still, sleep did not come easy.

I wished she had not mentioned them.

Santiago and Mateo had been two of Pepe's most trusted bodyguards. Both men were middle-aged like Pepe, good looking guys who were always dressed in a suit and tie. They did not wear dress coats well. Their muscular arms and shoulders strained the seams.

I returned to bed. Riana had not wakened. I tried to sleep, but the scene played behind my closed eyelids.

The night Santiago and Mateo died, Pepe had called me at home in Bogota and asked me to come over with an update on the past month. I brought

---

[14] Sister.

[15] Sister, I love you with all my heart.

[16] I love you, too, my love.

a ledger and a notebook with me. When I walked in, I could smell the liquor. I could tell he had been drinking, but that was not unusual. He was rarely completely sober.

He was at the big house in his study set up like a living room: his desk, plus sofas and chairs for seating for thirty-five. Truth is, I preferred when we had these updates with Camila around. He was alone, not even a secretary in the room. He was on a leather sofa that faced his desk. I kissed him on both cheeks and sat down beside him. That wasn't enough. He kissed me on the lips, not like a sister. It was not the first time. It didn't bother me.

He asked about the month.

I gave him a quick summary of my activity for the past twenty-one days, reading from my notes. I gave him the total for all bank deposits and the total for all purchases paid on behalf of Camila's activity. He wasn't paying attention. He kept staring at my body, avoiding my eyes. I saw that glazed look and my heart sank.

"*Eres hermosa.*"[17]

I kissed him lightly on the lips.

"*Gracias, Amor.*"

He put his hands on my biceps. It didn't take much for him to push me down. My feet were still on the floor, his position awkward.

My notebook and pen clattered to the floor.

I played it cool.

"Amor, you are a beautiful man. You have women coming out of your ears. I know you don't want to do this to me again."

The smell of alcohol on him was strong. I kept talking softly. I had vowed to myself not to let this happen again, to do whatever I had to nip it in the bud. He was drunker than I had thought at first.

"Stop, Pepe, please."

His hand was under my skirt. His fingers invaded between my legs. I

---

[17] You are beautiful.

heard my panties rip.

"Amor stop."

He ignored me.

I rolled off the couch and out of his reach. He lost his grip on me and was left holding my torn underwear. I stumbled to my feet.

"I'm leaving, Pepe."

I reached for my notebook and pen. His hand closed around the back of my neck.

I woke up naked on his bed, his weight on top of me. Between my legs, it burned. I had already been penetrated harshly. He was drunk, fumes coming off of him. He was groaning, barely coherent. I frantically tried pushing him off of me.

"God must be with me. You can't even get it up," I hissed. "*Cobarde!*"[18]

He slapped me once, then again. Naked, he got out of bed. He was hairy, and the least fit I had ever seen him. He called for Santiago and Mateo, and when they came in, they were uncertain, seeing him like that, naked, his cock at half mast, and seeing me on the bed with my clothes ripped up.

"Fuck her!" he said. "That's an order."

I had no intention of waiting to see how obedient they were. I ran across the bedroom making for the door.

Santiago caught me and flung me on the mattress.

Pepe stood next to the bed and watched Santiago mount me. Pepe jeered and cat-called, raucous hard words, and encouraged him like a spectator at a boxing arena.

I had given up the fight. I looked past Santiago like he was not even there. I watched Pepe, swaying like he was about to fall off of his feet, and swigging from his bottle of booze. His dick had wilted completely. Santiago moaned, and bounced and groaned, and emptied himself into me. He moved aside but did not leave. He sat on the edge of the bed while Mateo climbed on me. I had

---

[18] Coward.

flirted with Mateo before, but never with the intention of consummating any-thing. It was hard to believe these were the two guys I knew, but I shouldn't be surprised. They were Pepe's puppets.

I put my arms around him, and I kissed him, pretending a passion that I hoped would slam Pepe in the gut.

"Fuck me," I said to Mateo.

Pepe had stopped yelling orders. Mateo looked at Pepe as though to get an okay.

There was nothing from Pepe.

Mateo went deeper inside. I hurt all over, not just where he was invad-ing me. My face was still stinging from Pepe's slaps, and my neck hurt from whatever Pepe had done to knock me out.

Mateo got off then got up.

Pepe asked him if he liked it. He asked Santiago. Both of them were sit-ting there like a couple of yellow curs.

I managed to get myself off of the bed, feeling battered and bruised. My insides burned, but I wasn't thinking about how I felt. I wanted out. I thought I had a chance now that Santiago and Mateo were looking wringed out, and Pepe barely able to stand on his own. Surely the worst was over.

"Puta Callejera largate!"[19]

Pepe screamed incoherently, pointing at the sperm running down my legs. I grabbed a robe that was hanging on a chair and headed for the bedroom door without looking back. Behind me, I heard rapid gunfire. Deafening. I didn't know if the shots were aimed in my direction. I made it through the door, and saw Pepe with his back to me, a Smith & Wesson in his hand. The mirror showed me the grin on his face, the drunken swagger, the bloody blowback. I couldn't see Santiago and Mateo from where I was, but I knew by the manner their voices had been cut short that he had shot them in cold blood.

It took an eternity to get from the master bedroom to the entry of the

---

[19] Streetwalker Whore get out of here.

house. I was running, but it felt like I was in slow motion. I kept tripping on the long robe, scrambling forward, skinning my knees, slamming into door jambs, knocking over furniture. I passed his guards, ran outside, ran past his people who were pouring into the house. No one tried to stop me. And why would they? I am known to one and all as Olga Camacho, Pepe's little sister.

My guard opened the door to my car.

"Drive!"

In all the years I lived at the Camacho house, I had never been attracted to Pepe. He had been the sweetest step-brother a sister could want until I graduated from university and went to work for him. When I came back from school, something inside him had changed. It was like all that was good in him was dead.

After the first time he took me by force, I told him, "If you just ask me nice, I'll fuck you."

"I own you," he said.

"No one owns me."

"No?" He had laughed, flipped me to my stomach, and forced himself in my ass. I'd been young and stupid then and didn't even know that was done. There was anger and meanness in him, but I learned fast how to avoid him when he was at his drunkest. I did not miss Pepe. I did not regret giving the order. Maybe I missed the person he used to be before, but maybe not.

I moved closer to Riana. I was still haunted by the ghosts of Pepe, of course, and those yellow curs, Santiago and Mateo. Sleep still refused to come to me.

Milan February 22, 1988
Mario

Letty and Tangles proved valuable locating used aircraft that were certifiable as air worthy. They kept busy making cold calls and whatever else they were doing to drum up inventory.

An airliner crashed in the south of France. The old habits kicked in.

"Boss, let us handle the case," Letty pleaded. "I have this itch to do it.

Tangles and I want to, please. It just feels wrong to pass it up."

"Baby, Gonor is only paying expenses up front."

"We want to jump on this. It's close, and we know we can handle it. We won't come home with as many retainers as if you were there, but so what? Goner will be happy to get something more than nothing, right boss?"

"I'm burned out," I told Gonor. "The girls want to do this. I won't let them do it unless you pay them up front."

"How many cases can they get?" Goner asked.

"That's a dumb question. Who knows? Do I look like a fucking crystal ball?"

"Mario, take a couple weeks off, and go at it yourself."

"I'm out, at least for now," I said firmly. "Want to try the girls out?"

"I can't pay up front. You know that."

"Give them half what you used to give me, plus their expenses."

He snapped up the offer.

"Sure. That I can manage."

I didn't think they would bring home a lot of signed retainers. That meant Goner could manage the smaller volume and smaller payment, but he'd have something. The girls would be happy because they would be getting more with me out of the cut.

"The money you get from Goner is all yours. I have nothing to do with the case."

"Not fair for you," Letty said. "This is your business."

"I already spent too much time on this. Take it or leave it," I said.

They took it.

"Take us off the leasing company payroll," Letty said. "At least while we're not here."

"Go," I said.

I would miss them being constantly underfoot, but I didn't tell them that.

Goner faxed a retainer template for them to use, if and when they got a client. The next day they left on a commercial flight without their security guard. Letty assured me they were safe.

"Boss, you know I can take care of myself and Tangles. And we can call Juan in, if we need him."

"Bitch, I can take care of myself," Tangles said.

I kissed my girls.

Later that day at my office, Olga called. Gossip among my girls flies fast.

"Amor, Pixie said the girls went to the south of France on that crash. Is that true? They went on that crash without you?"

"Yes," I said. "I'm alone now. When you are coming home?"

Olga laughed. "Amor, I'm in Pasadena. Get on a plane, I'll wait for you."

I glanced at my calendar and realized it had been exactly year since the fire. I had not been to Pasadena once, but this was Olga's fourth trip there. Her stays were short, but I liked the idea that she was staying in what someday would be our home.

"If I get there tomorrow, how long will you be staying?"

"Four, no, three nights, counting tomorrow."

Three hours later I was on the DC9 I'd been flying around in closing leasing deals. I was getting used to the luxury of having the use of the big plane. I'd had some updates done. New carpet, new bed, new seats throughout. I would have done more if I had planned to keep it. This plane was GAL inventory, and whoever eventually leased the plane would be absorbing the cost of improvements.

I was making so much money for GAL that using the plane and the fuel at the business's expense was a legitimate cost of doing business.

Letty and Tangles had not been gone long but they had been my constant companions. I missed them sorely. I do not do well alone. I was not looking forward to a solo flight.

Andrea solved that problem. She got me two flight female flight attendants instead of one, but that was just a perk.

"You will like these two," Andrea had warned me. "You may not have anything left for Olga when you get to Pasadena."

My attendants Adea and Edi were probably a little younger than me. I did not ask their ages. It turned out they were from my neck of the woods—Los Angeles.

A sex-filled flight all the way to California was great way to break in the plane's new California king bed.

Chapter 5
Pasadena February 23, 1988
Mario

When I got to Casa Luna on Tuesday, it took me some time to hug and kiss my fiancée, then Riana, who looked more beautiful than ever. My testosterone must be running on high. I was ready for more.

My house crew was lined up as I entered the house. I'd never stood on ceremony with them, but it was a formal gesture on their part to welcome me home.

I hugged each familiar face in the line. Miguel was at the head of the line, and teary-eyed.

"I miss you, Boss, very much. I should be in Milan cooking for you."

"Hang in there," I said. "I may be back before you know it."

Olga was in earshot, but revealed no response, her smile in place.

I inspected the entire house and kept sniffing to see if there was any hint of smoke. There was none. The house appeared exactly as I had left it, even down to my desk, the same model Monteverdi desk and credenza. The contents of the drawers and my closet were the only things that had changed. Jo had even taken pictures of the bookcase shelves to replicate exactly what had been on them before.

Now that I was home, I wondered why I had put it off. Yes, it was smaller than the villa in Milan, but it was home.

I missed having a reunion with Pixie and Lainie who were on tour, but Betty showed. I kissed her passionately with Olga right there.

"I missed you," I told my friend, my masseuse.

"Oh, Boss, I missed you, too. I thought you'd never come home."

"Join us for dinner," Olga held out her hand for Betty. "Miguel is dying to have company for dinner."

You'd think I would have taken them all to bed, but I didn't. I wanted Olga all to myself. Betty gave Riana a massage. I didn't see her until the next afternoon when she returned to do Olga and me.

Olga and I were still in bed.

"My pussy is so sore," Olga told Betty. "Work it in when you do me."

"You got it," Betty told her. Both of them were laughing. "I have the perfect oil for it."

Over dinner, I told Olga, "Baby, I need your support to move the office to Los Angeles. I love Milan, but this is home."

"Amor, you're running the company. It's your call. Camila will say the same."

I liked hearing that.

"I'll work on it," I said. "Let me get fifty more leases on the books, then we'll talk about it, okay?"

I got a savory kiss.

"Si, Amor."

Letty called my cell. She already knew I was home in Pasadena and asked me to give her regards to her uncle. I did better than that—I called him on the intercom, and when he came up, I put him on the phone. When he handed it back to me, he was teary-eyed again, and looking like the proud uncle he was.

Letty was all business. "We're circling the hotel where the families are staying, like we do. Wish us luck, Boss."

"You don't need luck, Babe. You got skills," I said.

"I wish I was there with you."

"Next time," I said. "And we'll be coming home to stay."

At two in the morning, Pixie called. She didn't even mention my being home. She was over the moon about Lainie and Jason.

"Lainie broke up with him. She says she's keeping the engagement ring per her deal with him and all the jewelry he gave her." Pixie giggled.

"Baby, I thought you were all over their engagement."

"I am, I was, but it still stung. He left me because Lainie is twenty-two and I'm going to be forty soon. Fuck him."

"Maybe not," I said. "Maybe they were just a better match." Though I really didn't see Jason as a match with anyone but Sami. "It's good to be home. I'm sorry you're on tour."

"Are you home for good?"

"Not yet. Back to Milan in a few days."

"Then I'll stop and see you in Milan next month, I promise."

On our third night together, Olga, Riana and I smoked a joint and laughed like dopes, played a bunch of games, and went to my wine room. I didn't pull down the disco ball, but we played music on the juke box. Miguel brought us snacks like he was on a mission to make up for lost time. If I'd been with Letty and Tangles, I'd have hit the pool and my workout room. Olga was another story. She did have exercise in mind, though. Olga had already invited Riana to bed with us.

Olga's face wore a mischievous expression. "It's just me and her, Amor," she said.

"Mario, I'm starved for a big dick," Riana said.

"Charge her batteries." Olga said.

"I promise to give back," Riana said.

Olga laughed, then I felt two sets of hands on my thing.

I went to work. I took care of Riana. She was wilder than I could remember her being. I remembered that there had been a husband in the picture at one time, but she'd cut him loose before we'd ever met.

"I don't get enough," Riana kept saying.

That might be true, but if so, it wasn't for my lack of effort. A good time was had by all. I made sure of it.

Milan March 14, 1988

Letty and Tangles returned to Milan three weeks after they had left. They messengered eight retainers to Gonor.

"It's marvelous," I said, hugging them. They'd come home to the Milan house, and arrived in time for dinner. It was pasta night. Okay, in Italy, every night is pasta night, but the chef tried to cook according to our taste and so limited pasta to one night a week. We had plates of angel hair and some kind of red gravy that was delectable.

"Oh Boss, if you had been there, we would have knocked out forty retainers or more. We look too young and inexperienced," Letty said.

"She's right, Boss. Those eight retainers, they are men. Didn't sign a single family where the woman is the survivor of the decedent."

"Eight is still good," I said. "I figure he'll give you twenty-five thousand plus your expenses."

Milan is seven hours ahead of Chicago. I pushed away from the table and called Goner right away and gave him the numbers.

Right away, he wired them thirty thousand, plus expenses. "That kind of volume I can handle. I wish I could have more, but this is very good. Thank you, Mario."

"Don't thank me," I said. "It was all their doing."

The girls told me they were giving me half the money.

"No way José. We made a deal," I said. "This was your baby from start to finish, so stop with the nonsense."

We had dined Italian style which means lots of lazy conversation drawn out over the meal. We'd long since stopped eating.

"Okay, Boss, we're free until the next case. Want us on getting GAL inventory, or should we draw unemployment?" Letty asked.

"Fuck unemployment. I want you in the office."

"First, we need to catch up." Tangles said.

"Catch up?" I asked.

"Boss, don't pretend to be dense." Letty gave my shoulder a thump. "You know what she means."

If there was a way to have Olga and Letty for keeps, I'd sign in a minute. Sign what? I laughed to myself.

"What's so funny, Boss?" Tangles asked.

"Let's hit the wine room, first," I said. I didn't think I could explain that thought anyway. Fortunately, no one asked me to explain again.

"I missed that room so much," Letty said, already up and heading for the stairs.

Ricky followed us down.

The politics of relationships and business don't make much sense to me. I mean, I'm affianced to Olga, and everyone here knows it. They also know that Letty and Tangles are living in the Milan house with me. And while I spent time with Andrea, there was no hint of anything at the office. She came over to the house. Sometimes we just had dinner, other times we had dinner then ventured into one of the guest rooms. We never used Olga's master bedroom or my bedroom either.

Andrea didn't want to use a bed I shared with Olga or Letty or Tangles. We used a guest room.

When Letty and Tangles and I slept together which was almost all the time, we used my bedroom.

Los Angeles February 1, 1989

About two years into my contract with the leasing company, I stepped into my office on the 48th floor at the Twin Towers in downtown Los Angeles. We had leased half the floor and had an option for the other half when it became available.

I had placed one hundred plus leases with our partner bank consortium that Riana's father had put together. Half our leases were new planes, which had been a learning experience for me. I could never have done it without Jules, Andrea, Dante, and deep pockets full of Camacho money. Without the consortium, it would have been impossible.

When we moved to Los Angeles, the office in Milan employed thirty people. The new offices were so empty they echoed. We had this giant space, and only four of us worked there, at first. That didn't count Letty and Tangles pitching in.

I made a conference call to Camila and Olga from my new Twin Towers office to give them the update.

"I'm making Jules the manager of the office. They can feed us cases, and we can feed them cases, depending on where the lease requests come from. Andrea is moving to Los Angeles. She will be my assistant. Dante wants to stay in Milan but is willing to fly wherever I have a plane to check out."

"Well done, Amorcito," Camila said.

"Milan will miss you, Amor," Olga said.

"I'll be back and forth," I said. "Jules needs to know I'm watching."

"Letty, Tangles, if you want to stay in Milan, you can stay at the villa," Olga said.

"Thank you," Letty said. "We will let you know what we decide."

After the call, Letty turned a troubled face to me.

"What's up?"

"Boss, can I still live with you at Casa Luna?"

"Absolutely. My feelings would be hurt if you wanted anything else."

"I'm jealous," Tangles said.

"Liar," Letty said. "You want to live in your apartment."

"I do," Tangles said. She snuck a quick look at me. "Boss, your feelings aren't hurt, are they?"

"Not at all," I said.

"I want it to be like before, Boss, when I stayed as much as I wanted, but could go home whenever I needed or wanted to."

"I wouldn't want it any other way," I said.

The industry soon learned that we had an office in Los Angeles. The phone started ringing. Andrea hired two leasing specialists to work the phones. Sometimes Letty and Tangles came in to do filing work and other minor chores, and sometimes to man the phones showing our new staff how to get it done.

Mostly, Letty and Tangles returned to the routine of looking for small aircraft cases in the United States. By the time returned to Los Angeles, they'd handled three airliner cases. Their volume was low, but they never home empty-handed. Goner dealt directly with them. To my surprise, every so often I got a check from Goner for a percentage on an old case that we had partnered in. Letty and Tangles work in the fourth floor conference room at my house.

"We're making enough between us on the cases we're giving Goner," Letty said.

"Not to mention that you let us work out of here, so we don't have office expenses," Tangles said.

Everything that happens at Casa Luna is under Letty's direct control again, just as it used to be. I have always felt like Letty is the lady of the house. Olga probably thinks of it as a housekeeping position. I've never paid Letty for supervising the housekeeping staff except maybe when she and Miguel first came to work for me. It is a lot of work. She supervises the staff, except for Miguel.

Los Angeles February 14, 1989

On Valentines Day, Melina eloped with her liquor sales person, Ronnie. I got the news when Melina called me directly from the bathroom of her honeymoon suite.

"Cuz, I love you. Please don't stop being my friend because I got married."

"How could you do this, without telling me?"

"It was easy, Cuz. We got in a car and drove to Las Vegas and did it."

I thought of all the times we almost left for Las Vegas to do it and it never happened. Melina always backed out on the basis she was ten years older than me.

"I love you, Melina."

"I will always love you," she said.

"I'm crushed," I said.

"Cuz, please. You have a dozen chicks on your bed and at any moment you could be married to Olga, who, by the way, you should inform that she has nothing to worry about where I am concerned any more."

That night, Raul drove me to the Whisky-A-Go-Go. I once picked up a chick here, Jenny, who had a home up in the hills above Sunset. I saw her twice, maybe three times, even took her home with me. She was gorgeous, classy. I looked but didn't see her. I drank their nasty wine that I never liked, but I had to consume something in order to sit at the busy bar. Soon I was hit up by a high-end hooker. I followed her from the bar to a seat in front of the stage where a stripper was working the brass pole.

It was loud. Conversation was a huddled business with lots of yelling.

"They call me Emily. I'm twenty-three, and you are beautiful."

"Hey, that's my line," I said. "You're the gorgeous one." She was closer to thirty than twenty.

"I bet that Rolls outside is yours," she said, speaking close to my ear.

"There's a bunch of Rolls out front," I said with a laugh.

"Only one limousine," she said.

I could have told her it belonged to Pixie, but the noise level wasn't conducive to conversation. And after Melina's defection, I wasn't in the mood for a lot of conversation about my life.

"You have a good eye," I said. "Want to go for a ride?"

"Three hundred for the night," she said. "I'm worth it."

"Want it now?"

"I trust you."

"Do you have a place?" I asked.

"I do. It's trash. Can't go there."

For an instant, I thought about AIDS and all the controversy going on about protection. The buzz about AIDS was that it a disease of gay men, so I wasn't too worried.

"I normally don't do this," I said. "Let's go to my place. I warn you, it's pretty far. I live in Pasadena."

"You got me for the night. I'm game."

On our way toward my home, we drank wine. Late as it was, traffic was heavy. Without planning, we positioned ourselves on the seat. Ample room. The partition between Raul and us was closed. My legs are too long for me to lie down in the back seat. I entered her. She squirmed, facing me, her arms around my neck, my arms around her as she rode me.

I closed my eyes. Emily was not Emily. She was Melina. I didn't have to do much other than to keep my erection, and that was no problem. Just as we hit the Pasadena freeway, I felt her twist into an orgasm. I let go. Fucking in a car is always messy. I kissed her, reached in my pocket, gave her five hundred dollars.

I was tired, but I was done with her. It was a business deal that ended early. She seemed happy that Raul would drop her off anywhere she wanted. I told her to give him her phone number that I would keep handy. I didn't pay attention to where we dropped her off.

I had Raul drop me off outside the gates of Casa Luna. The gates opened. I chatted with the guard for a minute before walking down the driveway towards the house. I had looked forward to it, but Letty was off somewhere with Tangles, not waiting at the door like she used to.

When sleep found me, I was still brooding over Melina getting married. Letty joined me some time in the night. I did not wake up alone.

Mornings began as they usually had, sometimes very early if I wanted to get in steam and sauna before breakfast. My work out area had a plush mat and mirrored walls, bright lights, piped-in music, and a big screen. There was also a big screen in the weight room. The Milan villa had nothing to compare. Most days, if Letty was not traveling on a case, she and I worked out simultaneously, sometimes together. Sometimes Tangles came early to work out with us. It helped to have a group of us; it gave us witnesses for defeats and triumphs, and someone to raise the bar in case anyone got too complacent. We would sometimes cycle through the rooms together, each doing our own thing. I might be practicing a jump kick while the girls were mastering a karate routine; then we'd move to the weight room and spot each other; and then we'd follow up in the wet area with steam, sauna and a mutual shower.

"Mario, you could work from home again, like you used to," Letty said.

"No way I can handle this business from home," I said. "Too much banking, too many numbers, too much paper. Besides, I'm used to it after two years in Milan."

Every morning, instead of walking to the fourth-floor home office, I drove myself to my office downtown. I would work until about three and leave for home before heavy traffic kicked in.

I often thought that Letty was like a wife, though I've never had one and don't have anything to compare it to. If Letty was the example of being married, bring marriage on.

Los Angeles March 1, 1989
Andrea

I hope I am granted my legal work status by the immigration authorities. I love it here. My rent-free apartment is in Westwood on Wilshire Boulevard in a building owned by LAI. Instead of fighting traffic on the freeway, I drive down Wilshire to our downtown office. Mario approved a company car for me, a 911 Porsche. Red on red.

Mario's home is quite a distance from where I live so I don't see him much after hours, at least not at his house. He doesn't drive to my place either. We have met discreetly at the downtown Hilton on 7th & Wilshire, walking distance from the office.

In the thirty days since we opened in Los Angeles, we did three leases for new planes. In the same period, Jules signed six leases out of the Milan office. My guess is this company will soon become one of the largest aircraft leasing companies in the world. Give us five more years.

Los Angeles June 1989
Mario

In the four months since my return to Los Angeles and opening of the leasing offices, I had not seen Jack Fino. We talked on the phone, but it seemed that our weekly lunches were a thing of the past. I was busy leasing planes and Jack was trying criminal cases again.

"I'm afraid I lost some of the polish that made me a well-known trial lawyer," he said. "After two trials, I may be getting back what I lost."

"That sounds way too humble for you, Jack. With you being in court all the time, who is loaning money to all the needy lawyers?"

"Just me. I have a law firm that handles the loan documents, but I do most of it by phone. Thanks to the fax machine, I get applications right away."

"Amazing, Jack."

"Not as amazing as you. I hear you are kicking ass with the leasing company. That was a good article the Examiner did on you and the company."

"Let me tell you, I was scared to death that they'd do a retrospective looking at the people I've killed or bring up my ambulance chasing days. I got lucky. The reporter did me proud."

Melina called when the article came out in the afternoon edition of the Los Angeles Examiner. "Cuz, as Pixie and Letty would say, fuck-me. Great write up on you."

"Baby, tell me fuck-me again," I said.

"Proud of you, Cuz," she said. "Come over for lunch one day, any time."

Letty cut out the article and faxed it to Olga and Camila.

"Amor, we will get business from that article," Olga said.

"I wasn't looking for attention from this," I said. "I like low key."

"This is positive," Olga said.

Camila agreed. "A business this new can't get too much attention. There's no such thing, Amor, except...newspapers do not bode well."

The next time I talked to Olga, I relayed what Camila said.

"She hates the Times and Examiner. When Pepe was in jail awaiting trial, they wrote bad stuff about him."

"Got it."

I really didn't get it. The Camachos don't have a low-key bone in their bodies. They are all about flashy cars, huge acquisitions, big planes and cash.

Pasadena June 2, 1989

I left the office about three. Instead of heading home, I drove a couple blocks to the Hilton. The valet took my car, and I went into the main bar. Well-stocked. Good bar.

I ordered a bottle of Chateau Mouton Rothschild. As the sommelier poured the wine into a snifter to breathe, I recalled how Pixie could do that so delicately without spilling a drop. I missed her. Originally her tours had taken thirty days. Now, she went on the road for two months at a time, sometimes longer.

"Everyone thinks the money is in record sales. Not so. The big money is in the tours," she always said.

I swirled the snifter. Andrea arrived just as the wine was ready. She kissed me lightly on the lips and sat at my shoulder at a table in a dimly lit corner. The steward poured me a pinch.

I sniffed. Drank. Smiled.

Andrea and I clicked glasses.

"You're getting prettier and prettier," I told her.

I got a smile.

"I love Los Angeles," she said. "I only hope immigration loves me back."

I had it covered. The immigration attorney I had hired to handle her paperwork had assured me she would get her green card. In the meantime, she was on a visitor visa. When it expired, she would fly to Italy and return with a new visa. Andrea was essential for my continued success in leasing aircraft. After two years I should be a pro, but I knew I had a way to go. I expected Jules to be amazing, and he was. Andrea is way too young to know as much as she does about leasing airplanes, but she, too, is unbelievable.

Andrea is two weeks younger than I am. We get along perfectly at the office, and when I see her off the clock, we never talk office. It is simply sex. She is a different kind of wild than my team. Andrea likes extended time sixty-nine. Apart from anal, she says the best sex for her is oral. She likes to shower together, but it is different with her than with my team or Melina. Andrea was different, strange. I like strange.

In bed, having sex, I brought it up. "When I first met you," I said, "You and Camila spent the night together at the villa."

"I go either way," she said. "The first time it happened, I figured I couldn't very well turn her down if I wanted to keep my job. After that, it was easy. I dig her a lot."

Her words drifted, and she moaned. It was a few moments before she continued with any coherence.

"Actually, I miss her," she said. "She keeps saying she's going to fly in."

Before I left the Hilton at nine-thirty, I called Letty on her cell.

"Baby, what's for dinner?"

"I'm taking orders. What would Mario Luna like to eat?"

"Have Miguel fix me a porterhouse, a baked potato, and something good for dessert."

"That's all?"

"That's plenty, baby. See you in a bit."

"Did you leave anything for me?"

"Always," I said. I love that girl.

I had the windows rolled down as I took the Orange Grove off ramp from the Pasadena freeway. The signal was red. It was dark and the weather was balmy. I smelled freshly cut grass. Behind me, a pickup truck pulled up with its bright lights on. The light turned green. I turned left on to Orange Grove. About five minutes from home, I heard two loud blasts. I was showered in safety glass from my exploding rear windshield. The angle of the car and the draggy way it handled was like my tires had been shot.

We should have stayed in Milan.

The pickup honked three times and roared away, passing me on the passenger side. I rolled to a stop in the middle of the street. The pickup sped ahead of me with its lights off. I couldn't make out how many were inside or see a license plate.

There was no traffic on millionaire row—that's what they call Orange Grove Boulevard. I punched the accelerator and caught up with the truck. Its lights were now on. Only the driver was inside. I did not recognize him. The signal at Colorado and Orange Grove turned red, and the pickup ran the light. There was too much traffic. I braked to a halt. A car driving West on Colorado struck the truck broadside and pushed it thirty feet. The intersection became a chaos of shrieking brakes, honking, and smoke. A cloud of black smoke enveloped the truck and the station wagon that had struck it. I got out of my car, left it on the inner lane, engine running. I ran towards the pickup, more than fifty feet from me. The passenger door of the truck was smashed, but apparently the driver's side was not. The driver got out, saw me coming and veered west on foot toward the Colorado Bridge. A police car pulled directly in front of me, and I ran into it.

"Freeze," the cop yelled as he got out of his car, gun drawn.

"I was running after the perp who caused this. There's my car," I pointed to my car, with its headlights on, driver door open. Cop paid no attention. I could have fought him off in a split second, but that would have been stupid. He put cuffs on me, opened the door to his patrol car, and put his hand on my head as I stooped to get in.

I watched the aftermath through a dirty rear window of the patrol car, my hands behind my back, my head not hitting the inside of the car roof because I was bent forward. More cop cars came. Paramedics were attending to the driver of the station wagon who seemed to be in bad shape.

Eventually, a cop with stripes walked past. He looked through the window and opened the door.

"Luna, what the fuck did you do?"

His badge said Scott.

I explained what happened as I watched a tow truck positioning itself behind my Rolls. I figured it was just as well. It needed one or both rear tires, the rear windshield, and who knows what else besides that.

Fifteen seconds into my explanation, Scott had the patrol officer to remove my cuffs.

"I just read about Luna here in the Examiner. He's not the bad guy here."

"Thanks for that," I said, my hands free. I rubbed my wrists. "Officer, can I get that truck to tow my car to the Rolls dealer a block from here?" I pointed toward the dealership on Colorado, less than two blocks away from where we were standing. "I'll be glad to pay him."

"Get a police report from Luna about the shooting at the Orange Grove off ramp," Scott said to a patrolman.

I got in a call to Letty and asked her to come get me. She arrived while the patrolman was taking the report. A few minutes after Letty arrived, I saw Tangles's car drive up.

"Truck is stolen," Scott came by to say. "Found a shotgun in the car. I hope that it has a story to tell about who the shooter was."

This was like déjà vu for me. It reminded me of the biker back when he shot at me on the freeway, but he was dead.

"Luna, I'm putting the pieces together. You're the guy whose house got toasted and then the bad guys blew themselves up."

"I was on my way to Italy when that happened. February '87."

"Sounds like someone don't like you, Luna."

Scott didn't laugh, but there was humor in the lines of his face.

Three hours after I drove away from the Hilton, I finally arrived at home. I went straight to the shower and when I came out, the dining table in my bedroom was set for dinner.

"Hungry?" Letty asked.

"Starved."

Tangles poured us wine.

"We should have stayed in Milan," Letty said.

"Earlier I had the same thought."

Tangles said, "Boss, I'm sorry this happened." Tears ran down her face.

"I'm convinced he had no plans to kill me," I said. "Please don't cry."

"It's anger, Boss." She was trembling enough for me to notice. "Can I stay with you guys tonight?"

Bogota June 3, 1989
Olga

Riana and I were at my home in Bogota. She was asleep. It was late when got off the phone with Mario. The sun was not up yet, and I had not been to bed. I was upset over the dust-up in Pasadena. This cannot continue. It has to be the same person targeting Mario, but who? Why shoot at his car and not tell him why? Where is this coming from? Why is he being terrorized? If you want to waste someone, it's easy. I still hear the shots when Pepe killed Santiago and Mateo. It was over, just like that.

I didn't wake Riana but tossed and turned restlessly. It was afternoon when I told Riana about the attack on Mario. We were on the sofa in my bedroom.

"He's unhurt. He came home and had a steak."

"Good news. He's strong," she said.

"Strength means little if you are ambushed with a gun," I said.

"Letty, Tangles, and Betty are with him for support." Riana said.

"I'm sure."

"We could go there," Riana suggested.

"I'm waiting on something." I put my arm around Riana. "We're going to Turkey, then we can shoot to Pasadena."

"Let's go out," Riana said. "I want to get high and dance."

"Si, let's go, but high as in pot."

"Si," Riana reached for her cigarette case. "Let's take a few tokes and we can leave as we are, okay?"

I watched her light up. "I'm getting more used to this stuff," I said as she passed me the joint.

"We should take some hits of coke."

"Not a chance," I said. "You've been off that stuff. Why go back now?"

Riana kissed me, "You are right. This is good enough."

Bogota June 4, 1989

We danced until four Sunday morning and hit our beds an hour later. My cell phone started ringing. I ignored it. Again, it rang.

"Olga here. Who is this?"

The familiar voice spoke. "Your plane is ready to depart, Senorita."

I went into Riana's bedroom. She was in worse shape than me.

"We have to leave," I said. "Amor, get in the shower. You can sleep on the plane."

Riana stirred lazily, stretched, and did as I told her. It was another reason why I loved roaming with her. She never gives me a bad time.

"If I had just a tiny snort of coke, I'd be like new."

"No."

Riana and I followed two of my security team into the plane. Four team members were behind us. As soon as we were aboard, the stairs pulled away, the plane door shut. Guards took their seats in the front compartment, a separate area from the main cabin where Riana and I occupied two seats, a table between us. Stewardesses served coffee to both of us within a minute. Then wheels up. The plane cut through bumpy storm clouds. My DC9 climbed.

Before we reached twenty-five thousand feet, Riana and I got out of our seats and headed for the bedroom cabin.

"I'm so tired. I had an awful night. Three pots of expresso couldn't keep me awake, not that I want to drink three pots of expresso," I said.

"I want to crash too," Riana said, flopping on the bed.

I hit the opposite side.

It was too bad I couldn't head to Los Angeles first. I would have felt better that way. Pepe was dead, but we still followed his cautionary guidelines. If the voice–the man known as Jeronimo Valencia–called me, as he had this morning that my plane was ready, I could not include any part of the United States in my flight plan. We were headed to Amsterdam with one planned fuel stop. Until the last minute, I had thought we were headed to Turkey.

The bedroom door opened. Riana sat up. The only light was through the cracked door.

"Alonso, why don't you knock? What do you want?"

I listened but didn't sit up.

"*Te quiero culiar.*"[20]

---

[20] I want to fuck you

It was Cesar's voice, the same security team as Alonso.

I sat up. Alonso had already stepped in, Cesar behind him, then the other four guards, Cayo, Lago, Ysidro and Vidal.

I got pissed off. Riana was already on her feet.

"Alonso, get these men out of this room this minute," I said.

"Olga, we're taking over the plane. We are taking the cash and co-caine," Alonso said.

The others said nothing, stood there like stupid puppets in the suits and ties I had bought for them. I wondered where the suit coats were. So, this is how one dresses for a hijacking. This was all a stupid nightmare.

"What cocaine, stupid? There's no cocaine on the plane."

"Of course there is. There's always cocaine on your trips."

That was not true. Cash, yes, but no cocaine. My guards wouldn't know because it wasn't their job to handle cargo when and if there was cargo on board.

"Alonso, you will never get away with this. Camila is not one you want to cross."

He smiled. It was ugly, a complacent self-satisfied look, both amused and mean. His expression gave me chills. His teeth were as white as his heart was black. Irrelevantly, I noticed a broken front tooth. I wanted to break all his teeth. Give him a matched set.

"That's our problem," Cayo said, the newest member of the team. "We will deal with Camila when the time comes."

They had no guns, not even empty holsters. They were overconfident, which was a bonus. The pressure was on for me to think of something. I'd have to play it by ear. They must have some kind of plan to land the plane some-where.

They were in it for the cargo. Everything had been so secret for so long I wasn't surprised they believed I was hauling cocaine outside Colombia to the different countries I went to. I almost never knew when I had a load of cash or when I didn't until after I arrived at my destination. Pepe's strategy had been the less I knew the better. It protected me somehow.

"Eat my snatch," Riana hissed, poking a finger in to Alonso's chest. "I'm on my period. Come eat me." She poked him again. Alonso punched her in the stomach. She fell on the bed.

Before he could hit her again, I stood up and slapped Alonso so hard it hurt my hand. Cayo took a punch at me, but I dodged the full impact, and landed on the floor, pretending more injury than had happened.

I raised my hands in defeat.

"Stop," I yelled, as if that little bump was enough to make me give up.

Alonso put his hand out and stopped Cayo. He was wearing a cap and thumbed the brim while gazing down at me like a cat stares at a bowl of cream. "We're going to have a good time, you and me," he said.

"Okay, okay. We can have fun." I got up from the floor and sat next to Riana. She was curled up in a ball, her face contorted in anger. She had a snarl on her face. I caught her eye, shook my head slightly, hoping she would let me handle this. I looked from Alonso to Cayo. "Who's in charge?"

Alonso shoved Cayo aside and thumbed himself in the chest.

"Me."

"Let's come to terms."

"Deal," Alonso said. He loosened his tie and unbuttoned his top few buttons.

"I have some questions," I said.

"I don't have time for questions," he said.

Vidal said, "Too many questions, you'll get dead like Tomas."

My heart sank a thousand feet. Tomas was the relief pilot. I'd liked Tomas. He used to let me take the second seat sometimes and gave me flying lessons.

"The pilots are with us," Alonso said, "Busy flying the plane. You put smiles on our faces first. You can fix up the pilots when we're done with you."

I gave them all the once over, trying to put heat in my expression. I licked my lips. They weren't bad looking guys, all of them as fit as security guards needed to be. I wanted to throw up. These were the men who for so long had guarded me. Mario had built additional space in the personnel quarters at Casa Luna for them to lodge in when I was in Pasadena. I felt queasy. My heart was racing like I was having a heart attack.

"Riana, want to fuck these six dudes? "

"Fucking is better than getting punched," she said.

The idiot guards looked at each other with smiles on their faces.

"You want our cooperation. It will be better that way. Alonso, let's negotiate. Get your men out of here. They can stand outside by the door while we talk."

With a snap of his fingers, the men got out. Alonso was not a big man. He was middle-aged, a no-nonsense killer, and his men knew it. He didn't fight like Mario or know karate, but he was a street fighter who would use anything available. I knew the histories of all these guys except for the new one. Pepe had been full of stories about the atrocities our security guys committed at his command. I'd seem some things myself, as had Camila.

As soon as the door closed, I started taking off my clothes, like a striptease. Riana had no idea what I had in mind, but she did the same. We were having an effect on him. He wore a shit-eating grin and stared at Riana and me like we were ice cream sundaes, covered in whipped cream with fudge and a cherry on top. Alonso stood there like a mannikin with a hard cock and no vocal chords. Riana and I ran out of clothes, and he was still staring like he was going to get a lap dance. I guess he remembered where he was.

"I thought we were going to talk," he said.

"We are," I said. "Take your clothes off. Let's see it."

Alonso was out of his clothes in record time. His dick was raring to go.

I went down on the bed and spread my legs. Riana got on the bed near me and playfully kissed me on a sensitive spot. Alonso dick jumped.

"Come here, Alonso. Let's talk." I said.

He pushed Riana out of the way and got on top of me. I felt him go inside. I fought nausea. He tried kissing me with his broken-toothed Judas mouth.

"Kill your men. I keep the cash. You keep the coke," I said. I turned my face toward Riana. He nuzzled the base of my neck and pumped into me.

"Why should I do that?"

"Because you will get away with it that way. I will come up with a story." I hesitated. "The others, they arranged it all. You can be the hero. Camila will believe me. We don't have Pepe any more. Maybe you can be our new Pepe?"

Riana put her arm over him and kissed his neck. He groaned and worked his body on mine.

"I been wanting to do this for years," he confessed, speaking in Spanish.

I moved slow, to give him the feel that I was in sync with him. I put my hands on his face and our eyes locked. He was sweating, ready to explode.

"Kill them. We dump them, then blame them. There's not that much cash on board right now so the real value for you is the coke. Just think, you won't have to split it with anybody."

Alonso grunted. I could see he liked the idea of having it all. If Mario were here, he'd have already killed him.

"What about the pilots?" Alonso asked.

"They do what you tell them until we land somewhere and get rid of them."

"How do I know you will keep your mouth shut? And what about Riana?"

"We could care less. You know how we are." I wasn't going to try and convince him there was no coke on this plane now or ever, at least that I knew of. I played along. "This coke is not mine and neither is the cash, but if we do this, the cash is mine and Riana's. You have your coke worth millions."

He was thinking about it. He groaned again and finished. His eyes cleared of sex, and he gave me a satisfied smile.

There was a knock on the door.

"I'm busy. Don't knock again," Alonso said loudly.

I kissed Alonso, seriously thinking of biting his lip off. "You are the boss. You have the power."

He climbed off of me. Riana was still on the bed. She touched his limp dick.

"Later, Riana. More for you later," I said.

"Si, Riana," he said, looking from her to the door.

Alonso dressed as fast as he had undressed and left his tie on the chair.

"Si, Papi," I said. "Come back and fuck us both."

As soon as he went out, I got out my sweats and started dressing.

"If he does what you told him to do, the plane will explode," Riana whispered.

"Put your sweats on." I opened a drawer and took out a set for her.

Under my lingerie, I found my beautiful gun, a chrome 45 like the one Letty kept as a collector's item. I loaded it and put two rounds of spare ammo in my pocket.

"I haven't seen that in a while," Riana said. "Right now, I'm glad your father was Camacho's hit man."

"And he taught me everything he knew," I said. My family always protected the Camachos. I had been really little when Papi had started taking me out for shooting practice, maybe six or seven years old. He had me out there in the fields shooting till it was second nature. I thought about my father when he was teaching me how to shoot. How he taught me to be calm, how to handle the kick of bigger guns. This one would have to do.

I was nine when my father shot eleven men in our yard, and he never told me to look away. I knew it was my job to look. After they were dead, he gave me the gun. It was so hot it burned my hands. I could barely hold it. He said, "When it's you or them, use the gun. Always, *mi hija*."[21]

---

[21] My daughter.

"Mario doesn't know," I told Riana. "He was surprised when I piloted the helicopter. He doesn't know about my father's specialty, and he doesn't know how well I can shoot."

"Fuck secrecy. Kill them all," Riana snarled. "I am glad you can shoot. Shoot now. Worry about explanations later."

The words were brave, but I could see she was shaking.

"Don't be afraid," I told Riana.

"I'd be less afraid if I had some coke," Riana said. "Why do they think you have coke aboard?"

"Because they are stupid and know nothing. They are fishing, and I'm going along with it."

"I understand," Riana said.

"Amor, sit down and buckle up. No arguments."

I opened the door. The main cabin was off limits to them when we were airborne, but I could hear conversation from there. All of them were talking loud about how they were going to split the proceeds. I was not counting on Alonso killing the men. I hoped they would be grouped together around the main table where there were enough seats to accommodate them. I figured Alonso would take them there while he thought of what I had asked him to do. There really wasn't anywhere else to go.

The narrow hall I was in led to the cabin. They were embroiled in an argument—all of them but Alonso—yelling at each other. Good. I appreciated the distraction. I emerged through the door and faced the six traitors seated around the table, unnoticed until I started shooting. I was fast, mechanical. I wanted to cut them down where they were seated so that if the bullet went through, it would lodge in the bulky seats, and not go through the fuselage. I knew I would not miss. They had the table to contend with as the seat had to swivel for them to get up, and I gave then no time. Alonso was first, one shot to the heart. Then I shot, one, two, three, four, five. Alonso was already slumped over. Two died with seat belts on.

I dug into my pocket and reloaded.

The flight attendant Patricia came from the forward cabin. She had a black eye, a split lip, the sleeve was torn off of her GAL uniform, and the shirt she clutched to her chest had no buttons on it. There was blood on her uniform, but I don't know whose it was.

"Are you with them or with me?" I had the gun pointed at her, but to be honest it was a few seconds before my eyes registered what I was seeing.

"Tomas," Patricia said in a broken voice.

"I know about Tomas," I said sharply. "Go to the bedroom. Tell Riana that it's okay to come out."

I headed toward the cockpit. Patricia caught my hand.

"Don't go in there," she said, her eyes panicked. "They're bad."

"Patricia," I said softly, "Get Riana. I got this."

I waited till she went down the hall before I ran to the cockpit. The door was open. I could hear the pilot and co-pilot talking. They were joking around, talking about what they were going to do with their cut.

"I'm here to give you the promised blowjob," I said as I entered behind them. I stopped shoulder to shoulder with Tomas who was in the jump seat, slumped over. He'd been shot. His eyes were open, staring ahead, his face expressionless. I saw him in my peripheral vision and tried to act like he wasn't sitting there with a bloody, gaping hole in his chest.

"Where are the others? They finished with you already?" Hal asked, a copilot that I had always considered a friend.

"Wrong. I finished with them," I said, stepping forward.

I moved my gun to his chest and shot him. The bullet came through his body and lodged itself in the seat.

The captain looked like he was in shock. I put the gun to his head.

"Hello Carlos," I said. "Glad to see me?"

"Ms. Camacho," he said. He stuttered a little. Didn't say anything else.

"Call ATC and request permission to return to Bogota. You are having instrument problems. You may have a cargo port open."

Carlos did as he was told.

"Good boy," I said. "We're going to the military airport. Request coordinates."

"They may ask why."

"Do it." I was ready to kill the bastard.

Took five minutes for ATC to clear us. We were one hour, ten minutes away from the airport.

"You want to die now or wait until we land?" I asked.

He didn't answer. I guess it wasn't much of a choice. He tried to push me away, but my gun held steady. I shot him. Again, no damage to the fuselage. I looked from his body to the open door where Riana and Patricia were now standing. Riana was looking ok, but Patricia was shaking so much I was surprised she was still upright.

"Who will fly the plane?" Patricia asked in a quivery voice.

"Riana, Patricia, help me get these bastards off their seats. Shut up and do what I said."

The bodies were limp and heavy and buckled in. It felt like forever moving them. Dead weights. It took all three of us to drag them off, one at a time. Patricia wasn't much use. She was a basket case. We left them where they fell.

I got in the captain's seat.

"Sit in the copilot seat, Amor," I told Riana. "Don't be scared."

"I'm not scared. Patricia, give me a towel to wipe this fucking blood off the seat." Riana mopped up the mess.

"Tomas," I said to the dead relief pilot, "I hope you're as good a teacher as I thought you were. Let's hope my landing is as good as the last one you let me do."

"He's not going to answer," Patricia screamed hysterically. "He's dead!"

"I know that Patricia," I said, like I was talking to a child. "Go buckle yourself in a seat in the main cabin or in the bedroom if you don't want to see the bodies."

Patricia headed off. I was too busy watching dials to pay attention where she went.

Riana looked like she was about to tune up. I cut her short.

"I know how you feel. Suck it up. Don't get weak on me until we land this fucker," I said. "We have to keep it together. I need to contact Air Traffic Control. I need instructions. And I need you to ask them to get General Durazo. Hope I can remember what the fuck to do." I kept picturing Tomas walking me through the checklist.

It was a good thing that it was daytime. A night landing would have been impossible. I don't remember a thing on the dials, or what the hell I did, but kept a tense discussion up with ATC. We hit the runway with a bounce but managed to touch down without sending us to hell. It was close, but I brought the plane to a stop. It all felt unreal as I turned the plane one hundred eighty degrees and taxied to the tarmac.

General Durazo was an old friend of the Camacho family. He'd known my parents and me since I was born. He was waiting as Riana, Patricia, and I deplaned. The general saw that it was me and opened his arms. He frowned at Patricia's ravaged condition.

"We knew it was a Camacho plane, but I didn't know you were aboard. What happened?"

"We need to talk," I said. "Somewhere private."

We went into the general's office. I told him everything.

"Go home. I will take care of it all," he said. "I'll have a car drive you."

Riana and I returned to the plane and stood at the foot of the stairs.

"If you would wait here for a moment, I have to go fetch something," I told him. "General, do get Patricia's side of the story. I haven't heard it yet. Please call me before you do anything. I'm not sure of the cargo," I said, "But I'd just as soon let it remain where it is until the mess is taken care of."

We left him waiting at the foot of the stairs. Riana and I boarded the plane again. We returned, each of us carrying two large briefcases, one in either hand. I also had a plastic bag from the pantry that I'd put two bundles of cash into.

We came out and the general was waiting for us. I kissed him and handed him the plastic bag.

"This is for your trouble," I said.

"I will handle everything. I am so proud of you landing that plane. Your father would be so proud."

I reached Camila on her cell.

"Need you in Bogota."

Camila didn't ask why I wasn't on my way to Amsterdam as Pepe would have.

"I'll be there in fourteen hours."

Riana and I rode in a military car with a soldier at the wheel, and a soldier next to him in the passenger seat. Behind us, a military truck followed with ten soldiers. When we pulled up to the house, two soldiers from the truck jumped out. The general had given them their instructions.

I did not know who to trust.

Through the window, I told the two guards to turn their weapons over to the soldiers, to go home and wait to be contacted. Once we were inside the gates, two more soldiers came with us, and relieved the four guards on the grounds of their weapons and sent them away. The soldiers took over. Once Camila arrived, we would sort it all out.

After soaking in the tub for an hour, I showered. When I thought of Alonso touching me, I wanted to shower all over again, but instead, I walked over to Riana's bedroom. I found her in the bathroom drying off.

"Oh baby, your stomach!"

An angry purple mark stretched across her belly, striations of black and blue running across her creamy skin. The bruise reminded me of when Pepe would beat me. Once, I had holed up for weeks in Bogota hiding my bruises from Mario.

I hugged her. We walked into the bedroom and got on the bed. I tucked her in and kissed her. "Want anything?"

"I'm fine. Probably hurt tomorrow, but I'm fine. How about you?" she asked.

"I'm good. I douched twice. I will probably douche twice more before I go to sleep."

I rang a bell. Yuliza ran up from the kitchens. I ordered a meal for us.

"Nothing fancy," I said. "Pork sandwiches, cocoa, pastries. We will eat here."

I was sitting on her bed. Riana sat up and hugged me. "You're so brave, Olga. Why did you fuck him if you were going to kill him?"

"I didn't know what I was going to do. I was buying time."

"You are so brave. I love you all the more."

I hugged her in return. "I was thinking the same about you," I said. "You are one tough hombre."

"I'm not an hombre."

Yuliza brought the food on a tray, and we picked at it until Riana was all yawns. She fell asleep, and I tucked her in, and returned to my room. Normally, the after-smell of sex would keep me turned on. This was different. I showered again. I could not get the feel of Alonso off my skin.

Bogota June 5, 1989
Camila

It was after midnight when I arrived at Olga's. I was surprised to see uniformed soldiers at the gate and on the grounds as my car pulled up to the house.

The housekeeper Yuliza greeted me as a soldier opened the front door for me.

Yuliza said that Olga was asleep in her room. I made my way upstairs and peeked inside.

"Is that you Amor?" she asked.

Her bedside lamp lit up. Olga pushed to a sitting position.

"Are you okay? Why the soldiers?"

"I don't trust any of my security people. The soldiers sent them away. I'll be glad to let you sift through the mess."

"Hermanita, I will handle everything. I won't leave until everything is done. Now tell me what is this mess I am sorting through."

"We were hijacked," Olga said. "I was hijacked by my own men."

Riana joined us. I listened to them tell what had happened, tucked Olga and Riana into the same bed, and kissed them good night. I met with the soldier in charge of the general's men.

"I will call the general to send relief soldiers for you. I want a strong presence here at all times."

I reached in my purse and pulled out a bunch of hundred-dollar bills. He refused to take the money at first but took it after I frowned at him and insisted.

"Senorita Camila, we will guard her with our life. Do not worry."

"Do not let any of her security return to this property."

"Count on it," the leader said.

It was two in the morning when my driver took me home.

At four I was still up. I called in Estevan, the family enforcer, the man who now did the job that Olga's father once had done. We met in my study.

"Pass the word about what these *traidores*[22] did. Deliver the bodies to their families. A week after the funerals, I want every family member dead. Pepe is gone, but I'm not. I want it common knowledge that I am deadlier than he ever was."

"I will take care of it," Estevan said.

"There is no rest for you until all of this is behind us," I said.

"I don't need to sleep, Senorita."

---

[22] traitors

"General Durazo's soldiers are guarding Olga for now. Get your men to bring you every security guard that works for her. Ten hours from now, I want the ones who are trustworthy to be the only ones still breathing."

Estevan nodded his understanding.

I poked his chest with my index finger. "If this had happened when my brother was alive, you would have been the first he would have killed, because everyone that works for us is your responsibility."

"I will kill everyone going in the same direction as the traitors who caused Senorita Olga harm. I will put them down like the dogs they are. Count on it."

"You better, Estevan. I love you, but that doesn't mean I won't have you killed if you fail me."

"If I fail you, I will take my own life," he said, his eyes watering.

Chapter 6
Pasadena June 5, 1989
Mario

"Not a single cut on you after all that glass shattered all over you," Letty said.

"It was raining safety glass," I said.

"The service department said both your rear tires got hit, but the pellets didn't puncture them. They just embedded in the tires. You still need new tires and a new spare. There's body damage in the back, the windshield glass, and that's it. I told them to do the repairs. We're not reporting it to the insurance company."

"Good," I agreed.

"Boss, there is nothing in the Examiner," Tangles said. That morning the LA Times had nothing on it either.

"Wonderful news," I said.

Inside gossip started by one of the team is how word leaked out. I got calls from Melina and Jack Fino. Jo and Niley came over to touch me and make sure I was not hurt. Betty came over and went on for ten minutes complaining that I hadn't called her right after it happened. She would have come over to massage me, make me feel better, and maybe keep me from suffering from whiplash.

"You're here now, baby. Work me over."

We were in the office when I had Letty get Andrea on the phone. She stayed on the line as I told Andrea to stay at the office and take care of business instead of coming over to check on me. I was fine but planned on staying home for the day.

"I feel guilty that it happened when you were on way home after we were together."

"For all I know, it was a random event. This crazy guy decided to mess up my car. He got struck at the intersection and he ran off. Everything isn't necessarily a conspiracy."

"Oh, Boss, please," Letty said on the extension. "Give us a break. You were a target. It was planned."

"Amor, my plane is out of commission for at least a week," Olga said on the phone. "Camila couldn't drop me off in Pasadena because she was late getting to Budapest."

I wanted to tell her about the accident but not on the phone. Two hours later, I was on the company plane. On June sixth, I landed in Bogota at the international airport and was greeted by two uniformed military soldiers who drove me to Olga's house.

Five minutes after my arrival, I was in shock. For once, Olga gave me details—how her security team turned on her, how she shot them, how she flew the plane home, how Patricia had witnessed the relief pilot's death.

"I had uniformed soldiers guarding the house. Now I have a new batch of guards."

"Screened, I hope?"

"Yes. Let's not get into that. If it was up to me, I'd toss the security."

"She doesn't mean it," Riana said.

"Baby, you need security. Both of you are loaded with cash. You are absolutely targets."

"Targeted by my own people. The bastards were supposed to be guarding me, protecting me. Instead, they betrayed me."

Riana hugged her.

"No more talk about this, please," Riana pleaded.

"Let's go to Rio," Olga said. "Just for a couple days. Please Amor."

"We can sleep on your plane," Riana said.

Just like that, a decision was made to fly to Rio to that fantastic pad on the beach. I called the first officer of my plane and told him to ready up. Next, I called my office, spoke to Andrea who said everything was under control, then I called home.

"I knew we should have gone with you. Damn, we're missing out on the fun," Letty said.

"When I get home, I'll tell you about the crisis over here. What happened to me is nothing."

"Tell me now. I need to know."

"Not on the phone."

"Boss, damn. I'll be on edge until you're home."

"The crisis passed, and all is well now."

There was silence on the line, then, "Thanks, Boss. I feel better."

I waited for Olga and Riana to get ready. I passed on the offer of wine. I don't drink alone. The housekeeper brought me a coke.

I was spooked by the idea that Olga was transporting cocaine in her plane.

Olga had said, "I never know when the plane is loaded and when it is not. If the voice calls, I could not fly to the states but have to go where the shipment is headed. Payment is always in US currency and in hundred-dollar bills. I don't know how they hide it, or how it gets delivered. I never see who is picking up, or who is paying. The money boards in suitcases as luggage delivered by a messenger I never see."

On the plane, the three of us went to sleep on the Cal King bed. It was a bit tight, but so what. I think Olga and Riana found comfort in snuggling up to me as we slept. It took me a while to sleep. My mind kept racing. I was in this now whether I liked it or not. My own mind was assaulting me on two fronts: first, the idea of LAI being involved in drug trafficking; second, the idea that Olga had been raped. I wished Alonso was alive so I could kill him again.

The leasing company is a great job, but just a job. I could walk away from a job. Olga was something else altogether. Olga had grown on me. I wasn't walking away.

<h3 style="text-align:center">Rio June 7, 1989</h3>

Olga and I walked the beach in Rio, holding hands like the lovers that we were.

"It's peaceful here," I said. "Why don't you stay here and hang up what you're doing. The last you told me, you have millions. Let me do the work."

"Amor, three more years. I promise, three years."

"What if you get busted?"

"Won't happen. Please trust me."

I raised her hand and kissed it, still walking. "I trust you. It's that drug business I don't trust. I don't want to lose you."

It was her turn to kiss my hand.

"We're one, Amor. You will never lose me."

I stopped, turned her so we were facing each other. Olga was taller than Letty, but she still had to look up to meet my gaze.

"I love you, Olga."

"I got you beat, Mario Luna. I adore you."

"I feel helpless that you went through hell with Pepe and now this traitor, Alonso."

I knew all her guards. They'd been to Casa Luna many times. I remembered Alonso. I had a clear picture of this bastard.

"Amor, it was just a fuck. An expensive one for him. It cost his life."

Our feet were getting wet as we walked along the shore. I tried to concentrate on the feel of the sand underfoot. I heard sea birds, the rolling waves, and the fierce wind, but louder than that were the sounds of Olga's rape, in my imagination. I could not turn off the pictures in my mind. They made me angry.

"Riana said you got them all with one shot each. That's marksmanship."

She nodded.

"My father taught me how to shoot. I was seven when I started. He had everything. Rifles, pistols, all kinds of firearms, even a machine gun, the kind you see in gangster movies." She laughed. "I started to mention it a couple times when Letty showed me her collection of firearms, but there was no reason to rain on her parade."

"And you landed the plane. That's amazing."

She shrugged. "Not so amazing. I have millions of miles in a seat of a plane. When I used to travel alone, I got bored. I would always spend time in the cockpit. The pilots had no choice but to put up with me. I listened to the pilots talk to ATC as we entered different airspaces. And Tomas," she sighed, sadly. "He walked me through landing more than once. I am so sad that he was killed. We were lucky we survived. I touched down way past the safety point. Here I am. I made it."

"What a turn-on you are," I said, stopping.

We were alone on the private beach below the Camacho mansion. It wasn't dark yet, but sunset was close. I dropped my swim shorts and helped her out of hers.

Olga was beneath me as the waves moved over and under our bodies. Our kisses pressed so hard, it was a wonder we didn't damage our teeth. When we were done, we looked for our shorts, but they were nowhere in sight. I guess they were floating down to Ipanema. We laughed about it, walking naked up the private walkway to the house and jumping into the outdoor pool.

Andrea reported to me every day, always with the same advice.

"Enjoy yourself. All is under control."

Letty and Tangles were handling a plane crash in Marseilles, France. They called during breakfast. In the breakfast room in Rio, the house phone was on speaker.

"Boss, if you were here only for a couple of meetings, we could sign all the families," Letty said.

I could hear Tangles commenting in the background.

"She's exaggerating, Boss," Tangles yelled plenty loud enough for me to hear. "Not the whole plane but a whole bunch."

"Hey, don't underestimate me or yourselves," I said.

"He's not going to Marseilles on a plane crash," Olga said loud enough so Letty could hear.

"Boss, tell your fiancée to fuck off," Letty said.

"I heard that," Olga said. "You're on speaker."

"I'm not taking it back," Letty said.

Olga laughed.

"Get what you can," I said, "You don't need to sign everyone. Goner will be happy with whatever you get for him."

The few days in Rio turned out to be much longer. It took almost three weeks for the interior of Olga's plane to be redone. It must have been a bloody mess. In the meantime, Rio entertained us, day and night. We went out to night clubs and came home when the sun was coming up. We rolled around in bed, and got up when it was dark again when it was time to party some more. I had never had a long vacation to compare, except for the time I completely unplugged from my life, and took off for Europe for six plus months when I met Sami.

After three weeks, we flew to Bogota in the company DC9, and landed on the twenty-sixth of June.

"They stripped everything in Bogota and flew the plane to Miami for a retrofit of the interior. Camila saw the finished product. She's jealous."

I got a chance to go through Olga's refurbished plane. New everything, and I mean, everything. It looked like an entirely different plane.

"You are going to Amsterdam," I whispered in her ear. "Do you know if you have anything?"

"Amor, we're not going to do this every time."

"I need to know."

Olga looked serious.

"You are totally out of that part of the business."

I didn't want to agree. I needed to know but did not want the argument here and now. I could put a pin in it and talk later.

"I got it, baby."

"Amor, gracias. Now kiss me again."

Riana stood next to Olga, her lips puckered, playfully waiting to be kissed by both of us.

I deplaned. I turned on the tarmac and caught the kisses they were blowing from the open plane door.

I waved and again started to walk toward my plane.

"Mario Luna," Olga yelled out.

Both our planes had engines running. Planes were taking off and landing. The runway noise was deafening, but I heard her. I turned around.

"I adore you," she screamed.

Pasadena June 27, 1989
Letty

He's so busy with leasing. It's not like him to disappear in Rio and lose all this time. Finally, Mario is on his way home. He dropped off Olga and Riana in Bogota. Tangles doesn't think anything was wrong. I know better. It would be like leaving a case he was working on without finishing. Something is going on.

"Ease up," Tangles said to me. "With his money and her money, he can do anything he wants. I'm surprised he doesn't do this more often."

"You're right, bitch."

"Why bitch?"

I smiled at my friend. We had signed eight individuals, called it quits and came home. Without him, we can't reach the confidence level needed to get a family to sign a retainer. Goner was happy, and Tangles was happy with the money he paid us. I know we could have done better. Now all we had to do was wait for the next crash. We were walking in Mario's shoes.

"Let's chill on the small aircraft stuff," I told Tangles. "Lots of effort and we don't need it. If we can get three airliners a year and sign at least ten from each crash, we're set. Come on. I'll teach you how to bake."

"I don't want to learn how to bake. Boring."

"You sound like Pixie, bitch."

"Nothing wrong with that. She's getting so rich. I love that chick," Tangles said.

"Don't love her too much," I said.

"You are so jealous and possessive. You want Boss and you want Pixie."

I giggled. "I want you, too."

"Letty, do you really like girls more than boys?"

"I dig both. What about you?"

"You know the answer to that."

I was going through a cookbook to get ideas of what I wanted to bake. When she sat there quietly, I looked up at her, and caught her staring.

"We're alike. We like both. Not ready to go out and tell everyone about it and be called queer," Tangles said.

"So I'm bi. So sue me," I said. "Why do I have to declare one or the other?"

"I like the smell of pussy, and I love the feel of his dick in my mouth or buried in my pussy," Tangles said.

"You are so vulgar, Tangles."

Laughter. "Yeah, right. I'm so vulgar, bitch. How about you?"

"Did I ever tell you about the time he fucked me right here on this counter with peanut butter as the lube?"

"Of course, like a hundred times. The time that Olga walked in."

"Want to hear the story again?"

"Sure. Can we smoke a joint while I listen, and you bake?"

"If Miguel catches us smoking in here, he'll have a cow," I said.

Tangles got up. "I'll fetch a joint. It will be fun watching him have a cow."

I made brownies with way too many walnuts. I made half of them with way too many peanuts for the boss.

Catch this picture in the kitchen: we smoked a joint, and then we drank milk and ate brownies, giggling and laughing. Silly stuff. We made up a game of brownie hockey and batted a soccer-ball shaped brownie back and forth with our forks, jumping up and down, taking a bow when we made a goal. The goal was made of drinking straws that Tangles weaved together while I was baking. Then the brownie hit the floor. Tangles dived to catch it, and it splattered into crumbs. She looked as upset as if it had been a real disaster.

"I got this," I said, sweeping the mess with a whisk broom, and wiping up afterward with a sponge. "See? Good as new."

Something had jolted Tangles out of the playful mood. Maybe it was the pot giving her a bad buzz. I don't know.

"Do you think it's one person causing grief to Boss, or more than one?" she asked.

"I wish I knew who it was. I'd blow the head off whoever's responsible."

"You mean that?"

"Serious as a heart attack."

"Me too," Tangles said. "I'd want to get away with it though, not spend the rest of my life in prison or die in the gas chamber."

"You're such a drama queen."

Tangles turned defensive. "You're the drama queen, bitch."

"I'll slap you around like a bitch," I told her, laughing.

"You're on. Let me finish this brownie, then I'll give you a shot."

Los Angeles June 27, 1989
Andrea

"Jules, I have six new leases, and I could lose two of them because Mario isn't back. I need him to designate if we are partnering or going alone. He's been gone so long already."

"Do your job. If you lose some or all of them, it's not your fault. He put the decision on you. Don't lock horns with the boss. My advice to you."

"He does call every day and tells me to handle it. He says he'll back my decisions, whatever they are. When I push for his opinion, it's that it has to wait till he's back, or for me to make the decision. I don't want to make that kind of decision."

"Make the decision. What is the problem?"

I felt as though I were sitting across from him in Milan. My caution seemed foolish.

"I got you loud and clear. Thanks Jules."

Medellin, Colombia, June 1989
Olga

My flight attendant Kati closed the door.

"Go grab a seat, Amor," I told Riana. "I want to have a talk with the pilots."

Two pilots were in the cockpit. I went in and waved for the relief pilot to join us. He got up from his seat in the front cabin, and when I had the three of them in earshot, I spoke.

"My last flight in this plane was an experience I will never forget. I know you know about it, and I know Estevan vouches for you. But I want you to know that if I should be confronted with this kind of situation again, I will shoot to kill. I don't care if I blast a hole in the fuselage and send everyone on board, including me, to hell. I will never be subjected to blackmail or intimidation. Am I clear?"

All those years I had traveled without worry. That was over. Before taking my seat, I went in the bedroom and put my forty-five in the last drawer of my new cabinet, not yet filled with lingerie. I opened my canvas bag, took out a sawed-off shotgun, and put it in the second to the last drawer that was also empty. Each drawer had a keypad lock that had been installed during the remodeling of the interior. My nightstands also had the locks and eventually would hold firearms. I didn't want anyone else opening the drawers when I was not on the plane. When I was on the plane, everything was in unlock mode.

The flight to Medellin was short. We stayed at the Camacho house, big, but not nearly as big as the mansion in Bogota. Riana knew we were waiting for the call from the coordinator I think of as 'voice.' That's when I would know if we were going to Amsterdam or elsewhere.

The morning after we arrived, I got the call.

We were buckled into our seats, facing each other with a table between us in the main cabin area.

The blonde suede upholstery smelled delicious and felt lovely. I quite enjoyed the new design. The carpeting was a shade darker than the seating. It would be a bear to keep clean, but not my problem.

"Amor, I feel guilty that you are getting involved in what I'm doing," I told Riana. "I never planned this. Never would have told you."

Riana smiled broadly and blew a kiss at me. "I needed excitement in my life. Thank you for giving me that."

The plane began its take-off run. I smiled back at my friend.

"I love you, Riana." I put the palm of my right hand over my heart.

Riana did the same.

We stared at each other for a long time without saying a word. When we were wheels up, I asked Kati to bring us a bottle of red. Riana and I kicked off our shoes. The plane began the climb, and it was bumpy. Too bumpy.

"Kati, don't rush. Go stay in your seat."

I had to raise my voice over the noise of the engines, but she was already there holding a tray with two wine glasses and an open bottle of Merlot.

"I'm sorry, Amor. You could have waited," I told her.

"I'm used to this. Don't worry."

She handed me a glass then one to Riana and poured just a bit to taste.

"Amor, it's okay. Pour and go take a seat."

The captain's voice came over the speaker.

"Senorita Olga, we have run into a few bumps, I apologize. We will be out of this turbulence in a few minutes."

Riana raised her glass and leaned across the belt to click glasses.

"Don't you just love this life?" she said, grinning ear to ear.

"I love it, yes."

Soon after we leveled off at some altitude, twenty-eight thousand or thirty thousand feet, the turbulence disappeared. We were on our second glass. Kati provided mixed nuts for us to nibble on, plus crispy taquitos with guacamole on the side.

"I don't want to bring up bad memories, but I can't help thinking…" Riana said.

"Thinking what? I want to hear."

"When you landed the plane and then turned it three hundred sixty degrees on that narrow runway, I had an orgasm."

"You've been spending too much time with Pixie and Letty."

"I swear, I was just so worked up, I exploded. What about you?"

"I was just so relieved I had brought that big animal down without killing us. First, I was relieved, then I was mad at the turncoats again. I tell you this much though. When I find a pilot I really trust, I'll start practicing my landings."

Riana raised her glass for a click.

"Right on," she said.

Maybe it was the wine and the relief of being safe. We were silly and a little hysterical, but we laughed till our stomachs hurt. We ate then headed to the bedroom. The bruising was only now fading from Riana's stomach. I kissed her there, then moved beside her under the covers. We faced each other, the cabin dimly lit by two night lights, one outside the restroom, and the other by the door.

"I used to do all this traveling alone. Amor, thank you for sticking it out with me like you do."

"Your wine breath is a turn on," Riana said.

When we landed in Amsterdam, a car from the hotel was waiting for us. One of my guards took the front passenger seat after we got in the back. Two guards got in a second car to follow us. The three pilots would leave the plane shortly. Three guards would remain on the plane. At some point during my stay, they would come to the hotel. No matter where I landed, if the voice initiated the trip, the routine was the same.

"How long are we going to be here?" Riana asked.

"Until I get a call that my plane is ready."

Sometimes it was a day, sometimes longer. When I did return to the plane, there would be suitcases filled with cash in compartments located in the sleeping cabin, money I would have to deliver to a bank or banks in different places, sometimes close, sometimes far. Everything depended on the bank and the banker willing to accept cash deposits. Sometimes generous deposits, sometimes huge deposits. This is what I did best. I found a home for the cash.

"Let's get laid," Riana whispered in the back seat of the Mercedes limousine.

"Si," I said. "You got it coming, Amor."

I'd stayed in the same suite at that hotel so many times that I'd lost track. Two guards, one in front of us, one in back, walked us to our rooms, then took positions outside the door.

The guards were new and not used to me. One asked us to wait outside with the other guard while he checked the room. I shoved him out of the way and told him that I wasn't El Capone. I didn't need my room swept before I entered.

Riana was still laughing after we entered the room.

The bellman brought us our luggage. Always the same bellman, Lucus. We only had one bag between us. I planned to shop if we stayed more than twenty-four hours. I had all those empty lingerie drawers on the plane to fill.

The suite was all lit up, champagne in a cooler, strawberries in a silver goblet and chocolates in another goblet.

"Lucas," I handed him a hundred-dollar bill. "I need a favor. We want a little something extra after dinner." I turned to Liana, who gave him her order.

Riana had a list of qualities that ended with "...preferably not Dutch. Preferably from Africa."

Lucas's eyes widened, but he was happy to oblige.

Two hours later, after we had eaten a delicious dinner and luxuriated in a hot bubble bath in our own bathrooms, Lucas delivered two hunks, just as Riana had ordered for us. They were thirtyish, clean-cut, short-haired.

We didn't swing together. I kissed Riana. She went to her own bedroom with one hunk, and the other followed me. When the lights were dim, and the hunk was on top of me, I felt no guilt. I did adore Mario, but knowing him, he'd be doing something similar by now at Casa Luna. The difference is that it wouldn't be a manly hunk he was messing with.

Before long, I got in my favorite position, on top.

In the middle of the night when I was exhausted and empty, I showed him to the door. The sounds coming from Riana's room spoke for themselves. She was not done yet. I went to my bed and found sleep in a bed permeated with the smell of sex. When I woke up, Riana was naked in my bed, her back to me. I got close and hugged her, kissing her neck until she woke up moaning. I playfully slapped her ass and told her to get up.

"You've had enough sex," I said.

"Never enough." Riana stretched like a big cat. "Olga, thank you for hosting last night. He was a *Toro.*[23] I wonder if I can walk. He was bigger and thicker than your fiancé."

We laughed.

"Hey," I said, "Say Mario. Don't remind me you are talking about the man I'm going to marry someday."

"Right, sorry. This dude, as Pixie would say, was hanging heavy and thick."

We laughed.

"You haven't mentioned your hunk?"

"He was good, but not as good as my Amor."

"You didn't enjoy it? Damn."

"Hey, I loved it. Did you smell the room?"

We laughed again. It felt good to laugh so much.

"Let's clean up, eat, and shop. I got to buy clothes."

"This isn't Beverly Hills, you know," Riana said.

"I'll show you some great shops here in Amsterdam. Let's shower."

"Can we have just a little coke to wake up?"

"No coke. I hate the stuff," I said.

"You should be proud of me. The Toro had coke and I didn't touch it. He did rub it on my nipples."

"I will chew Lucas ear off when I see him. I told him, no drugs."

"Olga, it's just coke."

We were deep into shopping when I received a call on my cell.

"Miss Olga, your plane will be ready tomorrow morning at nine."

Amsterdam July 3, 1989

I called Pasadena. Mario was at the office. Andrea said he was on phone, that he had been that way for two days since he returned. I called his cell and got through.

"I know you're on the phone. Just wanted to check in."

---

[23] Bull

"Baby, I just got off that call. I have time. Always have time for you."

"Did you get a wild reception when you got home?" I asked.

"You know Letty. She baked a cake like it was my birthday. Actually, it was fudge brownies with peanuts, and a thread of peanut butter running through."

"Then what?"

"Hey, why you want to know details? What did you do in Amsterdam for four days?"

"Three days," I corrected him. "I shopped."

"What else did you do?"

"I fucked a hunk that the bellman sent up for me."

I don't know what made me tell him. I never tell him things like that. Not everything.

Mario was silent, but only for a minute. "Did you leave anything for Riana?"

I laughed at him.

"She had her own hunk."

"I did it with Letty," he said, a little sharp-voiced, "Then with Tangles, then with Letty and Tangles. Last night Betty stayed over after we got a massage."

"Amor. You sound upset."

"I'm not upset."

"Amor, it's sex for money. It means nothing."

"I'm not pissed. I know you love me. That's what's important."

"I don't just love you. I adore you. The guy was just a fuck, Amor. How about the girls you did it with? Were they just a fuck?"

Mario went silent.

"Amor?"

"Baby, you know my relationship with Letty, Tangles, Betty and the rest of the team. We love each other, but it is nothing serious. It sounds so empty to say that they are just a fuck. It's not the same as a one-night-stand you order like a nightcap from the bellman. My team, they are friends. Your friends, too."

It was my turn to be silent.

"You're right, Amor. It is not the same. I'm sorry for asking you that."

"Don't be sorry, Olga. It's like you and Riana, or you and Camila. It's personal. Not the same as sex for money." I heard him sigh. "We should get married."

"Amor, the piece of paper isn't going to change what you and I do when we are apart from each other. Let's be open, as when I told you what happened with the traitors and everything else. Si?"

"Si," Mario agreed.

"Amor, thank you. I'll let you go now."

Riana was watching and listening. She looked perplexed over the conversation and couldn't hold her tongue.

"Why tell him all that?"

"I don't know. One part of me wants to share. The other part of me wants to keep everything a big secret. Being honest is difficult."

Riana said, "Being honest is impossible. Look what happened to Enrique and me for being too honest with each other."

Enrique Vas, her ex, beat her up when she'd confessed that she wanted to swing. He had affairs going on daily basis, but he wouldn't give her the same freedom. And he was the one who'd gotten her hooked on cocaine.

Los Angeles July 11, 1987
Mario

"Boss, your car is ready. It's being delivered this afternoon. The service manager says the job came out perfect," Letty said.

"I been thinking that I don't want a Rolls anymore."

"Why?" Tangles asked.

"Someone out there hates me. Not sure if it's this house, my Rolls, my beautiful team, or what the fuck it is. I had two burned up, or was it three? I'll sell the car. I'll get a Lincoln. Or a Cadillac."

"Boss, don't do that. You are made for a Rolls Royce," Tangles said.

"I can't see you in anything less than a Bentley," Letty said.

"I like the Suburban. Big car. It's a tank."

They talked me into keeping the Rolls until I found something else big enough for me to drive.

The office had underground parking. My spot was on the first subterranean level. As I walked to the elevator, I looked behind me at my Rolls. It was a beautiful vehicle. It looked like it was straight off the showroom floor, chrome shining, paint glistening. The body shop had done a bang-up job getting rid of the buckshot dents.

Andrea came running to my office at 12:15.

"I just got a call from the parking lot attendant. Your car is burning up. The fire department is on the way."

The leasing office was on the 40th floor surrounded by heavy plate-glass windows. The sound of sirens is not unusual up and down Wilshire. I heard them the way you hear them when they cause your heart to race because this time, they're not for someone else.

It was masochistic because there was nothing I could do, but I rushed downstairs. The firemen were already at work. My beautiful perfect car was a mess.

After a tow truck had hauled my car away, I learned that the security tapes caught a man throwing an incendiary device. My windshield didn't break. The device went off, and flames immediately engulfed the front end of the car and spread.

I called Letty to come get me at the office.

"Just last night you were talking about buying another type car, and now this? Very fishy," Letty said. "I'll be right over, Boss."

The Los Angeles Police Department officer took a report. I didn't mention the shooting or the past problems. Let them find out on their own. My history is an open book. I assured them I had no clue who had done this or why. I was given a field report card with a number on it for reference. A detective would be in touch. This was a somebody's game, but I was not having fun. Being played is no laughing matter.

"It's our fault, Boss," Tangles said when I got home. "We talked you in to keeping the car. So sorry."

"I had no plans of buying a car last night. No matter what, I would have driven the Rolls to the office. And do you think if I'd driven a different car that the arsonist would have left it alone? Silly. Letty, here is the police report reference card for the insurance company. I'm getting another Rolls. Fuck the creep doing this to me."

"I'll handle it, Boss," Letty said. "What color do you want?"

"Black."

"Boss, all your Rolls have been black. Maybe you need to change color?" Tangles suggested.

"You think they're after my Rolls because it's black? I want what I want, and I want black," I said.

That night, one TV news show had a picture of the charred car on a flatbed.

"Arson at Arco Towers Parking Lot in broad daylight."
Pasadena July 12, 1987

The morning LA Times coverage had more background. The reporter wrote about the fire that took down my house a few years before and the fire at the same address two years ago. They said that the police had no leads in either case, and how did I feel about it. I didn't reply, because what could I say? At least in the one-minute interview I gave, the reporter quoted me correctly.

"Someone out there doesn't like me. What can I say?"
Los Angeles July 14, 1987

Two days later, Mason Cooper called.

My secretary Ava buzzed me on intercom.

"Mario, I have a man who says he just spoke to Olga on the phone and she asked him to call you. Want me to give to Andrea?"

I took the call.

"Mr. Luna, I'm a private investigator. My company is Mason & Associates. Your fiancée told me you are having a number of mysterious problems. Two days ago, your car was burned, and before that, a man took several shots at your car when you were on way home."

"How do you know Olga?"

"I don't know her. I did speak with her for thirty minutes. I was recommended to her by a Swiss banker who recently moved to New York."

"The cops have never been able to come up with any suspects over the years. What did you promise Olga?"

"I'm a psychiatrist and a licensed attorney. I don't practice medicine anymore. I never practiced law. As a doctor, I have been able to resolve countless mysteries for clients by profiling the kind of person who commits certain types of crimes."

"Where is your office?" I asked.

"I work out of my home in Pasadena."

"Well, I'll be," I said. "I live in Pasadena."

"I've lived in Pasadena for twenty-two years. I live on San Pasqual. Olga told me you were also in Pasadena. I want you to know I read the piece in the LA Times a couple of days ago."

I called Olga after I talked to Mason.

"Amorcito, forgive me for taking this in my own hands. I want someone working on this, not just the police. Mason has a tremendous reputation. He does work for banks in the United States and abroad. He investigates complex cases and solves them."

"I forgive you, baby. I am impressed he's a doctor, a lawyer and investigator."

"Oh, Amor, I'm so happy you are not mad at me."

Tangles stayed for dinner with Letty and me and had her own opinion of Mason.

"What a combination. He must be good to have fancy clients. If it's a nutcase or freak who is after you, he will know what to be looking for."

"What if he's not a freak?" Letty asked. "What if he is a common everyday lowlife son of a bitch?"

"Either way, he has some direction who to look for," Tangles said.

Betty came over. Tangles and Letty passed on a massage, so I got one that lasted three hours straight.

"You are fantastic," I told Betty. "But you must be exhausted."

"Not even," she said. "If Letty and Tangles each got a massage, it would have taken me longer. Besides, I dig these long massages. One minute your *Verga*[24] is at attention, then it mellows out only to rise again. Not sure what makes you tick, Boss."

"I know exactly what makes him tick," Letty said.

Even I laughed.

July 15, 1987 (Saturday)

At ten in the morning, Mason arrived at my house. I took the day off. Letty went down to greet him and bring him to my office on the fourth floor. We shook hands, and Letty went to fetch coffee.

Mason was about forty-five, a white guy, clean shaven including his scalp. He had on jeans and a designer t-shirt with a blazer. His shoes were Versace casuals that matched his blue jeans. Most investigators I came across didn't dress as well or look as well put together.

"If we do this, Mario, I need to have details. I have put everything on this list for you to answer." He handed me three typewritten pages. "Olga mentioned problems you had many years ago where you killed in self-defense. I need the particulars."

---

[24] Penis

I glanced over some of the questions.

"Mason, I wouldn't recall the relatives of the guys I threw out of a window ten years ago, if I ever knew their names at all."

"I know that, but you know the name of the persons you killed?"

"Yes, I do. One of the dead guys, his parents sued me, and my insurance settled. Wait—that was the follow-home robbery. These guys had followed my team returning home from Christmas shopping."

We chatted for thirty minutes, and Mason left. The girls and I went over the list.

"I need Pixie in on this," I said. "Some of this stuff goes way back. Also, Jo and Niley."

"I can help, too," Tangles said. "I want to."

I considered going to the office after the short meeting but stayed home for the rest of the day.

"How did it go?" Olga called to follow up. "Does he live up to his rep?"

"I like him. Might be a while before I see him again. He gave me homework."

"What?" Olga laughed, startled. "Excuse me?"

"I have to put together information he needs about my life. Pages of questions."

"I think that's wonderful," Olga said.

"I hope so."

"Be sure to include Janice, Oscar's widow in there," I said to Letty.

"Yes, Boss, I know who Janice the bitch is."

"Ungrateful bitch," Tangles said.

"Jo will know the particulars about the two I threw out my apartment window. Niley will have the details about the shooter I killed who killed her sister."

"Got it, Boss," Letty said.

"This Mason dude will have to get the information about the families of these men you killed in self-defense. Any one of them could be a suspect." Tangles said. She pried off the staples, went to the copier, and made several copies of the list.

"There's the home invasion dude you offed. His partner who survived went to prison. I need the details on the settlement you made with the family after they sued you." Letty said.

"Very good, Letty," I said. "These families have a reason to hate me."

"Remember what happened to Melina," Tangles said. "The brother got out of prison after more than a decade of being behind bars and went after Melina for killing his brother. Blood is thick."

"You weren't even around then," Letty said.

"Oh hush, bitch. I know the stories."

Before I met her, when she'd been a senior in high school, Melina shot and killed one of two armed brothers who robbed her father's market and shot her father. The surviving robber went to prison. She'd always feared he would be released some day and return to kill her. When she was shot outside her market, my childhood friend, Pélon, serving life in San Quentin for murder, told me the shooter had been the brother who had recently been released from prison. Pélon ordered him dead but not as a favor to me or Melina. Before leaving prison, he'd been warned to stay away from Melina.

"About Melina being shot, let's just write it up like it was. No need to mention Pélon."

"Got it, Boss," Letty said. "Keep going, Boss."

She was busy taking notes.

"On page one, it asks for your father's name. Do you know it?"

"Luna was my uncle. He married my aunt and adopted me. Ask Aunt Carmen. My mother was Elena, maiden name Garcia." I wasn't sure I knew my father's name. I'd have to look at my birth certificate.

"Lots of personal questions," Tangles said, studying her copy. "Mom's name, living, deceased, when, where, cause."

"My mother died having me. Better ask my aunt the rest. I'll call her and tell her why I need this stuff."

"Mason is a fucking investigator. Why does he need you to put your life on paper? Isn't that his job?" Tangles said.

"Shut up," Letty said.

"Let's give him what we can put together. I can tell him to dig out the rest. Frankly, I don't want to relive it like we're doing right now."

"You may have to relive it sooner or later when you find out who is doing this," Letty said softly.

She and Tangles were at the conference table in my office. I got up and kissed the tops of their heads.

At four, Miguel served us hamburgers, grilled hot dogs, and steak fries as a late lunch.

"I think this is dinner," I said.

Letty laughed. "I'll remind you of that in a couple hours when you are craving a steak, a baked potato and peanut butter ice cream."

"After going through all those questions and answers, this food is like an aphrodisiac for me," Tangles said.

I exchanged looks with Letty, who nodded slightly with her Mona Lisa face on. She had one of those little hints of a smile with a promise of more to come.

"Let's have a little wine, a little bit of a joint, and hit the sack for a little while." Regurgitating all these painful recollections made me feel all beat up. I could use a distraction.

A week after I got the list, Mason returned. We spent four hours going through the typed answers to his questions and he quizzed me on some individuals such as Janice, widow of Oscar, Carson, Jack Fino, my father Francisco Sanchez about whom I knew nothing, and many others who had crossed into my life's path.

Mason wanted to know about Luca Rossi, the now-dead biker who had confronted me on the freeway, confronted me in in San Antonio and torched my car at the airport. I told him about the sketch left on the Camacho New York apartment door, the shotgun taken from my car at the airport and left in Pixie's car, and Rossi's home invasion through my master bedroom balcony when Letty shot his extremities, and he went over the railing, landing in my koi pond.

"For sure, Rossi didn't do anything this year. The police found him with a bullet hole between his eyes. Whoever pulled his strings is probably still alive," I told Mason.

When we were done with the list, we weren't done.

"We haven't talked money," I said.

Mason got up. "Olga is taking care of it."

I didn't argue with him. I did have some questions for Olga.

"How much is he charging? Why not let me pay him directly?" I asked her.

"Amor, once I knew you were working on the list, I assumed you wanted to hire him. I sent him a wire as a retainer. Please let me handle his fees."

"Olga, thank you. I'd love to reimburse you."

"Next time I'm home, you can find a nasty way to do that."

"You're so hot, baby. I love you," I said.

In mid-July, Jason called me from London on my cell. "My source says they closed the Pepe case. The investigation ran into a wall in Colombia."

"They ran into a wall because he died in that plane crash," I said. "There was nothing to pursue."

"Lainie and I are going to make an announcement. We're getting married this year."

"Congratulations, Jason."

"Thank you. We're going over dates. Will let you know."

Pixie had already told the team and me about the upcoming event. Pixie was taking it okay. She was busy doing tours and had no free time to fret about her daughter marrying her one-time boyfriend.

After Jason hung up, I had Letty arrange a conference call with Camila and Olga.

"I talked to my friend in London. He says that matter we discussed is closed."

"Amor thank you for letting me know," Olga said mildly.

"There was never anything to investigate, *putos todos!*" Camila snapped, then said, *"Gracias, Amorcito por avisarme."*[25]

On the road August 5, 1989
Pixie

I was on my last night of a Latin song tour that had taken me through fourteen US states. The venues were large theatres where movies were shown. In Texas, a stadium with twenty thousand seats was a sellout. In Mexico and South America, my appearances were always in stadiums, the smallest audience ten thousand. Olga, my manager and Rialto, my promoter and studio who puts out my records, were determined to spread my stardom in the United States. I had a contract with Capital that worked jointly with Rialto. I did not know if Olga, Rialto or Capital gave away tickets in order to fill a venue when it wasn't a sellout. I knew that the disc jockeys that played my music over and over again were being taken care of. Payola is part of marketing. I don't care. The only thing that is important to me is performing, and not because I get a cut of the box office.

Olga is wonderful to me. I often think about whether she was making money representing me. She gives me so much. When I complained about Rialto's planes, she had Mario get me a practically new Learjet that had my name on the pilot's side of the plane.

---

[25] Thank you for letting me know, Amorcito

I am careful not to mess around with my crew. The media would have devoured me. Who knows what my fans would do? I keep it cool, but it's difficult. I find comfort in smoking a joint now and then, but I am careful. Everyone smokes pot, but I live in a fish bowl, and pot is illegal. I looked forward to returning to Pasadena.

On my latest tour, Olga landed in Lima to watch a show, then we went to her plane. Boy, did I get the sex overhaul I needed. I smoked so much pot that I spaced out. It was all good.

In Guatemala during a concert, a fan came at me with a knife. I took him down like a fly. A reporter in Mexico City dug up my karate awards. One reporter wrote that many of my male fans didn't dig my doing that, but that most people he interviewed said it was hot, and they respected me for defending myself. I should hope so. Would it be better to be a fainting flower who let the guy stab me? I think not. Bottom line, I was in the spotlight. Olga said the publicity helped sell records and tickets. After this tour, I'm going to have at least a month off.

Guatemala September 2, 1989

Late one night after a concert, I was at a hotel, home away from home. Just one more hotel room after so many. The lights were out, and I had the blackout drapes closed to block the lights of this strange city. I got on the phone and made a call.

"Mario, I'm coming home. I miss you and home so much. Tell me you'll make time for me."

"Baby, your scent is coming in over my cell phone. Hurry, I can hardly wait."

Pasadena September 7, 1989
Mario

Pixie spent her first night home with me; and her second night home with Letty, Tangles and me. There was no sex that night, but we had her talking till she was hoarse about all the things that had happened on tour. She was a sight for sore eyes. She's always been her own fashion plate, and that was still true. She came back with half blue hair, half pink hair, and feathers weaved into half of her braids. Letty and Tangles decided to unravel the braids, and it kept them absorbed while Pixie talked. Every so often, someone would ask a question that reminded Pixie of another story that would take an hour to tell. We got up halfway through the night, and continued the talk in the sauna, hot tub, and back into bed again. We fell asleep close to dawn. No one made a move till Miguel told us breakfast was on the buffet when the sun was high in the sky.

Less than a week after Pixie got home from her tour, she sent out invitations to a promo party bigger than any party I have ever thrown, and most of the people invited were strangers. She invited three hundred guests. My biggest party had been for Christmas once, and I feel sure I had not invited anywhere near a hundred people.

"My publicist invited people from all walks of life. Most of them I don't know. She says this will insure that they will never forget me."

Letty was wildly excited.

"Do you dig it?"

"I so dig it," Pixie said.

"Fuck-me," Tangles said.

"Hey bitch, that's my line," Pixie said.

Tangles went home with Pixie, leaving Letty and me alone.

"Talking about support," I said. "Olga and Camila are both flying in to attend."

"I know. It's wild. I'm so proud of Pix."

"That makes two of us, baby."

Bogota September 8, 1989
Camila

"I want an eye to eye," Olga said on the phone. I didn't ask why. It sounded urgent.

I arrived in Bogota last night to meet with Olga today. I held off having breakfast and waited for her to arrive. I opened my arms for a hug.

"Amorcito, so wonderful to see you."

Instead of a hug, Olga slapped me once, then again, stinging on my cheeks. The hurt practically knocked me off my feet. Not physical pain, emotional pain.

"Are you crazy?" I screamed.

Olga slapped me again.

The maid and manservant who were handing the meal looked like they wanted to help, but I pointed to the door, and they ran out of the dining room. I had no such easy escape.

"I've been like a maid to you for years," Olga screamed at me. "I have licked your pussy and ass for hours at a time. I ask you not to do something and you go right ahead and do it. I am so mad at you. I could kill you."

I was in shock. In all the years Olga has been with our family, she has never talked to me that way, nor has she ever shown the hatred I saw on her face. I had no idea what she had asked me not to do that I had apparently done anyway.

"What are you talking about?" I asked.

"You said Estevan was taking out the families of the traitors. But not the minors!"

I could have summoned a guard or fought back. I just sat there.

"Let's talk about this." My face was burning from the slaps.

"I don't want to talk about it. I don't blame Estevan for following orders. I blame you for giving them. Not the children!"

Tears were running down Olga's face.

I took a shaky breath. "You never leave a family member to grow up and come looking for revenge. Your own father taught me that. I didn't like the decision I made. I didn't like having to kill anyone. Pepe was always the person who handled protection, but now it is all up to me. I am the one. I have to protect what we own and you and me. Look what happened to you on the plane. Eight trusted staff turned on you. They figured with Pepe gone, they had nothing to lose. They figured I was just a woman with no balls. They believed there were no consequences. Estevan has taken care of it. No one is saying I am just a woman now."

Olga was still crying.

"I hate you," she said.

"Get over it."

"And what if I don't get over it? Are you going to have me snuffed too?"

"I would never do that." I got up. I opened my arms and walked up to her. She let me hug her.

"Tell me what I can do to make this up to you."

Olga sobbed. She did not answer, but she embraced me.

"I should have told you myself, I'm sorry, Olga."

I left Camila's house and went straight to my house. I wanted to let Mario know what I had learned, that Camila had ordered the hit on the families, including the minors.

We had promised transparency. I couldn't do it.

"Amor, I miss you," I said on the phone.

"Come home," Mario said.

"Soon, Amor. I needed to hear your voice."

"You sound upset."

"I'm just tired. I will call you tomorrow, Amor. Kisses."

"Olga, are you alright?"

"Amor, I'm fine, promise." I managed a little laugh.

When I hung up, Riana handed me a glass of wine.

"Let's go to a club. Sounds like you need to kill time."

"I feel miserable," I told her.

Riana moved next to me on the sofa. She caressed my hair, kissed my ear, then my cheek.

"You can't change what happened," she said. "You wanted to confront Camila. Now you have. It's done. Let it go." She nibbled my earlobe. Chills ran through my body chasing her touch. I felt comforted. We didn't go out.

Estevan called me the next morning. He had two new security hires for my detail and wanted me to meet them before he put them on duty. He faxed over their resumes, and I studied them before he arrived. They'd both had distinguished military careers with an earlier regime. I knew that General Durazo had vetted them, so I was feeling optimistic. The two well-dressed men, thirty-four year old Leopoldo and thirty-six year old Justino, physically matched my other security personnel. Looking stiff and uncomfortable in their new clothes, they stood in the living room across from Riana and me. Riana and I had dressed down for the occasion, both of us in soft old jeans and random t shirts and wearing silly matching house slippers that stayed here in Bogota. Riana's long straight hair was pulled up into a pony tail, and she was wearing a gold mesh and diamond choker that mimicked a dog collar that cost as much as a Cessna. I had no idea who of her admirers had given it to her. I was wearing a pair of dangling diamond and platinum earrings that Mario had given me on my birthday. Esteven sat between our respective camps like a mediator or matchmaker; if he turned east, he saw the guards, and if west, he saw Riana and me.

"Leo," I said. "Speak to me in English."

"I speak English, ma'am."

"What about you?" I looked at Justino.

"Tell me what you want me to say, and I'll repeat it," he said in perfect English.

"They have no record anywhere in the world. General Durazo has expunged their military histories." Estevan said. "They are well-traveled. They are expert with firearms and have martial arts training. Two years of Brazilian Jiu Jitsu.

"Can I trust you?" I asked them. They knew why they had been hired, knew about the families that had died, and that I had killed the guards and pilots who turned on me.

I looked toward Riana who was looking uncharacteristically solemn, but maybe she, like me, was remembering our final hours with my last security crew. The unwanted memory served to make this introduction to these new guards seem very important.

Leopoldo left his chair. He walked past Estevan to kneel at my feet and held his right hand to his heart.

"I will guard you with my life, Miss Olga. I will be loyal to you. I swear to you in my family's name."

I looked into his face. He was not especially handsome, but he seemed sincere. I nodded at him and extended my hand. He did not take it, but bent his head, not kissing but bringing his forehead down to touch my wrist. He stayed in place when I beckoned Justino, who did the same.

"Okay," I said, getting up. At my side, Riana followed suit.

The guards rose to their feet.

"This is Riana," I said. "She travels with me. She will get the same respect that you give me. Understand?"

Both men nodded. I could not help comparing this meeting with the feeling I'd had when Alonso was hired.

"I'll leave them with the men on duty. They are ready to travel. They have two bags in my car."

He sent them to fetch their bags and to meet with the men on duty. Riana quirked an eyebrow in my direction, and I glanced at the door. She took the hint and excused herself. I was alone with Estevan.

"How did you know I'd hire them?"

Estevan smiled. "I didn't."

I looked at the older man that I had known all of my life. He had lines around his eyes, and his expression was careworn. His stubborn chin was unchanged. "Why did you kill the minors?"

"Your father would have done the same," he said, his expression not wavering. "I'm sorry. I am always sorry."

"Did you do it yourself?"

Estevan shook his head. "No. No difference. I ordered the kills."

Normally I would have kissed him, but I couldn't. I walked past him to the front hall, Estevan behind me.

I got the call from the voice. In two hours, my plane was wheels up, headed for Vancouver. The guards—including the new ones—were in the front cabin, away from us.

"Leopoldo and Justino are so cute," Riana said. "Actually, they are all hot."

"No," I said firmly.

Riana saluted, reminded me of Letty.

Pasadena September 11, 1989
Mario

Letty, Tangles and I had breakfast by the outdoor pool. Letty brought me a phone with a police detective on the other end. He talked briefly about the hit and run, and Letty joined me for breakfast. Tangles showed up. I had done laps indoors for an hour, and though it was September, it was in the eighties, and the sunlight felt good against my skin. I brushed away the last crumbs of Miguel's breakfast burrito, a thing of beauty. Tangles tackled a grapefruit loaded with sugar. Letty tore into a tall stack of pancakes. Caro poured us a round of coffee, refilled our carafe, and went inside.

"Olga has her team of eight guards again," I said. "She just hired the last two."

"Eight. That doesn't count the guards she has at home in Colombia," Letty said.

"No, those don't count," Tangles said.

"What does that mean?" I looked at Tangles, waiting for her to explain.

"The important detail is the new one. They are unproven," Tangles said.

"These had better not turn on her like the others," I said. I wondered how Olga could ever trust any guard again, after her experience. "These had better be loyal."

"Have you seen Gloria?" Tangles asked. "Gena Rowlands protects a kid from the mob. In mob movies, the family gets wiped. That keeps everybody loyal."

"Oh please, drama queen," Letty said. "This is life, not a movie."

I wondered.

Pasadena October 6, 1989

"I think I'll fly to Milan and pay a surprise visit."

"Can we go?" Tangles asked.

"Sure. Let's invite Betty. Tell her she's a guest, but also she's there to work."

"Boss, I went to the same school she went to. I'm a masseuse," Tangles said with a nudge.

"You don't want Betty to go?"

"Sure, I want her to go. I was just reminding you."

"Letty, get on the phone. Get my pilots together. Wheels up at five this afternoon. That puts us in Milan Sunday noon. We'll catch some sleep and walk to the office Monday morning."

"I'm on it," Letty said.

Pasadena October 7, 1989

Pixie was leaving Monday morning on tour, but she still did a number on me when she learned we were not waiting until she took off to leave. I felt the guilt trip, big-time. I tried changing the subject.

"Should I ask about the wedding?"

"Invitations are being printed. Both of them are acting like kids. Won't say when or where. Got to wait for the invitation."

"Are you okay with it?"

"I know it won't last. Hopefully she'll get a chunk of his money when it ends."

"He'll want a pre-nup," I said.

"What the fuck is that?" Pixie asked.

I made a last-minute call to Olga on cell.

"I'm in Toronto."

"Canada. I don't hear you mention it very much."

"Amor, been here many times," she said.

"You're so close. I would cancel my trip to Milan if I knew you were going to hop over here."

"I can't Amor. That little vacation we took in Rio screwed me but good. I'm so behind."

"Don't stress, baby. It's not like you have to punch a clock."

Olga laughed. "You got that from me, rascal."

Pixie's driver, Raul, drove us in her Rolls while Pixie was in the back seat with us. The car drove right up to the plane. We climbed the stairs, Pixie right behind me. She had not been on this plane since I'd had the interior re-done. It wasn't a ground-up remodel like Olga had, but it was enough to make it look brand-new.

"I'm so jealous," Pixie said, poking Letty in the chest then a poke at Tangles. The girls laughed. "I wish I could go."

"Call in sick," Letty said.

"Yeah, right. My first stop is in Durango, supposedly 30,000."

"Supposedly?"

"It's hard for me to believe that thirty thousand people are going to drop everything they are doing and pay twenty dollars to see me goof around."

"Believe it," I said.

At the last minute, she gave me a hug and whispered in my ear, "I'm not really upset about your leaving for Milan now. We gotta do what we gotta do."

Times like this, I remember our being kids together, both of us with our lost childhoods, clinging together to keep afloat. I knew she was living her dream, but also how much she missed being on my team. Thing is, she told me she was kidding about being upset, but I thought she was a little too earnest, and her feelings went deep. After lots of kisses and hugs, Pixie deplaned. I told

Letty to track Pixie's concerts and arrange for Pixie to get some after-show bouquets from me at every venue.

Susie, one of two flight attendants, shut the plane door. We sat at a table in the main cabin, the girls in seats across from me.

"Too bad Betty couldn't come," Tangles said.

"More room on the bed for us," Letty said.

Betty had wanted to come, but her day calendar was booked for weeks ahead. We took a lot of her time, but she reserved all her after hours with us.

"You got to respect the way she runs her business," I said.

"She's always been stand up," Tangles said. "Who else would have turned down a free trip to Italy?"

"For once, you said something I agree with," Letty said.

As the plane pulled away from the tarmac, Tangles asked about the call I took during breakfast.

"That was a detective. No prints on the shotgun. Some prints from the inside of the pickup, but so far no match."

"I knew if it had been good news, you would have told us," Letty said.

"Olga has security teams all over the place," Tangles said, "I think you should have at least one security guy that packs a gun or two and travels with you."

"It's bad enough I have to keep security on the grounds of Casa Luna," I said. "I ain't no rock star."

Letty frowned. "I agree with Tangles. You take your safety too lightly. You know someone is targeting you."

"Boss, that's twice today she agrees me." She gave me a thumbs up.

"Suck me," Letty said.

"Right here in front of the boss?"

As we taxied, Susie poured us a glass of Spanish red wine from a case that Riana had given me. Susie introduced Tina, our second stewardess, who had been attending to the pilots. The attendants took their seats in the front compartment and soon we were wheels up.

Five hours later, the plane landed in Washington D.C. for refueling and customs. By midnight according to Pasadena on my wrist, we were in the air again. After takeoff, we went to bed. Somewhere over the Atlantic, Susie and Tina whispered to me about the turbulence. They got on the bed to fasten the custom-made belt that ran the width of the bed. Letty, Tangles and I were naked under the covers.

If I ever got a serious inspection, the belt would never pass scrutiny, but in the meantime, it made us feel secure. The attendants left it loose so as not to wake the girls. A little later I felt the turbulence, but the girls didn't budge.

My plane landed at the private airport where we kept the leasing company inventory. It was only twenty minutes from the villa. As we came to a stop, Letty was looking out the window.

"Boss, I think you've got a surprise waiting out there."

"What?"

I looked out my window where Letty was pointing and saw Olga standing, her sidekick Riana standing next to her. They were head to toe in fur, Olga in white fox, Riana in black mink. The only thing visible that wasn't fur-lined were the noise-cancelling muffs on their ears.

"She was in Canada, too busy to hop over to Pasadena," I said. "How the fuck did she get here so fast?"

I waited at the open door as the stairs extended to the tarmac, then I ran down and into Olga's embrace. I picked her up and gently swung her around, our lips together.

"You must have not been in Canada when we talked," I said.

"I sure was, and we dropped everything and headed out. We got here an hour ago and waited for you."

I kissed her again and set her down. I kissed Riana and gave her a hard hug. Olga greeted Letty, then Tangles.

I noticed two guards when we walked to the Lincoln limousine. One held the back door open. The second guard was in the driver's seat.

"Where are the rest of the dudes?" I asked.

"You mean security?"

"Yeah."

"Behind us."

A full station wagon was following us.

"How long will you be here?" Olga asked.

"It depends on how long you will be here."

"Amor, I leave tomorrow afternoon."

"You came all this way from Canada for twenty-four hours?"

"Amor, wouldn't you do the same?"

Our eyes met.

"You bet, baby."

We kissed.

"Is this a love story or what?" Letty said.

Riana said, "So romantic."

We arrived at the villa and made ourselves comfortable in our respective bedrooms where the staff brought us snacks and hot drinks. Olga and I went to her rooms and had a fireworks-filled reunion chased with red wine and skewers of shish kabobs.

"I haven't heard from Camila," I said.

"If you need her, call her," Olga said, her voice unusually curt. "She's got her cell."

I wondered if I had inadvertently done something wrong. A couple of frown lines crossed Olga's forehead. I did not know why she was upset. "Is everything okay?"

She did not explain but sat up in bed and moved on me.

"Amor, fuck me some more, please."

I was happy to oblige.

Milan October 9 1989

Olga left with Riana as planned. I didn't visit the leasing office until Monday morning. Pepe had certainly picked two jewels for this business. Jules was a meticulous businessman, doing a marvelous job unattended here in Milan.

Before the meeting, I lingered in my office. It had been Pepe's office, and I could still feel his presence there. I thought about Pepe, about how suave and smart he had appeared in public, but what a snake he had been. There was a bust of him in white marble sitting in a niche. I walked over to it without thinking. My hands clenched into fists, and I 'accidentally' shoved it out. It fell on the floor with a huge crash. The fucker didn't even chip. The man was bulletproof, even in death.

Julian was first to the door.

"Put this somewhere else," I said to Julian who made no comment. As he had a couple of workers haul it to the front desk, I remembered what Olga said Pepe had done to her.

I had a thirty-minute meeting with the thirty-two employees working under Jules, shook hands with each one of them, then I left. No need to return a second day.

We ate pasta, bread, and wine, polishing it off like we hadn't eaten in days. Afterwards, we took a swim in the indoor pool to burn calories. The butler arranged for us to have a massage. I had the tables all set up in my bedroom. Letty and Tangles opted for male therapists. I got Valentina, who had attended to me a number of times before when I'd been living in Milan. After the massage sessions, the three of us hit the bed. I was so tired from the twenty-four hours I spent with Olga and the day I'd had that I went right to sleep. I suppose the girls did the same.

Next morning before noon, we were wheels up headed for home.

"We came all the way to Milan and didn't fuck," Letty said.

"All you do is think of sex," Tangles said.

"We got hours to go," I said getting up. "We're not home yet."

"Seat belt sign," Tangles said, pointing.

"Don't be a sissy," Letty said, getting up and following me to the bed-room.

"I'm right behind you, Boss," Tangles said. "I was kidding about the sign."

A plane crashed in Detroit. It was all over the news. Letty and Tangles wanted to work it.

"I know you know this," I said. "An airliner crash in the US is not the same as a plane crash abroad. We have a whole mess of rules and laws that we do not want to test. You cannot solicit, period."

"Got it, Boss," they said.

"I can't count how many small aircraft cases we've worked in the states," Letty said. "The same rules apply, and we've never messed up."

"She's right, Boss. We know what to do."

The girls left for Detroit the next day on a commercial flight. They were excited. I was excited for them.

I was going to leave the office at my regular time—early enough to miss traffic—but I remembered the girls were not at Casa Luna. I stayed later than usual, and thought I was alone. I sat on my chair, raised my feet up to rest on my desk facing the beautiful view. More and more buildings were being raised all around us. I suppose that no one was thinking about earthquakes anymore. Los Angeles had always limited the height of a building to thirteen floors, but now the sky was the limit.

I let Miguel know I was working late. I would have been the last one out of the office except Andrea was there too. The two of us closed the place down for the night, took the elevator down together, and walked through the quiet halls toward the exit.

I asked Andrea if she'd like to have dinner.

"I have a date," she said. "I'd love for you to have dinner with us."

"No way," I said in good humor. "You got a date. Go for it."

"Are you sure?"

"Of course, go. Have a great time. You deserve it."

She kissed me. "You're late getting out of here. Please be careful."

I got home at seven. At the kitchen island, I ate a porterhouse, a sweet potato smothered with butter and brown sugar, peas, string beans and I passed on dessert. I read the newspaper. It was Friday the 13th.

At nine, Betty arrived. I'd forgotten it was massage night. Seeing her was a treat, especially since no one else was here. I don't like to be alone.

On the level with my indoor pool, I have some massage tables, a couple of showers, and what the girls call 'a wet area.' That's where Betty set up the massage. The music was piped in, radio tonight. She lit a couple of aromatic candles, but nothing to compare with what Letty did in the bedroom. Still, it was nice. We talked casually for the first hour or so. She entertained me with risqué stories about some of her clients, but not the one I wanted to hear about.

"You don't do Melina anymore since she got married?"

"Not at midnight and not at her house. Always in her office at one of her markets."

"Are you doing anything else tonight?" I asked after two hours.

"Letty told me I should look out for you."

"Really?"

"I wouldn't lie, Boss. She said she was going to be in Detroit and that you would want company."

"Want to steam or sauna with me?"

Betty was out of her clothes in record time.

"Can we do both?"

It was obvious that Letty was absent. There were no candles lit in my bedroom. Two lamps in the sitting room were all that was on, enough light to see our bodies in the mirror above my bed. We weren't looking though. We were under the covers, facing each other, still talking. Betty's hands softly stroked me between my legs. She rubbed my stomach and chest with her nails, lightly enough to arouse a dead man.

"Do you think Melina is happy with him?" I asked.

"Seems to be," Betty said. "She doesn't talk much about him. She's dressing casual now, though it is still designer stuff I could never afford like her jeans and shoes. She doesn't wear her elegant suits like before. She's really laid back. Gorgeous. She's never going to age."

"I want her to be the happiest woman on earth." I kissed her, testing the waters. Betty was receptive. I felt her tongue.

"You're so hot, Betty."

"You tell that to everyone."

"It's true, I do."

Her arms were around my neck, and she pulled my hair, just a little. "Ouch."

I rubbed her ass. "You're hot, Betty, and you have a fine ass."

"Umm, do that some more."

In the morning when I awoke, Betty was gone. I worked out, showered and had breakfast with my newspaper. I had Miguel sit down and have coffee with me. We touched base, something we did once or twice when the girls were out of town. He still had his body builder physique, even though he was a chef. Letty was always pressuring him to take up karate, but all he did was lift weights.

Letty called during breakfast.

"Boss, they have the families in three hotels. We're in one of them, checked in. Are you okay?"

"I'm good, baby."

"Did Betty come over?"

"She did."

"I told her to take good care of you, a body exploration, something different."

"Body exploration?"

"I just made that up. Did she give you a PM?"

"A PM?"

"Oh, Boss, a prostate massage."

"Not a chance. Are we done with this interrogation?"

She giggled. I could hear Tangles in the background urging her to hang up so they could get to work.

Pasadena Oct 14, 1989

When I first started, my car was my office. Then I worked at home. Now I drive to work every day. Did I like what I was doing that much? Was it the money driving me? I have a hefty salary and a promise that I would get an option to purchase stock. I never bought it after two years as I had planned, but I got to open the LA office and had another extended promise to review my options. If I settled for what I already had, I could take it easy. I have enough income to live in luxury the rest of my life without putting in another day of work. Was I after easy? I've always had this bottomless pit of ambition, and it was still unsatisfied.

My curiosity was also unsatisfied. Who was trying to kill me? Or scare me? Why?

When the biker had appeared on my balcony, he'd been there to do harm. He was there to kill me. I wondered if I was dealing with multiple puppeteers: one that wanted to scare me and another one that wanted me dead.

I had asked Mason that question.

"Damn good question, Mario. I'm working on it."

I was still using my CPA that I had for years and he was not getting any younger. Loyalty would keep me with him to the end. He kept me straight and out of the cross hairs of the IRS and the California Franchise Tax Board. The leasing company was presently being taken care of in Milan, but that had to change. We were leasing more and more planes in California and the United States in general. I had an appointment with a CPA executive named Jim who wanted the leasing company business. Olga had asked me to meet with him.

After two hours in my office with Andrea and Jim doing most of the talking, Jim said he'd get back to me with a proposal for his firm to take on our business. In the meantime, he believed that the company in Milan should remain as it was, and a new company be formed for the office in Los Angeles.

I called Camila and Olga on a conference call and explained. Andrea was not on the call but sat across my desk when I was talking to Camila and Olga.

"I want it to be the same company. The business generated in the US can go on the books in the US, and the business generated in Milan can just continue like it is."

"I agree with Olga," Camila said. "Let's find an accounting firm that is a heavyweight. Olga research that and give Andrea names. Someday we may go public with LAI; and if we do, we may want to do the same with the leasing company."

"Why don't we use the firm handling LAI?" Olga asked.

"I prefer to keep the leasing company severed from LAI. That's why Pepe formed a separate company. Amor, Olga will work on getting some firms to call you through Andrea. Tell this Jim guy to go fish."

There were several moments of silence on the phone. Olga and Camila didn't always agree, and this was one of those days. The call was tense, filled with tension for no reason I could discern.

After the call, I asked Andrea how her date went.

"One second and I'll tell you," she said. I watched her walk across the room to the double doors. She locked them, and returned, came around my desk, swiveled me around so I was facing her and not my desk. She went down on her knees, unzipped me.

"Let me," she said. "I quiver when I'm around you like this," she said, beginning to work on me.

Olga and Camila were thousands of miles away. Letty and Tangles were in Detroit. Besides, this was my office.

I got up, dropped my pants and pulled her pantyhose off. She bent over my desk and she turned around to watch as I disappeared inside her. I set a pace and rhythm that was teeth-clenching but backed off when I felt her orgasm, once, then again, and again. Then, it was my turn.

After I got home at four, Andrea called.

"Mayco has agreed to the terms of the lease. I'm so happy," she said. It was our first helicopter lease. Twelve brand new Bell helicopters. We were expanding into a new market.

"Congratulations," I said with gusto. "You are dynamite."

"Should I come over to your house and celebrate tonight?"

"Yes," I said. "We'll have dinner in the master bedroom."

"Oh, how fun. I'll be there."

Every woman is beautiful, with her own unique qualities. Andrea was kinky in some ways but that made her glamorous to me. I like a woman who tells me what she wants and what she likes. My team was exactly that way. Andrea was that way, naturally outspoken. When her glasses were off, and she stood naked, she oozed with appeal.

"My bottom is ready if you want a tight fuck like last time, or we can be ordinary, your pleasure."

"Let's toss a coin," I joked.

"Fun, yes."

There wasn't a single coin in the master bedroom. She looked in her purse. We were both naked, hunting for a coin. "I got a nickel," she said raising it.

"Heads in front, tails, bottom," she said.

She tossed the coin. A few minutes later I was inside her pussy.

"Twice in one day. I can't believe it," she said through her moans.

"You never told me how your date went?"

"Nothing to write about in my diary," she managed to say as I rolled over and put her on top. "I'm so happy about the Mayco deal. I'm going to explode any second."

I was enjoying her too much to tell her she didn't have to talk shop.

We were lying on my sheets exhausted but recuperating for another round when my bedside phone rang. The intercom line.

It was Betty.

"Boss, I'm set up downstairs. Do you want a massage?"

"You got enough energy to do two of us?"

"Always," Betty replied.

Pasadena October 16, 1989

Monday morning. We were on the balcony having coffee with Betty.

"Take the day off," I told Andrea.

"Thanks, but no. I have to work on closing Mayco. I'm going to be late though. I need to run home, so I don't have to make the walk of shame."

"Baby, it can wait a day. Go rest up. I'm the boss. It's okay."

Andrea left. I felt like taking the day off. I had missed my five AM workout. Betty was raring to give me a morning massage.

"A deep tissue will fix you up, Boss."

I was in the spa face down on a table, waiting. The anticipation made me sensitive. I felt little kisses, a tongue on my neck, then my shoulders. I got aroused.

"Hey, I'm never going to get to work like this."

"It's payback for all that you did to me last night. You are so special, Boss. You make me feel so, so beautiful."

I sat up. "You are beautiful." I pulled her to me and hugged her.

"You seem more sentimental than usual. Is something going on?" I asked.

"Two days in a row with you."

She smiled, pushing me lightly to lie down, and then she continued working my back.

On my way to the office, I got a call from Letty with Tangles next to her.

"We've been talking to two men who lost a mother and sister, and another who lost his wife."

"Take your time. It's too fast," I said.

"We're willing to sit here until Christmas. Don't worry, Boss. We're doing this by the book."

"Good," I said.

"I'm just worried about you," Letty said.

"Yeah, Boss," Tangles said in the background. "Are you okay without us?"

"I'm fine."

"You mean you don't miss me?" Letty asked, a little quiver in her voice.

"And what about me?" Tangles asked.

"I miss you, both. Stop worrying about me. Take care of the business you are there for. Got it?"

"Got it."

I would be lying if I said I didn't like the attention.

After I hung up, I wondered when Letty would find someone and leave me. Tangles liked dating. For sure, she'd probably be out the door before Letty.

"You forgot to mention to me at lunch that you'd given your private investigator my phone number," Fino said over the phone. He had called me at work, something he rarely did.

"I overlooked it, sorry, Jack. It was Olga's idea to hire—"

He interrupted. "Olga told me. It's a good idea. I told him I'd be happy to meet with him."

"He wants to meet with you?"

"If he's as good as Olga says, he needs to meet with everyone that knows you. Got it handled," Fino said.

"Jack, thanks."

Letty called to give me their progress.

I told Letty, "I'd love to be a fly on the wall next to Janice when Mason calls her."

"Fuck, I can imagine the cussing he will get out of that witch."

"If she's guilty, it may shake her ass up," Tangles said on the hotel extension.

"Too bad Betty hasn't done a massage on her for long time," Letty said. "Betty was pretty good at getting her undercover on with Janice."

"I don't want the people he calls to think they are suspects."

"Boss, hands off. Let Mason handle it," Letty said.

"Hands off?" I said mockingly.

"Sorry, Boss, that just squeezed out of my mouth."

She reminded me that while I was in Rio, Mason had spent three days interviewing all my personnel. Olga had insisted that I should not interfere, so I had given him permission. I heard he was planning to interview Jo, Niley and Betty as well. My brain told me that he was just charging up a storm of hours to get all he could from Olga. I didn't say anything to anyone else, but I did apologize to all of my help when I returned from the long trip.

"Boss, I dug it," Tangles had said. "I even asked him if I could consult him professionally to make sure I wasn't crazy or something."

Letty said, "Boss, she did. I wasn't there, but I know she did."

"Damn right. He's a psychiatrist. He said he doesn't practice anymore but could refer me to someone else."

"Baby, you aren't crazy, and you don't need a shrink," I said.

Tangles had laughed. "I just wanted a chance at doing him on the couch. I pictured me lying there like in a movie and then you know."

I may have chuckled, but I was a bit pissed. Not sure why. I couldn't possibly be jealous. And then Letty launched into progress on their retainers, diverting my attention.

Olga called.

"Fino is going to think I have him on the suspect list," I told her.

Olga laughed. "He will think no such thing."

"He said you told him about hiring Mason. Do you talk to him often?"

"Not too often. At the moment I have him hunting three good candidates for you to interview to handle the leasing company books."

"I see," I said. "Just wondered."

"Mason will find the person behind what has happened to you," Olga said. "One of his cases involved a painting stolen from a museum in France. I don't recall the artist, but it was worth a fortune. It was stolen in transit to the museum. Mason worked the case almost two years and not only solved who stole it, but he recovered it from the person who bought it from the thief. The thief never gave up the buyer. Mason found him on his own. He's good at what he does."

"I'm afraid to ask how much you are paying him."

"If he comes through like I expect, not nearly enough, Amor."

There was silence for just a moment. I didn't know what to say. I felt a rush of love for her, for her understanding, for her generosity.

"Olga, I don't deserve you."

"Wrong, Amor. We deserve each other. When you're bad, don't feel bad. I'm not perfect either."

"I love you, Olga."

"Mario Luna, I adore you."

Pasadena November 1, 1989

Letty called to tell me that they were done and were calling it quits at a retainer count of nine.

"We're at the airport, headed to Chicago to deliver and get paid. Be home tomorrow, Boss. These twenty-three days have wrecked me, I miss you so much."

Pixie was on the tail end of the short tour she'd started on the day I'd visited Milan. She was soon to be home, but as she was still on the road, Raul was available to pick them up at LAX. He drove Tangles to drop her stuff off at her apartment, then brought them home to me. They had half a day to recuperate from their trip before Jo, Niley, and Betty joined us for dinner that night. Jo's husband, TJ was on a job up north.

Miguel had set up hot oil fondue pots on the buffet. Individual cheese fondue pots lined the center of the table. Colorful dishes of partially-cooked vegetables were arranged on a cloth runner, and huge baskets of fluffy bread cubes. The table looked like something out of those home magazines Jo used to mark up and hand over to Melina. It was not the meal of my choice, but the girls were over the moon. And I was happy that Miguel was cooking filet and chicken strips at his meat station so I could concentrate on my guests. I could not help laughing when I looked at the foot of the table where there was a chocolate fountain surrounded with crystal dishes of fruit, angelfood cake, and Oreos. Caro had promised me to secrecy when she'd confessed how Miguel had tried and failed to invent a creamy liquid peanut butter concoction to go in a chocolate fountain.

"Nine is a great number," Jo told the girls.

"If Boss had been with us, we could have tripled that."

"If Boss had been with you, it would not be your case," Niley said with a grin. "Be happy. You did great, and the money you made is all yours."

Letty looked across the wide table at Niley. "Are you staying over?"

"I haven't been invited," Niley said.

"Boss, invite her already," Tangles said.

"Niley and Jo don't need invitations. They are family and can stay here as long as they want whenever they want."

"I'd love to, but I can't stay," Jo said. "Luckily for Niley, we came in separate cars."

"TJ wouldn't care if you stayed over," I said. "Would he?"

Jo just smiled. "He's out of town or he'd have been here too. I just have unavoidable obligations."

There was a time when Jo and I had fucked our brains out, anytime, anywhere. She had been the original member of my team and had trained Pixie in our business in the days when all we did was car crashes. There had been a time when we shared the love in bed with the rest of the team. As domesticated as she is these days, Jo is still wild, beautiful, and hot.

Merida, Yucatan November 2, 1989
Lainie

I just finished a music video filmed on the most beautiful beach in Merida, Yucatan with a local audience as part of the background. A stage had been built on the sand with fantastic quality sound equipment and generators powerful enough to light up a small town. I sang twelve songs and filmed day scenes, dusk and night scenes, and a spectacular light show for the close. It wasn't a one-shot deal. I sang each of the songs at least a dozen times over nine eighteen-hour days and nights before the director said it was a wrap. On the last tour, the same film crew had toured with my mother, and cut together a music video, which had given someone the bright idea to film me.

It was cold at home and in England, but I wasted no time getting on Jason's plane and taking off for London. The invites went out the week before. Less than five months to our April wedding day. I told Jason daily that we didn't need a big wedding.

"You deserve the best," he said. "If we do it another way, I would lose face with my friends, your new friends."

I didn't care about appearances. That was all him. I wish I could convince Jason that a ceremony with no fanfare would be so much better. It bugs me that every article written about me in the past year has included a mention about my boyfriend being old enough to be my father, and some have said grandfather. When a picture of Jason is shown, they cut me some slack because he's handsome, but they also talk about how rich he is, the English estates, the plane, and that makes me out as a gold digger and a trophy. No way to win.

I'm beginning to make pretty good money, but I work for every penny. I love to sing, and maybe someday act. It would take a whole string of heavily booked concert seasons for me to afford just the engagement ring on my finger or the forty-five-carat diamond bracelet I wear all the time.

My mother knows Jason better than anybody, and suspects that we have an arrangement, but I'm not admitting it to anybody. Jason is a director of a number of companies and it would destroy his image if it got out that he was gay *and* kinky. As much as I love Jason, the feeling is not enough to marry him if there wasn't an arrangement. Our marriage will discredit any gossip out there about his private life. He never fucked me. We had sex, but he never fucked me. By the time he told me his preferences, I had already figured it out.

On the wedding day, I get ten million British pounds sterling, and the title on the London penthouse. He'll lease me a new Falcon plane for five years. The amount of the monthly wife allowance hasn't been resolved, but that's extra. After five years, I can walk with a divorce, but there will be no alimony or cash settlement. If I choose to stay beyond the five years, we negotiate again.

Now that I know the truth, our sex gets pretty hot. He likes to watch me and a male partner or do a threesome with him on the guy. It's the male anatomy that turns Jason on. Every partner Jason has gotten for me has never had a problem getting an instant hardon and keeping it hard as long as I'm under, or on top, or just sitting around naked.

If any man Jason provides turns a rat, Jason will pay me five million pounds on any public exposure. I love this new life Olga turned me on to, making me a star, and my mother turning me on to her boyfriend, even though that was a freak of an accident. I just hope nothing happens to rock the boat. My mom says she's not pissed at me, but she's pissed at me. I think she's jealous, though I don't know why she'd be jealous, knowing what Jason is about behind closed doors.

Only one of my agreements is in writing—a handwritten one that says

I can keep the engagement ring if we don't tie the knot. He also trusts my promise that once we are married, I will never go out with another man in case I get caught by the media. It would be embarrassing to Jason, and it would defeat the objective of why he needs me. I can do that. After a tour or any business trip that takes me away from London, Jason will have a male or males lined up for me on my return, so that he can have his pleasure. Jason knows how to pick them.

My mother calls me every day and if she misses, I call her. But lately we've been having the same conversation over and over. It goes like this:

"Did you get the invitation?"

"I didn't get it," my mom says, but she's lying. I talked to Letty. Letty already got hers.

"Mom, I will send you another one."

"I may be on tour that day."

"There you go again, picking a fight with me."

"Honey, why are you marrying him? Can't you just keep it like you have it now? Why go through the hoops?"

"Mom, I love him. I want to marry him."

"Bullshit."

"Mom, stop it."

"Give me a good reason you insist on getting in to this circus with him."

"Circus? Mom, if I'm doing this, I have a good reason, and it's not just love."

"I hope it's worth it. I love Jason, too, but I wouldn't marry him."

"Mom, you were ready to marry him until I came along."

Silence.

"Mom?"

Then she hangs up.

Pasadena November 3, 1989
Pixie

I made it home from a tour and returned by stealth before sunrise to my place across from Mario's. I let the staff unpack for me. It was ungodly early, but my people get cabin fever when I'm gone, and go nuts making me feel at home when I finally get here. I had a long soak in a bubble bath. Mario's house is always the first call I make. Letty answered the house phone.

"Are you coming across the street to see me or what?"

"On my way."

By then, it was eleven in the morning, but night time in my master bedroom. She opened the door and stood in the light from the hall. Once I saw her, I knew I was home.

"How can you be in bed this late, and you call me lazy?"

"I've only been home since five this morning, and I got jet lag from concert hours on Mexico time. What's your excuse?"

I sat up in bed. She was just putting me on. Her clothes flew off, then she was in bed with me. We hugged. If we'd been vertical instead of horizontal, we would have been jumping around and squealing like a couple of teenaged girls. My eyes were accustomed to the dim light, and I could just make out her beautiful dark eyes. How I have missed her.

"What is it about you that pulls me like a magnet?" she asked me.

"My pussy."

"Bullshit," Letty said. "You're so dirty, I should leave."

I felt her fingers exploring me.

"You won't leave," I said.

"You mean you won't let me leave."

I felt three fingers, maybe four, and was beginning to squirm, wildly.

Out of breath, Letty said, "I want autographs, records, and videos."

"Yes, yes," I moaned, "Yes, yes." A long string of yeses, like an incantation.

I faintly heard Letty laughing as she teased me.

Mario does office hours now, so I might get more time with Letty. She hangs around the house with Tangles waiting on plane crashes. It's so easy to rile her up. I tell her she's getting lazy, and she gets all wound up to punch me out. She spends hours with Tangles working out in the gym. They are into boxing now.

Later we have a late lunch delivered by Raul, the only one of my help who does not gossip. He leaves the food on a folding table on short legs wide enough to fit both of us side-by-side as we lean against pillows.

Club sandwiches, fruit salad, cups of shaved ice ready for cokes. The small glass coke bottles sat in a champagne bucket filled with ice.

"If you weren't part of his life, I'd steal you and let you travel with me. I get so fucking lonely. I mean, I'd pay you."

"If he weren't part of her life, you'd be having Mario travel with you."

"True," I agreed. "Like I could choose between the two of you. Both of you could fly with me and do plane crashes where ever we go."

"Ha, like that could work," Letty laughed.

We both know it takes a while to handle crashes and would not fit in with my fast-track lifestyle.

Letty munched on half of a sandwich. She sniffed her sandwich, then her hand,

"My fingers smell like pussy."

"Let me smell," I said.

She put her sandwich down on the dish and pushed her palm against my nose.

"Yummy," I kidded. "I wasn't kidding when I said I'd steal you."

"I'm not leaving him until he shows me to the door."

"He's going to get married."

"You already know that Olga has committed that I can live with them."

"Sweets, I'd never take you away from him. I was just saying I'm here for you. I just want you to know that."

Letty leaned to the side a bit and kissed me.

"Olga once hinted about hiring me to travel with her as an assistant."

I reminded Letty, "When I spent that time traveling with her, she made me the same offer."

"Here's how I see it," Letty reached for another sandwich and took a bite. "She gets rid of Melina, buys this house from her and tells her to scat. Then she gets you discovered. It's great for you, but mostly, it fulfills her goal, that she gets you out of his everyday life."

"I owe my career to her, and I love her for it, but I'm not blind."

"I'm just saying," Letty said, shrugging like she doesn't care though I know she does. "I love Olga, too. I used to be afraid of her. Not just of her, her people too. I always thought how she got rid of Melina and got rid of you. How is she going to get rid of me?"

It sobered me up a little, but it would be crazy paranoid to think Letty was in danger from Olga. We showered again and crossed the street to Casa Luna. Boss would be arriving from the office soon.

Tangles's greeting was more of a tackle than a hug, then she jumped right in on me. Her hair was weirdly long and wildly curly, a flashback to the way she used to wear it—then I realized it was a wig. I had a little hint: she pulled it off for the shock value, revealing a cut so short it almost looked like a shaved head with a month's worth of growth. Come to think of it, she probably had shaved it.

"You don't answer your cell. I looked in every room of this house," Tangles said, dangling the sig in her hand. She can be a drama queen.

"Oh hush, bitch. You been kicking back, waiting for a big crash," Letty pointed her finger.

"I smell sex," Tangles said, "That fragrance you got on isn't enough to camouflage it."

"Bitch, we showered. The only thing you smell are your own fingers from playing with yourself."

We headed to the gym to work out, then I watched Tangles and Letty box with the big bag, showing off new moves. Cosmo had taught us how to use the bag to kick and tackle in a workout, but they had gloves on, and boxing moves were entirely different. I got a pair of gloves on, and Letty and Tangles gave me a beginner lesson. I was trying on the moves when Boss got home. He found us a sweaty mess, laughing away.

"Hey Mario, ever fuck a sweaty pussy before?" I asked.

Boss nodded and laughed. "Pix, what would your fans say if they heard you?"

"My fans aren't here. You didn't answer me," I winked at the Boss who was near the door. I dropped my gym shorts, turned my ass, bent over like a cunt.

"Want some?"

Letty and Tangles were in tears laughing.

Boss kicked his shoes off, suit coat, tie, shirt, trousers, underwear. He stopped at his socks. In stocking feet, he walked over, his dick standing at attention.

"Your fans are too here," Letty giggled. "Bet you that's your biggest fan right over there. Biggest, get it?"

Letty went over to the wall and pushed a button, telling Miguel to hold dinner for a couple of hours. Once, that announcement would have sent Miguel into fits, but he's a pretty smart guy. I'm betting he put dinner on hold as soon as he saw me walk in. He has a pretty good idea of what can happen on my first night home after a tour.

First time ever the three of us fucked on a gym mat before. First time since the rebuild, anyway.

Chapter 8
Pasadena November 3, 1989
Mario

After the mat workout, we steamed, dipped in freezing water, jumped in the sauna, showered, and wore robes to the wine room for dinner. Pixie picked out the wine and opened two bottles of Malbec. Miguel presented a platter of cheeses, biscuits, figs, and jams.

Pixie's cell phone rang. She ignored it. Letty's cell phone rang. She answered it.

"Who the hell is this?" You never know how Letty will answer the phone. In a split second, Letty's expression went from comical to concerned.

"Lainie, hi. Where are you?" Letty suddenly looked concerned. "Wait, I can't understand you. Why are you crying?"

"She's so spoiled. Give me the phone," Pixie said, reaching for it.

Lainie must have really sounded bad. One second into the call, Pixie pulled the same one-eighty as Letty.

"It's Mama. What's the matter?"

Letty muted the juke box. We were all silently watching Pixie listen to Lainie.

"Crying is not going to help at all," she said. "And I can't understand half of what you're telling me. Take a deep breath and start over from the top."

"What is it?" I asked.

Pixie raised her hand.

"Lainie, hold on. Let me tell Mario what's going on."

Pixie turned toward me.

"Jason's been arrested for grand theft and a whole mess of other crimes. The prosecutor has taken possession of Jason's house, the entire building Sami's penthouse is in, all of Lainie's jewelry. There's a lien on everything. It's all over the news in London."

I grabbed Letty's phone from Pixie.

"Lainie, where are you?"

"I'm at the Mandarin. Just got here. They held me at the house for more than ten hours."

Behind her choked sobs, I could hear a television in the background. I heard footsteps, a recording of Lainie singing, and a news anchor's voice over.

"I'm all over the news here," she said. "Not good publicity."

I heard the television turn off. No more footsteps. She must have sat down.

"Have you talked to Olga yet?"

"Not yet. I haven't talked to anyone else yet. She was going to be the next call."

"We're coming to get you. I want to check on Jason."

"Jason's in jail. I doubt they are going to let him out. He took millions from Sami's estate."

"What?" I felt my knees go weak and flopped down on the couch. I could hardly believe what I was hearing.

"He wasn't rich. He was using her money."

By the time I talked to Olga in Lima, Peru, she already knew.

"Go get our girl, Amor. I'm terribly sorry about Jason. I know how close you are to him."

Pixie, Letty, Tangles and I boarded my plane as soon as the pilots were able to fly.

"I spent so much time in his house. Lots of pictures of Sami and Jason, Sami growing up, Sami and her family. I never thought it was not his house," Pixie said.

Sami had told me of a big family mansion outside of London she'd grown up in, an estate where she couldn't bear to live, but couldn't bear to live without. Too many ghosts, and too far from city life. Before we'd met, she had purchased the penthouse and moved to live there full-time. I never visited the estate. Maybe that's the house Pixie was talking about.

Our flight time was just under eleven hours. At five AM on Nov 4, a hotel limousine from the Mandarin picked us up at the airport. A lawyer named Adolph Myers came to the hotel within an hour of our arrival at the hotel. Leave it to Olga to have connections everywhere. At six thirty, we met Meyers over coffee and croissants in the sitting room of Lainie's suite that was much bigger than mine.

Meyers had looked into the matter and read the media accounts. Sami's father, a physician in the United States, had passed away. During his lifetime, he had left all control of Sami's estate to Jason, who had been the executor of her will. Sami's father had been the heir but had no interest. His widow was another story. She'd asked Jason for an accounting. One thing led to another. The widow's attorneys were getting stonewalled. The widow's agents eventually talked to the prosecutor's office in London. They investigated and found transfers of assets and irregularities that revealed that Sami's estate was being bilked to the tune of millions of British pounds.

"Jason has very capable attorneys who are representing him," Myers told all of us. "Too soon to tell, but personally, I don't believe the judge will grant him bail before his trial."

Myers met me the next morning and took me to the jail where they were holding Jason. When we got there, Jason refused to see me.

"I think he's embarrassed," Meyers said. "We can't force him to visit with us."

I asked him to check on Ginger and Crispin to see if I could do anything for them. I wasn't sure if the liens would affect their lifetime jobs to maintain the penthouse or the two apartments Sami had given them.

I didn't eat for forty-eight hours. I was sick from what had happened to Jason, and to learn that he was embezzling money from the estate of my late friend Sami. She was smart. She must have known her estate was vulnerable, but Jason had been her close friend. She had chosen him as second executor if her father was no longer living or declined the position.

"What about the diamond?" I asked Myers after telling him that Sami had given me the ring that Olga now wore.

"That was a gift directly from her. I doubt you will have a problem."

We left London on Thursday, the ninth. Jason had refused to face me. Myers was right. Jason had been embarrassed.

It is a good thing the DC9 is a big plane because I needed to be alone. I had a hard time reconciling the Jason I knew with the Jason who had been an embezzler. Lainie and Pixie slept in the bedroom. The flight attendant opened two sofa seats that faced each other into a queen size bed. Letty and Tangles gave up trying to stay awake and crashed. I sat in a seat away from the others for hours, and finally, reclined the wide seat and closed my eyes. I went in and out of sleep.

I wanted to assure Jason that no matter what he had done, he was my friend. Who knows where I'd be today if he had not talked me into going after plane crashes. For years he fed me confidential information to make it easier for my team and me to find families of decedents, details that newspapers never printed. My career would never have happened without his initial encouragement. Without that career, I never would have been kidnapped in Venezuela, never would have been introduced to Pepe when Oscar hired him to 'rescue' me. If I'd never met Pepe, I would not now be running GAL US and I would not be engaged to Olga.

I never gave him a thing in return for all the years of his help.

Raul was at the airport and drove us home. Letty, Tangles and I were dropped off at Casa Luna then Raul drove across the street to Pixie's.

I was so tired that I went right to bed. After midnight, just before I went to sleep, I got a call on cell. It was Adolph Myers.

"Jason committed suicide. The bastards should have put him on suicide watch. He was distraught. It's expected. I'm sorry, Mario."

The news got me out of bed. I stopped by Letty's room and told her. She promised to tell Tangles and meet me across the street. Pixie and Lainie were still up when I cleared security and walked up to the front door.

Pasadena November 10, 1989

"Boss, what's up?" Pixie asked. Lainie was behind her. I went inside, put my arms around them and gave them the news.

I knew absolutely no one in Jason's family that I could call. No one answered the phone at Sami's penthouse.

"I'm not going," Lainie said. "The press over there is calling me a gold digger. He's gone. There's nothing I can do."

London November 12, 1989

Two days after we got home from London, Letty, Tangles and I were on our way back. Myers told me that the services were planned for Tuesday, two days after we arrived.

On my first night there, Adolph met me in the lobby bar in the Mandarin, and we had a glass of wine.

Myers explained that he was friends with the prosecutor, and therefore had an inside track on the events in Jason's case.

"Jason never transferred real property out of the estate. He paid himself tens of millions of British pounds for executor services. He took jewels that had been inventoried as assets of the estate. If you read the newspapers, you get different scenarios. That is all reporters taking liberties with the story."

"Jason once told me that Sami's father didn't want anything to do with the estate. I believe it. The day Sami gave me the ring, her father was there in her apartment, and so was Jason," I told Myers. "Both of them are dead now.

I'm not worried about it, but it's just the principle of the thing. The ring was a gift. She put it in my hands. I'm not returning the diamond without a fight. Sami gave me that ring. She gave it specifically for me to give it to my fiancée when I had one to give it to."

"Relax. At the moment, no one is asking for the ring."

"You knew Sami but not Jason?" I asked. I was surprised. I mean, it wasn't like Sami and Jason were joined at the hip, but they did run in the same crowd.

"Sami knew my name, but we weren't what you call friends. I saw her often at charity functions. I have a sister who knew her pretty well, but she worked at the hospital with Sami. My sister, like Sami, is also a doctor."

"Small world," I said.

"I never met Jason, didn't know he existed until now."

London November 14, 1989

Early Tuesday morning, Letty, Tangles and I were getting ready to go to the church, and Myers called.

"I guess we will see you at the service," I said.

"No, you won't," Myers said. He explained that Jason's brother had had the body cremated and elected not to have a service. "I can understand that a family of a mass murderer would not want any part of relative who died in shame, but Jason's crime was much lesser. He didn't kill anyone. Anyway, there's no service. I'm sorry you came all this way for nothing."

"It's okay. I got a chance to meet with you again, and I appreciate that very much. If anything comes up with this diamond matter, I may need to reach out to you."

"Mario, I'm at your service."

I conferenced with Pixie and Lainie at home in Pasadena.

"I feel terrible," Lainie said on the speaker phone. "I told my mother about the arrangement I had with him. It wasn't like we were madly in love with each other. He was concerned about the directors on boards that he was on, no doubt companies owned by Sami's estate, not him."

"Get a tour going," I said. "Keep busy. You'll feel better."

"She already has something coming up to promote her latest music video she recorded in the Yucatan. Wait till you see it," Pixie said. "Olga is fixing it so Lainie travels in Latin America until the press here loses interest. In Mexico no one cares about a scandal."

At least this flight home was not as gloomy as the last one.

"We need to move on," I said. I lifted my glass of wine. "To Jason, my dear friend."

We clicked glasses as the plane leveled off at thirty thousand feet.

"I imagine that Jason was ashamed to face his friends," Letty said.

"If they were friends, he wouldn't have to face down anything," I said.

"I don't think I could kill myself," Tangles said. "I do feel sympathy for how he must have felt."

"Jason was so smart. How could he not know that the fantasy life he was leading would have to come to an end?" I asked.

"He must have believed that Sami's father was never going to check on the state of things," Letty said.

"Exactly," I said.

"Lainie will get over it," Tangles speculated.

"I think Pixie was already over him," Letty said.

On December first, we were at my house having lunch. Both Lainie and Pixie were leaving on tour that evening. Both would fly to Mexico City. Lainie would be there one day, then leave for her first stop in Guadalajara. Pixie would stay at Olga's Mexican home for a week because she was needed at the recording studio. Her tour first stop was in Sao Paulo, Brazil.

We had scheduled to celebrate Christmas and New Years together, all of us flying down to Olga's home in Mexico.

"My publicist says there wasn't a single word printed in Mexico about Jason and me other than he had committed suicide in police custody. Nothing else," Lainie said.

"I wasn't even mentioned," Pixie said.

"I'm never returning to London. Those tabloid bastards called me a gold digger," Lainie said. "What a wasted part of my life."

Pixie said, "You gave the jewels back, but you had fun with him, and jetting around in his plane. He walked you down the red carpet a couple of times and looked nice on your arm. They can't repossess the fun you had. It wasn't a waste of time."

Pasadena December 7, 1989

A week into December, I had a call from a London lawyer who represented Sami's estate.

I knew it was not going to be good news.

After a minute of chit chat, he said, "The inventory of assets shows a diamond ring in your possession. I cannot locate anything that bequeaths the ring to you during Sami's lifetime. I assume you still have the ring?"

"I do. Sami gave me the ring on her deathbed in the presence of her father and Jason. I didn't ask for it. She gifted me the ring to use as an engagement ring one day."

"I'm sorry Mr. Luna, but I have nothing in writing to support that. Jason was the executor of the estate. He should have done his paperwork, but he didn't."

"Let me give you my attorney's name and phone number there in London. Please work it out with him."

Pasadena December 8, 1989

The next day I got a call from Adolph Myers.

"I told the idiot to file an action to recover the ring," Myers said. "We'd duke it out in court. The widow is out to recover everything she can."

Olga was in Paris. I told her about the problem.

"Amor, let's return the ring. You buy me another one. I don't need this ring. Please don't stress over this."

"It's not the ring or the value. It's that Sami gave me the ring. It was a sentimental piece that sat in my safe for years until I gave it to you. I'm not giving it back."

"Amor, in that case, let Adolph fight it out in court."

"I'm sorry," I said to Olga. "I told him to do that."

"Amor, don't be sorry."

Paris December 8, 1989
Olga

"Adolph, what are the chances we win in court over this stupid ring that means so much to Mario?"

"I haven't received a demand to turn over the ring. It will be difficult to win in court because there is no paper trail. Jason screwed that up. He was sloppy and didn't file anything that he was required to do."

"Eventually then, we're going to lose?"

"I'll give it everything I got," Adolph said. "Yes, I think we will lose."

"Thank you, Adolph. We never had this conversation."

When I hung up, I tried thinking of something other than the ring.

Riana went out to a night club, but I stayed behind in the hotel room. I walked outside and stood on the balcony feeling the bitter wind blow through my silk lingerie. The city looked so lovely, the dim yellowish lights making it look romantic and picturesque. But it was too cold. I stepped inside, fastened the doors against the wind, and got into a hot bubble bath to defrost. I didn't take off the ring. I could just imagine the trouble that would come if I lost it down a hotel drain. What a fiasco that would be. The damn ring means so much to Mario. I had to make sure he won that case.

New York December 22, 1989
Slim

I gave up burglaries, heists and murders three years ago and took off for my homeland, Cali, Colombia. But then I get a call from Olga Camacho. You don't say no to a Camacho. There is no way I can remind her I'm retired. Took me days to pin down this broad's penthouse apartment on Park Avenue. I high-jacked the alarm system to her place. So here I am, in New York City, walking quietly through the broad's house looking for the master bedroom. It's a ritzy place, carpets three inches deep. Everything looks like it's gold and marble. She must be loaded. Too much furniture in this fancy-ass apartment. The floor doesn't so much as creak. Not much room, but that's New York for you. A grandfather clock says one fifteen in the morning. My watch says one thirteen. Credenza full of gold plate dishes, paintings on the walls like it's the fucking Museum of Modern Art of Medellin. There are four bedrooms so far, and no one has been in any of them. Finally, the master bedroom, double doors on the opposite side of the other bedrooms. I slip in. It's dark, but I see two bodies on the bed. If this is the widow, she wasted no time getting a bed partner. I get close. The guy's eyes open, and I'm so close I can see tiny hairs on his forehead. I hit him with the butt of my 357 Magnum, and he goes out. The smack to his head is loud enough that the babe stirs. I stick my hand in my pocket to find the rag, and switch on her bedside lamp. Before she can scream, I shove the wash cloth in her mouth. One hand over her mouth. With the other, I pull the knife out. She sees it. Her eyes get big. I don't have a mask on.

"Emma," I tell her in a soft voice. "I see you have a bed partner. Didn't waste any time, huh? You're like all bitches."

Emma is frantic.

"This knife is real. Nod your head if you understand."

It takes a few seconds, but Emma nods. Her eyes are tearing now.

"I have someone wants to talk to you on the phone. You just listen. Understand me?"

She nods.

"Don't worry about this fucker lying next to you. He's not dead. You both will be stay breathing as long as you do as you are told."

This time she nods without my having to ask her.

I get Olga on my cell phone.

"I have Emma listening. One second while I put the phone to her ear."

I can't hear what Olga is telling her, but I see Emma's expression. She's nodding, but she should know that Olga can't see her.

I take the phone back and deposit it in my pocket.

"Emma, I don't want to return, but I promise, I will if I need to. If not here, wherever you are, when you least expect me."

Emma nods.

"Did you understand what you have to do?"

Emma nods.

"I didn't tie you up. I did not threaten you by putting the knife at your throat. I don't like messing with women, but I have a job to do. I hope I never have to come back."

Emma nodded.

"I hope I don't have to finish what I didn't do tonight. You're not going to call the police or tell anyone about this little visit, are you? Because if you do that, I'll have to come back."

Her eyes got big again, and she shook her head.

I took the rag out of her mouth, poured a spot of chloroform on it and held it over her nose and mouth till she was out. She tried pretending she was out, but I wasn't born yesterday.

I left the same way I came in.

I called Olga from a pay phone a block away. I gave the operator the pay phone number in the Netherlands where Olga was waiting and deposited one dollar and fifty cents in quarters.

"What you want me to do next, *Patrona?*"[26]

"Go home, Amor. I owe you."

"You owe me nothing, *Patrona.*"

---

[26] Patroness

Pasadena January 29, 1990
Mario

A month passed since the estate attorney filed a demand for the return of the diamond. Myers said it would take time, but it would be a difficult case. At GAL offices in the US, I was busy as ever working on three leases. I wanted badly to score them. New 747s. Big planes. Big money.

Adolph Myers called me.

"I wish I could take credit for what happened." He sounded happy. I could hear the smile in his voice.

"What happened?"

"The lawyers filed a dismissal. He was so nice I couldn't believe it was him. He's sending over the title on the diamond ring."

"Adolph, that's fucking fantastic!"

"I'm not an estate attorney, but you may have to pay a tax here in the UK. I'll let you know."

That night I talked to Olga. At first, she pretended not to know.

After I told her, she admitted, "Amor, Adolph called me with the good news. Congratulations. I guess I can keep my ring."

"I want to see you," I said. "When are you coming home?"

"Amor, probably three weeks. I dare you to fly over to Milan. I'll be there for two days. Flying there tomorrow."

"Make it three days, and I'll leave in three hours."

"Si, Amorcito, three days. Hurry."

I dialed Andrea on intercom and asked her to come in my office.

She came in with a notepad and pen, like some secretary in a fifties movie. I could see aviation notes on that pad. The hot pink pantsuit she was wearing would not have been around in the fifties. She'd been working on picking up some planes from a small commuter airline that was downsizing. Her big glasses had slid low on her nose, and she looked at me over them.

"Baby, I know you're buried in work, but I need a favor."

"Anything."

"I want to leave for Milan in the next three hours or so. I need the plane ready with a crew and one flight attendant. I'm going alone, so don't go crazy on any special catering for me. I'll eat what the crew eats."

"Is that all you need?"

"I love you, Andrea."

She grinned that grin that coaxed a dimple in her chin and headed for her desk.

I winked, picked up the phone, and dialed Letty on cell.

Milan January 30, 1990

Olga's pilots had dropped off Riana in Spain.

We were at the villa. She worked her schedule out so the two of us could have five nights together.

"I'm so relieved the diamond case is over," I said, raising her hand up. I kissed the stone on her finger. Her bedroom at the villa was as large as a house, but with the blackout drapery hanging around the bed, we were in a cozy little spot. A couple of gold sconces were in the space with us, so we weren't sitting in the dark.

"Me too, Amor." She kissed the stone, too.

"It's been long time since I saw Camila," I said. "How about you?"

"I talk to her regularly. I have to. I haven't seen her in months."

"Why not?"

Her eyes met mine. She looked away. "We had an argument."

I pulled her on to my lap, pushing a pillow aside.

"All these years, I don't think I ever heard you guys in an argument. I mean, not that you agree about everything, but not a real argument."

Olga shrugged. "This was different. Amor. I can't tell you about it. Please don't ask."

"No problem. Not another word about it."

"Thank you, Amorcito."

She was silent for a few seconds.

"But you talk every day," I said.

"She knows the leasing company is thriving. She mentions it. Andrea keeps her updated."

"Good to know," I said. I felt a little uneasy about Andrea talking to Camila about the leasing company I was running. Camila was the owner. It had to be okay, but it felt like Andrea should be following the chain of command. Most of the time, she acted as my assistant. Maybe I should clarify that role with her so that I didn't feel like Andrea was looking over my shoulder with Camila's eyes.

"Amor, I have Adolph Myers checking on some of the assets that are going to be sold out of Sami's estate. Remember, once Jason turned down my offer to buy the penthouse."

"Yes, I remember," I said. "Once I turned down Sami's offer to give it to me." Right now, I could not remember why I'd turned her down. Maybe because she'd been dying at the time, and I could not imagine that place belonging to anyone but Sami.

"The widow wants to sell as much as possible to recover cash. Jason hit the estate hard. One of the assets for sale is the penthouse."

"I wonder for how much? The penthouse, I mean."

"Don't know the minimum yet. It will be an auction. Adolph is not sure yet. There's a catch though. It's not just the penthouse for sale. It's the entire building, except for two apartments that are owned by Sami's chef Crispin and housekeeper Ginger."

"I never knew the people living below the penthouse were tenants. I thought they all owned the apartments."

"So, did I," Olga said.

"Let's try and get it," I said. "The property is stupendous. I'm not that familiar with real property values in London, but I did some fishing around years ago. It's expensive, but I'd love to see LAI own that building. Maybe you and I can buy the penthouse. Remodel it completely so it's a part of us, and not a memory of my dear friend. I'd like to have a piece of London we can call our own."

Olga's eyes brightened. She flung her arms around my neck. I drank in the hug and the sweet scent of her perfume.

"Amor, I adore you. Si, work on it. Get in touch with Adolph. We can buy it together, without LAI if you want."

"I forget you are loaded."

"Amor, you are loaded, too."

I thought of the penthouse. I pictured all the rooms as they had been before she got sick. The balconies overlooking Hyde Park. It was all Sami. Laughing, smiling, cussing, filling my headspace with her life, her joy.

"Are you thinking of her?"

"I was, yes. She was a bundle of joy. She wanted me to quit Los Angeles and come live with her. She wanted to support me. She said we could travel the world together. She'd buy a plane. It was never about getting married."

"She loved you very much."

"We loved each other. I'm not sure what you'd call what we had for each other. The love I had for her is different from what I feel for you."

Olga was still on my lap, her arms still around my neck, and we were still reclining on her bed. The talking stopped. I turned down the dimmer on the sconces so that the lighting was more romantic. We got to business, under and over the covers of her king-sized bed. The bedroom I used when she wasn't there was also huge but not like hers. Camila's room was as big as Olga's, but Pepe's bedroom was even larger. His door bore a sign: "DO NOT ENTER.

Milan Feb 4, 1990

On our last day in Milan, we boarded a small helicopter that was on the grounds of the villa. Olga had us in the air within five minutes after boarding. I was less anxious with her in the captain's seat this time around. The long ride in Bogota had given me more confidence in her flying skills.

"I can't believe you didn't tell me you could fly," I said.

"It was no secret. You would have learned it as a kid if you grew up as I did, where roads are often impassible," she said. "Big estates always had helicopters to fly over the mountains."

"I should learn how to pilot something like this," I said.

"You said that before. Amor, I can help you. Here, let me show you."

"Not this time, baby. Keep your eyes on the road."

We flew around the city that I had gotten to know so well. It was different seeing Milan from a low flying helicopter. After thirty minutes, we landed on the helipad above our Milan leasing offices. Jules and the staff were expecting us. We still had far too much office for the number of employees, but we were growing.

Lunch was catered in the conference room. We ate and chatted with Jules. I spent a little time with every person employed there but didn't transact any real business. When we were done, Olga and I got in the helicopter and zoomed away.

The sensation of coming off a building in a helicopter is one for the books. Lifting straight up without the forward-moving plane take-off that I'm so accustomed to—I'd have to get used to it. And with all the glass, there's visibility all around. Very different. I thought about what Olga had said about flying around big estates. I feel certain I could master piloting a helicopter if I had a place to fly one. It would never happen in Los Angeles.

We circled the helipad at the villa. Olga expertly landed our flying bubble. There's a step down out of the helicopter. I had just unbuckled. Two men appeared with guns just as the blade came to a full stop. At first, I thought they were her guards, then I realized that the guards who were at ready when we got in the helicopter were nowhere in sight. These men were not her guards. They were Latin, but not her men. They pointed their guns at Olga and started shooting.

I shoved Olga down, out of the line of fire. She landed hard on the grassy area around the cement deck where the helicopter landed.

"You fools!" Olga yelled at the two men in Spanish. "You are dead meat."

"Killer!" one of them screamed.

"They're crazy," I said to her. "Get down and stay down."

Both of them were running in our direction. One of them was yelling, "You are killers of innocent children and families. Putas, both of you. You belong in hell!"

Three of Olga's guards appear behind the intruders, too far away to do any good.I lunged at the men, managed to kick them both. The first one was a good square hit. It all happened in a few seconds. He went down, his gun in my hand. I threw the gun on the lawn and kicked the second man twice before he could raise his gun. One of them moved. He was lying on the cement helipad deck. He tried to get to his feet. I kicked his face. I was sure I killed him. The other bastard was not moving. He was dead when he hit the ground.

I ran toward Olga and skidded to her across grass that was as slippery as glass. Olga was on her side on the lawn. Three of her guards reached her with guns drawn, for all the good that did.

"Miss Olga, you were supposed to call us on cell before you landed," one man said in the chaos.

Olga was pissed. "Didn't you hear the helicopter? Fools. All of you are stupid fools!"

I picked Olga up and cradled her in my arms like a baby.

"I'm sorry, baby, I know I threw you hard. Tell me what hurts."

Her arms were around my neck as I ran with her to the house.

"My pussy hurts, Amor. Take me to bed. Tear my clothes off, check every inch of my body for bruises."

Inside the doors, I stopped running. She kissed me on the lips.

"You got balls of steel, baby," I said. "You were almost killed."

Olga hit my chest. "I have no balls. You have balls like a Toro."

She started laughing.

"Are they calling the police?"

Marty Lombardi of the regular villa security detail had followed us in. He was the one who had driven Letty and Tangles around. I'd never seen him out of uniform before, but he was in a leather jacket and jeans.

"I was off duty," he said, a worried crease across his forehead. "I came as soon as I heard. I don't know what is up with your men. We would never—"

Olga interrupted. "I know. My new guards are history. As for the mess, clean it up."

He nodded crisply and left.

She shrugged. "We are the police on this property. Take me to bed while they clean the mess up."

I've never felt violence was an aphrodisiac but this feeling, this was an aphrodisiac. I feel very alive now, very aware that Olga could have been shot and killed and taken away from me.

I did as she suggested. I checked her body. She was bruised, her knees, the side of her chest. Her face was untouched. The examination turned into fast and furious sex, then slow with more examination of her bruises. We were been in bed for about an hour and ended sitting up against pillows. It was late afternoon, the windows all open, the drapes around her bed strapped to the posters, and we were swimming in daylight. Her cell phone rang. She looked at me before she reached for the phone.

"Someone must have told you they shot at us. They screamed that you and I kill children and innocent families, called us putas. That was before my Amor killed them. It was like a movie."

I couldn't hear what Camila was saying, but whatever it was, Olga listened for a long time.

"I'm not mad anymore," Olga said. "If I had died out there it would have been terrible to leave this earth without making peace with you."

Tears filled Olga's eyes as she listened to whatever it was that Camila said, then she replied, "I love you, too, Amor. You know I do."

While she was talking, I started to think about the two guys I had just killed. I don't reflect often on the lives I have taken, and I guess Olga doesn't either. She shot and killed eight traitors. She hadn't brought it up since she told me about it. Now, she was talking away like nothing had happened a little while ago. I wondered what was going on outside these doors. Would the police come knocking at the door? If not, what would Olga's men do with the bodies? Those bodies were men, human beings with families somewhere. The intruders couldn't have been more than thirty years old. How did they get on the compound? And what was that they had yelled about innocent families and children? I might not have remembered it, but she quoted it to Camila. I wondered how Olga could move on so fast.

The next morning, Olga got a very early call. We were still in bed. As she reached for the phone, I was thinking how comfortably we had slept, and told her so.

She spoke in Spanish. "*Quiero despedir a los seis idiotas, por poco me matan esos hijos de la chingada. Fue culpa de los guardias.*"[27]

She hung up and snuggled.

I sat up and looked at the clock.

"Amor, you can go ahead and split. I have to wait for replacements again."

"We should have fired them last night," I said.

"Amor, leave it to mama. After you went to sleep, Marty and I spoke to the chief guard of the grounds. My trusted crew here dealt with the clean-up. As for my new security guards, Estevan will handle it."

"Estevan? Do I know him?"

"I don't think so. He's been with the family for many years, since my

---

[27]   I want to dismiss the six idiots. I was so close to being killed by those sons of bitches. It was the fault of the guards.

father's days. He's from Colombia. He will fly in and take them with him."

"I can wait until you head out. When do you think that will be?"

Olga hugged me.

"Amor, at least three days. Stay, si?"

"Si," I said.

"The six suspects are in the basement under lock and key."

"You have a jail down there?"

"Three cells. When Pepe got the house, they were already there. The seller didn't know why they were there. Must be as old as the house. Huge bars."

"You don't even know if they are part of any conspiracy. They might just be bad at their job."

"I'm taking no chances. Estevan recruits, and he recommended them. In the old days, he would have been killed for the failure of his men."

I kissed her. "Good thing it is not the old days."

"Estevan isn't going anywhere. He's like family to us," she said. "He can handle hiring and firing."

Milan Feb 8, 1990

My trip to Milan wasn't over yet. Four days later I was still there. We were on our way to the airport in a four door Lincoln limousine, a house driver behind the wheel, one of her newly hired guards in the passenger seat. Behind us, a GMC black SUV with a house driver behind the wheel and five newly hired guards.

"I'm flying to Spain for Riana," Olga said. "Then it looks like I'm going to Mexico City."

Our planes were next to each other at the airport but far away from the main terminals. The cars drove up between the planes. I was going to ask her if her plane was clean, as in cocaine-free or free of whatever other contraband she may be involved in that I didn't know about. I figured I better not. Questions about contraband would only piss her off. Instead, I held her and kissed her. A long, very wet kiss.

At the top of my plane stairs stood Isla, my stewardess. At the top of Olga's plane stairs were two women I had never seen. Hot stuff. I walked up my stairs alone, then turned to watch her.

Three guards walked ahead of Olga and three behind her. I believe her when she insists she never fucks with her security except that one time when it meant life and death. These new guards were good-looking guys, well-dressed, well-mannered, buff. They looked like cops.

Seven hours later, my plane landed in Washington, DC, to refuel and for US customs, a routine stop that seldom took more than an hour. Three officers came aboard. I handed my passport and my landing card to the young officer. The crew was in the front cabin with the two other agents.

"You indicate you're flying from Milan," he said.

"That's correct."

"Purpose of your trip?"

"Holiday."

"Anything to declare?"

"I brought nothing," I said. "I wrote in the landing card approximately two hundred dollars for anything miscellaneous I may have not listed such as bathing trunks and sandals."

"I'd like to have a look around the interior and a team is checking the cargo bins."

"Be my guest," I said. "Walk around freely."

I remained seated next to a window, a table in front of me bearing a cup of coffee and today's issue of the Washington Post that Isla had brought me.

The other agents that took care of the crew came through the main cabin, nodded hello to me and met up with the agent who still had my passport and landing card.

Looking out the window, I could see that we were refueling.

Isla appeared.

"New uniform?" I asked. Flight crews were usually in uniform, but I noticed that today Isla was not.

"Versace," she said. "It's from the new spring line. I lucked out in Milan. I hope it is alright. If not, I can change."

"No," I grabbed her wrist to keep her from dashing off to change. "It's lovely on you."

She beamed. It really was lovely on her—a layered dress of some kind. It was sleeveless. A black sash with gold stripes running down the front and six nautical-style gold buttons belted over a strapless black tube. The wide black and gold belt looked like something I might have seen Melina in once or twice. The outfit showed off a pair of wide shoulders with dramatic hollows, and her gold-toned skin.

"Something to drink?"

"I'll wait until we're done with customs."

"The crew is clear, Mr. Luna," she said.

"Good," I replied, wondering what was going on with the walk-through.

The three agents returned. The agent who had my passport found a page to stamp, then handed it to me.

"Welcome home, Mr. Luna."

As we started to taxi, I walked through the plane to where the agents had been and saw nothing out of place. The bedroom was intact. The bed and covers were fresh as housekeeping had no doubt left them.

"I'll have that wine," I said. "Let me see what we have."

I walked in the pantry, looked in the wine cooler, then shut the wine cooler door. There was plenty of wine there, but I wasn't feeling it.

"No wine. I'll have a coke, cold, no ice. Better still, in the bottle."

"Right away, Mr. Luna."

Before I walked out of the pantry, I tapped the tip of Isla's nose.

"How many times have I told you that I am Mario, not Mr. Luna?"

"Many times, Mr. Luna."

I turned around. "Do we have popcorn by any chance?"

Isla smiled. "I'm sorry, Mr. Luna, we don't. We have peanut butter."

It was my turn to smile. Letty made sure the plane always had peanut butter, just as she always packed a jar or two in my luggage.

"When we're airborne, I'll have toast, peanut butter and jelly. Forget the coke, make it coffee, black."

"Yes, Mr. Luna."

I returned to my seat. Here I was again in this huge plane, alone with the crew. I fastened my seat belt, closed my eyes, and a few minutes later, we were wheels up.

I woke up to the scent of toast. Isla had placed a tray on the table in front of my seat. A basket of breads included my toast and at least three other kinds of rolls and biscuits. A carousel of jams. A silver cup with two huge scoops of peanut butter.

I pointed at the seat across from me and looked up at her.

"Join me. You'll love this chunky peanut butter."

She had a beautiful smile. Her brown eyes were penetratingly beautiful. In at least six or seven trips together, I had never made a move on her, and neither had she on me. We were not always alone; sometimes we were with the girls.

"Thank you, Mr. Mario." She took the seat I'd pointed out.

"Wait. You can't sit until you promise to stop calling me Mister."

She froze halfway between standing and sitting.

"I promise, Mario."

I nodded, and she settled into the cushions.

"That's more like it, Isla. Did I ever ask you why your parents named you Island? Such a beautiful name."

"You never asked. I don't know why they named me Isla."

Within thirty minutes we were friends. Not sure why we laughed so much. Our conversation was chit-chat while we munched away. She got up three times: once to get a place setting for herself, once to bring more warm breads, and once to get us more coffee.

I suggested that we watch a movie.

"Anywhere you want," I said. "Either in the main cabin here, or in the bedroom cabin."

"Wherever you want," she said. "Please excuse me while check on the pilots. They probably want something."

"They should get up and serve themselves," I kidded.

She smiled. "Should I tell them that?"

Maybe it's what she was wearing that made her look so special that day. She was all creamy gold.

"No, go ahead." I knew she was just doing her job. "I'll check on the movies we have."

I knew what movies I had, but sometimes someone brought in new stuff.

About an hour and a half out of Washington, the movie *Cannibal Women in the Avocado Jungle of Death* was on in the bedroom, unwatchable except for the moments when Adrienne Barbeau was on the screen. I was naked on top of the covers, and Isla was naked on top of me. I cupped one of her breasts and when I touched her, a smile appeared.

"Why today and not before?" she asked softly, her lips near mine.

Los Angeles was home to my pilots. Acapulco, Mexico was home to Isla. Like many flight attendants, she got her gigs from an agency. We had our own pilots, but not flight attendants. Andrea had a short list of flight attendants.

Before we were on approach to the airport, I was in the main cabin with Isla sitting across from me.

"So now what? You wait for another gig?"

"Yes, I'll have one almost right away. The agency keeps me busy."

"When do you go home?"

There was that smile of hers. Smiles do things to me.

"I go home when I get a gig headed to Acapulco."

"So, you live out of a suitcase?"

She raised her right hand, showing me three fingers. I guess that means three suitcases.

Raul picked me up at the airport. Letty and Tangles were on a plane crash in Guadalajara, Mexico. I would have taken Isla home even if Letty and Tangles had not been away. Neither of us had had enough of each other, or she wouldn't have accepted my offer to hang out at Casa Luna until her next gig.

When we walked in, she was struck by my place. I don't know what it was—the bright chandeliers all lit up, the grandness of the entry level, or the sheer size.

"Mario, this is a palace," she said in Portuguese, then in Spanish.

"How many languages do you speak?"

"A bunch of small stuff that I picked up. English and Spanish are my foundation."

"It's not a palace," I said. "It's actually very homey. Isla, Caro will take you to your room. I'll meet you back here after you settle in, and we'll get something to eat besides peanut butter and jelly."

"Thank you," she said, following Caro to the elevator.

In no time at all, I showered and went down to the kitchen wearing sweats. Miguel was cooking a little bit of everything, munchies to start with, fried prawns so big that two could be dinner for a light eater.

I told Letty on the phone, "She reminds me of Tangles when she had long hair. Adorable."

"I'm jealous already. Don't tell me." Letty was bubbly like she always was on a crash case. Not that she has the wrong attitude with mourning families.

She does get lit from inside when she's working.

I heard Letty call Tangles. There was lots of background noise. They were in a hotel lobby with the families of victims.

"Boss has a broad over that reminds him of you. Isla, the stewardess. Remember her?"

Next, I heard Tangles talking. "Boss, I miss you. Tell me about the broad. Is she wildly pretty like I am?"

"She's not a broad," I said.

"Oh Boss, we're all broads. I remember her on a flight we had to San Francisco."

I heard Letty giggling in the background.

"Boss, she's not adorable as me, so it must be something else you went for."

Isla and I ate at the kitchen counter. She had sort of changed clothes. She still had on the black tube top that had been under the sash, but the rest of the Versace was gone. She also wore a pair of white shorts. She was wearing a pair of the slipper socks Letty keeps in baskets in the bathrooms for guests to wear. Some of them say "Casa Luna." Some of them say "Feet by Letty."

We stuck it out with the prawns, a salad and two chocolate milk shakes.

"I am speechless about your house," she said, eating with gusto.

"I'll give you a tour of the rest."

"I've always known you were special and rich. I mean, look at the planes you fly in. The agency loves you. But never in a million years, never in my life have I been in a home like this. My room is out of this world." She stuck out her foot and pointed her toe. "Thanks for the socks. I found them in the bathroom."

"That's why Letty puts them there," I said. "Wait till I show you the disco and the arcade. Maybe we can get a massage in the spa. Or a steam or a sauna?"

"Count me in," she said with the same gusto I was feeling.

"Wait till you see my bedroom." I said.

"I can hardly wait." She stopped eating and stared at me.

"Most men would be done for after what we did on the plane," Isla said, her eyes still on mine, a forked piece of shrimp in her right hand.

"You're too hot," I said. "My heart races just looking at you."

Isla's mouth opened for the piece of shrimp the fork delivered. It left a dab of sauce on the corner of her lip. I leaned over and licked it off.

"You said you're not married. This place is way too big for one person. Who lives here with you?"

I told her about Letty, Tangles. My team. I told her about Olga.

"I remember Letty and Tangles. Those beautiful chicks who fly with you. They live here?"

"You are engaged, and we did all those things on the plane?"

Her facial expressions were hilarious. I think she was trying to be funny, but I wasn't sure.

"I don't think you care that much."

"Doesn't your fiancée mind that Letty and Tangles live here with you?"

"She doesn't mind," I said. "And she doesn't care about what goes on in the plane. We have an open relationship."

"You got it made."

"Are you making fun of me?"

She shook her head slowly. "Not making fun. I won't take the chance of offending you—not till after I get the grand tour of this place. Can we start with your bedroom?"

Pasadena Feb 9 1990

The next morning, Isla checked into the agency by phone and got a gig leaving LAX at two in the afternoon. She was going to Miami.

"You got to be kidding," I said.

"I shouldn't have called."

"I wish you could stay."

"Invite me again. It will be a big sacrifice, but I'll manage." She laughed at her own joke.

"I'll make sure we keep requesting you with the agency," I said.

"Mario, I love your gigs."

"You got em. I promise."

"Thank you for your enormous hospitality," she said in Spanish. "You made me feel like a queen. I will think of this every time I close my eyes."

Pasadena Feb 16 1990

The girls returned from their trip filled with happiness and success.

Tangles beamed. "We got eleven!"

Letty's smile mirrored Tangles mood.

"We did good, Boss."

"Where is the Acapulco girl?" Tangles asked, pretending to look for her in a closet.

Letty looked under my bed. "She's not here," Letty said. She pretended to check the balcony and my dresser drawers.

"You missed a drawer," I told Letty.

Letty turned to the top drawer and checked it.

"Nope, she's not in there either," she told Tangles, laughing.

I had really missed the girls. They do liven up my life. "She stayed one night. Split a week ago."

"You feel like taking on two sex-starved chicks?" Letty asked.

"Boss, say yes, please. I've gone through two sets of vibrator batteries," Tangles said.

"She's lying, Boss," Letty said. "It was four sets."

About twice a month, I talked to Mason. He was always on cell.

"It's me again. Anything interesting?" I asked.

"Not yet. I am putting the pieces of the puzzle together."

"Mason, is that good or bad? You keep telling me about the puzzle. Give me a peek at this puzzle."

"It's good," he said vaguely, ignoring my request for a peek.

"Great."

It wasn't great. I hung up, feeling like a pussy. I still knew nothing. However much Olga was paying him, it was more than he was worth. I had a feeling it was plenty, and plenty means why rush it? The leasing company was very busy. Both offices running at full throttle meant I was very busy, with little time to think about who was after me.

My office hours flew by. Sometimes I skipped lunch, then couldn't remember if I'd eaten or not. I changed my workouts to every other day. I started leaving the house at six thirty in order to arrive at the office before anyone else. When Andrea caught on, she started coming in early, too. I used to go home before three PM to avoid traffic, but now, I didn't leave until I figured I'd finished whatever I'd been working on. Sometimes this took me until late afternoon, and sometimes it was well after dark. I loved what I was doing.

"Boss, I seldom see you anymore," Letty said, exaggerating. "Want me to do office hours with you until the next plane crash?"

We ate dinner together every night. We slept in the same bed.

Tangles still lived in her own apartment. She was at her home most nights, but she stayed with Letty until I got home. If I got there very late, the three of us would eat dinner together, drink, smoke pot and sleep together. I had a few lazy mornings, too, especially if I had two wild pussies in bed with me who wouldn't let me get out of bed. I loved my life. I wondered how long I'd be this lucky.

Nothing is forever.

My phone conversations with Olga lasted until my cell phone battery went dead. I always made time for her. I loved talking to her, thinking of her, listening to her voice, running movies of her in my head. Still, I wasn't ready to get married. I knew she felt the same way.

One night I had a horrible nightmare, the kind that makes you twist and turn. Letty said I was talking in my sleep until she woke me. I was sweating, drenched.

"Boss, I think you're coming down with something. You must have a fever," Letty said.

"I'm going to shower. Let's move to your room, baby. The sheets are wet."

She waited as I showered and put on clean sleep shorts, then we tromped down the stairs to her bed. The sheets were fresh, the room fragrant and welcoming with Letty's light perfume, the street lights blocked by blackout curtains, the mattress perfect. I should have been able to shut my eyes and drift off, but it would not happen.

Letty asked what I had been dreaming.

"I can't remember," I lied.

In my dream, I was hovering over the scenes as Olga landed in Miami. She wasn't greeted as usual. It was not an easy in and out. I was in the cargo hold watching as agents from customs and drug enforcement pulled countless bundles of cocaine from the walls of the fuselage. Olga was handcuffed and taken away to jail.

"I was framed! I know nothing about the drugs!"

She was screaming, but no one was paying attention. As they took her away, I noticed her stomach. Olga was pregnant!

I felt panic and prayed.

God, no, this can't be happening. Please, don't let them take her, she has my baby with her, God, are you listening?

When Olga returned to Pasadena, I told her about the dream. I didn't tell her right away. I held back until it was late, and the specter of sleep approaching. The dream and the fear that had been born in that dream had been haunting me. I couldn't believe that I was here, safe between clean sheets on my comfortable bed with Olga in my arms, and all I could see was some frightening future out of my worst imagination.

"I didn't want to tell you on the phone. We should be careful with the phones."

Olga laughed. "Amor, all we talk about is sex. Is that a felony?"

"I worry about you. I was devastated in the dream."

"Amorcito, it was a dream. I'm here. You just fucked me. Come closer."

I pulled her till we were skin to skin, spooned her and spoke in her ear.

"Olga, please be careful."

"Amor," she whispered. "I will never fly in USA airspace or land in this country with anything that could result in a criminal filing against me. You know this. Stop worrying."

I lightly bit her neck.

"I love you, Olga."

"I know you do, Amor. I adore you. You are the most important part of my life."

I was at the office. For once, Mason called me.

"You must have something?" First words out of my mouth.

"I believe so. I got a call from Detective Jenkins at Pasadena P.D. They arrested the guy who shot up your Rolls when you exited the freeway."

"How did they get him?"

"I helped them. They had two prints they lifted from the stolen pickup and were dragging their heels. I got Jenkins to speed up the process. When they got a hit, he called me, and let me in on who it was. He matched the profile of a car thief they had on record. The pickup truck had been used to rob liquor stores. And he robbed three people."

"You got my attention, Mason. Go on."

"I looked at his record and watched the interrogation at the station through a window. He's doing a lineup later this afternoon. One of his hold-ups was on the same night he shot at you. Two happened the night before. My guess is that they will identify him."

"Why did he shoot at me?"

"His records say he burned a neighbor's brand new car. He pled guilty in exchange for a year in the county jail. He told the judge he was jealous. So that's probably why. Jealousy."

"I have to digest this. Are you sure?"

"As sure as I can be. He looks like he's the one. As far as the court is concerned, he's innocent until proven guilty."

"You're saying this guy shot up my car on his own, not because someone hired him?"

"Exactly," Mason replied.

I guess I'm just a paranoid fool, thinking someone is out to get me. I wasn't expecting this to be a matter of being in the wrong place at the wrong time.

"I never got a good look at him. He wasn't that far when he passed me, but it was pretty dark, and I wasn't paying attention. And when he jumped out of the truck after he got slammed at the intersection, he was across a lot of pavement, not very close."

"Jenkins would like you to come take a look when they run him through the lineup. Just in case. Even if you don't recognize his face, you may see something. Maybe his body type."

"Where is this?"

"The Pasadena jail."

I wrote down the time and address. I had a stack of possible leases I was reviewing. It pained me to leave the office early. If Mason was correct, even if this guy is the one, it did nothing to narrow down who is responsible for all the other events that have happened to me. Still no suspects.

I was alone with Detective Jenkins and Mason behind the mirrored window when I viewed the six guys in the line-up. They didn't see me, and none of the other victims saw each other.

"His name is Larry Rogers. Age 34. Single. Charged with armed robbery," Jenkins said, showing me a photo later. He looked much older than thirty-four, white, mousey looking. He had skinny arms and legs, not much of a chin to speak of, and a beer gut. I'd seen him behind glass. It's hard to explain, but he looked like he smelled like beer.

"I have no idea if this is the guy who shot at me before he had a hit and run," I said. "I'd like to help, but I don't recognize anything about him."

On my drive home, Jenkins called me on my cell.

"The three liquor store victims positively identified Rogers as the man who held them up."

"He didn't wear a mask or anything?"

"No mask, and the liquor stores had no video, but his prints put him in the truck. He's going to do time for the robberies. Tomorrow is another lineup with six more alleged liquor store victims."

"He's been busy. I don't know if I should be happy or disappointed."

Jenkins chuckled. "Your investigator is one sharp son of a bitch."

"Yes, Mason is something else," I agreed. "Thanks for keeping me up to date, Detective."

"Without a gun, a liquor store owner would have run him out of the store with a broom. Skinny," I told Letty. We were in bed, the room flickering in the glimmer of countless burning candles. "Out of shape."

Letty sat up in the dark and put a cone of incense on the burner. I heard the scratch of a match, saw the flare of flame, smelled the stink of sulfur. I don't know what kind the incense was, but it smelled good, slightly exotic, slightly anachronistic. It reminded me of the sixties. She returned the burner to the end table, and lay on her back, looking up at the ceiling. The candles gave me a good view of her profile.

"I hope Mason is right that no one sent him after you. At least we can write off that one attack just like we wrote off the death of Jake."

"Still leaves all that other stuff unsolved."

"Boss, Olga has Mason full time on all your matters. He'll get it done."

"Fuck, she tells you more than she tells me," I said.

She cuddled close.

"Thanks for being here," I said. I kissed her and fell into a deep sleep.

Pasadena March 2, 1990

On the way to the office, I thought of my childhood friend, Pélon, who was serving life for murder in San Quentin. He told me that I shouldn't visit him any more, but when I needed something taken care of, I should contact one of his soldiers who lived in ELA. I had not visited him since he'd checked on a suspect for shooting Melina. A couple of years ago, his man Easy had delivered a taped confession to me from the suspect that shot Melina and killed her driver, Johnson.

When I got to the office, I called the number I had for Easy. I gave it a fifty-fifty chance that he would still be around.

A male voice answered.

"Hey, remember you came to a big house in Pasadena once? This is the friend of your friend."

"Ese, what you need?"

"The man up north once told me if I needed something that I should contact you?"

"When you want to meet and where?" he asked.

Pasadena—March 4, 1990 (Sunday)

Two days later I met him at the Pantry. It was noon, very busy, packed with the church crowd, and that's how I wanted it. I didn't dress up that morning, just jeans, t-shirt and loafers. The line to get in was fifty feet along the building, a mass of anonymous hungry people of every size, type and color. Church people, ragged people, baseball-capped loners shoulder to shoulder with whole families with babies in strollers. Standing in line was the perfect meet. Easy walked up in khakis, t-shirt and black combat boots. He looked a little worse for wear, older than the young kid who had come to my house to deliver the package with the evidence about the asshole who shot Melina. We nodded our hellos and stood side by side in line.

Speaking carefully, quietly, I told him about the shooter in the county jail in downtown Los Angeles awaiting court for liquor store robberies.

"My investigator and the cops say he shot at me just because he was jealous of my car. The cops don't care about my case. They have him on big stuff, robberies, break-ins, who knows what other shit. He's a busy guy. I need to know if he was hired to shoot at me or if it was really random."

"What's his name?"

"Larry Rogers." I gave the basic description.

"We got people in the county jail. I'll get him found. Is that all you want to know, or do you want something to happen to him?"

"For now, I just need to know if he was hired, and by who. I'm not gunning for his life, just looking if he's got a boss."

I slipped him an envelope with a thousand dollars [28]and a card with nothing on it but my cell phone number.

"Toss the number after you memorize it."

"I call you, but we don't talk details on the phone."

"That's for sure," I said. "No pressure. Next time I see you, there's more of that green for you."

"Alright, Ese. I'm out of here."

He stepped out of line and split. Five minutes later, I looked at my watch like I was pissed off at the line and went to my car, parked across the street. Inside, Letty and Tangles were waiting for me.

I got in.

"I'm hungry," Tangles said.

"Good idea. Let's go the Pacific Dining Car," I said.

"Ten minutes and we're there, Boss," Letty said, running an amber light on Figueroa and 9th Street, headed North. "We could have videoed the whole meet from where we were parked, but you said not to."

"You don't video people like Easy. He's on our side."

"He looks mean," Tangles said.

"I'd kick his ass in a split minute," Letty boasted.

"I said, he's on our side."

---

[28] $1,000.00 in 1990 is equal to $1,992.33 in 2019.

"She's kidding, Boss. She gets mean with the cramps," Tangles said.

"Bitch, open the window and tell everyone. Go ahead."

Tangles ignored her. "Boss, if you want, I don't have to home tonight. I'll fill in for a week, with pleasure." Tangles had a big smile on her face.

"Do you guys want to hear what he said? Or are we going to talk about Letty's cramps?"

Without taking her eyes off the road, Letty nailed me in the side with her elbow. It hurt, but I laughed aloud.

March was booming. In March, we leased six brand new planes to a growing Mexican operator that services direct routes between Los Angeles and Mexico City, and Los Angeles and Acapulco. The operator was certain they would be adding routes and would need more planes.

"There are no words to describe how proud I am of you," Camila told me on the phone. "Bravo, Amor, bravo."

"When I heard about you closing this deal, I had two orgasms," Olga said, calling from Madrid.

"I wish you were here with me," I said.

"Soon, Amor. I've been so busy."

"How is Riana holding out?"

"She's killer tough. I love her. I try to pay her, but she laughs at me."

"Her papa is a billionaire," I said. "What would she do with more money?"

We laughed.

"Riana digs being with me. I would be crazy from loneliness if I didn't have her traveling with me."

Riana was involved in everything, and although not a participant in the business, she knew or overheard everything. Olga trusted her. Did that mean Riana knew all the secrets? You'd think Riana would be afraid to fly around in a plane that at least sometimes was loaded with cocaine. For that fact, you'd think that Olga would have sense enough to be apprehensive. But then, Olga had shot her guards and the pilots, without batting an eye. She'd landed the plane with a little help from ATC—a cool customer under stressful situations. Two would-be killers ambushed us getting off the helicopter at the big house helipad, and fifteen minutes later we were in bed wrapped around each other making love. I don't know about Riana's grit, but as for Olga, she wasn't a martial arts expert like my team, but without any doubt, Olga is a tough cookie.

Pasadena March 28, 1990

Toward the end of March, Mason called me at the office.

"I don't know if this is good news or bad news for your ears."

"Spit it out."

"Larry Rogers is dead."

I wondered if Easy had him offed. I told him what I wanted, and it was not to off him. At least, not yet.

"What happened?"

"He was in a tank with dope addicts, all of them coming down from whatever high they were on. Some inmate took him out in a fight. I don't know the particulars. Detective Jenkins will fill me in when he gets the report from the sheriff."

Pasadena March 30, 1990

I didn't call Easy. Two days later, he called me.

"Rogers is dead. Just found out. We had nothing to do with it, Ese."

"I know," I said. "You should stop by the house like you did before."

"Nothing due," he said. "Later, Ese."

Was it all just coincidences? This vato gets in a fight and gets killed by another addict while in custody? Hard to believe. His death seemed awful convenient. I don't believe in convenient coincidence.

Letty shared my skepticism. "Do you believe this coincidence?"

"I believe Easy had nothing to do with it. I believe he was killed by another dude doing time for some stupid reason. The report from the jailers at County might hold some answers."

I wondered, though. He might have been killed to cover up whoever he was working for. He might have died as a result of a too-enthusiastic inquisition by one of Pepe's soldiers. Eventually I would learn the truth, but patience is fucking hard. I needed distraction.

"Fuck with the Boss, you end up dead," Tangles said, a bloodthirsty gleam in her eye.

"Don't say that," I said firmly.

"He could have killed you," Letty said. "Fuck him."

Fucking didn't seem like a bad idea.

I took a deep breath and walked out of my house, got in my car and drove away. It was seven and change in the evening. It was a little after eight when I drove up to the Whisky. I hate their wine, but wine isn't why I keep coming here. It's for strange pussy. I had phone numbers for two ladies I had picked up here. If I was going to get the distraction I was looking for, she had to be someone who wasn't a regular.

Strange turned out to be Lola. There were girls on the dance floor making eyes at me. I noticed two leggy girls sitting at a table, a brunette and a blonde. The brunette—Lola—saw me. She smiled in my direction and chased away her blonde friend. She patted the vacated chair for me.

It was still warm when I sat down. I could still smell the cloud of cheap perfume she'd left behind.

"Tiger, I'm buying. What's your poison?"

Poison was a good name for the vile wine I had in front of me. I raised my full glass of red swill and said, "I'm good. Thanks."

I extended my hand. "Mario."

She got up. Curvy body. Kittenish face. She kissed me on the lips. Bold for a stranger. She sat down after her kiss, a satisfied expression on her face like a cat with cream. I could picture her licking her paws and managed not to laugh aloud. The music stopped, and the sound of the randy crowd got a little louder.

"Lola's my name."

We smiled at each other. The music started again. A new dancer wiggled around on stage. It was like a scene in a movie I'd seen a hundred times before. The girls could have been different, or they could have been the same ones I'd seen here for years. I was busy looking at Lola.

I moved close. An intimate yell over the raucous noise.

"How much?"

Music was loud. Guys on the left and right of us were loudly enjoying the floor show.

"Two hundred, all night," she yelled back. "Hotel or your place."

I put my glass of swill on the table. We walked out to my car. The valet held the passenger door open as she slid in. She nodded her head at him like the Queen of England.

"Is this yours, or did you rent it?"

I didn't answer until the doors were closed. I put the car in drive.

"I didn't know they rented these," I said.

"I was joshing you. This is the first time I've been in one of these."

"You want to go to the Century Plaza Hotel or to my house in Pasadena?"

"No one ever takes me to the Century Plaza. Do I really have a choice?"

Lola said she was twenty-six. She was at least ten years older than that, or just looked it. Age never mattered to me. Melina is ten years my senior. My team had given me their twenties and were still gorgeous in their mid and late thirties. It was a short drive to the hotel. I don't know that much about lady fragrances other than the price tags on my team's favorites, but I knew what Lola had on was not cheap. Her attire wasn't cheap either. "Why only two hundred?"

Lola laughed. It sounded genuine, a great laugh. Made me want to laugh along with her even though I didn't know what she found so funny. I turned on to Sunset. The car was as dark as is possible when you are driving on Sunset Boulevard.

"I didn't want to take a chance you'd say no. You can pay me more."

"Lola, you are hot."

"So are you," she said. I could feel her staring at me as I drove.

I reached across the seat with my right hand. We held hands for a little while in silence.

"Is your name really Lola?"

"It's Lola Chavez. I'm really twenty-six."

"Want to know anything else?"

"I was just curious."

"Your problem."

"Are you hungry?" I asked.

"No, not hungry." We rode in silence for a while. I heard her stomach growl. She laughed. Embarrassed, I guess. "Starved," she confessed.

"We can go to the Playboy Club across from the hotel unless you want something somewhere else?"

Lola gripped my hand.

"I've never been to the Playboy Club. You must be a member?"

"I am. They have mean hamburgers, and their steaks aren't bad."

My phone rang.

"Boss, are you okay?"

"I'm fine. Are you okay?"

"Boss, you sound a little sassy. You left in a rush. I'm sorry if we did anything. So is Tangles."

"Don't worry about it. I love you both."

"What do you want for dinner? Miguel was asking me."

"You have what you want. I'm going to have something at the Playboy, and I won't be coming home tonight."

"Okay, Boss. Call me if you need me to drive you, or for anything."

I could feel Lola's eyes on me as I hung up.

"Sounds like you have a wife."

"Her name is Letty. She's not my wife."

"I didn't mean to snoop."

The Playboy gets noisy, but nothing like the joint we had just come from. There is no dance pole. The playboy bunnies are gorgeous. There is music, dancing, but you don't have to scream to make yourself heard.

I ordered a double cheeseburger with bacon and steak fries. Lola ordered a club sandwich. I ordered the good Merlot and two glasses.

"You work out?" I asked.

"No. Every couple days I run, but I don't work out. Why?"

"You look very fit," I said.

"You got me for the night. You don't have to be on your good manners." Her look was a tease. "I can tell you work out." She reached for my right arm and tested my bicep. "Solid."

By the time we finished the bottle and the dishes had been cleared, I already liked Lola. I wanted her, but I wasn't in a hurry. I was enjoying being with this soon-to-be friend. I asked more questions than she did. Small talk. More importantly, not once did I think about Rogers being killed in jail or wondering if Mason would ever figure out who was causing me so much grief.

When we walked across the street to the hotel where I had left my car with the valet, we got some bad news from the front desk clerk.

"I only have three rooms left, and they are standard size rooms."

I got a hundred out of my pocket, folded the bill and shoved it across the counter. The clerk very politely pushed my hand away.

"I'd love to have that bill, but I don't have any suites or anything larger than a standard. I'm terribly sorry."

I took out a twenty and put it on the counter and read his name tag.

"Thank you, John."

I walked toward the entrance of the hotel. Lola followed my lead.

"What's wrong with a standard room?" she asked.

"You deserve better, and I won't fit on the bed."

It was just past one in the morning.

"Okay, you've been to the Century Plaza. Now let's go to my house," I said.

"But what about the lady you talked to?"

"Letty will be asleep in her room."

I picked up my cell and speed-dialed her.

"Baby, change in plans. I'm on my way home with Lola."

"Oh, how nice Boss. Cute name. I'll light some candles in the bedroom for you."

Lola's jaw dropped when the gates to Casa Luna opened, and I drove in. I waved at the guard and continued to the front of the house.

"Why's a guy that lives here slumming it at a dive like Whisky-A-Go-Go?"

We took the elevator to the fourth floor and walked in the master bedroom. Letty had a dozen candles going. My favorite incense permeated the air.

"I don't know what to say," Lola said, her eyes wandering. Her hand covered her mouth when she noticed the mirror over the bed.

I pointed to a door.

"That's the lady's room. This one is the men's room. I think I'll take a quick shower."

"May I do the same?"

"Make yourself at home."

Just as I walked in the bathroom, the intercom rang.

"Boss, let me put Lola in a bathtub with a little Clorox, and if she screams you know her pussy is having problems."

"Letty," I said into the intercom. "Where did you get that from? No."

"I left some condoms in your bedside table drawer. I hear that may be protection against AIDS."

"Letty, I love you. Thank you for fixing up the room and your suggestions. Good night." I hung up. The last that I'd read, they hadn't figured it out yet, but AIDS was a disease of gay men. I wasn't as worried about it as Letty. Whatever Lola was, she wasn't a gay man.

Pasadena March 31, 1990

Just before noon I realized I'd missed going to the office. I wasn't feeling guilty or stressed. Besides, it was Saturday. The room was dark though two or three candles were taking their last flicker before dying. I wasn't alone. I moved close, turned Lola around, my hands on her breasts. Lola moaned, and pushed her ass against me. I got hard. I entered her and we had a moment, then we went back to sleep.

Pasadena March 31, 1990
Letty

I got nothing against sex for money. It's the haunting fear about who has AIDS and who doesn't. If you have a lot of sex partners, you are as vulnerable to catching it as if you share needles. Doctors don't understand it, so who fuck knows? Once all of us had a blood test to check if we had it and the results said we did not, but that was then, and this is now. Mario is way too smart to put himself, maybe all of us, at risk. It's not a good decade to go out to bars and engage the Lolas of the world.

I saw her this morning. She is pretty. I bet she could do something else to make a living. They were in bed almost eighteen-hours. He didn't go to the office. He had a late lunch in bed. Right in front of me, he asked her to stay another night. She said, "I need to pay my rent. Manager already locked me out before I met you last night. I don't want him throwing out my stuff."

Boss handed her a bunch of hundreds, probably five hundred. I doubt that's her price tag on even the best night, no matter how pretty she is. Some people work all week for one fifty. Boss left it up to me to take her home.

I had to map out where she lives on the Thomas Guide because Lola had no idea how to get home from Pasadena. At least that's what she said.

"What do you think about this AIDS epidemic?" I asked her. We had been quiet up until then.

"I hear it kills you," Lola replied.

"Aren't you worried?"

"I'm worried but I have to pay rent and eat. I don't need to take a bath in Clorox. I'm clean."

"You heard that." I said. I wasn't going to apologize. "Yeah, I tried to get Boss to let me put you in a bath with bleach. He didn't take me up on it."

"You must be a sicko." Lola looked at me. I turned my eyes from the road and made eye contact.

"I hear if you got something, just a little bleach in the water makes you scream."

"Disgusting," Lola said. "I'm a clean person. And bleach in the water would make anybody scream. That's fucking crazy."

"Not saying you aren't clean. Just worried. I don't want to catch your cooties next time I'm in bed with him."

"Telling the wrong one," Lola said. "He's the one who brought me in."

"Nothing personal, Lola."

I thought of my best friend, Pixie. Before I knew her, she'd been a street girl for years. I've kissed, licked and sucked every part of her body. Difference is, she isn't out screwing outside the team. Or is she? So stupid to think she's on tour for months at a time and not doing anything. We're all fucked with this mystery AIDS shit.

"Why do you call him Boss?"

"He's my Boss," I said. She was still waiting for more. "Been doing it years."

"What do you do for him besides drive his dates home and fuck him?"

"Hey bitch, I don't like your tone." Maybe I get agitated easy.

"Piss off," Lola said, looking my way again. I felt her eyes on me. "You wanted to dip me in a tub filled with bleach, and *you* get pissed because I ask a question?"

I couldn't help it. I started laughing. I turned to look at her.

She laughed.

"All of a sudden, you're so nice. Why?" Lola asked.

I took my right hand off the steering wheel and extended it to her.

"My name's Letty. I'm Mario's assistant. I do a lot more than drive his dates and fuck him."

We shook hands.

"Lola is my real name."

Her apartment was off Hollywood Boulevard, a multi-level building surrounded by buildings just like it.

"Want me to come in with you and make sure he lets you back in?"

"When he sees the cash, he'll let me in. Thanks for the ride."

I handed her my card. "My cell number is on there. Call me if you have a problem."

Pasadena March 31, 1990
Mario

I had dinner with Letty and Tangles in the disco, a beautiful room we seldom use these days. There's a juke box like in the wine room. The neon signs and lights make for a party atmosphere, and we had good wine for cheer. Our dinner wasn't fancy. Hamburgers, hot dogs and French fries with five different dipping choices.

"She's a looker," Tangles said.

"She is and she's different somehow," I said.

I glanced at a notepad Letty handed me that had messages from missed calls. Mason's message from a few days before reminded me of the dead suspect at the county jail. For all those hours I was with Lola, I had not given that guy any thought at all.

"Lola speaks her mind," Letty said. "On the way home, I gave her a hard time. She held her own."

"What did you say?" Tangles asked.

"Doesn't matter. I like her bark."

"Something about her," I said again. "Somehow she attaches herself, but in a good way."

Letty and Tangles were exchanging making-fun-of-me looks.

Lola had no phone at home and no cell phone. I had given her my card and written my cell number on it. I wanted to see her again. If she didn't call me, to find her, I'd have to take a run to Whisky-A-Go-Go or to her apartment. I decided to wait. If she enjoyed my company as much as I did hers, she'd call.

Pasadena April 6, 1990

Work was going on as usual at the tail end of the week. I had some paperwork to finish up before I called it a weekend. I signed off on some documents and handed them over to my secretary.

"It's been a long one," Andrea said. "Leaving soon?"

Andrea and my secretary Ava were in my office, sitting across from me. Before I answered, my cell rang.

"Guess who?"

It was Lola.

"I've been thinking of you," I said. I didn't really know Lola, but I wished I could help her so she wouldn't have to be hooking for a living.

"Thanks to the money you gave me, I not only paid my rent, I got a cell phone. You're my first call."

"I want to see you," I said.

"Where and when?"

"My house," I said.

I heard a soft laugh. "Only if you promise that Letty is not going to bathe me in bleach."

"How did you know about that?"

"Letty told me. But to be honest, I heard her on the intercom when she suggested it."

"She was kidding."

Still laughing, Lola said, "She was not kidding. I hope she knows that bleach is not a cure."

"Tell her yourself."

Pasadena April 6, 1990
Lola

Five minutes after I talked to Mario, I called Susan.

"I've been invited to the house tonight. I think he likes me."

"Get him to like you a lot."

"We agreed this was not going to be rushed." I reminded her.

Silence. "Are you still there?"

"Yes," she said. "Check in regularly."

I went to my walk-in closet. I keep it organized. One side has things for the house. The other has all the getups I could never wear to work. I picked one a guy would like. My plan was to shower here, get dressed, and hustle over to the dive where Mario was sending a car.

Pasadena April 6, 1990
Mario

"I invited Lola to the house tonight," I told Letty on the phone.

"Anything you want me to handle?"

"If you and Tangles are up to it, have Miguel prepare dinner. We can eat together."

There were no wise ass remarks.

"Always up to whatever you want, Boss. I'll do a number in the bedroom for you for after we eat. I got a new shipment of snazzy candles. And I'll ask Tangles to stay the night. We'll be in my bedroom. Wouldn't think of spoiling your little shindig."

"You sound more and more like Pixie," I said.

"That's a compliment, Boss. Thank you."

I heard Tangles in the background. "Tell Boss we could have a royal blast if he wants to do a foursome."

"He likes Lola. For the moment, no sharing."

I hung up without a goodbye. All the way home, I pictured the four of us in bed. Not a bad picture, but I wasn't ready to share Lola yet, not even with the team. Years ago, Olga had made it clear how she felt about other women.

She wanted me to go clubbing and bring strange pussy home. To her, that was preferable to my getting serious about one person. Melina and I had been serious once.

Letty and Tangles took themselves off the payroll after I took over GAL. They started making money without me, generating new business for Goner's law firm on their own. Letty still managed everything that went on at Casa Luna. She no longer did the house shopping herself, but she still managed it. There was no paperwork to do for the house. Payroll was handled by a service. Miguel handled the kitchen and all the purchases needed to keep the pantries, refrigerators and freezers well-stocked. Cleaning supplies were delivered by a janitorial company. Arrowhead Water company delivered large bottles of drinking water for the main house and staff quarters. The girls operated out of the fourth-floor conference room, as always. That's where they made and received their calls, sent and received faxes about air crashes big and small. Small in the United States, and big, worldwide. I charged them nothing.

"We do our business at all hours of the day and night, eat your food, use your phones, your resources," Letty said. "We should be paying you rent."

My reply was always the same.

"In that case, I need to put you on the payroll for running the house and managing all the things you and Tangles handle for me. Problem is, there's not enough money in this world to pay you for everything you do for me."

"Aw Boss," Letty said, and gave me a hug.

Pasadena April 6, 1990
Tangles

I wanted to ask Lola how long she'd been in the street business, but I didn't dare make Boss go nutty on me. I watched him and watched her. Letty and I made eye contact often. Boss was at the head of the table, Lola on his right, Letty right next to her. I sat on his left.

Her black dress was cool, but not what I would wear if I was hooking.

It wasn't revealing enough. No doubt she wanted to sit with Mario and look conservative, and she did.

I ate small bites of the baked potato smothered with chives, butter and sour cream. I carved small pieces of the rib-eye steak and had seconds of fried mushrooms. I ate like I was paying attention to the food, but I was really watching Boss and bimbo. I wondered if her eating with us made her a keeper, or if she would be one of his one-night wonders. Letty and me, we were quiet listeners. Boss talked about the plane leasing business. Lola asked short questions like she had a brain between her ears. She knew how to carry on a conversation. She knew what the shrimp fork was, which is more than I can say for myself, when I first got here. Her table manners fit Mario's table, not the dive where Letty said she lived.

Once I attacked Olga, though I don't really remember it because I was wasted. Letty told me I told Olga to her face that she can't love Mario like we do if she feels no jealousy. I still feel that way, though Letty's got my head straight. I know I have to keep my cool so Olga will be cool. But during dinner, I had fun in my head, picturing Olga walking in unexpectedly, and crashing our cozy dinner. I bet she'd be jealous as hell. If not, maybe she really doesn't love Mario as much as we do. If she walked in, I bet I could tell how she felt, even if she was trying to hide it. Too bad Olga called from Bolivia this afternoon and talked to Letty. She would not be walking in on us, not tonight, anyway.

Letty helped Miguel when he brought out a cart of desserts. She pointed out which of the choices she had made. She's a fantastic baker. It was like a restaurant. We—all of us—went for it. Letty sat down with a dab of everything. I played with my apple pie a la mode with two scoops of Miguel's homemade vanilla ice cream. I took my time, and when I was done, it looked like I'd licked my plate. Miguel's apple pie is unbelievable, but not as unbelievable as his ice cream.

"How do you stay so slim?" Lola said, looking at me and my clean plate. She had black coffee in front of her, and she hadn't had any of the baked potato, either.

I smiled at her. "I work my ass off in the gym."

She looked at Letty. "You too?"

Letty had just dipped a part of a chocolate chip cookie into a dab of whipped cream and chased it with a forkful of chocolate meringue pie. She nodded. "I do." She dipped a spork into something else, maybe tapioca or rice pudding. "Every day."

"You have hourglass figures," Lola said.

"How can you tell we have hourglass figures dressed like this?"

I looked at Letty critically. We had been in the garden earlier, and Letty and I were still wearing these cute gardening smocks. We hadn't been gardening though. Letty went out there with the intention of getting someone to put some fresh paint on a trellis near the guest house. Quito saw us and after Letty talked to him, sent Memo and Yoli to do the job. Memo and Yoli Munoz were always puttering in the dirt, even on their days off. Caro and Chete Garza always hung out in the back house on their days off too.

"I know," Lola said. "That top is cute, but I know there's a tiny waist under there."

"They do have hourglass figures," Boss said, concentrating on his ice cream topped with peanuts and swirled with peanut butter.

"Are you a swinger?" I asked.

"We agreed not to ask personal questions," Letty said, though I knew she, too, was dying to ask.

Lola smiled widely. "I'll do anything Mario wants me to do."

Mario shook his head. "I'm in for whatever you want to do," he said.

He waited until everyone's forks were down. He met Lola's gaze, then looked at Letty and then at me. "Too early to talk about bedtime. Let's go down to the wine room."

In the wine room, Letty fetched the wine that Boss likes, opened the bottle, and served him a sip just like when we are out and some fancy ass wine steward prances around with bottles and glasses and a stick up his ass. She's so damn gracious. He nodded over the wine. I wondered where the fuck she picked up those manners. I love him, but it's the same love he has for me. It's not to die for love. But I am grateful. If it wasn't for Betty turning me on to him, I'd still be giving hand jobs in that slimy one room apartment in Hollywood or giving head for a ten spot or twenty. I don't have Olga's money, Pixie's voice, Letty's style, and I sure don't have Lola's looks. This girl just oozes class.

Boss headed for his room with Lola. Pixie and I made out in the spa, and then took a skinny dip in the pool.

"You still want to dose her in bleach?"

She didn't answer, just swam another lap. She's more afraid of AIDS than I am. Maybe that's why she doesn't screw around. I know she loves him. No one can tell, but I know it. I hope Olga doesn't kill her one day to get her out of the way.

"Do you want to crash his party?" I asked.

She didn't want to. Boss is into group sex, or at least, group sex with girls. He's always the only guy on the bed.

We showered in the spa and wore towels up to Letty's bedroom. I have a bedroom at Casa Luna, too. It has some changes of clothes, and my favorite shampoo in the bathroom. I sleep in my apartment, or with Letty, or with Boss.

We put on some of her babydoll lingerie. Normally Letty controls the action when we're together, but this time, I did. If I do say so myself, I was inspired.

"I'm so turned on," I told Letty.

"Why?"

"Lola," I said.

"Really? I thought you were kind of jealous of her up there with Boss."

I shrugged. "I don't want to get to a point where I like girls more than boys."

"As if that's going to happen," Letty said, grabbing me there and starting off another round.

Letty said, "You don't need to work out tomorrow. I think you burned off dinner, dessert and seven breakfasts from next week. Maybe we should get up and take a quick shower."

"No," I whispered back. "The scent is a turn on."

"The scent is coming from the candles, bitch." Letty said.

"Oh, now I'm a bitch?"

We laughed.

We hugged.

We slept.

Milan April 6, 1990
Camila

"We haven't shared a bed in a long time," I told Olga on the phone.

We are both busy, but that had never before stopped us from connecting regularly. No doubt her hands are full with Riana. She doesn't make time for me any more. Maybe she's not over the elimination of the guards' families though she said she was over it. We haven't been intimate since. Pepe would have done the same thing, and we'd never even have heard about it.

"I miss you, Amor," Olga said. "Where are you?"

"Hotel Panama."

I didn't know how to read her. At least I knew where she was. Hotel Panama is one of our hotels.

"Are we okay, Amor?" I asked her.

"What do you mean?"

"What happened is over, yes?"

I waited for an answer. Seconds passed. I looked at the grandfather clock across the room, watching the slow pendulum. I'd had it moved from Pepe's office into the informal den.

"I love you, Camila," she said. "Nothing has changed."

"I'm in Milan. Come see me."

"I'm in Panama, and not done."

"Is Riana with you?"

"She is."

I bit my lip, holding back words urging her to come to me. "Amor, finish what you have to do." My voice was as calm as I could make it.

"Si, Amor, I'll finish."

She drew out the silence. I waited.

"I'll adjust my schedule. I'll see you soon."

Panama April 6, 1990
Olga

"What did she say?" Riana asked. "She got talking, you got serious."

"She's wondering why we haven't been intimate lately."

"I figured as much by your expression."

"She's feeling insecure."

"I don't trust your sister."

"She's not my real sister," I said.

"That tells me you're still pissed at her."

I looked up at the chandelier above us in the living room of the suite we are in. Nice chandelier. We'd bought the factory that made them. Then I looked at Riana.

"I'm not pissed at her. Doesn't do any good. She's not my sister, but I'd do anything for her. Always have. I've never let her demands or her impulsiveness bother me. I was just a kid growing up in her house. I helped her with her hair, her nails, her clothes, what she should put on. I did her makeup for the longest time. I comforted her when she had cramps. I massaged her feet. She loved that. Still does. I did her homework. I figured out how to have an orgasm before she did, and then I taught her. She had fucked and so had I, but we didn't know how to get off. Imagine the innocence."

Riana laughed. "Innocence? You were fucking. That's innocent? How old were you guys?"

I heard yelling. My guards? I heard shots.

I grabbed Riana's hand and pulled her toward the bedroom, away from the sound of gunfire.

"What the fuck is going on?" Riana asked, running with me. "Someone is shooting out there."

"I know as much as you do," I said. "Pick up the phone. Lie flat on the floor. Tell the operator to send security. Shots fired."

"What about you?"

"Just do what I say."

I took my forty-five from my suitcase and checked the magazine. I headed to the living room. It was quiet now. The shooting had stopped. The yelling had stopped. I don't think any bullets had made it through the door or wall.

No one was knocking at my door. Were my guards dead or what?

"Vincente, are you out there? Carlos?"

I heard a knock. "Si, we're here."

What the fuck was going on?

I looked through the spyglass on the door and saw both my guards.

"I'm going to open the door," I said.

Riana heard me and came running. She grabbed my hand and tried unsuccessfully to pull me into the bedroom.

"Don't open the door. Not till hotel security comes up."

I ignored her and opened the door.

"What was that shooting?"

Carlos said, "It came from down the end of the hall in one of those rooms."

"We didn't want to disturb you. We did not leave your door unguarded," Vincente explained calmly. "We called the front desk and alerted them, but we haven't seen anyone come up."

"I called the front desk," Riana said from behind me. "And told that fucking idiot we were being accosted. He said security would be right up."

"Carlos, Vincente, you did good. Thank you," I said.

I closed the door. Riana carefully took the gun out of my hand. I smiled.

"Sorry for pointing, Amor. I forgot I had it in my hand."

We walked over to the sofa and dropped on it.

Riana said, "That Vincente, he's hot. But you, you're really hot. I think I came."

"Lying fuck," I said.

Riana lit a joint. I thought maybe we should wait to see if security came up, but then my guards could talk to them. Fuck it.

"It sounded like it was right outside our door," I said, watching Riana take the first hit before she handed it over to me.

Holding the smoke in her lungs, she spoke. "I sure thought so."

"I thought for sure this was another attack. I never had to worry about shit like this," I said, inhaling. "This is like what happens with Mario. Being shot at, stalked, accosted by my own people."

"You went for your gun right away. You're a tiger. No question about it." Riana said.

"I'm going to start packing the shotgun," I said.

Riana nodded. "If this had been for real, the shotgun would have been better," she said, like she had experience with that kind of thing. "Maybe next time."

I could tell that Riana was feeling the high.

"What next time?" I said, making my hand into a gun, looking down at my knuckles to aim, and firing it at the door.

Riana got a fake-shocked look on her face and uncocked my finger from the trigger. She tapped my knuckle.

"Oh, you shot the guards!" and giggled hysterically.

I couldn't get through to Mario that night.

Early the next afternoon, I finished up the Panama business, and we headed to the airport. My six guards spread out between the car we were in and a car behind us. In Los Angeles, it was three hours earlier, about eleven. We boarded the plane. I used my cell while we were still on the ground. Mario answered on the first ring.

"Amor, tried calling you last night four times and got no answer."

"I'm sorry, babies. You should have called Letty. You know I don't always carry my cell around the house."

"Letty said last night you were sound asleep."

"I haven't seen her this morning. I didn't know you called. Is everything okay?"

"What if I wasn't okay when I called? We need to have an agreement that I can always reach you. The same goes when you call me."

He was quiet for a moment. "You've fallen off the grid before for weeks at a time. I have gone for long stretches of time when I could not reach you. What's wrong? Are you okay?"

"I'm fine. I asked Letty to wake you. She said she was in her room. I got the sense that she was covering for you and that is not necessary. If I call you, take my call."

"If you were here, you'd see the salute I just did," he said, making light of what I said.

"I'm going to hang up. Talk later," I said.

"What was that about?" Riana asked.

"Nothing important. Let's get the hell out of Panama. Buckle your belt, Amor."

I lifted the intercom phone by my seat and told the Captain, "Let's go as soon as you're ready."

"Senorita, seven minutes to wheels up."

I put down the intercom and stared out the window. Outside was tarmac, a runway, and beyond that, traffic on a road. But I didn't see planes and traffic and Panama. What I saw was Mario's room, candles lit, the muscles of Mario's back and arms flexing, his skin working up a sweat as he was fucking someone below him. Her face was in shadow, but I'm sure she was beautiful.

He must be fucking someone new. There's no way that he was asleep when I called. I'd interrupted Letty and Tangles doing whatever they were doing.

I could feel Riana's eyes on me.

"Olga, are you jealous or something?"

I ignored the question. I called for our flight attendant, Mercy to get us a glass of merlot. By the time our glasses were full, the plane started to lift. Momentum knocked Mercy off her feet, though she held the bottle upright, and did not lose a drop.

I opened my arms and she fell on my lap, my arm around her. Riana and I didn't spill a drop either. It was fun though. It coaxed a sorely-needed laugh out of us, and just then, I needed a laugh. Mercy put the wine bottle in a deep recession built into the table and excused herself.

The plane climbed slowly to its planned thirty-one thousand feet.

"You didn't tell me if you are jealous?"

"I'm not jealous. I have to know I'm the important woman in his life. If he's playing, fine. He needs to time out and talk to me when I call."

"He didn't know you called."

"You're sticking up for him. I didn't expect you to do that."

Riana held her empty glass.

"Sure," she said. "I love the way you let him fuck me."

"I love to watch," I admitted.

"Why make a big deal?"

I shrugged. "I don't know."

The glass of wine helped. A couple more would help more.

Riana squirmed in her seat. "My pussy is burning like I'm in heat." She sighed. She squirmed some more and looked at me plaintively.

"I have a cure for that," I said, holding my hand out. We walked to the bedroom cabin where my king bed awaited us.

"Should I open another bottle?" Mercy asked.

Without looking, Riana said, "Later."

Chapter 10
Pasadena April 20, 1990
Mario

Mason Cooper called me at the office asking for a face to face meeting. I asked him to come over for lunch. The lower floor of the building had shops and restaurants, and the twin tower across the way had more of the same. There was no shortage of places to eat. One of the larger restaurants was a steakhouse. My office had a conference table where I often had lunch with coworkers. Sometimes I ate alone. I met him in the downstairs steakhouse. Mason ordered steak. It was not quite as good my favorite restaurant. Pacific Dining Car was minutes away from the office, but I preferred not to mess with traffic.

"I work alone, but I outsource," Mason said.

I nodded. I'd still like to know what Olga was paying him, but I didn't want to ask and display my ignorance.

"I have personnel outside your house, twenty-four/seven. We're not watching you. We're watching everyone outside your wall, everyone who comes around. It's part of putting the puzzle together."

"I had no idea you had the house under surveillance."

"I'm watching others, too. I promise, you will know all the facts when we have facts gathered."

I nodded. I passed on a big meal and was making do with a chef salad.

I knew Miguel had a massive porterhouse marinating at home. I spooned too much dressing on my salad and stabbed at it with my fork. A perfect bite.

"Lately you have had an occasional visitor. A young lady. I believe you call her Lola."

I stopped eating. I looked at him. "You know her name."

"Her name is Nina Caputo, not Lola."

"I'm not surprised a woman in her profession uses another name. What about Nina?"

"Not sure yet. Lola keeps a run-down apartment in Hollywood, but as Nina, she lives in a much better neighborhood in West Los Angeles."

I stopped eating again. "I picked her up at a club in Hollywood. I pay her to come over."

Mason carved his steak. "You should not let on you know she's got an alias. I know you are smart enough not to confide anything to her that is sensitive."

I knew from the beginning that Lola was different.

"Do you believe she's a call girl?" I asked him.

"Since the first time you met in March, she goes home, that is to the shabby apartment to get her car then drives over to where she really lives. So far, she has not picked up any other johns."

"Are you watching Jack Fino?"

Mason chewed away. He met my gaze.

"Do you suspect, Fino?"

"You tell me, Mason. What would Jack Fino gain by having my house burned down or having someone shooting at me?"

"I'm not ready to say he's a suspect or not. He is strange though. And yes, we're watching him and that crazy lady Janice who refuses to meet with me."

"Janice is crazy," I said. Once I'd had a private investigator tap her phone and Fino's, but if Mason was as good as his reputation promised, he either knew that already, or would find out. "Why do you say that Fino is strange?"

"I interviewed him. You already know this. He speaks highly of you. He told me seven times in an hour what good friends you are."

"That's not strange," I said.

"He's strange. Give me some time. I'm not ready to tie it up."

I dropped the talk about Fino and started on Lola. "So, she has another name and lives in a better place. That's all you got?"

"For now, yes."

"If you had to guess, what do you think she wants if she's not a call girl?"

"I would have to interview her, and I can't do that and keep it confidential. She could be an undercover cop."

That stopped me cold.

"Why would cops be interested in me? I'm not doing anything wrong."

Immediately I thought about all the laws Olga and Camila were always breaking. How could I not think about the messy business that my fiancée is in? I wondered if Mason knew anything about Camacho business.

Our lunch and talk took all of two hours. I walked him out to the elevators. He rode with me up to the GAL floor. We were alone, and he took advantage of the privacy. He spoke in a low voice.

"When I agreed to take this case, Olga accepted my condition that even though she is paying me, I cannot, and will not release any information to her about my ongoing investigation or about the results."

I patted him on the back, shook his hand. I stepped out of the elevator. He remained inside.

"I look forward to our next lunch," I said.

The elevator door shut, and the lights above the elevator door tracked his ride down to the lobby.

At my desk, I stared at the contracts I was working on, but my mind was floating way out there in the stratosphere. I'd seen Lola a total of five times.

I could have tested Mason, maybe asked for his run-down of each visit. I did not find it amusing.

I tried to think of a movie where the undercover was a woman who had given up her body like Lola had given hers up to me. Some of the stuff she did to me, and I did to her. Fuck, no way that lady was that deep undercover.

I grabbed my cell and called her. She answered on the third ring.

"Are you coming over tonight?"

"I don't want you to tire of me."

"No chance."

"Letty and Tangles are getting jealous. I can tell."

"They don't get jealous."

"We should invite them to join us. What do you think?" Could it be an agent of the law talking like this? Not a chance.

"Are you there?"

"I'm here," I said. "Sure, I'd love to have three hot ladies in bed with me. Sure you want to do it?"

"I never say anything I don't mean," Lola said. "It will cost you."

Paying wasn't the problem. Hearing her say it bothered me a little.

"I'll send a car to get you. What time?"

"I wish I had a car," she said. "I hate to be bothering you like this. I'll take a taxi."

"Baby, take a taxi. I'll pay for it. Is that okay?"

When we were done. I recalled what Mason had said, that she got dropped off at the messed-up apartment building in Hollywood then she would drive her car to where she lived. She had just lied to me. Or maybe the car wasn't hers.

I left my unfinished work on my desk. I called Letty from my car for the address where she had taken Lola the first time, the same address where Raul went to pick her up after that.

"Get off on Santa Monica Boulevard then go East three blocks." Letty said. "I can go get her, Boss."

"It's okay. I'll explain later."

"Is everything okay?"

I chuckled. "Of course, babies. Everything is okay."

"Not like you to leave the office early and head to Hollywood to play driver for..." she stopped short.

"I'll be back to you soon. Ask Tangles if she wants to spend the night."

"Yeah, sounds like we may party?"

"Later," I said.

I didn't have the apartment number or any idea what floor she was on. I drove by the three-story apartment building that needed some love and care on the outside, and no doubt a lot of love and care inside. I'd purchased a bunch of similar buildings for LAI and for myself, but I'd always arranged for renovations. None of our buildings were run-down. I found parking for my Rolls a block away.

On the wall next to the front door, I found an intercom with buttons and names. The door was open. It was a mess, but I didn't smell anything too terrible. I knocked at the first door on the right.

A middle-aged Latina answered. She looked frazzled, with hair that was falling out of its pony tail. She wore a faded short-sleeved flowered cotton print dress with buttons that ran down the front. Her feet were bare. Her toes and nails were painted bright red and smelled of wet polish. She held her doorknob carefully to keep from ruining her obviously wet nails. A soap opera was blaring on the television behind her.

"Are you the manager?"

"Got no vacancies," she said, looking up at me. She waved her fingers in front of her face and blew on them.

"I'm not looking to rent."

The lady looked me up and down again. "What you want?"

"I'm looking for Lola. Don't know her apartment number."

"You a cop?"

"Just a friend."

I pulled out my money and peeled out a twenty. She took it like a starving cat snatches up a rat, expertly leaving her manicure undamaged.

"She ain't never here. Her place is number seven, end of the hall on this floor."

"Thanks." I started down the hall.

"If you looking for a fuck, there's others in the building that are here all the time."

"I'll let you know," I said.

I heard the door close.

No one answered number seven when I knocked. I tried the door. It was locked. There was grime on the door, and a smelly bag of trash sitting in the hall near an incinerator door that was nailed shut. Incinerators were banned here in the fifties, putting an age to the building. There was a threadbare carpet runner of indiscriminate color glued to the floor. Everything needed a good wash.

Lola was too classy to live here. So, what was this about? I contemplated the grime on the white-painted door. At least I think it used to be white.

"Hey you," I heard her voice.

I turned around and found Lola walking toward me. She was carrying a paper bag.

I had only seen the manager and not her fellow tenants, but I suspected Lola stuck out like a sore thumb. Hooker or not, her clothes weren't cheap or trashy.

"What a surprise. Did you come get me personally?"

I smiled.

"I thought I'd surprise you."

She stood on her toes. I leaned over, and we kissed.

"I'm surprised. Let's go."

"Don't you need to go to your place?"

"I got dressed earlier. I ran to the store. I don't want you to see the closet I live in," she said.

Thanks to Mason, I didn't believe her. Lola didn't live here. She rented this apartment. But the manager knew her name and that she was a hooker. Why else had she volunteered that there were others in the building who fucked? I played along. I was adding up two and two, but it kept coming up three and six. We walked outside.

"I parked down the street," I said.

"You're daring," she said. "Did you bring your Rolls?"

"I did."

I wanted to know what she was up to.

When we got in the car, she scooted up close to me and squeezed my already growing package at the same time as I turned the ignition switch. The power under the hood roared just enough to say it was ready for anything. I stopped being curious about who was beside me and concentrated to how badly I wanted to fuck her.

Pasadena April 20, 1990
Letty

"Boss says if you want to stay over, we might be partying with Lola."

Tangles was at her desk in the conference room. She had just hung up after a call from Gonor. She scribbled a note down on a post-it and tacked it on the bulletin board. "He wants us to call that couple from the medical evacuation."

I nodded, knowing which family she was talking about.

"What happened to the fear of disease?"

I shrugged.

"We're doomed if Lola is sick. We're still fucking him."

Tangles made a face at me. I sat on a chair across from her.

"I'm game," Tangles said.

"You're a whore."

"Takes one to know one," Tangles snapped at me.

"Does she turn you on at all?"

"Not at all. Not my type."

"What's your type?"

"Mario is my type. You're my type. Pixie is definitely my type. Olga and Camila are my type. Riana, my type."

"Okay, okay, I got it," I tell her. I thought about it a minute. "I don't got it. How is Lola different?"

"Not my type. She's not... savage."

"I didn't know you were into savage. Hey, I'm not savage."

"Do you know you?" Tangle laughed. "You're all about the passion, baby."

Pasadena April 23, 1990
Mario

It was early, six AM in LA but I was on the phone with an executive of an airline in Portugal where it was one PM. My assistant came in and did the wave to let me know that Olga was on the phone. I nodded and raised my thumb to let her know I understood. She walked out. I promised my prospect I'd call him back and switched phone lines.

"Baby, where are you?"

"Amor, good to hear your voice. I'm in Guadalajara."

"I miss you," I said.

Olga wasted no time to let me know the real reason for the call.

"Mason told you this floozy you are letting in your house does not check out, and you keep seeing her? What's going on?"

"I know you are paying Mason, but he told me he worked for me."

"Answer my question," Olga snapped.

It was obvious she was not happy. Well, I wasn't all that happy either. Why did Mason tell me he would not report to Olga, then go report to Olga? I don't like being played. I knew I was being played but hell, I didn't know what game it was, what Mason was up to, what Olga was up to, what Lola was up to.

"Years ago, you told me to go pick up chicks and bring them home. Lola is a chick I picked up and brought home. So what?" I kept my breathing calm.

"You are being stupid," Olga said. She never talked that way to me.

"Hold it," I said. "Watch your mouth."

"Mason is certain she's a cop."

"He didn't say that to me. He said she could be. He didn't know."

"You are smarter than this, Mario."

The conversation lasted another sixty seconds. By the end of it, I wasn't sure we were speaking the same language.

I dialed Andrea on the intercom.

"I have to fly to Mexico City yesterday."

"I'll set it up right away."

I called home, spoke to Letty. "Olga is totally pissed about Lola. She's flying from Guadalajara to Mexico City, and I'm flying out there soon as plane is ready."

"She doesn't even know Lola," Letty said.

"Apparently that is not an obstacle."

"Boss, are you ok?" Letty asked.

"I'm fine," I said. "Everyone's got an agenda but you. Babies, don't change."

I dialed Portugal, and finished up with my Portuguese airline executive, told Andria what kind of planes she needed to secure for him, and then I was out of there.

Mexico City April 23, 1990

On the four-hour flight from Los Angeles to Mexico City, I did a lot of thinking.

The Lola fling had been impulsive. I knew it. I ignored what Mason told me. I ignored the pieces of the puzzle that didn't fit. Hell, Lola was interesting *because* the pieces of her puzzle didn't fit. That was her whole allure, now. I wanted to figure it out.

If Lola was an undercover cop, she had to be a witch who had taken control of my brain.

After landing in Mexico, I was surprised to see Olga waiting for me on the tarmac at the bottom of the stairs.

"Baby," I said as I walked down towards her. She smiled. Maybe she wasn't as pissed as she had seemed on the phone.

We kissed, but it was a peck in comparison to our normal greeting.

We walked toward her helicopter. Our path was intersected by a customs officer. I shook hands with him. He took my passport and stamped it without even looking at the picture. No question. He belonged to Olga.

"Where is your security?"

"They're home."

"I'm not getting in this thing unless you swear you aren't going to kill me."

I was trying to make a joke, but it fell flat.

"I'm so mad at you, that's not a bad idea," she said with a straight face.

"Are you pissed because I fucked this so-called agent?"

"I'm pissed because you think with your dick and balls, instead of your brain."

"I don't think it's a good idea for us to have this conversation. I shouldn't have come."

I should be fuming but I wasn't. I felt cold all over.

"Get in. We'll have this conversation at the house."

I knew the drill, I put on my earphones, leaned over to kiss her. My lips ended up on her cheek.

"You got Letty, Tangles, and Betty and you still go out hunting for pussy. Is she that good that you shined on what Mason told you?"

Before I could respond, she shot back, "Oh, I forgot, and you got me."

The engine was noisy. I adjusted the headpiece to hear better. We lifted. The upward sensation made my stomach lurch. The landscape outside the glass came at us at a strange angle. I shut my eyes for a second and swallowed my stomach.

"Baby, let's talk about it after we land. Pay attention to the road."

"I'm so mad at you," she said again, in Spanish.

"Don't punch me until you land this thing."

I figured she'd laugh but she didn't.

Maybe Olga handled this thing like a pro, but my stomach and equilibrium were having second thoughts. She'd brought this helicopter experience with her when she took over the DC9. I know flying a plane is a whole other skill set, and it doesn't make her landing that plane any less impressive, but all I wanted was for the ride to be over. I didn't feel impressed right now and wondered if she was pushing the ride experience for me because she was mad.

Olga's home in Mexico City is a beautiful Mediterranean two story located in the exclusive area known as Lomas de Chapultepec. It was maybe half the size of my home, but it was a treasure. Tall ceilings throughout only three bedrooms, seven bathrooms. The kitchen was as big as Casa Luna's. Live-in help had a separate building close enough that driving by gave the illusion it was one building. The personnel house did not have the high ceilings, and did have more rooms: the laundry, eight bedrooms, nine bathrooms and three common kitchens. Olga's trusted Mexico security team resided there. They did not travel with her.

Mexico City April 23, 1990
Olga

I led the way to my study as soon as we walked in the house. It was almost noon, but I was holding off lunch until after our talk.

"No interruptions," I told Vincente as he closed the door behind us.

Mario came close to hug me, but I put up my hands.

"Talk first," I said, taking a seat on a sofa and gesturing for him to sit across from me. I offered him nothing to drink or eat. I didn't want to divide his attention. I wanted to get straight to business. "Mason felt compelled to tell me," I said. "He said that after he told you she could be a cop, she was over three days in a row."

"He only told me three days ago."

Mario just sat there. I don't give a damn if he's mad. He could totally fuck everything up. If Camila found out Mario was sleeping with a possible cop, she'd have her killed first and ask questions later. That's if I don't kill her first.

"I don't know what it is about her that attracts me," Mario said.

"I don't care what attracts you. If she's a hooker, she's not seeing anyone but you. Mason says she's a cop. Nothing else adds up."

"I've done nothing illegal. Why would anyone plant an undercover on me?"

"To get to me," I said.

"Why not just fuck what you have? That protects all of us, not just from a possible cop, but also from AIDS. I can't believe you kept seeing her, at your house no less. You should know better."

Mario looked down at the ground and rubbed his hair with both hands like he does sometimes. He sighed deeply, then looked me in the eye.

"I have no defense. You're right. I should have stayed away from her after Mason told me she could be a cop. I'm sorry, Olga."

I love this ape so much. I wanted to jump on his lap and smother him with kisses.

"Mason thinks it is unwise to keep seeing her. He wants to sweep your home for bugs."

"Oh, come on, Olga. Listening devices? Like in the movies?" He looked at me incredulously.

"Yes, like the movies."

There was a long silence. While I waited for him to respond, I realized that I don't remember the last meal I had. I was starving. Seconds passed, maybe a minute or two. He didn't say anything. He was restless. He stretched his legs and bumped the table that was between us.

"I said I'm sorry and I meant it. For years. I've lived with some unknown stalker who is trying to kill me or scare me or whatever the fuck he's doing. Now I have to worry about undercover cops getting at my fiancée through me. I don't like it. I've held my tongue, and I've held my discomfort. You tell me I should know better. You should know better. Even though I love you with all my heart and soul, I can't ignore it. I don't like you flying around the world with illegal cargos or whatever it is you are doing. I don't want to know the details. You're smart, and you're strong, and I know enough to know you should know better. I need to get away to think."

"Mario, you don't need to do it right now. Let's get something to eat."

"I'd rather not stay."

He had gotten up, and so did I. He kissed the top of my head, then our lips met.

"I love you," he said.

"I believe you."

He walked out my door.

Was he cutting me off?

Where was this going?

Mexico City April 23, 1990
Mario

I used my cell. I called Andrea in Los Angeles to round up my crew and get them to the plane. I had a security guard drive me to the airport in one of Olga's cars.

I didn't hear the familiar words, I adore you. That omission played over and over in my head.

The cleaning crew had just finished. I took a seat in the main cabin, a living room with seating for fourteen, but I've never had more than just my team with me. The first person to arrive was Isla. She wore a beret, her hair hanging straight below the fold of the cap.

"Jefe," she said with a smile. "I thought you were in for a night or two?"

"I'm sorry if I messed up your plans," I said.

"No plans, Jefe. Can I get you a drink? Maybe a hot chocolate, coffee?"

"Open us a bottle of wine. And don't call me, Jefe."

"Okay, Mario, you the boss." She walked to the galley, talking the whole way. "I thought you were upset at me all the way from LA to here, hardly talked to me."

"I'm sorry, baby. My head was scrambled. Still is. I was upset, but not at you."

She returned with a bottle and two glasses.

"How is your head now?"

I pointed at the seat across from me. She filled my glass first, then poured a little in hers. She put the bottle into the niche in the table, then she sat down.

"My head is still scrambled," I said. I lifted my glass toward her, but we didn't click. "I'll survive. It's nothing."

The pilots arrived. The senior officer said it would be about thirty minutes before departure to Los Angeles. The four-hour flight would put us in LA around five pm.

I called Andrea from my cell and asked her to get me tickets. Just before take-off from Mexico City, Andrea called.

"I'll have the flight plan changed to land at LAX, then you have one hour to make your flight. Both tickets are in your name."

"Love you," I said to Andrea.

"Mario," she said, hesitating in the middle of the sentence, "Do I need to know anything?"

She was my assistant at GAL. My eyes and ears when I wasn't there. I said, "Only that you are in charge. Lease a lot of planes. I'll be in touch. Don't be afraid to make decisions. I got your back."

Isla was watching me. I blew her a kiss. She raised her hand and pretended to catch it. I blew another kiss, then I raised my glass and leaned over to click hers.

After wheels up, I made no move to take Isla to the bedroom. We talked. We drank wine. She got up a number of times to check on the pilots, then returned to sit across from me.

"You have gorgeous legs," I said. I looked at her crossed legs. Her skirt was hiked up. She made no move to pull her hem down. I poured her more wine. "I'm taking off for a little while," I said. "There are two tickets on hold at TWA to Rome, an hour after our scheduled landing. Want to come along for the ride?"

"You are kidding me?"

"Not kidding you."

"What about my work?"

"I'll pay you for every day as though it was a gig. How's that?"

She took a sip of wine. "You don't have to pay me."

"That means you'll join me?"

"Why me?"

"Why not?" I drank. "I like you, and you're here."

"So honest, that hurt."

"You got your three suitcases?"

"Yep, always."

I hadn't brought a single suitcase. I hadn't gone home. I kept some clothes on the plane, but I would buy clothes in Rome.

"Why not just change the flight plan to Rome? Why commercial?"

I owned two planes, but both of them were leased out.

"This is a company plane," I said.

"But it's just Rome?"

I nodded. "Right. Just Rome."

I had two pairs of jeans, a sweater, a couple of shirts, underwear and socks packed in a standby leather duffel that I had kept in the plane. When I picked it up, I remembered when Melina had given it to me. I used to have a cloth duffle bag I carried around on trips. Melina had done a lot of things like that, made small changes in my life that made me look more like a man of business than a guy from ELA. Isla checked in her three suitcases. I carried on the one I had. The first-class stewardess gave us two small bags with toiletries, including toothbrushes, toothpaste and mouthwash. Good thing.

We had two seats three rows from the bulkhead seats. Nothing like my plane, but so what.

"Jefe," she whispered. "Does it feel strange flying commercial?"

"At some point I'll miss the bed, but my legs fit well enough. I'm cool. Are you okay?"

"I am okay," she whispered.

That was good, as the plane was still on the ground.

I must have not missed the bed very much. I was asleep before the wheels went up. It was a night flight after a very long day. I heard her talk with the stewardess about dinner. I felt when she put the sleep mask's elastic around my head. I stirred, maybe mumbled thank you, and fell asleep. I felt guilty that I had not called Letty and Tangles. I dreamed of Letty.

Mexico City April 23, 1990
Olga

Andrea told me she got Mario two tickets on a commercial flight from LAX. She does not know who the second ticket was for, and the airline won't give up the name. Letty has not heard from him.

"Did you guys have an argument?" Letty asked.

"Not really, no."

"I've never seen him just take off. When he gets irritated around here, the farthest he goes is to Whisky-A-Go-Go, but then he comes right back."

I had to say it. "That's where he picked up Lola."

Letty was silent.

"Are you there?" If there hadn't been some background noise on her end, I'd have thought she hung up.

"Sorry, yes, I'm here."

"I know all about Lola."

Silence.

"Are you there?"

"Olga, there's nothing to know about Lola. She's a hooker."

"Is that what you think she is?"

"She practically told me so, and Mario pays her for sex."

"Letty, you and Tangles must be losing it. Your pussy isn't enough for him, so he has to go scouting for hooker pussy?"

"I love you, Olga, but watch that tone."

I heard a click on the other end. At first I thought Letty had hung up, but I was still hearing background noise. Someone had picked up an extension.

I took a deep breath and apologized. "Letty, I didn't mean it, I'm sorry."

"You should be sorry." I heard Tangles voice.

"I'm sorry," I repeated. "I'm just upset."

"If you ask me, you two should just get married already and end this arrangement you two have," Tangles said.

I laughed but barely. "Neither of us are ready to get married. You should be glad. Gives you an excuse to stick around him."

"I don't need an excuse," Tangles said.

"Call back when the attitude is gone," Letty said. "I don't know what's up but wait it out."

"I love you two," I said. "Put up with me a little bit."

"Why are you sweating Lola?" Letty asked.

"Lola's real name is Nina. Mason doesn't have any solid evidence yet, but believes she's a cop."

I heard Letty and Tangles simultaneously. "What!"

"Don't mention this to anyone," I said, wishing I could take back the words.

"Does Mario know?" Letty asked.

"Yes, he knows."

"Is that why he left?" Tangles asked.

"Don't be stupid," I told her. "Why would Lola being a cop send him to Rome?"

"What she means is is that why you guys had an argument?" Letty said.

"We didn't have an argument. He shouldn't have kept seeing her after Mason told him she might be a cop."

"You think the other ticket was for Lola?" Tangles asked.

"I don't know."

"I'll go find her," Letty said. "I know where she lives."

I laughed for real.

"What's so funny?" Letty asked.

"Because that dump is where the imaginary Lola lives. Nina Caputo lives somewhere else. Don't bother trying to find her. Mason is checking to see if she's around."

I was wondering why I had told them everything.

Riana said, "You feel better now that you dumped it on them?"

"Yes," I said. "They are like wives to him. More so. They worship him."

"Olga, they don't worship him. They love him, like I love him. Are you jealous?"

"Damn! Yes. I'm jealous!"

An hour later I wasn't jealous. I was just mad.

"We'll leave in the morning," I told Riana. "Montevideo."

"A first. Uruguay. Very good, but why?"

"New banking connection, maybe."

"I'm in," Riana said.

I felt better after Mason called.

"She's at her house. She went to the grocery, stopped at the cleaners, and that's it."

"If she's there, who did he take to Rome?"

"Maybe he didn't take anyone."

After his call, I felt better. Thinking he had met up with this so-called Lola and took her to Rome is what had me mad as hell."

"Light up," I told Riana, "Just one. We're going out tonight."

"Where?"

"Dancing. We're going to have a wild Saturday night." I kissed her.

"I'll get a joint. What did Mason say that cheered you up?"

"I'll tell you later."

I had her summon my security guy.

"Vincente we're going out tonight. I don't want any chance of being kidnapped." No doubt he thought I was joking. "Let's take the six of you, but I don't want you hanging too close to us."

"Senorita Olga, we'll be ready when you say. Never worry about being kidnapped."

Riana came in with the joint. After he walked out, she whispered, "I'd fuck him if you'd say okay."

"No way do we fuck the help."

"Unless they are females?" Riana lit up, laughing.

"Right, we don't fuck them. We just play with them. Females are safe. Men are traitors. Assholes." I remembered the guards who took over my plane. Fuck them.

"You fucked that prick Alonso to buy time."

"Riana, don't get technical. Give me the joint already."

Where was Mario?

Who was he with?

Why did he split to Rome?

Does he figure we are done just like that? I looked at my ring.

Riana and I were buzzed by the time we got in the back seat of the GMC SUV. I had told Vincente one car, so my six guards were in the car with us. As much as I love Mexico City, it is dangerous. Anyone affluent is a target for kidnappers. In Mexico it is bad news to carry a gun. Only the military, law enforcement, or those with special licenses can carry firearms. It's expensive, too. Not many could afford the hefty *mordida*[29]. My guards at home had permits but not the guards with me that night.

Licensed or not, they were packing heavy.

Riana and me, we had a blast. We stayed at the first stop. Music was blasting away. The dance floor was bustling with gyrating people who left their troubles at the door as they walked in. That's where I left mine. That's where I left Mario, Nina aka Lola, the faces of the men I killed on my plane, and the two traitors who went after me on the Milan property. That's where I left the anger that Camila ordered the death of the traitors' families, especially the minors.

My ring was on my finger where Mario had put it the night he proposed.

The four hours we spent at the club seemed way too short, but closing time is four in the morning. When Riana and I got to the house, we were exhausted, drunk, high, exhilarated, and brand new. We went straight to bed. I had a wheels-up at noon. Our sleep would be only for a few hours, but we could always catch our shut-eye during the flight.

"Thank you for hanging with me," I said.

"Stop saying that. I love being with you," Riana said.

"I was wiped when we got here. Now I'm not even sleepy," I said.

Riana laughed. "You just want sex," she said.

Pasadena April 24, 1990
Letty

Tangles and I were in the gym for our early workout.

"You'd think he would call us," I said.

---

[29] Bribe

"Not us, at least call you to say he landed safely. What a fucker he is."

"Temper, temper, Bitch. I'll kick your ass."

Tangles laughed. "Come try, Bitch."

"Total mystery who he took off with. When we're done, I'll call the agency and see who was on that flight with him."

Stupid that I hadn't thought of that until now.

"Let's do it now. They're open. They're always open." Tangles stopped her workout. "Right on, Letty. Could be that one he brought over here when we were in Guadalajara. What was her name?"

"Isla, that's her name. She's from Acapulco."

I took off my gloves and got Rose on the speaker phone in the gym. Rose is at the agency we used for crew.

"Hey Rose," I said, putting on my boxing gloves as I spoke. "I was wondering if Isla had checked in. I had some questions for her."

Rose said, "Letty, funny you should ask. A man named Mason called wanting to know details about Mario's flight. I couldn't tell him anything because, well, who the hell is he? That's the flight that Andrea from GAL booked Isla on to Mexico City for one hour, and then back to LA the same day."

"Yeah, she signed Isla for the gig returning to Los Angeles that same night," I said. I figured that if she'd flown LA-Mexico City then Mexico City-LA with Mario, he'd probably flown with her to Rome. It was a very Mario thing to do.

"Rose, is Isla in Los Angeles?"

"No idea. I have not heard from Isla since her last gig to LA."

Tangles hung up for me and put her gloves on.

I was sure who had used that second ticket. I didn't have proof, but I know Mario. I don't know why being sure his companion was Isla made me feel so much better.

"He liked her. Remember the way he talked about the night she spent here," I said.

"She was on a flight or two with us. San Francisco was one for sure." Tangles said.

"I know who she is," I said. "Are you punch drunk or something?"

"You are so grumpy, and you aren't even on your period."

I punched Tangles, and she blocked me.

She threw a punch at me, and I blocked it with a kick.

She cried foul over the kick. I tossed my gloves in the corner, and we went from boxing to karate mode. We were soaked in sweat when we were done.

We went into the shower, then did a round of hot and cold and hot again.

"That work-out was worth at least a scoop of Miguel's ice cream tonight," Tangles said, laughing and groaning at the same time.

Rome April 24, 1990
Mario

The flight from LAX left at seven PM, and took thirteen hours. A taxi delivered us to the Hilton Hotel where we had no reservations. It wasn't difficult to get a suite on the top floor. I thought about Camila's huge mansion less than fifteen minutes away. I thought about Letty and Tangles at home, probably concerned I hadn't called. I thought about Olga, no doubt pissed that I left so abruptly. No doubt, she had Mason working on finding me.

"Are you tired?"

Isla put her arms around my waist. "I am if you are. I'm not if you aren't. Which is it?"

"We have two bathrooms. Let's shower then we'll decide."

Only one of the bathrooms had a tub. It matched the opulence of the suite. A window looked out to the courtyard—a weird place to put a window in a hotel room.

"Let's tub it together. Are you game?" The way Isla began in English and ended in Spanish reminded me of Olga.

The tub was roomy enough for me to almost stretch out my legs. That doesn't happen often at a hotel.

"We could have gotten a regular room. This is so expensive."

"Baby, no way."

"I've only been to Rome twice. Once was only for one day. Both were gigs."

"I know the city well, and I plan to show it to you."

I was leaning against the back of the tub, and she was between my legs, nestled in bubbles. She looked up at me. I leaned forward, and we kissed.

"I hit the jackpot with this gig," she said.

We opted to stay in, ordered veal parmigiana for two from room service, drank a bottle of wine and ate.

She beckoned me to bed.

I woke up just before midnight. My cell phone died in Mexico, but it had charged here at the hotel. I went into the parlor, closed the bedroom door and dialed Letty. It was almost three PM in Los Angeles.

"Mario, it's about time."

"I missed that voice of yours," I said.

"Then why did it take so long to call?"

"My phone died in Mexico. Long story," I said.

I heard Tangles in the background. "Let me at him before you hang up."

"We know the story. You're in Rome, and we know you're with Isla," Letty said like a know-it-all. "Admit it. She's with you, right? Tangles and I, we figured it out." She giggled.

"No, she's not with me." I looked over my shoulder toward the bedroom as if I could see through the door I'd closed. "She's asleep. It's almost midnight."

"Boss, what happened? Why did you run away?"

"Letty, I didn't run away."

"He ran away," I heard Tangles say. I heard the fax machine in the background and realized they must be working in the conference room.

"I'm going to kick back and do some thinking. I'm going to have my cell phone on. Call me whenever you want," I said. "I'm sorry if I worried you."

Tangles said, "Boss, we weren't worried. You're a big boy, but we were concerned. Got it?"

The girls couldn't see the smile on my face. "I got it, baby."

"Boss, Olga's not happy," Letty said. "She talked to us this morning. She insisted you hadn't had a fight, but we knew something was up."

Next, I called Olga. No answer.

I called Riana. No answer.

I returned to bed and slept until almost noon Rome time. I heard the shower, got up and let daylight in, watching Rome come alive in the busy street below. We were about a ten-minute walk from the Spanish Steps where we would go eat lunch. I went into the other bathroom, shaved and showered. It was a good thing the airline had provided us with a goody bag with toiletries, but I found more of the same in Hilton's brand on the bathroom sink.

Uruguay April 25, 1990
Olga

When we landed in Uruguay, the hotel sent an SUV big enough for the eight of us. Vincente rode up front with the driver. Estevan was very touchy about his selection of the men who would guard me this time around. Camila had threatened to have him killed for the failure of both sets of security people who had failed me.

"If he called me, I wouldn't know it," I said to Riana. "These stupid phones should have something to let a person know when we miss a call."

"Call him," Riana said. "Let it ring. He could answer."

We were taken directly to our rooms in a hotel I had never been in before. It had been two years since my last visit to Montevideo. The top floor of the hotel has two huge suites. Each has its own elevator to the lobby twenty-seven floors below. The guards would stay in pure luxury in the other suite on the same floor. I heard them joke around about it among themselves.

Two men were posted in front of the elevator door in the lobby, the only way in. After a quick look around, I called Mario.

He answered.

I didn't think. The first words out of my mouth were, "Amor, you haven't called me," followed by "Why Rome?"

"I called you and I called Riana," he said. "No answer."

"No doubt we were flying to Uruguay. Are you in Rome?"

"I am."

"You can stay at the house. Where are you?"

"Not at the house. Hotel is fine. Thanks for offering."

"Hey, are we straight or what?"

"I told you when I left that I needed to think. You and me, we are living in a crazy bubble. I worry about you doing what you do, and you worry about me hanging around with a street girl who works for the cops."

"She's a cop. Take that to the bank," I said firmly.

"I'm in Rome with a girl named Isla, a stewardess from the agency we use. Is she a cop, too?"

"You're so stupid," I said.

"You've been mouthy with me ever since your call about Lola. What gives? You think I'm a doormat?"

"Mario, lighten up. Don't try and turn this on me."

"Olga, I got to go. I'll be in touch."

"Don't you dare hang up on me," I said. I heard the click and held the phone for about fifteen seconds before I put it down.

I looked at Riana.

"He hung up on me."

"Maybe you just got disconnected. You can't tell with these stupid cell phones."

"Give me a break," I said.

We've been together, and all of a sudden, we were drifting apart. It was because of that bitch Lola. The cop. I know she's a cop.

It took a while for me to reach Mason.

"You got to get me evidence that she's undercover," I said to him. "I need evidence. Get me tangible proof, man."

"I got feelers everywhere. That I'm having such a time proving she's undercover is more proof to me that she is. Undercover, that is. She has no house phone for me get tapped. I suppose she uses a cell phone for everything."

"Including reporting in."

Mason chuckled.

"Do something. Go commit a felony in her presence and see if she arrests you."

"Very funny," he said.

Uruguay April 26, 1990

At eleven, I left the hotel with two guards to visit Chato the banker at Banco Uruguay. We had never met, and I wanted to make an impression. The dress I wore was more suitable for an afternoon yacht party than a meeting with a banker.

A banker I did business with in Rio knew Chato quite well and recommended me to him. Chato was probably hitting his sixties, but like his friend in Rio, he dressed well. I could see he kept himself fit. We had lunch in a private conference room in his office at a round table with a dozen chairs. Everything in the room was massive and manly. There was a lot of brown, a lot of wood. The food he provided was an Uruguayan sandwich that Chato called Chivito. It reminded me of a BLT with a little bit of barbecued steak in it.

"What you need to do is invest in money exchange outlets. Feed the outlets with cash and have them make daily deposits in to your accounts."

I did not tell him about the chain of check cashing outlets we had in Los Angeles. Money exchange outlets were not new to me. We had a lot of them in Mexico.

"Chato, that adds people to the business. The outlet manager becomes aware that there is more money coming in than he is taking in the teller window. If you can't handle large deposits, no pressure. At least we had a chance to meet and be friends."

He stared at me over the flame of his lighter as he lit his sixth cigarette. He took several puffs from each before grinding it out on the ashtray. He smoked all through the meal, but his manners were otherwise impeccable. I wanted him to do business with me.

"How much do you need to wash each month?"

"Chato, I don't wash money."

He took a drag from a new cigarette. "Of course, you don't. Forgive me, Olga. How much do you think the monthly deposits will amount to?" He put the cigarette down on the ashtray, made his fingers into a steeple and looked at me over his hand.

I smiled. "Ten or more, maybe twenty."

"That's a lot of money," Chato said.

"Imagine this, Chato. Twenty would mean one million for you a month."

"I don't need the money," he said.

I stopped eating. Smiled. "Then do it free."

"Not free. I'll do ten to see how it goes, for the million."

"Can't do it, Chato. Ten is five hundred thousand."

He set his dish aside, and his elbows went where the plate had been. He picked up his cigarette, but it had gone out. He crushed it and lit up another. "Bring twenty to open the account for a million and a half, then ten million a month for a year for the percentage you are offering."

I moved my plate to the side and stretched my hand out to him. He was sitting on left of me but there was plenty of room between us.

"Deal," I said.

"When do you want to do this?" Chato asked.

"I'm ready. Tomorrow morning."

He laughed. "You travel with that much money?"

"I said, I'm ready."

When I returned to the hotel, I was surprised to find Riana lounging around in her underwear watching television.

"I thought you were going out shopping?"

"If we're here tomorrow, we can go together?"

I sat next to her on the sofa in the parlor.

"Why aren't you in the media room watching a movie?"

"The sofa is more comfortable. Why all the whys?"

"Ooh, Riana is moody."

She kissed me on the cheek. "Not moody. Hungry. How did it go with the banker? Did he put his hand up that see-thru dress?" She laughed.

"I would have let him," I said.

"Did he agree to a deal?"

"He did." My smile got bigger.

Riana hugged me. "I love seeing you happy."

"Amor, I love you so much."

"If you loved me, you'd give some coke."

"You don't really want any coke so why do you keep bringing it up? It's been a long time without the crap. You can't still be hurting for it."

"Only when I get depressed."

"Why are you depressed?"

I put my arms around her and gave her a hug. She relaxed a little, and let out a little moan, not a sexy one.

"Because I have terrible cramps."

I laughed. Riana took a gentle punch at me.

I reached under her loose shirt and rubbed her stomach with my long nails.

"Don't stop," she said. "You know I love that."

Uruguay April 27, 1990

The next day, just before noon, my guards brought four large Louis Vuitton suitcases to the hotel. Four hundred forty pounds of hundred-dollar bills. Twenty million dollars. We went from the hotel to the bank, which was huge and busy. All around us, everyone was engaged in their own business. I followed the line of my plain-clothed guards, each one carrying a suitcase. We walked through the lobby to the vault under escort by a bank guard. From my vantage point behind them, it did not look like anyone noticed us at all. I took the elevator to the third floor to Chato's office where ten minutes later, he handed me a bank-stamped receipt for $18,500,000. I signed the new account card as an officer of LAI. LAI was the name on the account.

Chato came around his desk with a cigarette in his mouth. He took my right hand and kissed the top of it.

"When you come next month, maybe we can have dinner or do something exciting," he said

"For sure, Chato."

I moved forward just a little and softly kissed his lips.

"Thank you, Chato."

His reply was a smile.

Chapter 11
Rome April 27, 1990
Mario

The whole time in Rome with Isla was like being on a date, though it has been so long since I dated, I'm not much of an expert. We talked very little about ourselves. Once she mentioned my fiancée. My short reply made it clear that I didn't want to converse about Olga. We spent four hours at the Spanish Steps doing the shops and filling shopping bags with our purchases. Fun stuff. I could not find anything my size except for a couple of shirts and a light sweater.

"We should jump over to London," I said. "I have a tailor there who can measure me one day, and I pickup the stuff the next day."

Isla had said she had only been to Rome twice, but she went out on her own and found a seller of marijuana. She brought it back to the hotel and rolled up nine joints. Smoking pot in Rome is against the law, but we didn't think anyone would pay attention in the hotel.

"I like your company," I said, already wasted by the tokes I had taken.

She took a drag, held then exhaled, turning her head so it would not blow on me.

"I like your company, too."

Instead of London, the concierge fixed me up with a tailor two blocks from the hotel. I had three sport coats, six shirts and four pair of slacks made and delivered within twenty-four hours. The tailor gave me an address for a shop that had tall clothing ready-to-wear. Isla and I took a taxi there, and I found jeans, socks, underwear, odds and ends, and two belts.

"Let me buy you some serious stuff," I said to her.

She was wearing a plain black cotton shirt, jeans, and a loose violet cashmere sweater that showed off her eyes and complexion. What I had said made her laugh.

"What is serious stuff? I have everything I need already in my suitcases."

The idea of shopping for serious stuff struck her a funny. She broke into lilting laughter. Laughing, lively, beautiful Isla.

"I'm not turned on by lots of clothes," she said. "I can only carry so much. Do you think I look like Raggedy Ann?"

"I don't know her."

"I like you, Mario Luna."

"Ditto," I said.

She made a face. "What does that mean?"

"Me too."

We took a hotel car to a concert at the Coliseum. The driver said he would be on call nearby to pick us up.

Isla took out a ten-dollar bill from her purse and handed it to the driver.

"We're going to walk after, and then take a taxi. Thank you so much."

The car pulled away. We walked toward the Coliseum entrance.

"What was that about?" I asked.

"We don't need a big car to drive us around. It's more fun to flag a taxi or walk. I'll show you, after the show."

She reached around my waist and walked by my side.

During the performance, when her attention was on the stage, I snuck looks at her. I wondered how often she went to concerts. In her line of work, she hosted exclusively on private planes, which meant the people she dealt with could afford their own planes. You have to be a class act to put up with rich snobs. Away from work, she was simple, undemanding.

We returned to the hotel's bed, blackout curtains drawn. We lay facing each other, lips close. "Let's not make love tonight," she said. "Let's just cuddle. Is that okay?"

We kissed. I thought of Lola aka Nina, how much I enjoyed her every night she came to the house. That she was a street girl didn't bother me. It didn't even bother me if she was a cop.

Isla was also in a class of her own. Eventually we went to sleep, in a cuddle.

Rome April 28, 1990

During breakfast on the balcony, she answered her cell phone. I heard her apologize for not checking in. I was sure the caller was an agency person. "I was planning on being off at least another week or so," she said. She was silent for a long time. The caller on other end of the line was doing most of the talking.

"Okay, I understand," she said. "Let me get a pen and paper."

She went into the parlor and finished her call in there.

"I've got a gig," she said. "At least a week gig. A rich Texan I've worked for before is here and is going to be hopping around Europe. I've got to be at the airport in three hours."

I knew Olga must be pushing buttons with the agency. I didn't mention it. Isla was committed.

"It's okay," I said. "Maybe you can come back, or I'll catch up to you next time."

She sat on my lap, arms around me. "I'm sorry, Mario."

"It's okay, really. Of course, I'll miss you."

"And I'll miss you." We exchanged kisses, but I had the feeling her mind had moved ahead to the upcoming gig. I was positive that I saw little stars sparkling in her beautiful brown eyes.

"I'm sorry that I interrupted your breakfast." She returned to her chair and resumed eating.

"Mario, after we eat, do you want to shower together?"

In the bath, we made up for what we didn't do the night before. Isla was giving, and I gave right back to her. We dried each other off. She played funny and got on a bench that was in the bathroom so she could dry my hair from up high while I dried all her private parts. I kissed her belly button before kissing her in that very sensitive spot.

When she left for the airport, she was dressed to kill.

"I want to kiss you again but don't want to mess your lipstick. You look like a model out of Vogue."

"Kiss me, macho man. Don't worry about my lipstick."

Mexico City April 1990
Pixie

Luisito is one of the most famous up-and-coming stars in Mexico. He's twenty-four, and his voice makes me come. He has twice as many records out as I do, and in the last two years, he's been in a number of movies filmed by Guzman Studios here in Mexico City. I'm at least twelve years older than him, but this kid likes me. The way he looks at me, I know what he's thinking. His manager talked to Olga, and they cut a deal that we do three shows together. I do very well on my own, but a show with Luisito will put me over the top.

Estadio Azteca where our show is has a capacity of more than eighty thousand. I would not be at this huge venue without a Luisito. Maybe someday, but not now. Lainie will come here on her own someday.

My cell phone rang. My assistant Rene answered, told someone on the other end that I was getting makeup done, that I was taking no calls.

"Who is it?"

"Letty."

I took the phone. Juana, the makeup babe, stopped. I was anxious, ready to spring out of my skin.

"Bitch, I'm getting ready to sing to something like eighty thousand. Fuck-me. Ha."

"You got me and Tangles on the speaker phone. Just want to wish you good luck. We should have come to see you."

"You should have. Next time, I'll send the plane for you."

Rene took the phone away and told Letty we are almost ready for show-time.

I said, "I love you" loud enough for Letty and Tangles to hear.

The phone rang again. Rene went into a roar.

"Cool it," I told him in Spanish. "I can't handle the pressure already."

"Sorry," Rene said and answered the phone. "It's Lainie."

I grabbed the phone.

"Sweetheart, I love you, but mama is down to fifteen and I'm not ready yet."

"Mom, tell me the truth. Have you fucked him?"

"Is that any way to talk to your mama? No, he's too young for me."

"Bull, mom. You either already fucked him or will."

I laughed and returned the phone to Rene.

"No more calls," I said. My makeup artist Juana was making faces because I was laughing and disturbing her artistic work.

Luisito and I kicked some royal ass that night. He gave me more time than what was planned. I even got to do my trumpet routine while Luisito stood by and watched the audience go wild. His hammed-up reactions while I sang and danced had a hell of a lot to do with the crowd's reaction.

After the concert, the almost-forty bitch—that's me—was driven to Olga's magnificent house Thirty minutes later, Luisito arrived in his limousine to shake the hungry press people.

"Someday I will have a house like this," Luisito said to me as he walked in. No question, he's beautiful. Fuck-me.

We hugged.

"With all your money, you can buy what you want."

He laughed. "Maybe I could." He looked up at the high ceilings. "This is magnificent. Your manager has wild taste."

We sat in the living room. Olga had so many workers on duty, you'd think we were having a party with lots of people.

"Wine?"

We sat on the sofa and faced each other. He kissed me lightly.

"You were something tonight," he said. "Mesmerizing talent. I couldn't take my eyes off of you."

I shook my head. "No, Luisito, you were something."

"This was a good idea to meet here. With all this security, no reporters can get close."

"That's for sure."

The guard let in Luisito's valet with clothes in a hanger bag and a small suitcase. The plan was that he could shower and dress down, then have dinner.

After a drink, Olga's houseman showed Luisito to a guest room and I went to Olga's bedroom where I undressed, and I stood in front of a huge mirror. I checked my body out carefully. I was sure I was more toned than Luisito and hoped that would not be a turn-off for him.

When I first got started, there was a lot of press about my abs. Not all men like an athletic-looking female body. Eventually, the press let it be. I look solid. One thing for sure. I don't look my age. I headed to the shower.

In the morning, my security reported a horde of press people outside the gates. Neighbors' security forced a number of paparazzi down from their perches on trees ringing the property.

Luisito said, "I'll just get down on the floor of the limousine."

"There has to be a better way," I said.

I called Olga. Even though she was in Panama, she knew about the mob.

"When he's ready to leave, my chopper will take him over to a hotel where they can land, then he splits from there. I just checked with security, and there are no helicopters around, so right now may be a good time for him."

That meant the goodbyes were coming.

I sat, and Luisito stood next to me. He kissed the top of my head. His hand caressed the back of my neck. I admit I checked out his fine ass.

Fifteen minutes later, the helicopter roared to life, and lifted in the direction opposite from where the mob was waiting. Luisito and his valet were on the chopper. His driver, two security men and the limousine he had arrived in the night before were left behind.

Thirty minutes after he left, he appeared in the lobby of the Hotel JW Marriott. The news spread to the media outside Olga's. Eventually, Olga's security team gave the all clear. The street was a mess, but the mob was gone. Finally, the limousine carted off the rest of Luisito's people, and I was left alone.

Rome April 28, 1990
Mario

Isla had not been gone thirty minutes when my cell phone rang.

"Amor, too bad your friend had to leave."

I was cool about it. "You did me a favor. I was getting tired of her. I knew you orchestrated that call from the agency."

"Why would you just take off with her?"

"I didn't just take off with her. I took off. Without planning, I asked her along. How is that different than me taking a hooker home from the Whisky? Tell me, is Isla a cop like Lola?"

"I wish I could hate you," Olga said.

"Olga, I love you. Why would you hate me?"

"I do hate you. You are making fun of me!"

She hung up.

I looked at my phone.

I nearly called her back. Instead I got up and walked over to the closet full of the new clothes I had bought. I needed a suitcase. I took a walk to the Spanish Steps and found the right size valise at Louis Vuitton.

London April 28, 1990

Three hours later, I was on a British Air plane headed to London where I checked in at the Intercontinental Hotel. I rented a suite. It was very nice, but not grand as the Hilton suite I had slept in the night before.

I called Letty so she and Tangles would know where I was.

Letty asked what was next on my agenda.

"I'm probably coming home in a couple of days."

"Good news, Boss," Tangles said.

"Not good news, Boss," Letty said. "Not if you aren't ready."

"I don't even know why I headed to Rome. I got too much going on to just pick up and leave like I did before. Hang in there. I'll be home before you know it."

That night I had every intention of going out to play, but instead I crashed on the sofa and watched an English drama on television. I had room service bring me a bottle of wine, then I called them and asked them to send me four Coca Colas with a bucket of ice. I drank the coke instead of the wine. I have no fun drinking alcohol alone.

I don't know when I went to sleep. The doorbell to my suite rang and woke me up. I got up, still in stocking feet, and opened the door.

"Amor, Surprise!"

Even half-asleep, I realized that Olga's appearance meant she had eyes on me. Mason must have had someone watching me in Rome and London. Even if the girls had told her that I was here, she would not have known the hotel name or room number.

Still, I opened my arms, and she came into them.

I picked her up, cradled her, and kicked the door shut, leaving her guards in the hallway. I kissed her passionately.

"Amor, I'm sorry for being a bitch. I'm so sorry, Amor. I adore you so much."

I pressed my lips closed and said nothing.

I carried her to the bedroom.

"I love you, Olga."

"I've never been jealous before, and I don't want to be jealous now, Amor."

"I get crazy at times," I confessed. "I get even crazier worrying you are going to get busted on one of your trips. And then what will become of you and me? What will become of you if you are detained, put in some jail somewhere. You don't need to be doing what you are doing. You have more than enough money. I have money. Camila is set for a hundred lifetimes. What are you two looking to get that is worth the risks?"

"You keep believing I am moving coke. I'm not moving coke. I'm not going to get busted. I'm a consultant. A financial consultant. LAI is a billion-dollar company and GAL will become as big or bigger. I'm not going to jail. Stop worrying."

I was worried. I wasn't naïve enough to believe that if something happened between her and the law, that it couldn't take me down along with her. I worried what she might have to go through if something went wrong. Who would have thought that her security team would take over her plane? It happened. Shit happens.

Olga's warmth permeated me. I felt the love. We fucked around outside of our relationship by mutual consent. The only time there had been friction had been when Olga felt that I was getting serious over what should be an overnight affair. The whole fuss about Lola hit her a different way. She wouldn't be so worried about cops if she weren't breaking some kind of law somewhere. Something she was doing had to be kept hidden.

Hawaii April 30, 1990

The next day we were off in her plane to Hawaii. I had never been to that house, but years ago, Camila and Olga had taken the girls there for some days in the sun. Hawaii is a long way from Rome.

"How is it that you can take off like this? Why not do it more often?" I asked.

"My assistant is rescheduling everything."

Riana said she was going home to Spain. I assured her that she was not going to be in my way. I could see that Olga was happy she was coming along. I called home and told the girls to pack up something tropical. I was really glad we landed in Los Angeles and picked up Letty and Tangles.

There was only one real bed aboard, but there was plenty of seating that lay flat and one long sofa that opened into a bed. Besides, Hawaii from LA is just a jump.

It was not only my first time to Camila's home in Hawaii, it was my first time in Hawaii. The house was in Honolulu. After two days there, we started clubbing. The clubbing didn't come close to our clubbing in Rio de Janeiro, but it was fun.

"Will Camila keep this house?"

"You mean because we get no use of it and maintaining all this help is an expense for nothing?"

We were on the beach under a huge umbrella, lying on wicker mats on sand, and each of us holding something tropical with a little paper umbrella and bits of speared coconut and pineapple. Her staff brought out bowls of fruit salad and a pile of sandwiches, many of them made with spam.

"The house is deeded to LAI as a guest house for client entertainment."

"Where is LAI headquartered? Where do they file tax returns?"

"We file tax returns in every country where we do business, Amor. This house is part of the company's US assets. We file in Delaware for all United States assets. Anything else, Amor?"

I kissed her. "No more shop talk, baby. We're on vacation."

"Amor, the biggest asset in my life is Mario Luna."

Letty applauded. "Bravo, Olga."

Riana clapped and so did Tangles, all of them lifting their glasses in a toast.

Olga said, "I love all of you with all my heart."

Pasadena May 7, 1990
Mario

We flew home. Letty, Tangles and I hung around in the plane with Olga and Riana while they refueled in LA. The cleaning crew worked around us as best they could.

"You should stay at least a day," I said

"Amorcito, I've played hooky a long time now. Don't want Camila to have a baby."

Everyone laughed.

Riana said, "I talked to her yesterday, and she was not happy."

"She'll get over it when I let her know I'm on my way to Bogota."

Hugs and kisses later, we were in Pixie's car with Raul at the wheel on our way to Casa Luna.

Pasadena May 7, 1990
Letty

Last month, Mario had Mason bring in a team of men to check the house for bugs and devices that Lola may have planted. No bugs were found. No calls from Lola-Nina. Big surprise. Why would anyone want to listen in on Mario's life? It's got to be Camila and Olga who are doing something crooked and someone is trying to nail them. It couldn't be the past ambulance chasing or the few cases Tangles and I get now and take to Gonor. It can't be that Mario is leasing planes out to operators across the globe.   I saw Olga and Mario looking at each other as they ate their sandwiches, giving each other google eyes like honeymooners.

Am I jealous of Olga?

Why now?

Fuck me.

Pasadena May 7, 1990
Mario

"Thank you for taking me along," Tangles said.

"That's a ditto from me. When you said to meet you at the airport and bring Hawaiian clothes, I thought you were joshing," Letty said.

I sat between them, one hand on Tangles' thigh, the other on Letty's. I gave each a squeeze to let them know I heard them.

My gas tank was totally full of Olga. She made more of an impression on me than I could remember from another time. Neither Lola's or Isla's name came up once.

Pasadena May 8, 1990

The next day Mason showed up at the office. He was too early for lunch. He joined me in my private conference room.

"I want to apologize for letting Olga know about your continued visits with Lola after I reported that I believed she was law enforcement. I was stepping across the line and—"

I raised my hand. "Mason, Olga is going to be my wife. It's okay."

It really wasn't okay, but I wasn't really pissed any longer. The time I spent with Olga in the past two weeks had cooled my temper.

"I apologize for having you followed in Rome and London, and letting Olga know where you were all the time you were away."

He sat across the table from me. I watched his expression. I can read people. I didn't need to be a master in karate or judo to know that whatever he might tell me, he was Olga's. No big surprise. She wrote his checks.

"If you want to terminate me, I totally understand."

"Mason, I accept the apologies. I don't want to terminate you."

I didn't want him checking up on me, but I wasn't fooling myself. He was on Olga's payroll, not mine. I did want him to tell me who my stalker was.

My secretary brought a carafe of coffee and a basket of muffins. She poured us each the first cup and left us alone again.

"Did you get any evidence?"

"No. Lola she stays in her apartment almost as though she knows she's being watched. She goes to the market, the pharmacy, the cleaners and twice a week to a salon, and that's it. I can't get to her phone because I can't tap a cell phone."

"Does she have visitors?"

"Not a single visitor."

"I had no calls at the house or through my exchange from her. That's strange. I didn't tell her I was leaving the country when I first left to Mexico City, and I never called her while I was gone."

Mason said, "Another reason to suspect her. No doubt she has eyes on you somehow."

"But you would know that?"

Mason nodded. "Now, yes. Not when you first left to Mexico City or when you took off to Rome that same night."

I told Mason about the sex I had with Lola. If he had not been bald, I'm sure his hair would be standing up, even though he's a psychiatrist.

"If she's a cop, can she do this as part of the cover?"

"It would be frowned on by a jury if you had proof, but I imagine that anything goes if the agency wants someone bad enough."

I shook my head.

"It just doesn't seem right."

Mason took a drink of his coffee. "Sometimes it's not right."

"Have you figured out who the target might be if it's not me?"

I would have thought that Mason would be more careful, but his answer was direct.

"Probably something to do with Olga and Camila or their affiliation with LAI."

"I'm at a loss," I said. "There's nothing Olga and Camila or their companies may be doing that is illegal."

Mason shrugged. "Nor do I know of anything," he said.

I could tell that Mason was lying. He knew more than he was letting on. At least he told it to me straight that the target was probably not me. I doubted he was looking all the way back, like at who might have been pulling the biker's strings. The biker was dead, but whoever sent him was still alive.

I walked Mason to the door. We shook hands.

"Are you planning to see her again?"

"No plans at all," I said.

"That's good, Mario. I will keep watching her and let you know."

"We didn't discuss how the other matter is going."

"I have nothing new to add. Some of your friends are hard to read. Your past friends don't seem to fit the type of person who would go to the extreme of what has happened."

"Any clues?"

"You will be the first to know when I have it pinned down."

Mason had already proved that he was a snitch. He had people watching. How many people? He had me shadowed in Rome and London. How many did it take to do that job? What was the cost? I still didn't know what his services were costing Olga.

I had a private lunch served in the private conference room for Andrea and me.

"I have lots to report," she said, carrying in a foot tall stack of files.

"After we eat. Put your stuff down and enjoy the feast I ordered for us."

"No argument from me, Boss."

"Hey, not Boss."

"No argument from me, Mario."

Andrea had done a marvelous job while I was away. My desk was clear.

"There's something different about you," I said. "Not sure if it's the hair or the dress." I saw a blush. "Maybe that boyfriend is not bad after all, huh?"

"No change here," she insisted.

I got serious.

"You did fabulous while I was gone."

I hadn't yet looked at the files she brought in, but I had examined the computer database. The leases that were pending when I left were now active, and nine new leases were pending.

"Thank you, Mario."

"Andrea, it's about me thanking you. I would not know a damn thing about leasing were it not for you."

"I'd say if you want to give credit to someone, Jules is the person."

"You are way too modest," I insisted.

Andrea smiled.

I smiled back. "Let's eat."

Hours later when I was getting ready to leave for home, I got a call on my cell.

Lola.

"Tiger, did I do something wrong?"

I sat down.

"Lola, what a surprise. A pleasant surprise."

"Almost a month and no word from you."

"I was away for several weeks, but I didn't hear from you either."

"I should have called," she said. "I didn't want to be pushy. I figured you would call if you wanted me."

I laughed and took off my tie. Unbuttoned my top button. I got comfortable. I was at my desk, alone in my office.

"Did I say something funny?"

"No, no. I started to call you so many times. I had too many people around and couldn't do it, then I figured I'd waited too long, and let it go."

"Too many people can only mean you were with your fiancée?"

It took a few seconds for me to reply.

"You guessed right."

"I understand completely."

"What are you doing tonight?" As soon as the words were out of my mouth, I knew I was walking into hell.

"I have something going on. Does tomorrow work?" Lola asked.

I told myself that I could see her, just not at the house. When Mason snitched this meeting to Olga, it would for sure prove he was keeping tabs on me. Would Olga care if I saw Lola away from the house? I knew she would, but it's not like she was going to plant a listening device on my body.

"Are you there?"

I snapped out of it.

"Yes, I was imagining you, courtesy of my brain. I'll call you tomorrow and see if you are free."

On my way home, I kept looking in my rear-view mirror for a tail, but there was so much traffic that it was impossible. Besides, if Mason was having me followed, it was by a professional that would be hard to spot. Mason claimed keeping eyes on me was his way to spot others, i.e. Lola/Nina watching me. Still he had no evidence.

After an hour drive, I was home, out of my suit and in sweats, seated across from Letty having dinner.

"You're beautiful," I told her, then focused on the feast prepared by Miguel.

I told her about Lola calling me.

"I'm thinking of seeing her, but not here. At a hotel where Mason won't worry about bugs."

I laughed.

I looked up. Letty was not laughing.

"Wouldn't it be smarter to go out and pick another hooker than take the chance that Mason and Olga are right, and this broad is a cop?"

"Baby, easy, your voice sounds mean."

I kept eating. Letty was staring at me. This was not Letty.

"Boss, if you're horny, I will drain you tonight. Will that keep you away from her?"

"Letty, easy."

I stopped eating. Letty was pissed.

"You can't be jealous," I said.

"Don't flatter yourself!" I had never heard her shoot a one liner at me like that. She got up. "If you don't start paying attention to where you put your dick, you'll need to use a condom if you ever want to fuck me again."

I got up. We were both up. Facing each other with a table between us.

"Condom? What makes you think that's protection?"

"AIDS is out there, and it is killing people, and you don't even care that you're putting us all at risk. A condom isn't perfect, but it's better than just washing it off with soap and water and pretending it's safe."

I was left there trying to think of a come-back, but she was gone.

I didn't sit down to eat. I went to the gym and worked out for more than an hour, my second workout of the day. Good thing I hadn't eaten much. I ended up in the spa. The sauna was good and hot. I wondered where she was.

After a shower, I went up to my bedroom. The candles that would normally be lit were just there. I walked into the sitting room and turned on the television. I dialed Letty's room on the intercom. No answer. I called the guard house.

"Letty drove out one hour forty-five minutes ago."

I called her cell. No answer.

The gate guard informed me that Betty had arrived.

"She's with another girl named Storm."

"Storm?"

"I let them in, Boss. Hope that's okay."

"Of course, she's with Betty. It's fine."

I expected that I would be getting a massage. Maybe a two-hour massage or a three-hour massage. Maybe by then, Letty will have returned.

I stayed where I was sitting, upstairs in the sitting room adjoining my bedroom, television on. Betty came to the threshold of my door and stopped.

"Boss, is it okay to come in?"

"Sure."

"I have a friend I want you to meet."

I stood.

"This is Storm, Boss. Someday I may want to take a vacation. If you like her, she will cover for me."

Storm was gorgeous. Storm was hot. Hotter than hot. Her streaky hair reminded me of Farrah Fawcett.

We shook hands. I never shake hands with a girl. Another first.

"I love your name," I said.

"Thanks."

"I worked out and showered. That's why I'm up here early," I said.

"Where's Letty?" Betty asked.

"Somewhere."

Betty said to Storm, "You can get lost in this house. It's easy."

Storm seemed a little nervous.

"How about a drink?"

"Maybe later, Boss. We're fine." Betty said. "Should I bring a table up here or we going to the spa or your bed?"

"Am I getting four hands?"

"Not if you don't want," Storm said.

I smiled at her, then looked at Betty. "I can have a table brought up," I said.

"Oh Boss, no. We'll go fetch a table."

While Betty set up the table near the bed, Storm opened up a case she had, and asked, "Want to smell some different oils?"

"Sure," I said. Betty never asks what oil I want. She knows I like a cream with no fragrance.

"Boss, that's not like you."

"Let me smell your favorite," I said to Storm.

I'd had many four hand massages in my life, but this was sweet. While it was going on, I thought of Olga and Mason. They'd get wind of a new girl at Casa Luna, and I'd never hear the end of it. Would Storm be a suspect? Would Mason follow her around to make sure she was not a cop? The thought was entertaining. I wanted to laugh. I thought about telling Storm to deliberately lead Mason's shadows on a wild goose chase. Then I did laugh.

"Are you okay, Boss?"

"I'm fine," I said.

"Must be the four hands," Betty said.

"Maybe I'm getting ticklish in my old age."

"What are you," Storm asked, "Like thirty?"

"Forty-ish," Betty said.

Forty-two but I didn't correct her. When I was alone with Betty, I would get the run down on Storm. Betty was smart. She knew we were careful. Storm had to be trustworthy.

Pasadena May 8, 1990
Letty

I hadn't stayed at my apartment in ages, but I had a housekeeper come in weekly to clean, wash and change the linens, and air out the place. It took the housekeeper four hours.

I had no liquor, only cokes in the fridge. I sat on the living room sofa, turned on the television, put it on mute and dialed Tangles.

"You mean you're at your place?"

"That's what I said, you dope."

"Why didn't you come over?"

"I was so pissed I figured I'd come to my own house for a change."

"It's still his complex."

"It is, but I pay the rent each month just like you do."

"Can't argue about that. So, what are we going to do, talk on the fucking phone, or you come here, or I go there?"

I thought for a moment.

"I got nothing in the fridge here but cokes. Maybe I should shoot over there?"

Her apartment is a ten-minute drive from my place.

She had pretzels, mixed nuts, and a white wine that was chilled and savory.

"Why you get so pissed because he wants to fuck Lola?"

"It's not just his fucking Lola. It's ignoring what Mason is saying about her. It's the circus between him and Olga over this broad. If he just wants to get off and doesn't want to fuck, I'll jack him off. He's a nut case is what he is."

Tangles eyes opened wide. She laughed a bit.

"I can't believe you are talking about him like this. Are you okay? This is not you."

"That's what he said when I blasted him. I believe Mason. This bitch is a cop."

I poured her another half glass of wine and the same for me.

"What the fuck does it matter if she's a cop, anyway? No one at Casa Luna is breaking the law. At least if she's a cop, it makes her less likely to have killer cooties."

I hadn't forgotten I'd been starting to like Lola. "You got any weed?"

We went through the wine and a joint.

"I must be getting nutty," I said. "If he wants to fuck her, what's the difference to me? Nothing. He sticks his dick in Andrea's asshole, then he comes home and fucks us."

"You make it sound horrible."

"I told him if he's going to fuck Lola, he can't fuck me without a rubber."

Tangles started to laugh. I started to laugh.

I ran to the bathroom to pee and Tangles was behind me, at the door.

"Hurry, bitch." Both of us were dancing and walking funny we had to go so bad.

I felt good after the laugh and relieved after the peeing.

"Are you sleeping over?"

"I'm sleeping over," I replied.

"I'm going to make you feel so good," Tangles promised, leading the way to her small bedroom. At five in the morning, I returned to Casa Luna.

I figure if he gives me any lip, it will be the same as showing me the door. I'll pack and leave. At five-thirty I was in the gym. He wasn't there. At six, Tangles joined me in our daily routine. We hardly got any sleep, but no one would be able to tell judging by the energy that flowed between us. We were just leaving when he came in.

Pasadena May 9, 1990

"Morning, Boss," I said as though nothing had happened.

"Morning, Boss," Tangles said. "You're late."

"Morning," he said, all smiles.

He looked at me. "Are we good?"

We bumped fists. "All good, Boss."

"I'm going to do a quickie here. Want to have breakfast?"

"We'll wait for you," I said.

We went to the spa and left him in the gym.

We ate at the end of the kitchen counter to stay out of Miguel's way.

"Did Betty show last night?" I asked.

"She showed with another therapist named Storm."

"She called to ask if it was okay, and I told her yes after she assured me they were tight. I was going to tell you after dinner, but—"

"But you left before we finished eating," he said with some humor. "It's okay. Storm is nice. I had a two hour four-hand massage."

Tangles asked, "Any extras?"

"None that I want to discuss in front of Letty."

He said it while looking me straight in the eye like it was the punch line to a joke.

Miguel keeps large bibs hanging in the pantry that we use with crab or Italian food. Mario uses one sometimes during breakfast to save him from having to change suits. The bib caught a splash of stray coffee. Underneath, he had his tie on, but not his suit jacket. I couldn't see it, but the white shirt he was wearing was pristine.

"I'll cover my ears," I said, cupping my hands over my ears.

He took my wrist and pushed it down to the table, leaned over, and said in my ear, "No, I didn't fuck either of them."

He fucked Betty or both, because the gate log on the computer said they drove out at two thirty-five in the morning and got here at ten. I said nothing. I love sex but hadn't fucked anyone other than Mario since I landed the job with him. What a dummy I am. My love for him is never going anywhere. It's one-sided.

All I have is now.

"Are you okay?"

"Totally," I said.

"You had that lost-in-space look," Tangles said, then bit into a piece of bacon.

"Fuck you," I said, but giggled.

"Letty is fine," Mario said. Smiled at me. Leaned down and kissed the top of my head, went around the counter and kissed Tangles on the lips. "I got to get to the office."

"Hey, I get a sister kiss, and Tangles gets a wet kiss?"

Mario returned and kissed me on the lips.

"Have a good day, Boss," I said.

He started to walk away.

"Boss, you forgot something." I pointed at his chest. "The bib."

I heard Miguel laugh.

"What would I do without you?" he asked, his beautiful eyes staring at me.

"You'd show up at GAL ready for all-you-can-eat crab night at Red Lobster."

He laughed, tossed the bib at Miguel, and came back to give me an honest-to-God kiss. I wanted to tell him I was never going to leave him, no matter how pissed I got, and no matter how many others he took to bed. Yes, I'm a fool, but at least I managed not to say so out loud.

Pasadena May 9, 1990
Mario

I got to the office almost at noon and greeted everyone I passed with a good morning.

"Rough night?" Andrea asked.

"Not at all. I just ran late getting out of the house. Did I miss anything?"

We had five leasing agents who worked phones. At the close of the day, each one turned in a report to Andrea of calls that they believed were serious leasing inquiries. In the morning, a summary of the calls was prepared. I was reviewing the reports while Andrea sat in my office.

"The call volume seems to be growing," I said. "Why do you think we're getting so much continued interest?"

"The word is that we are not as strict as our competition."

"You mean we stretch on credit worthiness and earnings?"

"Exactly."

"We've been lucky so far," I said.

"I think we're safe. Your idea of getting a bigger deposit from those that are not very strong is good, because if they go belly up, we can go repossess the planes. The deposit covers a lot of the costs."

"Hopefully, all of our costs," I said.

"We have a sound operation, Mario."

I placed the printed report on my desk and looked at her. "Thanks to you and the team here, and Jules and his team there."

Andrea got up. "Yes, Boss."

"Easy with the Boss thing."

She looked back as she walked to the door. "I meant, Mario."

At three I got a call from Lola.

"I thought you were going to check in with me today?"

"I was. You just happened to beat me to it."

"Are we on?"

I gave it no further thought. I'd had it with overthinking. I'd decided last night, period.

"The Hilton on Figueroa and Wilshire at six. Does that work?"

"No Casa Luna?"

"If Hilton is not okay, you choose."

I walked from my office to the hotel. That would throw Mason's guys off if they were tailing me. I registered as Mickey Mouse and paid a cash deposit for the suite on the seventh floor. As planned, Lola called my cell at six to get my room number. I had wine and two shrimp cocktails delivered by room service.

I never touched the wine or the shrimp cocktails. Minutes after she entered the room, we were undressing on the way to the bedroom.

"I'm hungry for you," she said, beating me to the bed, raising her hands for me. I had a lot more to take off than she did, including a tie. I was so hard I had to pull my briefs down, up, and around.

"Let's see how hungry," I said. I forgot about the warnings, remembering only Lola's mystery and secrets. It was mystery and secrets that first drew me to Camila then to Olga. Lola was a mystery I wanted to solve, and it had nothing to do with her profession, whatever it might be. I had nothing to hide and nothing to share about Camila or Olga.

Afterwards, she dressed. I watched her do it. Pixie would have watched me watching her dress. She didn't. She managed to dress just for me while seeming completely oblivious of my presence. She didn't look like a hooker. She looked like someone about to go spend an afternoon at the opera house. She didn't show all that much skin, but what she had on fit her figure just a little better than office casual. Her legs were incredible, and I had a warm moment thinking of how they'd just been wrapped around me—almost warm enough to keep me from going home for another hour or two. I might have kept her busy for a couple more hours, but she picked up her purse the way a woman does when she's one minute from walking out the door.

"How much?" I asked.

"Is two too much?"

I reached in my pocket and gave her five one hundred-dollar bills.

"No one is this generous but you. I can sure use this."

She kissed me.

"Thank you, Lover."

Lola left to catch a taxi outside the lobby. I went down, checked out and walked to my office building. The parking lot on the first level under the high-rise was empty of cars and had no attendant. I got in my Rolls, and took off for the Pasadena freeway. If Lola is a cop, I am John Wayne.

Pasadena May 9, 1990
Lola

I had almost given up on him. Three weeks without a word.

I walked out of the hotel on the seventh street side and walked north to my car two blocks away. It was a beautiful night. The sky was clear, and I could make out some of the stars. Not too much traffic was out on the road. No one was walking ahead of me. I would be gone by the time he came out of the hotel. When I parked, I'd squeezed in between two cars. I'd have to squeeze out. I stepped off the curb, unlocked and opened the car door.

"Nina."

I heard my name spoken loud by a man behind me. I did not recognize the voice. I turned and heard two muffled shots that sounded like a couple of angry bees. I felt burning pain in the center of my body. One second I was standing. The next I was flat on my back, facing a towering figure holding a gun pointed at my midsection. I heard the next shot, and the lights went out.

Pasadena May 9, 1990

Mario

I got off on Orange Grove, the same place where the pickup driver shot up my Rolls then sped away. I made the turn, and no one took a shot at me. I called Letty.

"I'm ten minutes away. Are you in?"

"Dinner can be ready in twenty minutes. Miguel is waiting."

"Fire it up. I'm starved."

"Tangles is here. Can we have dinner with you?"

"Silly question," I chuckled. This was more like Letty.

I pulled up to the gates of my house.

In my neighborhood, the street lights hang like old lanterns. They were illuminating a black Plymouth parked across the street with a man behind the wheel. He was not looking in my direction. My guess is that the man in the car was working for Mason. Now that I knew to look for his agents, they were obvious. If the man in the car were a threat, my guards would be outside my property and on the street. The car was parked in plain view of two hidden cameras on the wall. It's possible I'd missed someone tailing me before, but if Mason had a tail on me when I was away from the house, I never saw him or her or them. If he had a tail on me earlier when I walked over to the hotel to see Lola, it was a ghost.

Normally when I drove up to the house, the security guy in the guard-house would see my car on a monitor and open the gates. When that didn't happen, a tap of my horn would get his attention, and the two tall gates would open inward.

I tapped the horn. I happened to look to the left. A large sedan was barreling at me. I was glad there were no bucket seats—I slid fast to the passenger side as the car came to a stop, inches from my where I had been seated. A masked man jumped out of the car. His rifle that reminded me of some kind of submachine gun, like the machine gun in those pictures of Patty Hearst back in the seventies when she was arrested.

I bailed out of the passenger-side door and landed flat on the street. A storm of shots hailed around me, exploding and thudding into my driver door. Under my car, I could see the tattered running shoes of the man firing. He didn't shoot under the car or walk around for a better angle. If he was trying to kill me, wouldn't he have done that? I stayed flat, feeling trapped. Any second, he could come around the side of the car. I had an unexpected ally. Mason's plant, the guy in the Plymouth, came out of his car, a big target with his flapping overcoat. He had a shotgun, and ran toward the shooter.

The shooter turned tail and ran for the open door of his car. I was on my feet right behind him.

"Mr. Luna, let me handle him," Mason's guy yelled.

Too late. I punched the shooter in the back, hard enough to crack something.

"*Hijo de Puta!*" He screamed in pain.

I grabbed the gun. The barrel was very hot. I didn't want it—I just didn't want it being fired at me. I jerked it out of his grip and tossed it into his car. I had a choke hold and pulled him toward me, resisting the impulse to snap his neck. A dead man couldn't tell me who sent him. I squeezed till he passed out. I took my free hand that burned like hell and yanked his hood off. He was Latin, a middle-aged hefty piece of meat that I had never seen before.

The gates to Casa Luna opened. Two guards came out with guns drawn; another came out with my dogs on leashes. I released him, and the unconscious shooter fell like a broken puppet on the street. Mason's guy rolled the bastard over, face down, and cuffed him. One of my guards assisted him, and the other tried to help me.

"I'm okay," I said. I felt myself shaking. Adrenaline was like fire in my blood. It wasn't fear. Anger permeated me to the bone.

Letty and Tangles appeared from behind the property gates coming at me at a run, caught in the flashing red lights of an approaching cop car.

I heard sirens.

I heard Letty.

I heard Tangles.

Time did that slow fast slow thing it does sometimes during a crisis. The girls frantically checked me over. I didn't see the ambulance arrive. A paramedic confirmed that I only had minor cuts on my hands and the back of my neck.

"I'm fine," I said at least ten times. My hand stung from the burn, but it wasn't bad.

The shooter was handcuffed to the gurney and taken away by ambulance, accompanied by a police officer. The man was Latin for sure. His Spanish had no accent that I could detect.

My street was like a circus, but it wasn't fun. The Fire department had two vehicles plus paramedics, and there were three police cars, my shot-up Rolls, the shooter's car and a slow parade of rubber neckers. Neighbors I only see during a crisis were craning their necks to get a better look and converging in little groups to discuss what they saw. Police closed the street from both sides. I always wondered if I could close the street and have a block party. This was not a party.

The officer in charge was the same sergeant who handled the shooter that I went after, the one who ordered me uncuffed after the patrolman stuck me in the back seat of his cruiser.

"Sergeant, can I go in and clean up really quick before we talk? I'd like to shower off some of this broken glass."

"Go. I'll go inside and talk to you after I get the rundown from my boys out here."

I walked between Tangles and Betty. They were sobbing.

"Don't cry," I urged. "I'm fine."

"I know you're okay," Letty said between hiccups. "I want to kill that bastard so bad."

"Me too!" Tangles said.

"I think I broke something in his back," I said. "He's lucky I stopped when I did."

Twenty minutes later, I was dressed in sweats and tennis shoes, sitting in the kitchen with the sergeant. Miguel had served him coffee at the counter.

"I'll have one, too," I said, taking a seat across from him. Tangles and Letty were outside talking to the neighbors. How many times violence had happened here: Olga getting rear-ended by a stolen truck because the driver thought she was me, the home invasion fiasco, being shot at by strangers, getting firebombed by a passing helicopter, and firebombed before that by passing strangers. We were getting to be old pros at surviving the unknown stalker, going back for years. These events had to be a pain in the ass for my team. Back when I'd been kidnapped in Venezuela, I'd come home resolved they learn how to protect themselves. I'm glad I did, but I wonder if without me in the picture, would they even have a reason to fear for their own safety? Who else in the world has to worry about getting caught in the crossfire or bombed by a helicopter?

Two detectives arrived not long after, and we moved to the living room. The sergeant sat in on the questioning. Everything they asked me, I had already discussed with the sergeant. I walked them out to a street still filled with action. Reflector lights were being powered by a noisy generator. I offered to hook up their lights to my power, but they declined.

It was past midnight, and my neighbors were probably wondering when the circus would shut down.

"I'll be inside," I said. "Don't hesitate to come in."

In the house, you couldn't hear the noise.

"I hope it's as quiet for the neighbors," I told Letty and Tangles. We were at the kitchen counter. My hunger from hours ago had not gone away. Miguel had a porterhouse on the grill.

"What about you guys. No food?"

The girls shook their heads and sipped their tea.

"Let's see what the detectives can get out of this bastard," I said.

"My bet, nothing." Letty said.

"Remember that bitch that worked me over in my apartment?" Tangles asked. "She got bailed out and no one ever saw her again."

"I remember," I said, "Long time ago. You see this as a connection?"

Tangles said, "Boss, I always figured it was Olga who did it to get back at me for bad mouthing her."

"Oh please," Letty said. "That record is broken already."

"It wasn't Olga," I said. "I think it was a burglary gone bad." I said it now and I had said it when the cops had made that conclusion, but I didn't believe my own statement. I said it to keep the peace. It didn't make sense that a burglar broke enough to steal from Tangles's barren apartment would have the resources to come up with twenty thousand dollars for cash bail, much less be flush enough to forfeit it when the burglar didn't show up to court.

"I agree," said Tangles. "Water, bridge. Forget I brought it up. I love Olga."

"Where were you tonight?" Letty asked.

"I worked late."

"Boss, just say none of your business." Tangles said.

"None of your business," I said with a laugh. I heard Miguel laugh. He was getting ready to serve the huge steak.

Both girls were facing me across the counter.

"Cop out, Boss," Letty said. "You met up with Lola."

After I ate, I realized it would be a long night. The girls and I sat around the living room and called all those who mattered, waking them up and telling them what had happened.

"Better I tell you I'm okay than you read it in the paper tomorrow and wonder," I said to my Aunt Carmen.

My next call was Olga in Sao Paulo, Brazil.

"Amor, you should have never moved back to Los Angeles. You should have stayed in Milan. This is horrible."

"Baby, we're building a giant leasing company here. This is home, not Milan."

"What good is it if one day you get killed by whatever maniac is doing this to you?"

"This guy was not out to kill me," I said.

"Carrying a submachine gun? Amor, get serious."

Chapter 12
Pasadena May 10, 1990
Mario

Tow trucks took the cars away. The street was reopened. The gawkers finally went home. After I was interviewed by the sergeant and detective, I complimented Mason for the savvy guy he had out in front of the house. I told him how bravely he'd performed, and how his shooting had turned the tables, giving me the opportunity to take down the whacko with the big gun. Just before five in the morning when I would normally be getting up to work out is when I finally went to bed.

I slept five hours. Letty woke me.

"It's Mason, Boss. He says it can't wait."

"What's up?"

"I didn't tell you last night. I wanted privacy, and it was chaos here."

"Tell me what?" I sat up and took the phone. "Shoot, Mason, why the dramatic prelude? What is going on?"

"As you know, I have someone watching Lola round the clock."

Here it comes, he knows about the Hilton.

"Yes, you told me."

"She parked two blocks from the Hilton downtown. My man parked nearby. When she returned to her car, a man shot her."

"What? Say that again."

"Lola was shot. The shooter took off running. My guy had a choice, either give chase or help Lola. He carried her to his car and delivered her to the hospital, still alive."

My heart does not race often. I can work out for two hours and I stay below ninety. I know my heart was going faster than that. I put my hand over the mouthpiece and told Letty what the call had been about. She froze. She looked queasy, like she was seasick, and asked in a small voice, "Is she dead?"

I relayed some of what Mason had told me.

"Mason is at the hospital greasing the wheels to get information. The police have questioned him. He identified himself, said that he's on assignment, is watching her, and told the officers what he saw. She's alive. The nurse says she made it through surgery. It was touch-and-go. They got the bullets out."

Who had put a hit out on Lola?

Olga?

She was the first person who came to mind.

I don't think Camila knew about Lola. If she knew about Lola, Camila could be responsible. But if they suspect she's a cop, would either of them be stupid enough have a cop shot? If she's a fed, she should know agencies hunt out the responsible parties.

"Are you there, Mario?" Mason asked, still on the line.

"I'm here."

"Look, if she's a cop, she could have a lot of enemies."

"Did your guy have a description of the shooter?"

"He was short, about 5-foot-seven, stocky. He was in a suit and tie. Jacob—my PI—was too far away to be able to recognize him, but he said that there was a silencer on the gun."

I was still feeling shell-shocked. I'd thought she was taking a cab from the hotel. I couldn't remember if I assumed that or if she said that. Lola and I had not discussed how she got to the hotel.

"Did you tell any of this to Olga?"

I wanted to strike Olga from my mental list of who was responsible. When I talked to her last night, she mentioned nothing about Lola being shot.

"I only talked to her about what happened to you, and I talked to her again after you spoke to her."

"Call immediately and let her know. Tell her you just told me about this, that I asked you to call and give her the news."

When I hung up, I filled in the gaps left by Letty hearing the conversation one-sided. I went into the bathroom to shower. When I came out, Tangles was in the bedroom with Letty.

"I feel terrible that I threw that shit-fit about her," Letty said.

"You should," Tangles said.

"This is no joke."

"Alright, I was just saying."

"I hope she pulls through," I said.

"Want breakfast or lunch?" Tangles asked, changing the topic.

"I need ten minutes at my desk. I'll see you downstairs."

"Did Mason call you about her?" I asked Olga.

"He did."

There was a long pause.

"And?" I asked.

"And nothing. Am I supposed to say something?"

"What bit you?" I wanted to ask if she had anything to do about it, but not on the phone, especially on international call.

"Amor, forgive me. I am speechless."

It was a short call, and unsatisfying. I hung up the house phone. My fourth-floor office was high enough to have a perfect view of the beautiful mountains. I walked over to the windows overlooking the grounds, and just stood there, watching this expansive property of mine and the mountains beyond. I never take the time to look at anything around me. That saying that life goes by so fast is crap. We make life fast. It's our fault. Everything is wound up to a rapid pace like a sprint. Sprint to Milan. Sprint to Rome. Sprint to Mexico. Sprint home to Pasadena. No time to breathe. Back and forth, and I bounce around like a target in a rifle range with that stalker taking pot-shots at me. And now Lola.

Who the fuck wants me dead? And who shot Lola?

Letty buzzed me on the intercom, so I came down. Miguel was cooking breakfast and lunch.

"I didn't know what you wanted, Boss. I have a feast coming up."

I patted his shoulder and went into the breakfast room. Tangles was having coffee. Letty was pulling pastries out of the oven. They smelled enticing.

"I'll have biscuits and the croissants," I said. "No meat."

"You got it, Boss." Letty said.

"Tangles, I want to call one of the detectives."

Letty said, "I got their cards in my purse."

"I got it, Boss," Tangles said. "Which one you want me to dial?"

Cops were getting better cell phones than everyone else. Within minutes I was connected to Sergeant Scott out in the field. He promised I would be his next stop.

Scott arrived in plain clothes with a small, fair-haired detective I'd seen him with before. Letty brought them up to my office and joined Tangles at the conference table in their usual routine of going through air accident faxes. Between the conference room and my office, there's a glass wall, and though they looked very engaged in their work, you can bet the girls were paying more attention to the doings on my side of the wall than what was in their faxes.

"This afternoon we'll be talking to him again," Scott said. "He gave us nothing."

"Did he have identification with him?" I doubted but asked anyway.

"He has a Mexican passport, and he's on a tourist visa. It will take several days to see if his prints verify who he is. He is going by Marciano Perez."

"I don't understand. You have a passport. That isn't identification enough?"

"Mr. Luna, a passport and visa issued by a consulate in Mexico mean nothing."

"You mean that it could be fake?"

"Exactly."

"Marciano Perez—if that is his name—was hired to do this. I never saw this man before. I don't understand why the hood. I didn't recognize him."

"If you had any threats of any kind from anyone, you would tell us. Is that correct, Mr. Luna?"

"Of course," I said, uncertain if I would or would not. "I have never had any threats leveled against me in person or on the phone."

"From all appearances, you are a victim," Scott said.

"Yet you have a rap sheet as long as criminal," the lightweight detective said.

"Hey," I said, feeling adrenaline and anger. "What are you saying?"

"He means when we run your name a list of occurrences come up," Scott said. "It's all in a database. Self-defense resulting in the death of four people, your burning house, burning cars, shootings on the freeway. Let us help you, Mr. Luna. Are you sure you are telling us everything?"

"Look, everything I told you, and everything in your database is all there is to know. I don't know who hates me enough to be doing this. I don't know if it's one person or a dozen people who have decided to make my life difficult."

The two detectives exchanged looks and stood.

"He had a freaking machine gun, and I came out of it with three or four little cuts from the window glass. I don't believe this shooter was out to kill me, but I would sure like to know who sent him."

"I'll call you after we talk to him again," Scott said. "We're going to arraign him tomorrow."

The detective reported to me in the early evening. The shooter wasn't talking. He was having trouble moving around. Apparently, I hurt his back but not bad enough to put him in a wheelchair.

Too bad.

Pasadena May 11, 1990

Friday evening, Detective Scott let me know Marciano Perez was arraigned on attempted murder and eight other charges. The judge set bail at $100,000 dollars.

"He'll never make bail," Scott said. "He's being transferred to the LA County jail downtown. His next court appearance is in three weeks."

"And that's it?"

"We're going interrogate him every chance we get."

Too bad I couldn't be the one questioning him.

My car was history. Saturday, I didn't go to the office. I worked from home. I had Andrea on the phone for an hour, then I let her go have a weekend.

"Boss, you want to go in and pick out a car down on Wilshire or want me to handle on the phone?" Tangles asked.

"Letty is letting you handle this?"

"It's about time, Boss. She gets to do it all, I'll never learn."

"I want the same color, same car."

"Live a little and get something new." Letty walked in. "Are you sure?"

"I'm sure," I said. It was the third or fourth car insurance would be paying for. I expect they will cancel me.

"Boss," Tangles said, "Mason is on the line."

I picked it up.

"Are you in the office today or home?" Mason asked.

"Home. I haven't replaced my car yet. Are you coming over?"

"If it's okay with you."

He must have been at his home which is also in Pasadena. He got to

Casa Luna in no time at all. I met him in my office, alone. I banished the girls. No chore for them. They went downstairs for sunbathing, a swim and whatever Miguel felt like whipping up for lunch.

"You'll probably be hearing from the detectives."

"What happened?"

"Marciano Perez made bail."

I remembered the trespasser who had attacked Tangles in her own apartment. She'd been released on fifty thousand bail and had never been heard from again.

"Who would put up a hundred thousand for this guy?" I stood and looked down at Mason who was splayed out on my leather sofa. "Why are you smiling?"

"We know who put it up," Mason said. "It's all good. When the cops call to tell you he made bail, play it like you know nothing."

"I do know nothing."

"If this works, we will find out who sent that creep after you."

It dawned on me what Mason was saying and not saying.

"Olga must know. You didn't do this on your own?"

Mason got up, a shit-eating grin fixed on his face. "I'll let you know how it goes."

I got up too. "I'd like to question the bastard."

I wasn't stupid. Mason or someone in his employ had bailed him out and taken possession of Perez.

Mason gestured with his hand to keep it down.

"You got the heads-up I was told to give you. Don't blow it. Lots of people are on the hook. And just so you know, Olga doesn't know about this."

When Mason referred to Olga, every word was a lie. Who else would have gone through the trouble, the risk, the expense? It had to be Olga. I loved her all the more for stepping up to find out who was after me.

Two hours after Mason left, I got the call from Detective Scott.

"Perez made bail. Got any idea who would foot that kind of bail for a nobody?"

"Detective, I don't know the chump. How would I have any idea about how he managed to get out?"

"I'm betting he never shows up for court," the detective said.

Pasadena May 14, 1990
Letty

Tangles and me were doing a very late workout to make up for the early morning one we didn't do, and to get away from him. He spent all day on the phone with the office and, for the longest time, talking to Olga.

"You think the bastard Perez will come here?" Tangles asked me.

"He's a nothing. Why would he chance it?"

"That gun they confiscated is one we never tried out," Tangles said.

"He's something packing a gun like that."

"It's an oldie, movie stuff."

"He totaled the fucking defenseless Rolls. Boss disarmed him. What good was the gun?" I said.

"Are we going to talk or work out, Bitch?"

We got in to the swing of things but still talked through it.

"My guess the bastard will turn up dead like the biker."

"The biker had a name. Luca Rossi."

"We haven't heard about Lola in three days," I said.

"That is probably good news. He gets updates from Mason but doesn't always tell us."

"He used to tell us everything."

Tangles said, "He still does. Why are you so gloomy?"

"I keep wondering when the next attempt on his life is going to be. I want to be there."

"Why the drama?" Tangles asked.

"Not drama, I mean it."

"Hey, I can kick ass like you. I ain't afraid."

After a shower, we rested in the spa.

I said, "Let's get dressed, and I'll bake us some goodies."

"We'll be in Miguel's way. It's almost dinner time."

"The kitchen is big enough for him to put up with us," I said.

"Okay, what you going to make?"

"Your favorite cookies."

"Something else. We just had cookies."

"Okay," I said to Tangles, the brat with a sweet tooth. "Anything you want."

Bogota May 14, 1990
Olga

Camila's plane landed at a private airport primarily used by owners of executive jets. Since Camila would not be leaving Colombia with delicate cargo, that airport was appropriate. My plane landed at the military base in Bogota about ten minutes later.

At the family mansion, my chamber girl had prepared me a hot bath. After a twenty-minute soak, a pretty girl scrubbed my body. On my way to the master bedroom, I stopped in to see Riana who was still in her bathtub.

"Do not worry about me," Riana said. "I'm eating right here in my room and turning in early. Enjoy your time with her."

She blew me a kiss. I blew her kisses back.

The master bedroom had many memories for me. It had been the bedroom used by Camila's parents. When they were gone, Pepe had renovated and made it his bedroom, the same bedroom where Pepe had shot his two bodyguards after he ordered them to have sex with me. Now that Pepe was gone too, Camila replaced all of the furnishings in the bedroom, repainted the walls and ceilings, and adorned the windows adorned with new drapery. It was all the color of dark red brick, red draperies, cherry wood floors topped with a gold and red patterned carpeting, and gold accent pieces. The ceiling was flat white, with gold leaf crown molding, everywhere but over the bed. A round crown of red and white and gold spanned the ceiling over the huge four poster bed, and the inside of the crown was hung with gold fabric. It was all very grand, from the bed to the maroon couch with its gold velvet pillows, to the massive zebra-wood desk edged in gold leaf, and the square squat black and gold chair whose seat was upholstered in cheetah fur. This is the bedroom where Camila and I met, an hour after our arrival.

Camila and I hugged for the longest time. "It's been too long," she said.

"Much too long," I said, before I kissed her. For the first time in all the years we had known each other, intimate to the fullest, I was uncomfortable. I tried not to show it. If she felt the same way, I could not tell.

"Promise me we will meet more often," Camila said.

"You're the boss."

"We're the boss," Camila said.

Camila was the boss, and she knew it. She was the head of the family, except she was the only family. She'd inherited and controlled a tremendous empire.

The master bedroom was twice the size of Mario's. His bed was unique. Camila's bed was also unique, maybe even a work of art.

"Should we have dinner?" Camila asked.

"After," I said, moving close. "I want to hold you."

We dined on the bedroom balcony overlooking the lit-up grounds that were like no park in Bogota. Pagoda lights, benches with walkways, gardens filled with trees and flowers illuminated with hundreds of lights. The bedroom's sliding glass door had full brick-red draperies which had been released from their ties, and now hung thickly, isolating us outside. The round table where we ate was wrought iron, covered with linens and fine dishware.

"Pepe was ready to sell this place," Camila said. "He was getting out of Bogota."

"He chickened out," I reminded her.

"Still, he was going to dump it."

The servants had brought us each white rice, red beans, shredded pork, chicharrón, chorizo, morcilla, fried egg, avocado, arepas and plantain. It was the peasant food I'd grown up on, and it tasted like home. It was good that we were both hungry. We ate silently for a while, and then I asked her the question that had been on my mind.

"Tell me, Amor, did you have anything to do with the suspected cop in LA?"

"Amor, what are you talking about?"

Give me a break. I gave her a look and kept eating.

"Your fiancée is a stubborn pussy-chasing crazy who doesn't listen."

"I agree." I suspected Camila was capable of the Lola hit, but also that she would never take the chance of doing anything that would make her the target of a US federal agency investigation.

"I heard she's alive," Camila said.

"Mason told me yesterday that me she's on the edge," I said. Yesterday's word was also that no one had shown up at the hospital. Her purse had not been taken, but there was no money found. Her identification had the Hollywood address that is not her actual address.

I said to Camila. "Amor, I'm curious. Was it done from here, or did Mason handle it?"

Camila paid little attention to my question for two minutes while she continued to eat.

"Why do you need to know, Amor?"

"Only one reason, Amor."

I extended my hand toward her. The balcony table was large. She was too far away. She also put out her hand, but our hands did not touch.

"What reason?"

"You and me, we have no secrets," I said.

Our eyes met.

"Mason had nothing to do with it. I took care of it."

"Okay," I said. "Are we having dessert?"

"Now or after?" Camila asked. She took a deep drink of wine. Her lips were stained red, the color of blood.

Pasadena May 16, 1990
Slim

I'm retired and this was the second time I was sent to a country I prefer to stay away from. Camila sent a puppy instead of a toro. He fucked up. Three bullets and the woman doesn't die.

"Amorcito," she said on the phone, "I need to see you in person right away. I'll be in Bogota tomorrow."

I met her at the mansion. She gave me the assignment of eliminating the woman who refused to die on her own. She handed me an envelope thick with cash. I refused it. She got mad at me.

"Patrona you can count on me. You don't need to pay me. After years in your service, I have more money than I can spend in what is left of my lifetime." It was not all in her service, but the service of her family. I date past her brother, her father, all the way to her grandfather.

"Take the money and shut up," she said. She kissed me.

"Don't fail me, Slim."

Forty-eight hours later, I was at the hospital. Under my white physician's jacket with the stethoscope in my right pocket, I wear a suit and tie, but I would feel naked without my holstered gun with a silencer. It was not difficult to find her room at the nurse station.

Lola Chavez.

She was in the intensive care unit. I passed two nurses. We exchanged smiles. I walked confidently as if I knew exactly where IC-15 was located.

I expected to find a guard outside the curtained doorway, but no one was there. Stupid police. They must believe she was a random victim and needed no protection. I stepped inside. She was on a breathing machine or something. She wasn't alone. A man got up from a chair next to the bed. He faced me. No uniform, but he smelled like a cop.

"You want me to step out?" he asked.

"I won't be long. I'm surprised the nurses let you in here," I told the man.

"I'll wait outside."

The curtain closed behind him. Camila said no one had been in to see her. It's a bad sign when the intel is off. Who was the guy watching the mark?

I should fuck up the machine she was on, but it might have an alarm. A pillow over her face would do. Still, I reached inside my doctor smock under my suit coat and grabbed my gun. My fingers fit around the holster like an old friend. She was probably going to die anyway. Why didn't she die?

I felt a blow to my back. The man was back.

"What the fuck!" he said, his eyes on my gun.

A blow to my neck. He threw me off balance. I turned and my gun went off. I missed him. I shot again and hit his right shoulder. He writhed in pain, but he wouldn't let go. His gun came out. He shot once.

Like a careless amateur, I came into this without planning. The price is this.

Blackness.

Bogota May 16, 1990
Camila

I wonder if Olga can see how happy I am that we are together and that the disastrous argument we had is behind us. I wasn't sure it would ever go away. I actually considered eliminating her out of fear that she would betray me. Foolish and stupid of me. I could never hurt her.

Breakfast time for us was noon, Bogota time. We were both in casual jeans and fitted shirts. I broke the news to Olga that the shooter who got arrested after shooting up Mario's car is in Bogota.

"Mario said the shooter was out on bail. He's so careful on the phone but hinted around that I may have posted the bail in order to get my hands on him. I don't know how he implied it without saying it, but that's what happened," Olga said. "So, you had him bailed out. How did you get him here?"

I gave my sister one of those I'm-not-going-to-tell-you smiles. "I'll explain later. Let's eat and you can helicopter us over there."

"This is brilliant, Amor. We can get to the bottom of Mario's close calls."

"I've always worried that one day an attacker will come after him when you are with him and..."

"Thank you, Hermanita, for doing this."

"Please, Amor, don't thank me. Thank Mason. Our all-round asset."

"How much does Mason know?"

"He knows nothing and everything."

"Are you going to tell me where we're going?" I asked.

"Remember the house over by the lake we used to like running away to?"

"Yes, of course. Plenty of space to land."

I looked over to my beautiful Olga. "Thank you for last night, Amor."

Olga reached over with her right hand for a second and touched my face. "I thank you Amor."

As we circled to land, I wondered if it was a good idea that we make an appearance. It seemed stupid. I told Olga what was bothering me.

"Once he sees us, he can't go back," Olga said.

The chopper touched down. The engine came to a stop. Three security people ran toward us.

"I have a good person questioning him. Maybe we should stay out of the way."

"You got it, Hermanita."

I opened the door and spoke to Juanito.

"Is everything okay in there?"

"Si Patrona. We were waiting for you."

I told Juanito to get the information we need and then come to the house to give me the information. I didn't go into the room where he was being held.

"Patrona, count on me."

"I would have liked to see what he looks like," Olga said as she started the engine.

"I have pictures, Amor. He's a nothing. Apparently from Mexico."

"Mason told me the passport and visa might be fake." Olga said.

"He looks Mexican," I tell her with a laugh.

"How does a Mexican look, Hermanita?"

We left the big house. I went to mine, Olga and Riana to Olga's. Riana joined us for dinner that night at my house.

While we were sitting around having a drink and passing a joint, I got a call from Mason.

"Someone tried to take out Nina at the hospital," he said.

"You mean Lola?"

"Yes, Lola. I've had a man there waiting for her to come out of the coma. We can befriend her and find out who the hell she is. This stocky old guy almost shot her. My man intercepted, wrestled him down. He's dead, and my guy was shot in the shoulder."

"I'm sorry to hear that. Is your man okay?"

Olga and Riana were looking at me intensely. I raised my hand up telling them not to worry.

"My man will be okay. The cops are curious about the shooting at her car. Before they figured it was an armed robber. Now, they have a guard outside her cubicle in the intensive care unit while they figure out who the dead man is."

"I'll tell Olga. She's here with me."

"I haven't told Mario yet. Give me an hour before you talk to him."

"Of course, Amor. Call him, but don't worry him. I'll be in touch shortly."

When I hung up, I told Olga what was going on. Riana listened, but asked no questions. Olga didn't say it, but I could tell she knew I had sent someone to take care of the unfinished business of doing away with Lola. When Riana went to the restroom, I told Olga that Slim was dead.

"Oh, that's terrible. Why did you send him?"

"He never failed us."

"He's old now."

"Was."

"Will they connect us to him?"

"He would not have left a trail. After dinner I'll figure out how to put Slim to rest."

Pasadena May 18 1990
Mason

When Camila and Olga need something delicate, they speak in riddles on the phone. I prefer meeting in person, but they're in Colombia. I'm in Pasadena. This is an emergency.

"Are you by your fax machine?"

"I can be at my home office fax in a few minutes."

The fax said, "Body must disappear immediately."

At two AM, an unknown dead man was cremated at the LA County Crematorium. The deputy who mislabeled the body may lose his job for messing up a homicide case. At least his service netted him a nice pay day.

I called Camila to let her know that the crisis had been handled.

"Amor, thank you."

It would be a nice pay day for me as well.

Bogota May 18 1990
Olga

"Slim is resting in peace," Camila said, lifting her champagne glass. "That woman is still alive."

"Hermanita, you can't send someone again. Give her a chance. She could stay in a coma or die on her own."

"I'm not sending anyone. My intent was to take her out of Mario's reach since he wasn't listening. If she dies and the police are interested in him, they'll just get another person in there."

"Too bad about Slim." I took a drink. "He handled something for me, and it went smoothly."

"You sent him to visit the widow about your engagement ring."

"Only Slim knew." I frowned at her. As Camila was bringing it up, it's obvious that she knew about it. I had wanted it to be a secret from everyone.

"Amor, your sister knows everything."

Mason called after dinner. Long after dinner. It was four in the morning in Bogota. Riana had nodded out on a loveseat, leaving Camila and me alone. We were in Camila's living room, Camila and I side by side.

I know her so well. I read the look on her face when Mason told her it was done.

Pasadena May 18, 1990
Mario

It would have been better if Mason hadn't called me to tell me about Perez getting out on bail. Some strategy was at work that Olga didn't know about.

I called Olga in Bogota.

"We're having dinner at Camila's. Riana and me. How are you, Amor?"

"I'm okay," I lied. A guy like me doesn't get anxious, and I was anxious. "Just wanted to hear your voice." I was waiting for her to say something about Lola, but she was too smart for that. I wanted her to admit everything she know about Perez and tell me if he snitched out whomever had hired him.

No such luck.

I worked out. I paced. I was still anxious and turned to Letty.

"Want to go with me to the Whisky?"

Letty nodded. "Sure, but why?"

"It's Friday night. I feel like getting out."

"Boss, Tangles and I can dance for you like they do over there."

"Are you telling me you don't want to go with me?"

"Boss, I don't want to go to that club or any other club."

Tangles was never too far away.

"Boss, you got everything here. But I'll go with you."

"Kiss ass, Bitch," Letty said.

The way they talk to each other, it's hard to tell if they are joshing or serious.

"Okay," I said, "Let's plan a fantastic dinner. We'll take a swim while Miguel cooks and we can spa like we got money."

I wanted to get out of my gloom, and who knew if this might do the trick.

"Deal," Letty said.

"Let's call Betty to come over with her magic fingers," Tangles said.

I thought of the new girl. "Have her bring Storm."

"You see, Boss. No need to go to Whisky," Letty said, all smiles. "I'll spread some cheer in the bedroom. Wait till you see the new candles."

We swam naked in the indoor pool. Not unusual. I am the luckiest guy in the world. I just wish the shooting would stop. I didn't want to kill anyone else. And I sure didn't want anybody else to kill me.

Betty and Storm joined us for dinner. There were no massages that night. From the dining room, we went to the wine cellar, drank, smoked, and ended up on my bed. Picture this: Letty, Tangles, Betty, Storm, and me. I took care of them and they took care of me.

Sometime during the night, Betty and Storm left. Tangles was asleep behind Letty, Letty was right beside me, candles still glowing.

"Boss, what if Storm has AIDS?" she whispered. "We don't know her."

I turned to face her. I whispered, "Then we're fucked."

"I heard that," Tangles said sleepily.

"You're supposed to be asleep," Letty said.

"Let's all sleep," I said, feeling Tangles clamber over Letty and me, putting me between them.

The silence lasted five minutes.

Letty said, "Betty has a boyfriend. If she's fucking him, maybe she got AIDS, then what?"

"Shut up," Tangles mumbled. "I was just falling asleep."

Pasadena May 21 1990

I finally went to the office. Didn't get there until noon, but I got there. Andrea followed me in and sat across from me, my desk between us.

"Welcome, Boss."

"You never call me Boss."

"But you are the boss whether I call you that or not."

"Okay, did you miss me?"

"Yes. I'm so happy. Boss, wait till you see the report for the month."

I didn't want to burst her bubble, but I watched the progress from home while I was off, and it had not been that long.

"Show me, baby. First, order me lunch."

Andrea said she'd already had lunch. I didn't move from my desk. I ate a double cheeseburger with bacon and avocado prepared by a high-end burger joint in the lower level of the building.

"You eat with such gusto," Andrea said.

While I ate, Andrea went through the leases that had closed during the last thirty days. The month was analyzed in the pages she was going over with me. The report tracked millions of dollars paid out for planes and paid in by companies leasing. The accounting department had grown from two persons to nine in no time at all. In Milan, the staff was double what it had been when I moved home to Pasadena. Jules was kicking ass.

I called Mason twice but got no answer. That was unusual. He always answered his cell phone. Maybe he was dealing with poor reception.

I was getting ready to split for home when Andrea returned.

"Mario, have you got a minute?"

I sat down. "All the time in the world for you," I said.

She blushed. Her calling me Mario was a clue that her news might be serious.

"I'm going to get married." She raised her left hand, and I saw a diamond ring.

That was unexpected.

I vaulted over my desk and hugged her where she stood.

"Congratulations! Why didn't you tell me earlier?

With the difference in our height, the way we were standing, it was awkward. Andrea had to crane her neck to look up at me. Being six five has its drawbacks. I sat down so she did not have to be a contortionist to look me in the face.

"And who is it?"

"You don't know him. I barely know him. I met him couple months ago. He has an apartment in my building. His name is Dan Jones. He's an architect. He works for a big firm in Beverly Hills. He's two years older than me and we like the same things."

I loved Andrea in my own way. I was happy for her, but not very enthusiastic.

"You love him?"

"Not yet, no."

I made a face. "Baby, then why get married?"

"I don't want to risk being thrown out of the country someday because I can't renew my tourist visa. Dan knows I have a deep admiration for him. If he loves me like he says, I will give him my love in return. In the meantime, I'll get my green card."

"Baby, there are other ways to get a green card. We have Lopez working it for you."

Andrea smiled. "Lopez will still work it out for me, only after I'm married to Dan, it will be easier."

We'd been intimate. When you've done the things to each other that Andrea and I had done, it is okay to ask if the sex was good.

"It's good." She licked her lips. Melina used to lick her lips, a turn on for me.

"I'm not going to lose you here, am I?"

It was her turn to make a face.

"Of course not. I'm not having any babies any time soon. He works long hours. I will be here. I will keep you busy."

"Baby, you do need to be here. I would totally be lost without you. You've put us on the map."

She blinked, and I saw a tear.

"Are you okay with the news?"

I got up and went around my desk again. She remained seated. I leaned over and kissed the top of her head and put my arms around her. I kissed her right cheek, then her left. I felt the tears.

"Don't cry baby," I said.

"I'm happy, Mario."

I felt a lump in my throat.

I hugged her tighter, my lips against the top of her head. I pressed my lips against her hair. We were silent. I didn't straighten up until she'd stopped crying.

"I love you, Andrea."

"I know, and I love you. You have been so good to me. The position you gave me, the salary, the car, the apartment. You are so generous. Thank you, Mario."

She had to realize how much I've learned from her. All she had taught me was worth more than money could ever be. There would be no way to compensate.

"You got to bring him over and let me meet him."

"Yes, I want him to meet you and the girls."

"Set it up, anytime," I said. She dabbed her eyes with a tissue and looked at me. Andrea is beautiful. Dan is very lucky.

I drove myself home in my new Rolls, the second time I'd driven it. I kept wondering when the insurance company would cancel my policy or advise me they were going to exclude the car from the policy.

I called Letty. "Just getting on freeway. Want to hear the news?"

"Wait Boss," Letty said.

I heard the click of the phone going on speaker. The room echoed on speaker, and sometimes gave shrill feedback.

I heard Letty and Tangles, "Yes."

"Andrea is getting married."

"What?" Letty gasped, sounding surprised. "Is she leaving?"

"No, she's not leaving," I said.

"Good for her," Tangles said.

"Who?" Letty asked.

"Some guy named Dan. She has a ring on. Says she's happy."

My gates were open, a guard on either side. I felt it was a tragedy that all these precautions were necessary.

I talked to the girls until I drove in and parked in front of entrance. "I'm here," I said. "And I'm starving."

"That makes three of us," Letty said.

I walked in the front door. They were running in my direction. When I married Olga, would Olga greet me like this? If so, for how long?

At eleven, we were sipping wine in the wine room. No weed. I got a call from Mason.

"Are you up?"

I said, "I'm up."

"Can I come over? I'm at home. I can be there in fifteen."

"I'll be here," I said.

"Why this late?" Letty asked.

"Maybe they found out something," Tangles said.

"Play it like you know nothing."

"Boss, we haven't mentioned it to anyone, not even Pixie."

If Lola was really a cop, my phones might be compromised. Mason had had the house lines checked and they appeared to be clean. His expert said that listening in on cell phones was more difficult and probably illegal, even if the cops had a judge's order.

I met with Mason in the living room without the girls.

I asked about his PI that had gotten shot at the hospital.

"He's tough. Shot twice in the service. He was a marine for twenty years."

Miguel brought a tray with coffee and pastries, poured, and split. I don't know what smelled better, the buttery pastry or the coffee. Maybe it was a toss up.

"Are you here about Lola?"

"No," Mason said.

"Before we get into why you're here, give it to me straight. How is Lola?"

"Still in a coma. Doctors are hopeful. I can't have a man there because they have a uniformed cop now, twenty-four-seven. I'm still paying our contacts there for medical updates. I have a copy of her medical chart up to yesterday."

"I forget you are a doctor."

I drank my coffee black. It was hot, and strong and bitter.

"Not that kind of doctor. But still, I want everything I can get on her."

"I had a good friend who was shot. The bullet in her stomach was so bad they induced a coma for long time. She came out of it," I said.

"They got all the bullets out of Lola, but if she hadn't gone in a coma on her own, they would have put her in one," Mason said.

"If she was a cop like you think, wouldn't they come see her or move her?"

"Depends on how deep undercover she is. Look, I'm here on something important."

"Tell me you got something out of the guy on bail?" I sat across from him. I wondered if he psychoanalyzed me every time we saw each other. On my end, I was sure trying to figure out what made him tick.

"Perez is on his way to the county jail."

I said, "Thought he was out on bail, and there was a strategy?"

Mason lifted his cup. "That was three days ago."

"Bottom line, Mason. I'm anxious as all shit."

"We have a lead on who paid Perez to do what he did. Before I get to that, here's what happened—"

I interrupted.

"First tell me about the possible lead."

"Mario, be patient."

"Okay. But you're killing me."

"Perez was brought back to Tijuana from . . . wherever." He winked at me. "He crossed the border on foot. Once he was on the US side, a bounty hunter that works for the bail bondsman here in LA took him into custody. He doesn't need a reason. A bail bondsman can ask that bail be revoked, and Perez goes back to jail."

"Fuck, I'm lost."

"Perez agreed to cooperate. He agreed to return to jail until we could verify his story. If everything checks out, we'll bail him back out and let him run to avoid going to trial for what he did to you."

"Why the bounty hunter?"

"We needed a way to get him back in jail. Bondsman is a friend of Jack Fino, but even if he wasn't a friend, it would work this way."

"Okay, I got it."

"He told the interviewers that he was hired in Mexico city by a rich businessman and loan shark. Perez is in debt to this prick, and the way he works down his debt is by doing collection work for him in Mexico, including murder. His trip to Los Angeles was his second job on this side of the border. They are gearing up in Mexico City to interview him."

The interviewers were connected to Camila and Olga. I knew they had to be. Mason was their puppet, and he was all up in this business. The interviewers in Mexico City would also be people who took orders from Camacho.

"Why would anyone in Mexico City send someone to Los Angeles to harm me?" I asked Mason.

"Perez said he assumed you owed the loan shark money, and his orders were to scare the shit out of you but not to harm you physically. He said when he got to Los Angeles, he picked up the car he was driving three blocks from your house. The door was unlocked. The keys were under the seat as the loan shark had told him. The gun was also in the car. It's not his, but it's one he is familiar with."

I picked up the phone and dialed the intercom to broadcast.

"Letty, bring me a bottle of Louis XIII and two glasses."

"None for me," Mason said. "I'm okay with coffee."

"Look, I never drink the hard stuff unless I get hit by a bat like you just did."

"Have you ever seen a psychiatrist?" Mason asked.

"Yeah, every time I talk to you."

"It might do you some good. You seem stressed."

"You need a degree to deduce that?"

Letty came in with a bottle in one hand and two glasses in the other, Tangles right behind her.

"What's wrong, Boss?"

"Sorry to have alarmed you."

Letty set the glasses and the bottle on the coffee table between Mason and me.

"Want me to pour?"

"I'll do it."

"Anything else?"

I shook my head. "Baby, thanks."

Mason waited till the girls left before he continued. "Camila told me to see you as soon as Perez was in custody in the US."

"So, Camila did this?"

"She told me I could tell you. Olga knows now, but she didn't know when the plan was initiated."

"So now what?"

"We wait. We cannot talk about this on the phone."

Mason stood. I extended my hand to him.

"Thanks," I said.

"I'll call you when I know something."

I walked him out of the living room and returned to the wine room, brandy untouched.

My trust for Letty and Tangles was unlimited. I told them what I'd learned.

"I'm staying over," Tangles said.

Bogota May 27 1990
Olga

I walked Camila up the stairs to her plane. My plane was ready to fly, a hundred feet away. The international airport has had a Camacho hanger for many years.

"It was a wonderful week, Amor," Camila said.

"It was, Amor. Thank you for taking it upon yourself to help Mario find out who is after him."

"Don't thank me, yet. If that Perez is lying, he will die in jail."

"Let's see what Juanito and his boys can do in Mexico City. I'm at a loss why someone in Mexico City would want to get to Mario." I shook my head.

"Safe travels, Amor," Camila said. "As soon as I hear from Juanito, I'll be in touch."

Bogota May 27 1990
Camila

Before I left my house, I sent a fax to Mason.

"No matter what, watch but don't touch hospital."

If she pulls through, she will know this was a message. If she wasn't a cop, she'd keep thinking that it was incidental, but that would provide her no explanation for the attempt at the hospital. This whole situation had not worked out at all. I lost Slim. Pepe had been better at this than me.

I had a talk with Juanito the night before about his mission in Mexico City.

"He gave you what to expect when you go see the loan shark?"

"I believe him, Jefa. He knows his family in Mexico will also pay the price if he's lying. The man we're going to question is protected at all times by two men. I will handle whatever I encounter," he said in Spanish.

I hugged him lightly.

"I lost Slim. I don't want to lose you."

Juanito is as tall as Mario, but where Mario has muscle, he has fat. Like Slim, he was fast and skillful with guns and knives.

"I will get this done. The man will confess, then I kill him."

"Go," I said. Juanito nodded his understanding and walked out of my study.

Pasadena May 28 1990
Mario

I should have found a way to see Lola, even if she's in a coma. She's fighting for her life. For all I know, I'm partly responsible. It doesn't make sense for Mason or his people to assault her at her car. At the hospital, his man got shot. Olga and Camila are connected, I'm sure of it. It's hard for me to believe they would be stupid enough to kill a person suspected to be a law enforcement officer. In another country, maybe, but not here in the states. I told Letty how

I was feeling.

"If you went to see her, she wouldn't know you were there, Boss."

I called Mason.

"I forgot to tell you, call me three times a day, and let me know how she's doing. Got it?"

I hung up without waiting for a reply.

"I'll bet you he's reporting her condition to Olga."

"To Camila as well," Letty said.

"Come here, Letty. Let me hold you. What would I do without you?"

"You'd have another chick here." She giggled. "But never a chick that loves you like this chick."

She came over and sat on my lap, her legs hanging over the arm of my office chair. She kissed me.

"Where's Tangles?"

"She's downstairs in my room. You want her?"

"I just wondered. Stay where you are."

I got another kiss.

Later, the three of us had dinner together.

"Boss, want to hear us speak French?"

"He knows we been doing the tape lessons."

"Yeah, I want to hear. Do the lessons work?"

"I think so," Tangles said. "I spent two hours today."

"Oh, you did not," Letty said. In French.

"Fuck you," Tangles said in English. "I spent two hours today practic-ing."

At six I drove us to El Cholo, a Mexican restaurant.

"Mason's guys are not obvious," I told the girls as I drove. I lost sight of the guy following us, but I had a feeling he hadn't lost us.

"Boss, take it in stride. I think it's great, and so does Olga," Letty said.

"Yes, Boss, especially, Olga." In French.

It was warming up, almost perfect weather for late May. In June it gets overcast and is only sunny some of the time. My cell rang. I handed to Letty to answer.

"It's Mason."

I took the phone.

"She's doing the same. Her vitals are good. My contact says her wounds are looking good. Healing."

"Mason, thanks. Call me in the morning or anytime if something changes, good or bad."

We took a seat at a booth. The juke box was playing Rock Around The Clock. We ordered a beer. The mugs were chilled, and for once, beer hit the spot. We had one beer then switched to cokes.

The waiter took our orders.

"Miguel could have fixed this," Letty said, once in English, once in French.

"We don't know what 'this' is, yet. The idea was to get out of the house," Tangles said, doing the same.

"For once she's right."

"Hey, enough of this double-speak. You know French never stuck on me," I said. "But sounds like you babes got it good."

"We do, Boss." Letty said.

"Are you planning to go to France?"

"You tell us, Boss," said Tangles.

"Let's see, you took Island to Rome."

"Her name is Isla," I said.

"That is Island, Boss," Tangles said.

We laughed.

By the time we got home, I felt like the gloom and guilt had fallen away.

"It's early, Boss. Let's watch a movie. What do you say?" Letty asked.

"I'm in, if I'm invited," Tangles said.

I put my arm around them and walked between them to the media room.

"Deal," I said.

"Good Fellas or Pretty Woman?" Letty wanted to know.

"You pick," I said.

The media room had a projection television with a big screen. There were ten reclining chairs on tiers like a movie theater, but we never had that many people in. We took three seats on the front row after Letty dimmed the lights and put on Good Fellas.

Twenty minutes into the movie, Letty got up and paused the action.

"I want popcorn and a milk shake."

"Call Miguel," I said.

"He's already in his quarters. Give us ten minutes, and we'll do it," Letty said.

Tangles followed her to the kitchen.

I dialed Olga. I wasn't sure where she was, so I had no idea the time. I got her on the third ring.

"Did I wake you?"

"I slept on the plane. Just got to Rio."

"A week in Bogota on vacation and now Rio?"

"Amor, I'm here on business and to check on the house."

She was building a house of her own about a mile up the coast from the Camacho mansion. Building in that part of the world takes forever. I hadn't really been keeping track of it, but it seemed like the project had been going on for two years, and it wasn't close to being completed yet.

"I missed you. Watching a movie with Letty and Tangles."

"Good, Amor. I miss you as well. I had a good visit with Camila. We needed it."

"Everything good now?"

Olga said, "Si, Amor, all good. I ignored Riana for an entire week, but

I will make it up to her."

"I wish I was there to watch," I said, laughing.

"You could be."

"I got to get with it. Andrea is doing all the work."

"She's getting married," Olga said.

"Yes, she told me."

Three bowls of popcorn and three huge shakes came around the corner on a rolling cart. Mine was chocolate. I love my life. I would love it more if I didn't need all the guards. I would love it more if I could freeze tonight in time.

Pasadena May 29 1990
Tangles

I stayed over, of course. I should move in like Letty. He's always telling me I should move in, and I'm always saying no. I'm always here. I dig it big time. It's not just this big house and the amazing life. I bitch and complain, but I love it. This is my family now. I love him. I love Letty. I love myself. It took a long time to get here.

We went to bed and joked and rolled around with Mario. He's so big. Wrestling around on the bed is not the same as on the mat when he's gotten in there with us to give us a workout.

"No sex," Letty said in my ear.

"I know."

"We don't need to have sex every time. We don't need to drink or smoke pot every day."

"Are you getting religious or something?"

Letty palmed my pussy.

"Oh, that feels good. I ain't admitting anything."

"Shh, you're going to wake him," Letty said.

When I was a kid, my dolls were all girls. I asked my mother why I didn't have any boy dolls. Truth is, in those days there weren't boy dolls anyway, except maybe GI Joe. I had a big collection. Regular soft dolls to play with, and fancy ones that stayed on the shelves, just for looking at, made out of china bisque with painted faces, and fancy dresses.

I love being under a man while he makes love to me. I can eat a pussy or a dick. Whatever works at the time, but I always wondered if my dolls had anything to do with my liking to be with girls. Like Letty, like Pixie, like Betty. I never told her, but I had a doll that looked just like Letty. I used to pretend the doll was my sister. Those same beautiful dark eyes, brown around the edges, darker in the center. They opened and closed depending on how you held her, and her eyes were so real, long curling lashes over some kind of artsy glass that was like looking into a living soul. She looked so real, with her dimple in her rosy cheek, like at any moment, she was going to break out of her silence and start telling all her secrets. The same long brown curls, creamy skin, the same cupid's bow mouth.

"Why you lying all clenched like that?" Letty asked.

"You told me to be quiet."

"Don't be ridiculous. Get comfy," Letty said.

We kissed, and she went around to sleep on his right side.

Chapter 13
Pasadena May 29 1990

Mario

"Boss, I hear your cell phone ringing. Might be important. It's the third time. I'll get it."

I sat up, squinting at the clock. It was three am. The phone was charging with the others in the dressing room.

"It's Olga." Letty handed me the phone.

"Something wrong?" I asked.

"Amor, check your fax right now. I sent you a love note."

"Love note?"

"Hit the lights," I said to Letty.

The glare blasted my eyes, shot straight into my skull. I sat up, putting my bare feet on the floor.

"Amor, fax. Hurry."

I dropped the phone on the bed and told Letty, "Olga sent a fax."

The air conditioning was going full blast. I grabbed my robe off the back of a chair and flicked off the lights when I trudged out of the bedroom wiping sleep from my eyes. I expected Letty to get back in bed. Good thing the office was on the fourth floor. I didn't even turn on the lights when I opened the office door. I barely had my eyes open, but there was enough light to see my way to the fax. Letty and Tangles were behind me, each carrying a robe. Letty had my boxers.

The fax was in Olga's handwriting. I put the page under the bookcase's backlighting to read it aloud.

"Amor, something went wrong in Mexico City. Interviewer reported by cell that he had the information. It was someone who lived near you. Camila heard two shots, and the conversation ended. No phone talk on this."

Letty handed me the boxers. I put them on.

"Someone who lives close to me?"

"This is torture," Letty said. "Why don't they just use a name, for God's sake?"

"I need to call Olga. Please get me some coffee."

"I'll get the coffee," Tangles said, running out of my office.

I picked up the office phone and dialed. "Thanks for that," I told Olga.

"Wish I could write better love notes, Amor."

"Thank Camila for me."

"No need, she knows. Amor, go to sleep. Take a sleeping pill. Skip your workout and sleep late."

Tangles came in with a coffee pot and cups on a tray.

"You have a sleeping pill I can take?"

"She's a drugstore," Letty said. "Sure, she has sleepers."

"I'll go fetch you one. Don't drink the coffee. Meet you in the bedroom."

I walked to my bedroom arm in arm with Letty and feeling like I had just been defeated in a karate tournament. Two shots heard meant that the guy with the answers had been silenced.

Mexico May 29 1990
Olga

When I heard from Camila about the mess in Mexico City, Riana and I headed out of Rio. My connections are good, but not as good as General Durazo in Bogota. I called him from a pay phone just before boarding.

"Amorcito, Juanito went to Mexico and I think he had a problem. I'm worried about his cell phone. I am worried that something happened to him."

"Mi Reina, yo entiendo, yo me encargo, no te preocupes."[30]

Riana and I boarded the plane. I met with the crew. We would make one fuel stop during the eight or nine hour flight.

Six of my security guys were in their seats near the cockpit door.

"Get some rest," I told them in Spanish. "Relax and enjoy the ride."

Dulce and Margarita were our stewardesses.

"We are exhausted. Don't bother me unless you need me for something important."

Riana followed me to the cabin where we crashed under the covers.

"I owe you, Amor."

"I'm so glad you're with me, Amor."

"Let's go to sleep kissing," whispered Riana.

If my team turned on me on this short hop, I would be dead. I was dead tired and would not be able to defend myself.

We slept most of the way and passed on eating. The only thing we drank was water with cucumbers and lemon. When we landed, we taxied to a hanger LAI rented from the airport authority. A customs officer came up the plane stairs and at a rapid pace stamped the passports of the crew and my security team, then came to the main cabin where Riana and I were waiting.

"Amor," I said to the familiar young man who smiled shyly. I got up and kissed him on the cheek, and he blushed. He found a place on one of my passport pages and stamped it. The smile hung on his face while Riana teased

---

[30] My Queen, I understand, I take care of it, do not worry.

him and gave him a pinch.

Two black Range Rovers driven by security men from my house were waiting for us next to the plane. Four guards got in one car, two in the car with Riana and me. In no time at all, we were headed for home.

"Got to eat soon as we get home," I said.

"Can you hear my stomach?" Riana said.

"That's my stomach, Amor."

I dialed the house and talked to Frida, my cook and filled her in.

"Prepare a feast for two. We are starving. Have some guacamole and chips ready the minute we walk in the door, Fix anything else that's fast that will hold us."

Riana said, "Just listening to that made me hungrier."

The men in the car were totally silent.

Just before we got home, my phone rang. A call from the general.

"You will have a visitor from the Federal Police tonight who will inform you of all the details. His name is Manuel. A good friend."

"I love you, *Mi General.*"

I closed my flip phone to disconnect. I took Riana's hand and clasped it. We were getting somewhere with the mystery of what happened. She squeezed back. I was still anxious though, because whatever it was, the news had been something not meant for a phone.

Riana and I ate a great dinner that Mario would have liked because there was a lot of steak involved. I excused myself and met with the high-ranking federal officer that the general had sent. He was about sixty, dressed up in a suit and tie that matched his gray hair. He asked me to call him Manuel, then sat with me in my study and showed me pictures of the crime scene. Juanito had come to interview the loan shark. The pictures showed the loan shark's place of business. Two men, bodyguards of the businessman, were found dead, their guns next to them. The so-called suspect who had never been convicted of any crime lay next to his desk. A picture of Juanito was between the two dead body-guards and the desk. Manuel believed that Juanito shot the boss and got shot when he turned his back on the body thinking he was dead.

I refused the copies of the pictures that the officer handed me, but I did want the brown bag carrying four cell phones. One of them had been found in Juanito's hand. Another bag held Juanito's two guns, a 357-magnum and a 45-caliber.

I handed the officer an envelope holding twenty thousand dollars. He kissed my hand. I put both hands around his neck and kissed him lightly on the lips.

"Amor, you are my friend. I will never forget tonight."

He touched his heart and smiled.

After he left, Riana and me, we took a bubble bath in my suite. We splashed around in the hot bubbly water and talked.

"Pepe never trusted Mexico," I said. "But I love Mexico. It is thanks to Mexico that we know what we know now. And I am so relieved to have Juanito's cell phone. Such things can only happen here and in Colombia."

"Please don't mention that bastard, Pepe," Riana said, her face twitching in anger.

"I hope he's burning in hell," I said.

"Burn, bastard," Riana said, reaching for glass of wine. We tapped glasses and drank deeply.

"Are we going to Pasadena to tell all this to Mario?"

"I didn't finish what I had to do in Rio. I think we need to head out to-morrow."

"Can you fax him?"

"I don't want to get used to faxing. I am not fully confident it is so safe."

"I think we need to fly to Pasadena, tell him, then we go to Rio,"

Riana had a cap of bubbles on her head that made her look like an elf.

"You're right, but it will have to be a fast trip. I have a pissed-off banker in Rio that I need to make peace with."

"Why pissed?"

"We left Rio without meeting with him."

Riana blew a bubble in my direction. I added a handful more bubbles to her pointy elf ears, which got heavy and dribbled down into the water.

"I'm melting," Riana said sadly. We refreshed the bubbles with a new blast of hot water, played for a while, and made a mess of the marble floor. We got out of the tub and rinsed off the rest of our bubbles the shower.

Mexico May 30 1990

At two in the morning, Camila surprised us with a visit. We were still awake, in fact, not even dry from the shower.

Even though I had told Riana what the officer had said, I met with Camila alone in my study and gave her the rundown. "I didn't want the pictures, but I'm sure you can get them if you want."

"I feel so bad for Juanito. I told him I didn't want him to die here."

"*Hermanita,* I don't think he planned it." I smiled just enough to tease out one of Camila's smiles.

"We can't send him back to Colombia."

"I can arrange to have him cremated right away," I said. "I told the officer we may want to do that."

"Amor, you are wonderful."

"*Hermanita,* it is you that is wonderful. You tried so hard to find the truth to free Mario from this cloud of misfortune."

"I love him because he loves you, Amor. He's like my brother."

I laughed and said thoughtlessly, "You don't fuck him like a brother."

Her face froze for a moment, and I remembered that Pepe had abused her. Her own father had abused her. "Oh my God, I'm sorry."

Camila raised a hand. "It's fine you say what you want. If you hadn't fallen in love with him, I would have married Mario. I loved him from the beginning."

"I love you, Camila."

In the morning we parted at the airport. Camila's plane took off first. With her were the guns and cell phones that the officer gave me. Three hours after wheels up, we landed in Ontario. As soon as the stairs were rolled up to my plane, Mario ran into my open arms. Riana got a big hug and we sat down in the main cabin. Riana and I were on a sofa for three, and Mario sat in a chair across from us.

"Baby, you're in a big hurry."

"Amor, I have to go back to Rio." I explained how we had flown to Mexico City and gave him all the details from the federal officer, friend of the general. "Camila and I figure that Juanito shot the loan shark, and then he called Camila from his cell. We think the loan shark was not dead and got two shots at Juanito before dying, killing Juanito before he could finish telling Camila what he'd learned. He told Camila only that the person re-sponsible for having Perez shoot up your car was someone that lived near you or real close to you."

Ontario California May 30 1990
Mario

The plane was fueled quickly. The pilots had done their walk around outside the plane, and it was time for Olga to leave. I was aboard for less than half an hour.

"I'm sorry to have brought you all the way here. Damn phones. If we could only trust them."

"No matter, Amor. At least I got to see you."

I kissed her passionately, hugged Riana, then kissed Olga again as I was about to debark.

"I love you," I said.

"I adore you, Mario Luna. Be sure you get in touch with Mason right away, and tell him everything I told you."

"I'll have him meet me at the house."

Soon I was on the freeway headed to Pasadena wondering who lives close to me. Melina? Jack Fino? Pixie? My workers? My neighbors? It would have been better not knowing Juanito's last words. It was a bigger mystery now, and one that made me suspicious of everyone. The bodies keep mounting up. Perez was in jail for the attack, another life wasted because someone wanted to kill me, hurt me, frighten me.

I met with Mason at my house.

"Too bad Olga didn't get the pictures. I'd like to see the loan shark."

"You know who to call if you need them," I said. "I can't see what you'll get out of looking at a dead man's face."

"You'd be surprised." Mason stood before he finished his sentence.

"So, your stalker is someone living close to you."

"Yes, whatever that means," I said with frustration.

"I'll check out the neighbors."

"Mason, don't interview my neighbors. They've been bothered enough over the years."

"I won't disturb them. I promise."

The next morning, I was up at five, did my workout and got out of the gym before Letty and Tangles finished their routine. I showered, and Miguel served me breakfast at six-thirty. The girls joined me.

"All dressed up. Must be going to the office?" Letty said.

"I got to get back to my life."

"Boss, we should go work at the office. Not much is happening with crashes. Can you use us for anything?"

I got up, kissed top of their heads.

"See you in the office at nine."

"Fucking-A," Letty said. "Thanks, Boss."

"Dig-it, Boss. We'll be there."

Just before noon, the receptionist rang me on intercom.

"Mr. Luna, you have two detectives here to see you."

I didn't know them. After introductions, they showed me a picture of Lola.

"Do you know her?"

"I know her, yes."

The other detective said, "Do you know she's in a hospital, and fighting for her life?"

I figured I'd come clean. I had nothing to hide, anyway. "Matter of fact, I do."

"A week from last Friday, did you see her?"

"Look, I have a private detective who is investigating crimes that have been committed against me. I know she was accosted at her car, and that a PI that works for my PI delivered her to the hospital. What else do you want me to tell you?"

The detectives looked at each other, like they were surprised that I told them all that in one mouthful.

"When did you see her last?"

"The day she was shot, I saw her."

"Where did you see her?"

"At the Hilton Hotel."

"How long have you known her?"

"I met her around the middle of March," I said.

I almost asked if I needed a lawyer, but I thought better of it.

"How do you know about me?" I said.

"Security tapes at the hotel showed her in the hallway on the fourth floor, knocking at the door of a room registered to you. Just curious, Mr. Luna. Is she a call girl?"

I shook my head. "Why would I tell you anything about her that is personal to her or that can incriminate me?"

"Hey, we don't care if she's a call girl. We're not vice. We could care less."

They were in my office for an hour. I was not a very good host. Never asked them if they wanted something to drink or eat, and no GAL employees came to do it either.

After they left, Letty, Tangles and Andrea came to see me. I told them what had gone on.

"The receptionist should keep her mouth shut about who comes to see me," I said. I wasn't upset, but it was crazy to think that people in my office knew the men I was meeting with were LAPD detectives.

"It wasn't reception," Andrea said. "I asked your secretary."

I shrugged. "No big deal."

"Did they ask if she was a hooker?" Tangles said.

I nodded.

"Did you confirm it?" Letty asked.

"Not a chance. I'm not a snitch."

"Right on, Boss." Tangles said.

I needed to get out. I stood. "I got an idea. Let's go eat at PDC. Been too long."

Letty drove us in my car—a short drive. On the way, I called Mason and told him about my visitors.

"If there had not been that attempt on her life at the hospital, no one would have bothered with this case."

"Come on, Mason. She was shot and could still die. What do you mean they wouldn't have bothered?"

"After the attempt on her life, they put a guard on her 24/7. Until then, nothing."

"Anyway, you got the picture in case they contact you. I'm sure they will."

"I'm flying to Mexico City tomorrow to get what Olga didn't. I'm coming right back."

After I disconnected, Tangles said, "What didn't Olga get and from who?”

"Let's go inside and eat," I said without replying.

A smartly dressed valet attendant opened the door for Letty. I got out of the passenger side, and Andrea and Tangles came out of the back.

"I never get out of the office for lunch," I said as we walked toward the entrance of the restaurant. "Got to change the routine."

"As long as we're there, we'll remind you, Boss." Tangles said.

Mason called me at home that night.

"Are you in Mexico City?"

"No, that's tomorrow," he said. "I need to see you."

Letty escorted him up at nine. I met him in my home office.

"Hopefully you have good news," I said.

"Just news. I got a call from my night contact at the hospital. In what he described as a cloak of secrecy, Lola was collected from her room by four men and a woman. They rolled her up to the roof where a helicopter flew them somewhere. No idea where."

"Am I awake?" I asked Mason, shaking my head in disbelief. I remember when Melina had been in a coma. Her doctor had ordered Melina transferred to Cedars Hospital because the coma care was better there.

"The hospital computer has it that she transferred to another hospital, information pending."

"What's your take on this?" I asked.

"She's a cop, and they came to get her."

"Mason, this isn't a movie."

Mason stood. He looked tired. He looked like a man who had not slept in weeks.

"Got to run," he said. "I have an early morning flight."

"You going all the way to Mexico City for pictures?"

"Olga arranged it. I can use everything I can get. Nothing makes sense."

I patted his back as I walked him to the door of my office. "You the man, Mason."

I met the girls in the disco room downstairs. They were sitting at the bar, the juke box playing.

"I say it all the time," I said. "We should use this room more often. A happy room."

"Boss, what did Mason want?" Letty asked. "He always looks so serious."

"I got a bottle all ready for you, Boss," Tangles said. Letty moved over, and I sat between them. I told them what Mason said.

"She's got to be something special," Letty said.

"Did I see this in a movie?" Tangles asked.

"That's what I said to Mason."

"Oh, Boss. Now I think she's a cop. But why was she poking around you?" Letty asked.

"We've discussed that a dozen times before," I said, taking a good long drink of Bordeaux.

"Should I light one?" Tangles asked.

I nodded.

"We been talking about everyone we know close by, wondering who your bad guy is," Letty said.

We both looked over at Tangles whose head was drooping. She looked a little dazed. Tangles laughed a little. "Sorry, I'm smashed."

"Did that joint come from Olga?" I asked.

"Of course. Where else?" Letty said.

"Seems stronger, different. I feel it to my toes."

"Let's just go to bed, smoke another one, fuck all night, and forget all this shit," Letty said, getting off the bar stool.

"I didn't notice until now you're packing. Are you okay?" I laughed.

"Look at Tangles. She's packing, too."

"But we're home."

"Boss, you never know."

We headed to the fourth floor.

The girls had been asleep for hours, but my mind was racing. Where was Lola flown to? Was Mason going to track her down? If she's a cop, would he be able to find any proof of it?

Rome May 30, 1990
Camila

I was at the Rome house. It was a beautiful morning. Mason said to check my fax machine. The typewritten note said, "I had every major hospital checked and nothing. She's in critical condition somewhere."

I sat in the solarium, still in my camisole and robe, and thought about the two failed attempts to get rid of her, cop or not. Who is she? Is she just a whore like she made herself out to be? What a fool I am if that is true. Damn.

"Senorita Camila, would you like your breakfast served in here?" Ana asked.

"Be sure the omelet is well done, and sausage burned. Yes, in here is fine, Amor."

"Mango juice?"

I nodded.

"You look magnificently beautiful," Ana said. She was slim with straight hair she wore pulled back, and eyes that turned up a little at the corners.

"Go away you liar. I just got up."

"I go, but you are beautiful."

Ana went out of the room humming. Most of the help is rather stiff with me, almost afraid, but not Ana. Here in Rome, Olga is the mean one who works the help over like a dictator. Sometimes I wonder what would I do without her. She oversees the houses, does the banking and makes us an avalanche of money. I love her. I wonder if things will change when she is married. I need to get married soon too. Here I am in this immense home, alone with thirty workers.

Olga called me. "Amorcito, I was thinking of you," I said.

"I think of you all the time."

"As busy as you are, how do you have time to think of me?"

"What are you doing?"

"Waiting for breakfast."

"Did you make the deal on the building?"

"Not yet, Amor. I will meet with the group again tomorrow at noon. It's their last chance to take my offer."

Olga laughed. "Amorcito, you can tell them that if you want, but I know you better. You want that office building bad."

"I do. It's beautiful. Good income. Fully rented. The fools, they are so difficult."

"Let me know if the deal goes through. I'll come and arrange payment."

"Si, Amor, I can wait for you if it happens. If not, I'm going to New York."

"Any word from Mason?"

"Yes, the person disappeared from the face of earth."

Pasadena June 30, 1990
Mario

Lunch at my office with Mason. We were discussing how strange it was that the detectives from LAPD that had come to the house had never called me again. Neither had they made any attempt to see Mason.

"She's an agent, probably federal. They would have asked local to back off investigating because they had it now."

"Sounds too simple," I said. "I hope she makes it. She's the most beautiful federal agent in the world."

"You agree she's a cop, then?"

"I don't agree. I was just saying."

"I am profiling six neighbors on your side of the street, nine across the street, and if I don't get anything interesting from that bunch, I'll start west of Pixie's house. She had four neighbors on her side, seven across the street from her," Mason said.

"I'm dizzy just listening. Do you really think it's a neighbor?"

"It's a shot."

"Mason, I like you. It doesn't matter how much Olga is paying you, but just out of curiosity, what is this costing her?"

"A bundle. I have fourteen people working with me on this, and four working twelve hours shifts following you around and sitting by the house and your office."

"That doesn't tell me how much."

Mason was quickly becoming my friend, though I'm not sure he felt the same way. It had taken a while for me to pick up on it, but now I was certain he belonged lock, stock, and barrel to Olga and Camila.

"A bundle, that's what it's costing her. Ask her."

I laughed. "I'm asking you."

"A bundle. What's for dessert?"

"Cookies and milk," I said.

I rang Letty in her office. She brought a quart of milk from the breakroom fridge, and the tin of pastries and cookies she'd brought from home when we came in this morning. Mason snagged two paper cups from the water cooler and went wild over Letty's oatmeal-peanut-butter-raisin cookies.

Before he left, I asked if he learned anything from the photographs that he'd collected in Mexico City.

"The so-called loan shark was a hoodlum, a bastard who didn't mind killing someone over an unpaid debt. He was also the go-to person if you had a dirty job that needed doing. He wasn't at the top of the food chain. Someone went to him to shoot you up, and the shark sent Perez."

"When you finish putting the puzzle together, please let me know."

I patted his back and walked him to the elevator. We shook hands, and he was gone.

I dialed Olga. Four rings later, "Baby, it's me."

"Amorcito, I called you earlier. Tangles said you were lunching with Mason."

"I haven't seen Tangles. Didn't know you called. How much you paying Mason for all this work he's doing, and is it worth it?"

"Amor, don't worry about how much I'm paying him. Yes, it's worth it. I trust him. Camila trusts him. He'll find whoever is responsible for the grief you have been put through."

"Baby, I can pay Mason, no matter how much."

"Must we discuss this again? Let's talk about something else. Do you miss me?"

Ten minutes after I was off the phone, Tangles passed me in the hall. I could tell she was on the way somewhere by the way she kept looking at her watch.

"Boss, Olga called when you were at lunch. Want me to get her on phone?"

"Thanks, baby. I talked to her."

Letty joined us.

"How was your lunch?" I asked.

"I didn't do lunch. I've been on phone talking to Carlos," Letty said. "He's in plane acquisitions with an Asian operator."

"You picking up on the business, huh?"

"Andrea is a bitchin' teacher. I want to make the commission on this deal. He's looking to lease three 737s, new."

"Andrea must trust you to put you on that big a deal," I smiled at my pal.

"Hey, Boss, I'm good at whatever I go after. Just watch."

"I'm a believer. What's Tangles doing?"

"She was going out to lunch with a lawyer from the firm down on eighteen. Dude is named Dario Gonzales. Mexican guy. Too old for her, but she digs lunch dates."

"Okay, get to work, and let me get some stuff done. Then we can discuss dinner plans, yes?"

I got a thumbs up.

"And get something to eat to tide you over," I said as she walked out the door.

"I had a cookie and a glass of milk when I brought them in to you and Mason," she said. "I'm good but thank you for thinking of me."

The way she smiled, I was almost blinded for a second, but then Andrea waltzed in, and I shifted seamlessly into work mode. Andrea was in and out of my office at least twenty times a day for one thing or another, never for too long.

"How much consortium money are we using?" I asked.

"About a hundred twenty," she said. "I can get the exact number."

"That's okay. All I needed is a ballpark figure." One hundred twenty million. Riana's father had encouraged me to keep partnering as many leases with them as possible. I purposely kept the partnering low as possible as long as Camila didn't complain about how much money I was using from her funds. Without partnering, the returns to GAL were astonishingly fantastic. I kept thinking of the income generated from a plane lease like an rent from apartment building. It's not a good comparison, but for years I had invested in apartments. From the apartments I had, the rental income was a lot of money. The less I owed on each building, the more of the rental income I kept. It is the same as a plane lease. Without the consortium as a partner, the return on the investment was entirely GAL's.

My intent had been to take the girls out to dinner, but we ended up at home.

"We got it all right here, Boss," Letty said. "Want to eat in the disco, or how about the wine room?" We ended up in the bar on the entry level near the kitchen. I showered and put on shorts and t-shirt as though we would eat out by the pool. It was a hot night. We sat at a round table near the granite bar with its fancy modern stools and the Wurlitzer juke box, which was off. We ate hamburgers, hot dogs, French fries and onion rings, all homemade. We had cokes instead of wine and no pot.

"Dario says that if you use Trojans when you have sex that you can't get AIDS," Tangles said.

"I've heard that, too," Letty said. "But they don't stop pregnancy one hundred percent, so why think it would stop AIDS one hundred percent? Sounds like a guy talking somebody into sex. Anyway, who knows for sure? Remember, first they said only gay men got it. Now it's anybody."

"Trojans. You mean condoms?" I asked. "That's who makes them," I said. "They are condoms."

"If Dario is right, we should buy stock in Trojan," Tangles said.

"Not a bad idea," I said.

"Dario wants to ball Tangles," Letty said, rolling her eyes at both of us. "You never heard a guy use a line before?"

"He does want to," Tangles admitted.

"Is that why you had a condom conversation during your lunch date?" I asked.

"It wasn't a date. Boss, it was lunch."

"It was a date," Letty said, still making faces at us as she bit into her hamburger. She looked over her burger, watching Tangles as she put on a pair of latex gloves before picking up her burger.

It was not the first time. She took a bite, put the burger down and meticulously wiped her lips.

Letty had stopped chewing and was just watching.

"What?" Tangles said defensively. "It's messy. I don't like food on my hands. I get this icky feeling, and I can't eat right. I don't like meat juice on my hands. So what?"

"Hon," Letty patted Tangles on the arm with fingers damp from her juicy burger. "I've seen you put a whole lot juicier things than that burger in that mouth of yours."

Pasadena July 30, 1990

Letty had closed the first lease she'd done entirely on her own, and we were celebrating. Tangles was on a Friday night date with Dario, and Andrea and her fiancée had other plans, so it was just Letty and me eating at Yamashiro's. The restaurant is just high enough above Hollywood to provide a view all the way to downtown. Letty was so happy that her smile lit a path from Yamashiro's to the Capitol Records Building to Beverly Hills and all the way to the Venice Beach boardwalk.

The waitress brought us crab cakes and avocado sashimi for our starters.

"Boss, I told the Chinaman that I'd do anything if he would just close the deal already, so we could order the planes. I may have to fuck him if he shows up."

"How do you know he's Chinese?"

"His last name is Wong. I'm pretty sure he's not Scandinavian. What else could he be, Boss?"

"Well, you can worry about it if he visits LA."

"I can do it with Trojans like Tangles."

We were sitting side by side to enjoy the view and the ambiance of the candlelit tables and the colored lights in the landscaping. When they brought us our Wagyu steaks, it was like cutting butter. Every bite was melt-in-your-mouth delicious, but I wondered what Miguel would be able to do with Wagyu if he could get his hands on it. Everywhere lazy fans circulated the slight breeze, maybe from the Pacific Ocean although that was twenty-five miles away. I put my arm around Letty.

"Letty, you got to get a life outside of me. It's unfair that I continue to gulp up your best years."

"Oh, stop it," she said. "We're here to celebrate. I love my life just as it is. You aren't stopping me from stepping out. No reason to feel guilty, if that's what you are saying."

She lifted her glass of wine.

"Salud, Mario."

I gave her a light peck on the lips. "Salud, Letty."

I felt stone cold sober after the two cups of black coffee I had with the house Crème Brûlée which was almost as good as Miguel's. (He puts a little peanut butter in his.) I drove us home.

"I can give you head while you drive," Letty said.

"You don't want us to crash, do you?"

Letty laughed, and didn't pay any attention to my cautions.

I had enough trouble staying on the road that I had to pull over.

"I feel so good. Thank you, Boss."

"That's what I should be saying," I said. "What happened to Mario?"

"Oh, Boss, you'll always be Boss. It's just who you are. I love it."

At home, we got in the steam, chilled in the cold jacuzzi, showered and went to bed.

"Can we just cuddle?"

I reached for her. She spooned herself against me. It's a good thing the air conditioning was set so high that the sheets were like ice. Where our skin touched, heat bloomed. She felt like home.

"How's that?" I asked. The blackout curtains were pulled shut. We were embraced by the dark. It made our little nest cozier.

"I love it, Boss."

We had just gotten into the perfect position, and she pulled away.

"What is it?" I asked.

"I'm sorry I didn't do the candle thing. I'll fix that now."

I pulled her to bed.

"Dark is good," I said, squeezing her close. I drifted off to sleep with the scent of her shampoo in my nose. At least I think I fell asleep.

My phone rang. The only line that rang through to my bedroom was my private line. I untangled myself from Letty who stirred just a little. I was a little disoriented in the complete darkness and fumbled for the phone. I managed a clumsy grab while still lying flat on my back. I didn't bother opening my eyes.

"Hello?"

"Mario, it's Lola."

I snapped out of sleep as though I was under attack. I sat up, flicked on the light.

"Lola, is it really you? I'm so pleased you're not dead."

I heard Letty say "Lola?" in a sleepy voice.

"Yes, it's me."

"You sound good. Are you well?"

"I'm getting there. I can't talk right now. I'm okay. Much to explain later."

"When will you call me? Where are you?"

"Later, Mario. I have to go. Just letting you know I have a heartbeat."

I dialed Mason immediately. I woke him up. It took a few minutes for his brain to check in to the conversation.

"Lola called me." I told him what she told me.

"Strange," Mason said.

"That's all you have to say?"

"Let me digest this. I'll see you tomorrow."

What was running through my mind? A one-sided conversation with the missing Lola. Lola, who are you? Where are you? Why did you call me?

I didn't call Olga or Camila. Mason would be taking care that right away. I turned off the lamp and got under the covers where Letty was keeping the bed warm.

I pulled Letty to me.

"I can't believe she called you," Letty said. "I thought she didn't make it. They took her from the hospital at the end of May."

"I think Mason is right. It's strange."

Letty yawned, "I'm not sleepy anymore. Want me to do things to your… master of ceremonies?"

Her hand was communing very effectively with the aforementioned 'master of ceremonies.'

"You scoundrel," Letty said. "Lola calls for sixty seconds, and you're hard enough to saw wood."

"Baby, not true. I've wanted you since we were at the restaurant."

She guided me in, and I proceeded to prove myself a man of my word.

Mexico City July 31, 1990
Olga

"*Hermanita*, we should have let the woman alone and watched her more closely. There is nothing at Mario's or inside Mario's head that can hurt us. If only we could do it all over again."

I expected an argument from Camila.

"*Amor*, she's an agent. Mason has never been wrong before. I agree that what happened to her was too much, but only because it did not succeed. I may have made matters worse."

"It's done," I said. "We will weather it. Why would she call him?"

"They want to send her in."

I laughed. "*Hermanita*, you have it all figured out."

"I lost two good men over the *puta*. I acted too quickly."

"What's done is done," I said. "What now?"

"We wait. If she returns, let's see what your man does."

"He called Mason and let him know she called," I said.

"Yes, he did."

"I want him to look at her as a possible enemy. He can be such a fool," I said.

"Not a possible enemy. An actual enemy. It was the way he scoffed off the warning from Mason that pushed me to extinguish her."

"*Hermanita*, we're on the phone."

"Cell phones are safe."

I said, "I hope it doesn't come back to bite us in the *culo.*"

In the morning I was in Mexico City. Before my meeting, I called him.

"Amor, are you okay?"

"Baby, I'm okay. And you?"

"Wondering why you didn't call me after you got that call last night."

"I figured Mason would bring you up to date."

"What a cold answer. Amor, are you okay?"

He laughed. I pictured his beautiful face and teeth.

"Not cold, baby. I'm sitting at my desk. You have my undivided attention."

"So early?"

"I get here early when I can. Business is good, baby."

"Amor, jump in your plane. Come see me. A late lunch, an afternoon *Cojida*[31] that I need so bad, Amor. Please don't say no."

"Start the clock. Figure six hours."

"Amor, *Si*, we have dinner, then we spend the night *Cojiendo, Si...*"

"*Si*," he replied. "Olga, I love you."

---

[31] Fuck

Chapter 14
Pasadena August 21, 1990
Mario

At eight in the morning, I was on my usual route to work making my way along quiet residential streets towards the Pasadena Freeway. It was so quiet here, it almost seemed deserted. I caught some action in my rear-view mirror. A block behind me, two unmarked cars with red lights stopped a familiar car. I was sure it belonged to Mason's man who followed me around. A car pulled out of a side street and pulled in front of me, and I came to an abrupt stop. It was a good thing I wasn't going fast, and that the street were empty of traffic at this time of the morning.

Before my brain processed why a car had stopped broadside in front of me, a woman in a silky-looking shirt and black slacks stepped out of the car, and stood in my way, unmoving. It felt like slow motion. The sun was behind me. I had a perfect view. I blinked and took my sunglasses off to make sure.

It was Lola.

I left my car running. Got out. Walked towards her.

"Mario, follow me," she said, raising her hand in a greeting.

"It's okay. I'm not going to bite you." She flashed her great smile.

I looked toward my car. A slow station wagon hesitated behind my car for maybe thirty seconds, then pulled around it. Two minutes after I started following Lola on foot, my cell rang.

I reached the sidewalk and answered it.

"Hello Mario," Lola said on the phone. She was ahead of me on the same sidewalk, a good twenty feet away, but had stopped walking. Weird to be talking to her this way.

"You're a cop," I said. I headed in her direction fast.

"Long story. Let's go have coffee. We can talk."

"Drive to the Ambassador. Big parking lot or valet, either way, your car will be lost there."

"Lead the way," she said.

I accelerated and walked past her, crossed the street and headed back to my car.

"I'm surprised you didn't have the meeting place planned," I said.

"Oh, I did have it planned. We can do it your way. How and where is not important. It's just us."

I sprinted to my car, still sitting in the middle of the street.

As I pulled into valet parking, my phone rang. Lola again.

"I'll meet you in the coffee shop," she said.

The restaurant was packed with people eating breakfast. The air smelled of pancakes, coffee and bacon. I had stayed at the hotel so often that the hotel staff knew me. I pointed toward the corner. Host Patsy gave me a menu and the inconspicuous corner booth I wanted. Waitress Jan poured me coffee. Lola sat down across from me. Jan filled her cup and left a second menu.

"You look great," I said. Nothing in her face and demeaner revealed she had recently been knocking at death's door and in a coma.

"You look great as well."

She reached across the table and took my hand.

"I'm sorry I ambushed you on your drive to work."

"Not only me," I said.

"Your boy wonder that follows you around is safe."

"He's not my boy wonder. If you've done your homework, you should know."

"One of Mason's men saved my life and got shot in the process. I'm trying to figure a way to pay him back," Lola said. "I owe him big time."

"You were in a coma. How would you know he saved your life?"

"I know everything."

"Want do you want from me?"

"Your body for starters, and your cooperation."

I drank my coffee and picked up a spoon. I rolled the spoon between my fingers.

"Cooperation?"

"Your fiancée is dirty, and so is Camila. One or both ordered me killed."

"You been watching too many movies, Lola."

"I like movies," she said. "You and I, we watched Scarface during a fuck break, remember?"

"I liked you better between the sheets. I don't know Lola the cop. Or is she Nina? When you called me, I was the happiest guy on earth. I am pleased you are not dead."

"Want to see the scars?" she asked.

Her tone was a little sharp. Maybe she was angry. Then again, maybe I was imagining it.

"Want to see mine? I've been there. Bullets hurt. Hospitals suck. I know."

"Mario, your woman is a drug trafficker, and you can help us."

"She is not a drug anything," I said, with some anger of my own. I shook my hand free of hers. "If she is, prove it. You said you know everything. Why do you need me?"

"Because she's slick."

"You pretended to be a prostitute. Took my money for sex, time and time again. All you wanted was to get information on Olga."

Lola laughed, reached across the table for my hand again, but I kept it in my lap.

"It was fun. I always wanted to get paid for sex."

"You did well," I said. "You should take it up professionally."

"I knew you wouldn't lead us to anything. I kept telling my boss a different story. I wanted to be around you. It had nothing to do with the case."

"How could you be a cop and do everything we did?"

"You made it easy. Here's the problem: if your woman had not had me shot, I would have been pulled away, and that would have been the end of it. Now, it's a different story. I'm not back officially yet. I told my boss I want to convince you that helping us would be your best move. Get her and her stepsister out of the way. You would control the empire. Get us the assets we can't latch on to."

"Lola, I'm not interested. You blew your cover. Go away. Come back when you retire."

Jan returned to the table and poured more coffee.

"Are you ordering anything, Mr. Luna?"

"No, just coffee," I said.

"I want to order if that's okay," Lola said.

I couldn't believe the performance going on. Was I being taped by a hidden microphone? How many cops were in place in this diner?

Mason was right, she was a cop and I hadn't listened. I had shined it on. It was my fault. I had put Olga and Camila at risk. Put us all at risk.

Jan took her order and left.

"You are not involved in the business," Lola said. "Nothing in your Casa Luna was part of what Olga is involved in. I can't say the same about the house where Pixie lives. Olga and Camila are dirty, dirty like Pepe Camacho was and his father before him. Their legitimate empire is one they've built with dirty money coming from a genius money laundering scheme that we have never seen before."

"Lola, you said you know everything."

"If she goes down, and there is even a hint that you have knowledge, it could be a life sentence. Think about that Mario. This is RICO. Very serious."

"Did your Boss tell you to tell me all that?"

"She did. I told her you wouldn't turn on them because you've never seen them do a blessed thing, and you think they're fucking angels."

"So why come back?"

"I wanted to see you."

I stared at my coffee. "I should get up and leave," I said.

Jan brought her a waffle, and a side order of bacon, and put a white ceramic dish of syrup at the corner of Lola's plate.

Lola didn't try to take my hand again, just looked at me with her beautiful eyes, eyes so deep a man could swim in them.

"Don't leave, Mario. Keep me company while I eat. I get it. You aren't going to help us. Fine. She—they—ordered a hit on me. Why should you care that I almost died? It's a miracle I am here today."

"Of course, I care. Of course, I'm glad you made it. Quit trying to mindgame me into whatever you want me to do. I'm sorry you got shot, but they had nothing to do with what happened to you."

She cut off a corner of her waffle, speared it, and dipped it into the white dish.

"Maple," she said. "Try it?" She held out the bit of waffle, syrup and butter dripping on to her plate. Her temperature changed, and the bite was not about breakfast. It was about sex.

I shook my head. If it had been truly Lola, I would have been tempted. But this was Nina, the cop who was after my fiancée.

The bite disappeared into her mouth.

"I'd rather see them fry for their drug business than attempted murder," she said.

I got up, looked down at her.

She looked up at me, right hand holding her empty fork. She sliced off another piece of waffle. This time she didn't dip.

"It doesn't really need syrup," she said. "Want to know who burned your house? Sit down and I'll tell you."

I was motionless long enough to see her the fork deliver another piece of waffle to her mouth.

I sat down.

"How can you know something like that?"

I wondered if cops were listening to this conversation.

"I should bargain with you, but here it is. The first time it burned, Pepe Camacho was behind it. He was jealous of you getting close to his sister and Olga. He didn't want to kill you, simply wanted to give you a bad time. He groomed you to become his acquisition. You were more valuable to him alive then dead."

"How would you know this?"

"Do I really have to tell you?"

"I don't even know why you're telling me this. Pepe is dead, not around to defend himself, doesn't make sense. He couldn't have been jealous. No way."

"Okay, don't believe it."

Jan arrived and I let her put a fresh cup in front of me. She poured. Jan got a fresh cup for Lola, filled it, then we were alone again. It was like intermission, and I needed an intermission because my mind wasn't computing. Facts seemed to be in conflict from what I knew.

"Officially I'm not back. It might be another month or two before I am. Doctors won't release me yet. You have some time to think about helping me nail those bad people."

She stopped eating. We were looking at each other. She looked the same. She was still the same beautiful, classy looking prostitute who fucked my brains out, only she really was a cop. Her hair was straight, pulled into a low pony tail, businesslike. Light makeup. Had she always worn light makeup? I couldn't recall. She was as beautiful as she'd ever been.

"Tell me how you know about the house, and what else you know."

"Never. Not unless you work with us. You work with us, maybe I'll tell you. If you're not working with us, then I'll get up and walk out the door, and you will never see me again," she said, nodding her head.

She took out a pen and unfolded a paper napkin from the table. She wrote on it: *Too many people listening. I will call you.*

"I will be in touch," she mouthed, a finger to her lips. She bunched up the napkin and touched it too her lips.

"The answer will be the same, Lola. Or whatever your real name is."

She finished her coffee, looked down at her half empty plate, and smiled at me. She pocketed the napkin, and without another word, got up and walked away.

I watched her leave. I stayed seated. I waved Jan over and gave her a twenty. Told her to keep the change. I took my cell out and called Mason.

"I think your man got detained this morning?"

"He said he looked ahead and noticed you were also stopped. Where are you?"

"Going home. See you there."

I stood there waiting for valet to get my car. I was running on autopilot, but my brain was racing. I tipped the attendant and drove home in a fog. I know I did those things because I made it home in one piece. Meanwhile, my mind was prancing around, wildly. Pepe's face played hide and seek in my brain, laughing at me, making fun of me. Had the fucker actually burned my house?

Pasadena August 21, 1990
Letty

When he came home and brushed me off, I knew something was wrong.

"Mason is on his way. Send him up when he gets here. I'm getting out of this suit."

He ran up the stairs from the second floor where we were. Tangles and

I exchanged looks. Sure enough, a few minutes later, the guard called that Mason was waiting to see Mario. Tangles took him up the elevator. I followed a few minutes later with a tray, two coffee cups, a pot of coffee, cream, sugar, and two baskets of pastries—one for savory, one for sweet.

I walked in the office just a minute before Mario. I poured coffee for them and walked out. Tangles was by the staircase waiting for me. She looked as curious as I felt.

"I'd like to be a bug on the wall in there," Tangles said.

"You snoop," I said with a laugh, knowing I wanted to be a bug, too.

"He'll tell us," Tangles said as we walked down three levels to the game room.

"Yes," I agreed. "Pinball or Pacman?"

"Both," Tangles said, and started explaining which was her favorite and why. Tangles was talking away, but I was paying no attention. I was too busy trying to figure out what could have happened between the time he left this morning, and when he came back an hour later.

Mason's visit was extremely short. For once, the game room juke was off, and no movie was playing. With the door open, we heard Mario leave Mason at the front door. You can't normally hear, but Tangles and I took turns eavesdropping on the front door from the best listening spot under the stairs.

Mason said, "Have a safe trip."

Tangles shot me her what-the-fuck look.

A trip? Where-the-fuck was he going?

We ran up the stairs. No knock, we never knocked, just walked in. He was on the phone. He pointed to the Queen Melina wingback chairs across from his desk. (They're queen somebody, but it was Melina who picked them out.) I sat in one, crossed my legs, copycat crossed hers. It's not like he could see anything with that huge desk between us. I playacted being prim and attentive because that could always make him laugh, but I was playing to an empty room. He was wrapped up in the phone call. He looked so serious I got worried.

I cooled it and just listened as he talked to Olga.

"It's important we meet, the three of us."

I couldn't hear what she was saying, but I am sure it was yes.

"I'll fly wherever."

He looked at me, then he looked over to Tangles.

"Milan is good. Yes, I'll leave tonight or late this afternoon. Will let you know."

He listened while she said something.

"I love you, Olga."

When he hung up, he raised a finger like a motion to wait. He dialed, and a minute later, he was talking to Andrea about prepping the company DC-9. He put his palm over the mouthpiece.

"You can go to Milan with me, but no questions about why I'm going or anything else." He looked from me to Tangles. "You can hang around with Riana. I'm sure she's going to be with Olga."

I reached over his desk and gave him a high five, and so did Tangles.

"Andrea, add Letty and Tangles to the manifest."

He was serious, but not upset. It only made me wonder more. I wondered if Mason had found something out, or if there had been something Boss discovered this morning.

In a couple of hours, we were on the way to Ontario Airport with Pixie's driver Raul at the wheel of Pixie's limousine. As usual, she was away on tour. I had packed one suitcase for him. Tangles and I had one suitcase each. Ours were a little larger than his.

"You don't look pissed, sad or bothered," I said to Boss.

He gave me that smile, nudged me, then nudged Tangles who was showing teeth.

"Here's what I'll tell you. Mason was right. Lola is a cop. Not sure what agency. Probably a Fed. It doesn't matter as I have got nothing to hide. More later."

I was surprised, not about Nina/Lola since we had already talked about that. I was surprised that he told us so suddenly, without any argument, begging or wheedling from us. I guess it was sympathy from him because the curiosity was eating us alive.

Tangles put her hand right on his thing. I saw her squeeze.

"It's okay, Boss. We'll help you weather the storm, whatever it is."

There was the smile again. He is such a big guy. Sitting between us, he looked like a giant, even in the cushy leather softness of the Rolls seat. My hand went there too, rested on top of Tangles' hand.

"Yeah, Boss, we got you covered. Whatever it is, we've been through worse. At least you don't look heartbroken."

"Not heartbroken," he said in a low, thoughtful voice.

For the rest of the thirty-minute drive, none of us said a word.

Milan August 23, 1990
Olga

Camila was in Rome. She beat me to Milan by a few hours. Riana and I were in Paris. It took almost two hours to take off from the congested airport.

After the hugs and kisses, Riana went to her room to shower. Camila and I met in the study. She handed me a fax from Mason and watched as I read the short, handwritten note that came through quite faded on thermal paper.

"I told Mario that I would not give you a heads-up on the phone. He says not to trust cells. As far as I know, Lola surfaced and forced a meeting this morning. He will explain. She told him she's what I've said she was all along."

I looked up. "I'm not a bit surprised," I said.

"Two men tried to kill that whore and failed," Camila said angrily.

"She can look as deep as she wants. Mario is clean. LAI is clean. The leasing company is clean."

It was like when you tell someone drive carefully. Meaningless words of comfort. I was telling Camila what she already knew.

Mario arrived with the girls. They took off for the rooms they always occupied. That left the three of us in the study. We sat at the large conference table.

I handed him the fax from Mason. He glanced at it and pushed the note to me.

"We know, Amor," I said.

"I wish he would not take chances with phones or anything else. Lola seems to know everything."

"Tell us," Camila said.

Milan August 23, 1990
Mario

Olga has been around me and the girls so long, she said, "It's like right out of a movie."

Camila laughed. Olga laughed too. I didn't laugh.

Olga said, "No doubt she's part of a task force."

"That's how they got Pepe," Olga said. "When he was jailed in the US for a year, it was task force with agents from the FBI, Customs, ATF and several local agencies that built the case against him."

"My guess Nina is FBI," Olga said.

"Does this bother you two at all?" I asked.

"Certainly, Amor," Camila said, "but we have nothing to hide that this lady cop can use against us."

The truth is, I really don't know anything solid. I know only that sometimes Olga's plane may be carrying something, and that even she doesn't know what it is.

The silence in the room stretched out for minutes. Olga and Camila exchanged looks I could not read.

Camila said, "Amor, there are no drugs."

I shrugged. "I never thought there was."

"You are such a liar, Amor," Olga said.

"Amor, we deal in money," Camila said. "Cocaine went out when my father died. There were times when Pepe got involved in something big, but he always kept us out of it."

I raised my hand and got up.

"You don't need to say any more. You are family to me. I believe you. The problem is not me. It's this Lola and whoever she is working with."

"Amor, sit down, please," Olga said. "Before you got here, we decided to tell you. You can stop worrying that my plane ever carried coke."

I sat down.

"I'm listening," I said.

This is what I learned: Olga was a money launderer for five major drug cartels. These mob guys knew how to make millions and millions of dollars from cocaine production, but nothing about putting the money in banks where they could use it. The deal was that Pepe had agreed to stay out of the cocaine business that his father had left him. In return for abandoning his massive cocaine business, Pepe agreed to clean the cartels' money. It started in major cities in Colombia, because the Camachos had connections with local banks. After Olga got out of school, she'd flown around making bank connections. The fee to put cash in the bank was a sweet thirty percent. That percentage, plus the money Pepe and Camila's father left behind, enabled the Camachos to amass billions, and found LAI and GAL which were both by now legitimate multi-billion-dollar companies.

I thought of my original deal with Pepe. Early on, he paid me ten percent on all projects I could purchase with green cash. I'd known that Olga made a cut, but not the particulars. I didn't ask. All this time, I had figured it was drugs hidden in the plane. I was just relieved that Olga was not flying around with bundles of coke.

"I feel safe," Olga said. "I always have recent legitimate bank receipts to cover any transactions."

Camila had this great big smile and pretended to clap her hands.

"Worry not, Amor," Camila said.

At the conclusion of our meeting, we agreed not to discuss anything unless we were behind closed doors.

I got out of a long shower, put on sweats and knocked on Olga's bathroom door.

"Why you knocking? Come in, Amor."

She was standing near a mirror, nude, her maid helping her dry off.

"You look comfy," Olga said. "I'll put on the same. Give me two minutes, and we're out of here."

"I'm starved," I said.

"I'm starved, too, Amor, for you and for food."

Her maid showed no sign of understanding, but I knew her. She spoke good English.

When I'd been living here, we used the study as our dining room, but Camila and Olga preferred the big dining room. We sat in the dining room to eat—a big formal room with a huge table and fancy dishes, tall candles in sconces, crystal glassware, and plenty of servants to tend to our every whim.

The girls had gone to their rooms and changed from fancy dresses to sweats, and so did Camila. Once we were settled down, everyone was comfy in sweats in this formal setting. We talked a lot, but it was all about nothing. I was acting as if everything were normal, but I was reeling from my new knowledge. I felt much like Adam must have when Eve gave him the apple.

Ricky brought out prawns, served them formally, and then put the rest in a chafing dish on the buffet. He came out with a vegetable salad, and several meat dishes and at least one pasta dish. The piles of food on my plates grew.

"Boss, don't you like the prawns?" Tangles asked.

I took a big bite and demolished one.

"Delicious," I said. I held out my wine glass and one of the servants filled it. Camila always matched the white wine with fish, red wine with meat, etc. I filled my fork with greens from the salad. Greens made me think of green cash.

I questioned the legality of money laundering. Both Olga and Camila agreed there was risk, but believed the risk was tiny compared to the risk of being a drug lord. I didn't agree with their reasoning, but at least when Olga's plane was loaded, it was full of money, not cocaine. It was not that big of a relief. Money laundering for cartels—they weren't flying around with puppies.

"These stuffed potatoes are great," Letty said. "I have to get the recipe to give to Miguel." I noticed she had passed on the pasta.

Camila said something about the chef being very protective about his recipes.

"Trust me," Olga said, assuring Letty. "I'll get him to talk."

I looked from my plate to Olga.

Olga must be a genius to be able to track the money from each person she was moving money for, banking it under beneficiary names that the money owner requested. The thirty percent that was Camacho money either stayed in cash, was turned into assets, or went to a Camacho account.

I felt a touch on my shoulder, and realized Letty was standing there with a bottle of wine. She was holding it over my now-empty glass. I glanced at the slices of rare roast on my plate.

"Boss, you ok?" she whispered. "You seem preoccupied. I called your name three times. Did you want some of this?" She turned the bottle and showed me the label. "It's that Argentine red you like so much."

I saw the concern on Letty's face. Olga, Riana and Camila were deep in a discussion about something, and not even looking my way. Letty's worry was more than just about wine. I wondered what part of the dinner conversation I'd missed, consented to the glass, and tried to focus on the conversation. From that moment on, I talked too much about nothing, ate way too much food and consumed too much wine.

Maybe they lied, but I don't think they lied. Pepe may not have just been involved in the money laundering, but I could see that he may have even packed the plane Olga flew around in with not just cash but also coke. When Pepe was alive, he had standing orders were that she could never fly to United

States if the voice called her. I didn't know the mechanics of how the plane was loaded or unloaded or where the cash went, exactly. I was fucking curious as all hell, but I would never ask her.

In the morning, Olga and I joined Camila in her master bedroom. Breakfast was served on the balcony. Simple, really, just strong coffee, good Italian bread and butter.

"There is something I didn't tell you," I said bluntly. "This is the reason I came here: Lola said that Pepe had ordered my house torched."

Camila exhaled like she'd been punched in the solar plexus.

"She is out of her mind," Camila said.

"I told her as much," I said. "She said that Pepe was jealous that I had become important to you two."

Both of them started talking at once. I raised my hand so I could finish. "I told her no way and asked where she came up with that idea. She didn't say how, just that she knows everything. I thought of telephones, like the movies. So easy to tap. Mason checked my entire house for bugs, you know this. He found nothing. Did he check your house? Did he check Pepe's?"

"How long has this she been nosing around?" Olga asked. Two spots of bright color appeared on her cheeks.

"She never said how long. My house was torched the first time years ago. I'm sorry I didn't tell you during our meeting last night. I didn't think of it. Last night, I felt guilty about it. You were so open with me. I should have told you. I am embarrassed now to tell you this."

Olga said. "It's fine, Amor. We know Pepe was no angel, but why would he burn your house? And what about the other fire and all the other things?"

"I don't know. She dropped this bomb and left in a hurry."

"I don't believe it," Camila said.

"It's done. It's over. I've moved on," I said, though when I looked her in the face, I thought she did believe it. She, more than anyone else, knew how he schemed. "Doesn't even matter. I've always worried about others getting hurt by being around me. There was the biker, Luca Rossi."

"And the bastard that hit your car with a truck when I was on my way to the airport," Olga said.

"They were after me, remember? My PI Tricia was driving, and heard them swearing because I wasn't in the car. They were after me, not you." If Pepe had been in charge of that, he must have been furious that Olga had been hurt in that accident at my gates.

It's a long flight from Milan to Pasadena. On the way home, I told Letty and Tangles about Lola and what she had revealed. I trust them without reservation and don't like to keep secrets from them. I felt sure that Olga would tell Riana about Lola. But I only told them about Lola. Olga's secrets are her own. I did not share that Olga was a laundromat for at least five big cartels, or that what was left of the Camacho family made a neat three hundred thousand plus on every million they placed. Years ago, Olga told me that Camila's father had left warehouses and houses filled with cash in all the countries he did business in. She'd told me then that her job was to turn that money into assets or put it in banks. I'd never felt that was the whole story. The dates of the money she handed over to me did not support what she'd said, but maybe it was partly true. What was fascinating to me was that Olga was a stone, unafraid. The thought of her made we want her right there and then, but I was on a plane headed home. The girls were asleep beside me in the dark cabin on my big bed.

Pasadena September 1990

For the next two weeks after I got home, I met with Mason five times. He pumped me about Lola. He wanted to know everything between us from the start, stuff he already knew, a great deal about sex between us, and especially about the meeting at the hotel restaurant. I cooperated.

I believed that Mason was using his knowledge of the human psyche to figure out Lola.

"If I could sit with her for a number of visits, I could figure here out, but obviously I can't do that. You can help me. It's important we know how she feels about this job she's on. It's interesting she said that she owes my man big time for saving her life. That tells me something. It could be she wants out of the job she's doing. With you, Lola escapes from her job. When you two are having sex, that's an escape. She could not do what she does with you as part of her job."

I laughed. "Mason, I've been saying that from the start."

"What you said back then is that she couldn't possibly be a cop, and do the things she did to you, and let you do the things you did to her."

"Mason, it's the same thing."

We couldn't agree that we were saying the same thing.

I got home from the office, and Olga called from Budapest.

"We should think about getting married," I said. It wasn't something I planned to say. It had just come out of my mouth on its own.

"Amorcito, what made you tell me this today?"

"I'm in love with you," I said feeling like a high school kid who was talking to his girl on the phone.

"I adore you, Amor."

I looked up and there was Letty.

"I wasn't being nosey. I just came in to tell you dinner was ready."

I saw her eyes were moist.

I opened my arms. "Come sit on my lap," I said. I hugged her. It took a minute and she hugged me back. "I love you, Letty. Our relationship is so strange. I wish I could understand it."

"Boss, I recognize the love you have for her." She sighed with a teary little hiccup. "I love you." She kissed me. "Darn. I don't want to cry."

I felt my eyes burn. A tear of mine ran down her cheek as she pressed against me. And then there was another kiss with tears slowly falling between us. I was lost in space and didn't try to figure it out. A big guy like me, still not sure where I get being as emotional as I sometimes get. Eventually I got up with her hanging on my neck. She giggled and stood on the couch to mount herself piggy-back. I ran with her all the way to the wine room where Tangles was fixing our table for dinner.

"Hey, not fair," Tangles said. "I want a ride too."

Pasadena September 14, 1990

Friday, I had been in the office for an hour when my secretary, Alicia, called me on the intercom.

"Boss, a lady named Nina is at reception. She says you know her by her nickname Lola. She is not giving a last name."

I felt like someone threw a punch at me. I turned in my chair to face the door.

"Show her in, and hold all my calls no matter who it is."

She walked in. Alicia closed the door behind her, leaving us alone.

"Nina, what a surprise. Every morning I keep expecting you to drive up from a side street and ambush me."

I knew enough about women's clothes to know the suit she had on had not come from JC Penny. Lola was a snake, but she was a well-dressed snake.

"You thought I was dead, and then I blocked the intersection and walk toward your car. Exciting, no?"

"You called me before that, so I knew you weren't dead."

"Got your attention, didn't I? And you got your meeting."

"You've been here sixty seconds and picking a fight already."

"Not picking a fight. I'm on medical leave. Are you going to ask me to sit down or what?"

I pointed at one of two chairs across from me.

"No kiss, no hug, nothing?"

"I don't have any cash on me."

"Being your whore was fun. I did love it."

"You weren't my whore," I said, annoyed.

"I was your whore. You paid me every time."

"Is this official? Are we broadcasting today?"

"I'm off duty," she said. "No wires. I'm flying without a net."

"Is this what you came over for?"

"Temper, temper. I'm the one who should be pissed. I almost died."

"Cops have enemies. Anyone could have come after you."

"Wake up, Mario. It was Camila."

"Oh, the last time we met it was Olga."

"Camila ordered the hit at the hospital. Not sure who ordered the hit at my car. I came to take you to lunch at the Hilton. It's walking distance, right?"

I vividly remembered the afternoon when I met her at the Hilton. I had walked because I didn't want Mason's guys to see me. I thought she had taken a taxi, but she drove herself and parked on Wilshire Boulevard and walked two blocks to the hotel. Mason told me this after she got shot that night when she was returning to her car.

"I know what you are thinking," she said, staring at me.

"Yes, you know everything."

"You're thinking of the night you fucked me for three hours at the Hilton."

It's possible I blushed. I felt my face get hot.

"Nina, Lola, what do you want from me?"

"Today, just lunch. No one is listening to us. I'm not on duty and, who knows, I may never go back."

Her words made me think of Mason and what he had said.

"It's not even eleven. Too early for lunch."

"We can eat after."

"After what?"

"After we do it for at least three hours."

What does a mocking smile look like? "Stop trying to bait me, Lola."

"I'm not baiting you. I'm here to take you to lunch."

"I don't want to be rude, but I have a busy day."

"Pretend I'm just a cutie that you picked up. Pretend I'm Lola, sex for money. Fuck me and pay me. More fun that way. I loved being your whore."

"Stop saying that. You were not my whore." I got up.

She remained seated.

"You are one tall mother," she said, tilting her head up to look at me, a smile on her face.

"Are you wired?" I asked.

She laughed. "Wired. Where'd you learn that word?"

"You're being a wise ass," I said.

"I'm having fun. I think I'm getting you pissed."

"I'm not having fun," I said.

"You want fun?" she asked. She kicked off her shoes. They were heels, not the scarlet stilettos Tangles might wear, but simple high-heeled sandals that probably cost her two weeks of a federal worker's salary.

She got up and started unbuttoning her suit jacket.

"What are you doing?"

"I want to show you I'm not wired."

I stood there and watched. She probably expected I would tell her to stop, but I didn't. Her bosses down at the federal building should see her now. She wore no bra or panties, and stood on my cold marble floor, her bare feet making her look somehow vulnerable. She stripped down to her skin, and pretty skin it was too except for the ugly marks left by bullets. Her shape was as lovely as ever, but the surgeries had left angry red scars like zippers burned into her creamy skin. The damage reminded me poignantly of the scarring left on Melina's abdomen from the attempt on her life. I couldn't help it. I felt terrible. Her bikini days were over. Then again, maybe not—maybe lady feds were different from other ladies. I knew nothing about her. She might think the scars are trophies. I have scars of my own, but they don't bother me.

I kept thinking that if Letty and Tangles had been here, they would have barged in. They were the only ones who did that now that Pixie was off singing, and Niley and Jo were managing my apartments. At least Letty and Tangles were at home today.

Lola stood naked. I figured that was as far as she could go, but she wasn't done. She took a gun out of her purse, and a wallet with her identification, and placed the two items on the chair where she had been sitting. She held the purse upside down, and the contents fell out and scattered on my desk.

"Enough," I said. I was a hypocrite, saying this while looking at her nakedness and she knew it. She had a lean, elegant torso. She was slim enough to seem delicate, though her ribs did not show. I remembered her butt and breasts as being rounder. They had been that way before the coma.

"They haven't invented bugs for pussy, but you are welcome to check. Should I bend over?"

I heard myself say, "Yeah, bend over and spread them."

I'd seen that in a movie more than once, and experienced it myself when as a kid, I checked in to Terminal Island Prison for what I'd thought was going to be a long time.

"You bastard," she laughed. "Tell me you believe me, or I won't get dressed."

"Good, don't get dressed." I said, walking over to her.

I picked her up, walked a few steps to my private conference room where I often had lunch. I locked the door while she was still in my arms.

"What are you doing?"

"Tell me to stop and I will," I said, as I lay her on the table.

When she realized it was going to take some time for me to get out of my suit, she sat up and watched me.

"You can tell me to stop," I said, calmly unbuttoning my shirt. My jacket was already folded over the back of a chair. My pants quickly joined the jacket.

"Hurry," she said.

I climbed on the table, and she got on top of me.

"I don't want to hurt you," I said. She pressed against me.

"Stop talking. I'm fine."

Mason was right about one thing. Like me, she liked sex. She respected no boundaries. I am no better, but I'm not a cop. At least she was off duty.

Fuck it. I enjoyed the moment. And I was sure of one thing. She had no bugs on her.

In the heat of the moment, I stopped and held her down on me. I was deep inside of her.

"Tell me why you said it was Pepe who burned my house."

Lola was breathing rapidly.

"Bastard, don't do this."

I wouldn't let her move. If it had been Letty, she would have climaxed, but Lola needed movement. "Tell me," I said soft as I could. I'm not made of steel. I wanted to move as much as she did.

"I will, I promise."

"When will you tell me?"

"Before I leave. I promise."

I stopped holding her back, cupped her ass, and let her ride again. My fingers went where she liked it. She screamed her release, her hips gyrating wildly, and then slowing and subsiding.

The conference room has two doors, one to my office, the other to my private bathroom, a full bathroom with a big shower.

"You can have the bathroom in five minutes," I said sliding off the table.

She was still breathing heavily. I showered quickly and returned with a towel wrapped around my waist. As she showered, I dressed and collected her clothes. When she came out of the bathroom I was back at my desk, and her clothes were all neatly laid out on the conference table.

My watch said it was almost one. It was hard to believe that the under-cover fed who had lied her way into my life was in my bathroom, and I was pretending to be busy when all I could do is wonder how much longer it would be until she told me what she knew about Pepe.

She came out smiling, her short hair dry and neat as though nothing had happened.

"What a setup. I wish I had a bathroom that fancy at home. If you take me out to eat, I'll tell you what you want to know."

She sat across from me again.

I opened a drawer in my desk and took out a menu from the steakhouse on the first level of the building.

"We can eat where we fucked," I said. "The food is excellent."

"What a mouth," she said, taking the menu.

"I don't know why I said that. Sorry."

"I know you hate me. You aren't sorry."

"I don't hate you." I didn't like how she was playing games. I did not like her saying she had it in for Olga. I had liked her a lot when she had been simply Lola, but there was no point in telling her that.

She looked up and smiled. "You're lying." Her attention returned to the menu. "What's good?"

I dialed the restaurant and ordered steaks, salad, potatoes.

"In thirty minutes, we'll have our food. Plenty of time for you to tell me."

"Can I smoke in here?"

"I didn't know you smoke."

"We smoked lots of weed, you and I."

She walked over to my desk where her things were scattered, and returned everything to her purse, wallet, keys, badge that said her name was Nina Caputo, Federal Bureau of Investigation. And her gun. She picked up an unopened pack of Winston cigarettes.

"I don't mind. Smoke if you wish."

I got up, and unlocked the door, then dialed Alicia.

"Please bring me an ashtray."

"If you like it smoke free in here, I don't have to smoke," she said.

"It's up to you. I never smoke here, but it doesn't bother me."

She lit up. Took a drag.

"I heard Pepe on a taped phone call. He told the kingpin that it should be done by amateurs, nothing sophisticated. The 'it' he referred to was the fire. The kingpin wanted answers. He asked why he was going after you. Pepe said you were fucking his sister and Olga. If he hadn't needed you for some business he had in mind, he would have put you down. That was the only reason he didn't do away with you. But after the fire, he was pissed off. He cussed out the kingpin for having burned down the house. All he wanted was to put a scare in you. He said that you could have been burned up with the house. Pepe made threats. Another mistake like that, ever again, he'd be the one to burn."

I stared at her as she spoke. I felt a chill, probably from anger.

"I'm at a loss," I said. "I don't think you're lying."

"I'm not lying."

"Why did you tease me with this at the restaurant, and why did you tell me now? This is not the kind of thing the feds talk about."

Lola laughed. "Simple. Now, because I promised. And because I know how much you need to know who burned up your house." She took a long drag, then crushed more than half of the cigarette.

"You could get in trouble for telling me."

"It's your word against mine. Besides, the team is no longer. They've all been reassigned. Only reason I'm still here, I'm on medical leave, and my doctors are here."

"Then what?"

"I'll go to Florida."

"Why did they pull out?"

"Once they knew you weren't cooperating, there wasn't a chance we'd get authority to keep spending money for nothing. It's a wonder they didn't yank us before. We like it here in California. Our reports always hinted we were on to something. In the meantime, we lived high on the hog. It was expensive to keep up with you. And the trio."

"I'm at a loss why you keep talking to me."

"I want you to trust me."

I laughed. I laughed so hard I couldn't stop.

Lola laughed too, but not as much or nearly as hard. She still had the kittenish face and the vulnerability that had always appealed to me.

"Lola, you got balls."

"You just fucked me. Did you feel or see any balls?"

I must confess, her words hit me between my legs. At least she could not see my response behind my desk.

"No, I didn't see any balls."

"The troops pulled away. There had to be more than one team. You said trio, that had to be Pepe, Camila and Olga. Pepe died so, now it is just Camila and Olga."

"Yes, one team split up. I stayed near you and your people."

"Hard to believe," I said. "I can't think of anything I've done that is illegal."

"You were never the target. The Camachos are. The next team may not be as kind."

"Next team?"

"Oh yeah. Camachos are not off the radar. Eventually, a new task force will be put together, and they will start all over again."

"Why are you telling me this?"

"I want you to trust me."

There was a knock.

"It's our food. Hold that thought," I said.

Two waiters came in. They knew their way to the conference room. In a few minutes, they filed out, following Alicia. "It's all set up," she announced.

"Enjoy your lunch."

Lola and I walked in to the room together.

Alicia had set us up across from each other, a good six feet between us.

"If this table could talk, what would it say?"

"My table is not a snitch. It remembers nothing."

I laughed first.

"*Provecho,*" she said as she sliced into the wedge of lettuce.

I said the same.

I wished I had a video camera in this room to record the lunch scene where I sat across from a woman who was no doubt an enemy, as though it was perfectly normal to do so. A woman who had been targeted by Camila or Olga. If that was true, Lola had every right to be wanting revenge.

It had been Lola's job to put them in prison long before she got shot so was that just part of her job, or was it personal? She had been on the case for a long time, long enough to get to know the life the Camachos lived. Does that turn an agent jealous? Does it turn a job into something personal?

"There have been other things that happened to me since the first fire. After Pepe was dead, there was another fire. A helicopter with two dummies dropped Molotov cocktails on the roof of my house and crashed on my lawn. Their bodies were so badly charred that the FBI couldn't get an ID on them."

"I don't have any idea who orchestrated the second fire," Lola said.

"You know everything," I said, mimicking her. Our eyes met.

"Pepe used an associate of your friend Fino to provoke you. He accosted you on the freeway once, torched your car at the airport, followed you to Texas, but made no moves there because he got orders from Pepe to do anything. Luca Rossi. A two-bit hood. Dead now."

"How do you know this?"

I stopped eating. I knew the name. Luca Rossi had done those things, as well as breaking into my house. I threw him off my balcony into my koi pond. He'd disappeared from my property, but the police had found him later, shot in the head. I could picture one of Pepe's men making that shot, but it was hard to know why. It had only been after Pepe was dead that I'd realized how much crazier he was than I'd ever guessed. I had only ever seen Pepe manic, and happy. I'd never seen or known Pepe's dark side, though surely I must have realized he had one, considering what he did for a living. I can't help it. I'm drawn in and dazzled by money and power.

Lola stopped eating and said, "There's more."

"There is?" I was feeling a little blindsided. I guess she really *did* know everything.

"Want me to go on, or want to interrupt some more?"

"Go on," I said.

Lola gazed across the table at me. "Under Pepe's orders, the same two-bit hood got another guy to ram your car as it came out of your driveway. When Pepe learned it was Olga in the car, he went silent with this guy. We heard nothing for a very long time."

I put down the knife and fork. My stomach churned. I remember my cameras had captured a security tape of Luca Rossi during that incident, but we'd never figured out who was pulling his strings.

"Go on, Lola, please."

"What am I going to get for all this?"

"I'll pay you whatever you want."

"While we are on the subject of money, I want a million dollars from Camila and Olga for having me shot and for attempting to kill me at the hospital. I have Camila on tape admitting to Olga that maybe she acted hastily."

"We can discuss money. Finish telling me about Pepe. Did Fino know Pepe hired this client of his?"

"I have no tapes of Fino. He was not part of this investigation. He's just one of the mobster's lawyers. Rossi was his associate. You have to figure that he made him available to Pepe."

"But you don't know for sure?"

"No tapes."

"Lola, finish telling me what you know."

"The next tape we have of Pepe contacting him, Pepe seemed drunk. Rossi was a coke freak, always high. The papers and the cops had it wrong. Rossi did not come down from a helicopter to your balcony. He did not arrive or leave there by helicopter. We don't know how he got in, but it was not by a helicopter or any kind of aircraft. I wanted to arrest that bastard many times, but I had nothing federal to arrest him under, and my bosses were not interested in him."

"You must have heard Pepe talk to this guy?"

"I did, the team did too. We were always two steps behind, but there was nothing we could do."

"I could have been killed and you did nothing."

"I've been watching you for a long time, Mario Luna." She gave me a wan little half smile that gave me a chill. She'd been around for years with her eye on me. "Luca Rossi was a nobody. I knew you could handle yourself against more dangerous threats. Our team knew you wouldn't let this punk kill you. Besides, Pepe never told him what exactly he wanted him to do."

Lola smiled after dabbing her mouth with napkin.

"I want to believe you, Lola."

She shrugged. "I don't care if you don't believe me. Let's talk about the million dollars your two loves owe me."

"Lola, you are trying to trap me somehow. Why are you doing that to me?"

"No trap. I am owed something for what I went through. If I could use what I have as evidence in a civil case, I would get much more than a million dollars. Those girls of yours are seriously loaded and seriously unbalanced. If I wanted to arrest Camila for ordering the hit, I can't use the tape because we had no warrant for that particular tape. She was in Colombia."

The plate that had held her six-ounce strip steak now only held a green garnish. The wedge of lettuce was gone, as well as the potato. My food was relatively untouched, but then my stomach was churning.

I became pensive and quiet. "Let's go in my office."

"Aren't you going to eat?" she asked, her eyes flicking to my face, and then away. She almost looked concerned for my welfare.

"Maybe later."

"Get me the money, Mario. I want to quit. I deserve that money. It sure beats my federal pension."

I stood and opened the conference room door. She followed me into my office and returned to the chair she'd sat in earlier.

"Are you setting me up?"

"No, I am not setting you up. I can see why you'd think so."

"What if I can't get you the money?" I was back at my desk. She was where she started across from me.

She lit up a cigarette. She held her chin with her thumb and forefinger, tapping, like she was thinking about it.

"If I don't get the money, I will quit my job, and I will kill both of them." She spoke quietly and sounded deadly serious. "I'll tell you one more thing," Lola said. "I befriended Pepe. I did what Tangles did. I flew around with him for three days and ended up at his Milan mansion where you stayed when you went to work for the leasing company."

"You got to be kidding."

"Not kidding. When I want in, I get in. The team didn't let me stick around because it was complicated. I had no business going outside the US, but I did it when I was following Pepe around. I almost blew my cover, but I turned it around, and he went hands over heels over me. I have a diamond at home that he gave me. Of course, I never put that on my report. I was lucky to get out of there with my skin intact, and so was Tangles. And so were Olga and Camila. He was one crazy bastard. I hope he never did to Tangles the shit he did to me. Hell, I even hope he didn't do it to Camila and Olga, and those two belong behind bars. But Pepe, he was mean down to his bones."

She got up, picked up her purse. "Get me the money."

"I'll work on it, I promise. You're a cop. You can't just kill someone because you think they tried killing you."

"Mario, I am mad to the core of my soul. I will get in, and I will do away with them."

I shook my head. She had to be bluffing. Didn't look like it.

I got up and walked her to my office door. She gave me a peck on the lips and a light hug.

"I hope I can walk," she said.

"Give me one second," I said. "Wait."

In my office, I opened the door to my walk-in closet where my safe is located. It's not a vault like the one I have at home, but it's big enough. I opened it and took out a bundle with ten thousand dollars in hundreds. I put it in an envelope, and half minute later I was with her again at the door.

"Here's a gift, like old times when you wanted me to pay you." I smiled. "Only this is a bit more than your asking price used to be."

She took the envelope, took a playful sniff, pretended to bite the envelope like it was made of gold, dropped it in her purse, then she kissed me hard on the lips.

"You didn't think I was going to refuse cash, did you? I don't turn down money."

"Actually, I wasn't sure."

"Thanks, Mario. Whatever you gave me, it's appreciated. I can use it. I have...expenses."

"By the way, are my phones safe to talk now that your team is gone?"

"As far as I know, your phones are safe. I can't say the same about your lady friends because it's a big world. There are probably others in and outside the US keeping an ear on them. Best you never trust a phone, no matter what kind it is. Take care of you." She winked. "There might be a Lola listening."

I couldn't stop thinking about how she got in with Pepe, got a diamond from him much like Tangles had. It could be that Lola was lying. It could be that Lola had listened to a phone conversation about Letty getting a diamond and used that to make her story credible. But her responses about Pepe being a crazy bastard reflected a side of him I'd only heard about. I tended toward believing her story, at least the part about shacking up with Pepe for a while. It seemed in character, or at least what I thought I knew of her character.

Barcelona September 14 1990
Olga

Mason sent me a fax. His man reported seeing her come and go.

Then Mario called to say we had to meet.

"I'll go wherever you want."

"Can we discuss it on the phone or fax?"

"No."

We agreed to meet at the apartment in New York. He would be alone. I was in Barcelona. Riana would stay in Spain until I returned for her. At the last minute, I decided that Riana would fly with me to New York and stay at the Waldorf Astoria until I could pick her up.

I wasn't sure if Camila would be there, though we'd talked about it.

"All of a sudden he wants to have these meetings," Camila told me on the phone. She was calling from Peru. "And it can't wait. But I have wall-to-wall meetings tomorrow and the day after tomorrow."

"Amor, this is Mario asking. Besides, we do this, I get to see you again so soon," I said.

"When he's around, we don't do anything anyway, so don't play that card."

"Amor, it's up to you. I'm going to be there."

Silence. I knew what she was doing, pictured her facial expressions as she thought this out. If there was a mirror around, she'd be watching herself. It was one of those things she'd done since we were kids. Minutes passed, then she finally said something.

"I'll do what I can to get there."

"Si, Amor. I hope to see you. It must be important."

"It's about that bitch. You heard it from Mason, too. She went to see him at the office this morning."

"She was there for three hours," I said.

Less than an hour after taking off from Barcelona, Riana and I went to bed to try to sleep and backtrack the six-hour difference between Spain and New York. Not a big deal. We were experts with time zones and jet-lag.

"Thanks for not staying in Barcelona," I said.

"It was your idea," she said, snuggling. "All this secrecy. You should tell them I know what's going on."

"They know, but they don't know," I said. "Best that way."

"I love being with you," Riana said.

The cabin was dark. There's something about the sound of a plane that makes sleeping so much better. And the bed was nice and comfy with Riana in it.

Chapter 15
Pasadena September 15, 1990
Mario

There was no big scene at the breakfast table. Letty and Tangles playfully nagged, but not seriously so. Tangles tended to chase indulgence with some new health kick every so often. Following too much ice cream last night, Tangles was drinking some blended concoction the color of alfalfa. Letty and I were having eggs and bacon.

"Why can't we go? You took us to Italy on the last secret trip. What's so different this time?"

"The apartment is small. It's not like Milan where you can get lost. I'm going alone."

"Well, okay, safe travels, Boss."

Letty smiled before she said, "We could have done things all the way to New York and back. You're just tired of us."

It was a claim too ridiculous to even deny. I used the toast she had buttered for me as a base for a mouthful of egg, and nothing else was said.

For once, I didn't have Raul drop me off. I drove myself and left the car at the airport.I was deep in thought for the flight to New York. I had two glasses of wine, and exchanged smiles with Lisa, my flight attendant, every time she came by to see if I wanted anything. I was in some kind of limbo, way out there somewhere, and Lola was responsible.

Though I had timed my departure from Los Angeles to coordinate with Olga's arrival, when I arrived at the apartment, it was clear that Olga and Camila had beat me there. I saw the familiar faces of their guards posted outside the building and in the lobby, and a pair at the apartment door. I thought of Lola promising to kill them if they didn't pay up. I wondered how she planned to get through their armor.

There were lots of kisses among Olga, Camila and me. If I wasn't there on such a serious mission, I would have hit the bed with them right off. Three pizzas in the kitchen were piping hot, plus a huge bowl of pasta in sauce, salad, and an ice barrel full of coke bottles.

"The guards wanted pizza so we got some, but we can order whatever you want," Olga said. "The barrel of ice the cokes are in is borrowed from the downstairs restaurant."

I smiled. "Baby, I love pizza and an icy Coca Cola."

"Me too," Camila said.

We were in the living room eating pizza on fine china plates. Camila used a knife and fork. Olga and I used our hands, philistines that we are. I chugged my icy coke straight from the bottle. They're so good, I wonder what's in them. I really didn't want pizza, but I polished off a slice before I dumped the story about the hours I spent with Lola. Maybe I was too honest. Olga took it well. Not Camila.

I couldn't remember a time when I'd seen Camila so pissed off. She hopped up from the table where we were eating. She couldn't sit still. She kept getting up and walking around the room, cussing and promising to kill the whore cop. Olga would talk her into sitting down, and Camila would comply until rage got her feet moving again around the room. Over and over again.

Olga tried to calm Camila. I'd seen her do this before. I'd seen her play the role of mediator between Pepe and Camila, between Camila and staff, between Camila and guards.

"Amor, let's think this through. If she has a recording of you saying this, you must have been talking to someone.”

"So, what? Mario just said she admits she can't use the tape. It's the threat that angers me. No one has ever threatened me, ever.”

I doubted that was true. Maybe no one threatened her to her face. And I'm pretty sure no one tried to extort money from her. At some point we talked it out. Camila said she was not going to pay a nickel to Lola.

"Mario, don't you dare give her one penny,” Camila said, "Let her try and kill me. Let's see who dies.”

I wanted to ask if either of them had anything to do with the attempts on Lola's life, but how could I ask? I couldn't before and couldn't then. In private I would ask Olga, but I had done that before. Olga can be evasive when she wants to be.

"It's interesting that this team was pulled away,” Olga said.

"We don't know if any of this is true. Just because she stripped to show him that she wasn't wearing a wire doesn't mean they didn't send her in.”

"That's true,” I said. "I'm just telling you what Mason's man can't report because he wasn't inside my office.”

Olga smiled. "You are right, Amor. Mason wrote us faxes and told us she had visited your office and spent three hours there.”

"I think it's time Mason pulls his people away from following me around. It's a waste of money and a total intrusion on my privacy.”

"It's up to you, Amor,” Camila said. "Olga thinks she's protecting you, but it's up to you, of course.”

"Let's talk about that later,” Olga said. "Tell us again her claim that she was with Pepe for a short time and spent time at the Milan house.”

I told them again.

"I'm going to get her picture from Mason, and show the help in Milan,” Camila said, fuming.

"Yes, Amor, do that. But what good is it? It's past tense. We can't change what happened. Pepe no doubt liked her looks and did what he did best—romanced her, flew her around, and dumped her."

"She says her people pulled her out. Not sure he dumped her."

I heard Camila hiss in anger.

"Anything else, Amor?" Olga asked looking at me hopefully.

"Yes," I said. I gave them a change of topic.

I told them about Pepe sending the biker after me. They had already heard that Pepe had my house torched. I told them how she told me the story. Some things she knew because her team had been in fact listening to phones and bugs and wires and who knows what other means were being used.

"And you believe that?" Camila, said in a high-pitched voice.

"I don't necessarily trust Lola," I said. "On the other hand, she speaks with a straight face about this. I've been trained to read people who come after me, face to face. I'm pretty good at it."

"And you think she's not lying. Is that what you are saying?" Olga asked. Her voice was calm, and I had the feeling she was trying to appear calm for Camila's sake and maybe for mine; but one of her hands was working a paper napkin to shreds. Her hands were not the hands of a calm person.

I could see from their anxious looks they were both waiting for me to reply.

"I want to believe her. It would be good to clear up some of the mysterious things that have been happening to me for years."

"The fire when the helicopter crashed in your yard, Pepe was dead already." Camila said.

"I know," I said. "She said she doesn't know who was responsible for that."

"We know the guy in Mexico City was involved in some way, but he's dead. We'll never know how he fit in. Pepe can't be blamed for that."

"For sure," I said. At the moment, neither one looked like they hated the departed Pepe. I knew Olga claimed to hate Pepe. If everything Olga had told me about him was true, and he had done and what they said he had done to Camila, she should hate him too. But he was Camila's brother. Family can be funny that way.

There are gaps in my knowledge of Camila and Olga. Many of their doings are cloaked in secrecy. I have heard things that I do not understand. I used to ask questions that Olga answered with half-truths or evaded; and there are some times when I have never asked for explanations. Like when the two men that were waiting for us in Milan when Olga landed the helicopter, there was something they said: that Olga and Camila were killers of children. There were bullets flying. It wasn't like I could stop to ask what they were talking about. I heard them, and I wondered what they were talking about. I didn't ask what they were talking about, but I did not forget their words. I killed both men, and ten minutes later Olga and I were in a bedroom fucking like nothing had happened.

My stomach twisted. The cokes and pizza were not sitting well on top of my conscience, if I have one.

I was as sick as any of them.

'Not paying a penny to the whore-cop," Camila said, at least a dozen times. She was still muttering that in the car when she left late that night for the airport. She had to return to Lima.

I know she had as many meetings waiting on her as Camila, but Olga stayed the night. We were both mentally drained by all the drama. I was not going to call for any special meetings in the future. Fuck it. Camila had looked at me like I had wasted her time making her fly from Lima to New York to hear bullshit told to me by a cop. I held Olga close, and we went to sleep. In the morning a car took her to the hotel where Riana was staying. I knew they would soon be off to the airport. A car delivered me to the airport, and I was on my way home.

"Short trip, Mr. Luna," Lisa said.

"Yes," I agreed. Our eyes met.

"Can I get anything for you?"

"Black coffee, an almost burned bagel, and cream cheese please."

"Coming up," Lisa said.

I had left my car at the airport. On my way home, I got a call from Lola.

"Are they going to compensate me for the tyranny they put me through?"

"No," I said. "How did you know I went to see them?"

"I didn't know. Did you?"

"Lola, you are playing me again."

"I'm not playing you. I like you too much to play you, Mario."

"Oh, now you like me?"

"I've always had a crush on you. I watched you for months and months, long before you picked me up thinking I was a whore for hire. You have no idea how often I waited for you at the Whiskey."

"Lola, if you really need money, tell me about it, and I can help."

"You don't get it. I don't want handouts or loans. I want compensation."

If there's one thing I understand, it is getting a victim just compensation. That's been my livelihood my whole life. "I get it," I said. "When will I see you?"

"I'll be in touch. They could change their mind. How can I reach you?"

The line went dead. I tossed the phone on the passenger side of the car.

"Lola, do me a favor. Don't ever call me again. Don't come to see me again. Just stay away."

I was alone in the car talking to myself. Without thinking about it, I took a chop at the steering wheel. It went CRACK.

I'm not in the habit of breaking the steering wheel of my Rolls. I just pulled over to the side of the road and stared at it for who knows how long.

Pasadena September 18, 1990
Letty

I couldn't get him to answer his cell. I couldn't get Olga and Camila to answer theirs. I called Andrea so I knew he was flying in. Tangles had stayed over. We had worked out early in the morning and seriously considered whether we needed to get a job between plane crashes. Sitting around Casa Luna was great, but the routine got old with Mario away. Lately he was always away at the office or on a trip. What bugged me was this secret trip. We figure he went to New York to see Olga and Camila because Lola surfaced again.

"I think he's getting tired of us," Tangles said.

"Maybe. Maybe not," I said. "He's got two pussies here at home anytime he wants to do it."

"It doesn't sound like you."

"It sounds like me being pissed we didn't go on this trip, short as it was."

"Oh fuck, we had a good time last night, didn't we?"

I looked at Tangles. "We did, yes. Ignore my bitching."

When Mario got home, he gave us each a tiny kiss and went straight to the gym. Tangles and I exchanged looks. Normally he'd take a shower. He hated to work out this late. It was three in the afternoon. We walked in the gym an hour later when we knew he would be finishing up. He smiled and appeared to be in a better mood.

"Letty, the steering wheel broke. Drop it off at the dealer and get it replaced for me. I have no car."

"Sure, Boss. Tangles can follow me. We'll do it right now."

"How did it break?" Tangles asked.

"I whacked it," he said.

"I hope it was cathartic," I said.

Mario gave a quick bark of laughter. "That's a ten dollar word," he said. "Where'd you pick it up?"

"Oprah," I said.

He laughed for five minutes. I didn't wait for him to stop. "I hope they can get a replacement right away. Who knows if they keep them in stock?"

I drove the Rolls. Tangles followed me. The steering wheel was not totally broken off, but the shape it was in made it interesting to steer. The dealer said it would be a week to get the wheel and twenty-four hours more after that to install it.

I left the Rolls, and Tangles took me home in her car.

"He must have been pissed at something."

"All of a sudden, everything seems like a mystery." Tangles said.

"Ever since that lady cop came into the picture. Fucking undercover bitch. If I had half a chance, I'd bitch slap her till Thursday."

"She may not be the pushover that you think. She's FBI. She must have some kind of fighting training. And you liked her until she was a cop." Tangles laughed.

"Just for saying that, I'll bitch slap you soon as we get home," I said.

"Right, you'll try, bitch."

By the time we got back, he was showered and dressed. I told him about the car.

"Tomorrow I'm going out to buy a Ferrari. I drove Pepe's for almost two years in Italy and did okay. I fit in it."

"Bitchin'," I said. "I want to go with you."

"And me," Tangles said with excitement in her voice.

"Let's get a great dinner going," Mario said. "I'm starved."

"Great dinner coming. Check out this, Boss," I said, and I ran up to the kitchen and got the book. The book is a three-ring binder with a bunch of take-out menus from local restaurants. I ran back down to the wine room and handed over the book.

"You want take-out?" Boss asked, misunderstanding.

"No, pick out anything you want and then have Miguel fix it."

"Ah, got it," Boss said. He winked at me, got Miguel on the line, and read aloud from a random menu, "Tuna Tartare, served with scallions, yuzukosho and red wine reduction, and a quail egg shooter."

Miguel didn't respond for a second, then all he said was "Boss."

I heard pure excitement in Miguel's voice. I could tell he would love fixing something different, but this order wasn't something he'd expect from Boss.

One of the menus fell out of the binder. Boss rolled it up and thumped me over the head with it, laughing. He gave me back the binder and tousled my hair.

"Just kidding, Miguel. Three steaks, you know how we like 'em, twice cooked potatoes. You can get as creative as you want with the salads and desserts."

"Sure thing, Boss," Miguel said, laughing.

Two hours after a dinner of perfect steaks, Betty gave Mario a two-hour massage. Tangles and I passed on a massage, so Betty left.

"I think it won't be long and we will have to start using her backup for massages. The boyfriend thing is getting serious," I said.

"Letty, she won't give up this gig just because she hooks up with a guy. The backup is for days when she can't make it," Tangles said.

"Let it go," Boss said with a chuckle. "One day at a time."

"Okay," I agreed. "Are we hitting the wine room or the bedroom?"

He looked at us without saying which. We followed to the wine room.

Pasadena September 18, 1990

Tangles

There was a time when I looked forward to the escape to my little cubby hole, even after I surprised that burglar bitch who beat me up in the living room. I had to keep going back in order to get over the fear. With Letty's help, I got serious about martial arts and guns. I'm good enough now I dare anyone to be in my apartment when I get home.

I go back to my apartment most of the time though I like being here with Letty, with him, and with everyone in this big house. Every day, I hope I'm asked to spend the night. I have my own bedroom with some of my stuff. I could invite myself but that's tacky. I don't do it. I know I'm not going home tonight. We are on the second bottle of wine. That's not a lot of wine for three people when one of them is Mario. Still, it's good wine, and good wine gets me tipsy pretty quick.

"Want a joint?" he asks Letty and me.

I reach for the gold cigarette box that Pixie gave Boss. I light up. I pass it to him to take first drag.

"You go first," he says. I take a hit and hold and pass it to him. He's across the round table. Letty and I are next to each other, facing him.

"I want to apologize that I didn't tell you this before I left for New York." He looks so serious, his brows always kind of lift. I want to jump over this table and devour him with kisses.

Pasadena September 18, 1990
Mario

These ladies are more than my friends. They are family. Pixie, Melina, Jo, and Niley were also close to me, each in her own way. Pixie had been my best girl growing up; Melina had been my girlfriend, almost my wife; Jo and Niley had been part of my team, but now they ran their own business renting out my apartments—but I hardly saw them any more. Letty and Tangles were a part of my daily life, a part of me, especially Letty. I love her enough to take care of her for the rest of our lives.

How could I not share this with them? I should have done it before I went to New York.

I told them about Lola coming to the office. I expanded on what they already knew that she had said and bought them up to date. Told them about Lola's visit, start to finish.

"Pepe arranged it with the fucking biker? If that man wasn't dead already, I'd kill him. Hell, I'll dig him up and kill him all over again," Letty said.

"Hush the fuck up," Tangles said, "Let Boss finish."

"I told Camila and Olga about this when I went to New York. Olga didn't react. Camila was pissed off. She made it clear that Lola won't get one thin dime from her. She was hopping mad, practically daring Lola to come after her, not that Lola could hear it." I shook my head. "I didn't want to burden you with secrets, but I wanted to come clean with you. I can't have secrets from my girls now, can I?" I finished. I put my arms out. The moved, one sitting on either side, tucked under an arm. I hugged them that way.

"Thank you for your trust," Tangles said.

"I feel so close to you, Boss. There's nothing in this world that I would not do for you," Letty said.

It was the way she looked at me, the way she spoke. I got a chill throughout my body.

Much later, we left the wine room for the spa. Four enclosed showers are in the spa, but we walked past those to the gym shower that has shower heads on both walls so that you can have five showerheads spraying the front and another five spraying the back.

We followed up with the ice-cold jacuzzi. It sounds cold, and it is colder than it sounds. We walked to the master bedroom in robes.

"No candles, baby," I told Letty who was ready to start her nightly ritual of lighting candles everywhere. "Let's enjoy the dark."

I saw her look in my direction, smiling, her face lit by the match she had just struck. For an instant before she blew it out, the light touched her face, and made the gold highlights in her brown eyes sparkle. Her eyes were warm on me.

We lay on the big bed. I was in the middle, hugging them close. Half of my body was pressed by Letty, the other by Tangles. I kissed them and they kissed me, passionately, in silence.

Pasadena September 19, 1990
Letty

I feel so fucking guilty that I was mad at him for not taking us to New York. How can I know the pressure he was under? He's calmer now. His breathing is shallow. He's sleeping solid. And Tangles. Tangles could be dead for all I know. I have to move up close to check if she's breathing.

I send a mental note to him just before I fall asleep.

"I love you."

Chapter 16
Pasadena September 19, 1990
Mario

The next morning, the three of us had breakfast. Raul picked us up in Pixie's Rolls and drove us to a Ferrari dealer that had a single car in the showroom. The car was in high-demand. I sat in it, got out, got back in.

"This works in Milan but not here," I said.

We went to a Mercedes dealer. I picked a black four door that I drove the girls home in it. I fit just right, and it was a great drive.

"I can swap cars now and then," I said.

"Boss, I loved the Ferrari," Tangles said, pouting.

"What is not to like about a Ferrari?" Letty said. "Of course you loved the Ferrari, you dope."

"I like it too, but I look like a freak in it."

"You don't look like a freak in it, especially with the top down," Letty said.

"Yellow is not my color," I said.

"They could have ordered one for you," Tangles said, still pouting.

"Stop already. I like this car."

At home, I spent an hour with Andrea on the phone going over what I was needed for at the office.

"I'll probably be in tomorrow," I said. But then I called Andrea back.

"Baby, please get a crew together for me. I'm going to Rome soon as you can arrange it. Manifest includes Letty and Tangles."

I called Olga. "I feel beat up like I lost two tournaments in a row. I'm taking the girls to Rome for a few days."

"Amor, good for you. Break out of there. Maybe that whore-cop will stop making surprise visits."

"I'm not going for any more surprise visits. I heard enough."

"Amor, I wish I could join you, but I can't. Stay at the house."

"I was planning on a hotel."

"Funny man. Stay at the house. Let the help do something for a change."

"The help has plenty to do taking care of that monster," I said.

"I'll call and tell them to expect you. When are you leaving?"

Then I sprang it on the girls.

"We're going to Rome. Just for fun, no business involved. I have you on the manifest so you can't say no."

Screams, laughter, high-fives, kisses, hugs. Letty and Tangles were jumping up and down like they had springs on their feet. It was a joy just to watch them. Fuck, even I got excited. We're going to Rome!

Our flight was perfect until the descent. The gift of rain in Rome produced fifteen long minutes of non-stop turbulence, bumping us all over the cabin until the wheels struck the runway. We would have been bouncing off the ceiling if our attendant hadn't insisted on seat belts.

"All the flying I do," Letty said hoarsely, her face the color of the blindingly white pillow she was clutching to her chest. "Hate turbulence."

I patted her hand.

"Chicken," Tangles said, looking at me. "What are you smiling at?"

"Glad to be in Rome," I said.

Carlos, one of two drivers at the Rome house was at the airport in a station wagon to pick us up. We came out of the plane and went into the wagon. He stood at the passenger doors and let us in. He closed the car door, and remained standing, looking from the terminal to the company plane.

"What are you waiting for, bub?" Tangles asked. "Santa's not coming. One of his reindeer had a flat."

Carlos looked understandably confused. He looked in my direction. I was seated between Tangles and Letty in the middle of the back seat. I was ready to translate Tangles' joke when he asked a question.

"No security?"

"Carlos, no security," I confirmed. "We left them back in Pasadena."

No telling if Mason's people were here or on their way. They didn't hide, but I wasn't always sure if or when they were around. Mason was a nice guy, but he had to be loving this assignment with a client like Olga who paid his invoices without reviewing them.

Carlos started the car. We were on the road. The mild rain looked much less of a storm that it had seemed while we were in it. There was heavy cloud cover, but the clouds were all white, and looked non-threatening. The girls were chattering about Rome in the rain. I turned my cell on and called Olga.

"Wish you were here," I said.

"I wish the same, Amor. Please relax and enjoy yourself. The help is waiting for your arrival and will look after your every need."

"Baby, thanks," I said.

I passed the phone on to Letty who switched from chattering at ninety miles an hour on rain in Rome instantly to Olga-talk without missing a breath or a syllable, and then passed the phone to Tangles.

The Rome house personnel greeted us. No hugs, lots of handshakes. I knew all of them from previous visits. The butler made it clear we could pick any bedroom we wished. We stayed in the rooms we were shown to—each one felt special, fresh, squeaky clean and new.

"I'll see you in about two hours," I told the girls. "I want to relax a little, and then we can decide on dinner."

I kicked off my shoes and crashed on the bed fully clothed to catch a nap. Ten minutes in, I heard a buzz, and opened my eyes. It was my cell phone.

"Mario," I said.

"This is Lola."

I sat up, instantly wide awake.

"You mean Nina? Or is Nina not your name either?"

"You didn't used to be this grouchy. What a grump. You must have had a bad flight."

"I thought you weren't watching me anymore."

"I'm not watching you. I'm still on sick leave. I told you, the team is no longer."

"And where am I?" I asked.

"In Rome, at the bitches' pad no less. Bitches is plural."

"I'm going to hang up, Nina. I don't need this crap."

"Is that payback for telling you about your house and the creep who stalked you for years?"

"For all I know, you told me lies."

"Ungrateful son of a bitch," she said.

I heard a click. She hung up on me.

I never mentioned Lola's call. I didn't plan on telling Olga or Camila either. The thought of all the unnecessary drama that would engage turned my stomach. I wasn't letting anything—not even Lola's shenanigans—spoil this trip.

We stuck around the house for the next two days. Therapists were brought in to take care of us. We had massages without having to wait for each other to finish. We hung out in the gardens, drank lots of very good wine. We laughed over a lot of Italian-dubbed spaghetti westerns. Letty read aloud the badly translated English captions. Her voices for the characters had us all laughing till we cried. The girls disrespected their bedrooms and ended up in mine every night. On the third day, we got out and wandered around Rome, and spent hours at Spanish Steps, shopping. At Tiffany's, as I bought and had a watch engraved for Olga's upcoming birthday, the girls admired a set of jade and sapphire earrings with matching bracelets. While they weren't looking, I got them each the set they preferred, and put them in my pocket. Carlos our driver hung behind us and carried our purchases to the car as we paid the store-keepers. Now that's the way to shop—no lugging of bags. It was wonderful. We had lunch, then sat on the steps and savored three scoop ice cream cones. The highs were in the eighties, so the ice cream didn't last long. It was a race to the finish, though Letty refused to rush, and ended up covered in melted ice cream. Tangles called her a show-off. All along, Carlos was snapping pictures of us. People stopped to watch, thinking we were on a magazine shoot or something. That's how gorgeous the girls are, even covered in melted ice cream. I did hear some 'crazy Americans' out of some of the gawkers.

My phone rang. That instant I was sure it was Lola and switched it off. After a second, I thought better of it, and switched it back on again.

Letty said, "We better cool it. We're scaring the natives."

Tangles threatened to moon them. I saw panic in Carlos's eyes that she was going to do it—once Tangles explained what mooning was—and he herded the girls toward the car. I followed behind them laughing. Tangles and Letty were having a ball driving Carlos nuts.

Tangles had bought an ugly tourist-style *See Roma* towel from a man in a cart, and Letty snatched it from her to wipe off any traces of ice cream. Tangles called her loco.

"What a fun day," Letty said on our way back to the house.

"I dug every single minute. How about you, Boss?"

"Loved it," I said. I would have sounded more convincing if my phone hadn't rung. Ever since I'd refused that call, I had been wondering if that had been Lola, if or when Lola would call again, and why I hadn't told the girls.

I put my arms around them. "We tore it up with all the shopping we did," I said, with more energy than I felt. "And Letty…"

"What Boss?"

"Tangles is right. You're loco."

That sent the girls into peals of laughter.

Before we made it to the house, my phone rang.

"Sweetie, tell the bitch, I missed her on purpose. Next time, maybe she won't be so lucky. I want compensation." She hung up before I said a word.

"Letty dial Camila. I'll call Olga. Just do it. Don't give me the third degree."

"Olga, are you okay?"

"Yes, why? What's wrong?"

Letty knew when I meant business. She dialed and handed me the car phone. I put Olga on my left ear.

Letty said, "Boss, here's Camila."

I grabbed the phone, held it to my right ear.

"Are you okay?" My voice was as calm as I could make it sound.

"Amor, yes, I'm okay, why?"

My mind was racing but Olga and Camila were okay. Lola was playing me.

"Amor, are you there?"

"I'm sorry," I said, "Just checking on you. Where are you?"

They both answered at the same time. I heard Buenos Aires and Mexico, though I wasn't sure who said what.

They both asked how I was.

I managed to laugh at the dual conversation. "I'm okay, yes."

I managed to hang up with Camila before any conversational disasters occurred and continued with Olga.

"Sorry," I said again. "I was just checking on you."

Letty and Tangles were looking at me with great big question marks on their faces. When I hung up, there were going to be questions.

"Surprise!" I said, "First one into the hot tub gets this," I said, pulling a single earring out of my pocket. I dangled the earring in the air, sending them into squeals; then they were off racing through the house, clothes flying everywhere. Of course, I would give them each a full set, but I was having fun with it. I followed behind them taking my time, getting into swimming trunks, and having the staff send wine, then later, a light dinner in the garden.

We returned to Pasadena seven days after we left.

"Boss, I want to be just like you when I grow up," Tangles said as we got out of the car at Casa Luna.

"He's three years older than you, dummy. That's it," Letty said. "The man ain't your Grampa."

On the top stair on the front porch, Tangles grabbed my ear and pulled my head down to her level. I was a couple steps lower, leaned over her way. She kissed me on the top of the head, her eyes glinting at Letty. "Thanks Grampa," Tangles said.

"You're welcome, kiddo," I said, faking a quivery, elderly voice.

"Boss, I love you," Letty said. "Thank you for taking me along. Nothing in this world I wouldn't do for you."

Letty was joking, I know.

"Oh, stop kissing ass, bitch," Tangles said.

Yes, I was home with the girls.

Tangles went home that night. Letty and I relaxed in the big house like a husband and wife might. I couldn't imagine that a husband and wife could have the relaxed life we led if we were married. I couldn't picture Olga and me kicking back the way Letty and I did. Olga was high octane and high maintenance, like that yellow Ferrari. It stressed me to think that way. I switched gears.

I was on my second glass of wine. It was getting dark. In September in Pasadena, twilight hits around six thirty. Miguel was holding off cooking our steaks till seven. Caro had just come to the landing where Letty's suitcases were waiting when Olga called.

"Baby, I missed you in Rome," I said. "Thank you for letting us use the house."

Letty yelled in the direction of the phone, "It was marvelous. Thank you, Olga."

"Did you hear her?"

"Of course," Olga said. "Tell her no need to thank me. We're family."

"I heard that," Letty said. "Thanks a bunch, Olga. Love you."

Caro picked up Letty's two suitcases and got in the elevator. I watched as Letty raced up the stairs to sort out her clothes for the closet or the laundry. The second suitcase was stuffed with new clothes from Rome. I knew Letty and Caro were going to dish over those new clothes, and that Letty had picked up scarves, shoes and watches for some of the staff, including her uncle. It was always an effort for Letty not to immediately give everybody everything the second she walked through the door.

I said, "Baby, you and me, we have to practice how it will be when we get married. Are we going to sit around and have wine, smoke pot? And what else?"

"Amor, we're going to have babies."

I thought about my age and her age.

"That's right, baby," I agreed. "We better hurry cause we're getting older every day."

"Seems like you and Letty practice the husband and wife thing plenty. Right, Amor?"

"Is that a question, Baby?"

Olga laughed. "Amor, don't get me started. I called to see if you got home all right."

"Thank you, baby. We got home heavenly."

"I wish I was there enjoying the wine and smoking a little bit with you two, si?"

"Si," I said. "I totally miss you, Olga."

"Amor, I love you even more when you call me by my name."

That night Letty slept in her room. I had my big bed to myself. I didn't try to figure it out. I passed out the instant my head hit the pillow.

Sometime later, my private line rang next to my bed. I fumbled for it in the dark.

"Yes," I said, barely.

"Oh, I'm sorry to wake you." It was Lola. She was not sorry to wake me.

"Stop calling me," I said, coming awake.

"Be glad no move was made against the tramp. That can change. I want what I've got coming."

"Lola, Nina—whatever your name is—who is the tramp, Camila or you?"

"I'm going to make you a believer, Mario."

"Fuck off," I said, "Some fucking cop you are. Blackmail and threats of murder."

"Why don't you report me?" she asked. Cocky daring voice.

"If I was a snitch, I would," I said.

"No one would believe you."

The line went dead.

Pasadena September 29, 1990

In the morning, I had Mason come over for breakfast. We sat in my breakfast nook, just the two of us. Letty and Tangles were working out. Miguel brought out breakfast pastries and coffee for Mason, and breakfast meats for me. I was on a no carb kick for a week, working off all that Italian pasta. It was no chore. What Miguel can do with breakfast meat is probably illegal in some places.

"Fix it so I can record calls on my phones," I told Mason.

"How many lines do you have?"

"I want to record my personal line. It rings in my bedroom, my office and two or three other places. Can we get that done?”

"Want the recording to be active all the time or just when you want it on?”

"Easier if it's always on.”

"Want me to tell me about it?" Mason asked. He drained his coffee cup.

Miguel refilled it, put the pot on the center of the table, then left the room.

I didn't answer until we were alone again. "Lola is still making threats.”

"I'll have it done today. We won't be able to use it as evidence," Mason said. "If you tell her you are recording or we install a beep, there's a better chance to get it in as evidence.”

"Mason, I'm not looking to prosecute her. I just think there should be a record of her reckless threats.”

"Say no more. Consider it done.”

When Lola called again, she was on my cell. The next time she called, it was on cell again. It was as though she knew the private line was bugged.

Olga made an almost unannounced visit.

"Amor, I just landed in Ontario. We got each other overnight. Are you excited?”

"Hurry," I said. "I'll leave the office now and beat you to the house.”

"Si Amor, just got in the car. Riana is with me.”

That night, there were too many candles to be dark, but the ambiance and aroma was sensual. During a sex break, we faced each other, lying on our sides, talking.

"Lola keeps calling, keeps making threats.”

"Ignore her, Amor. Let's not talk about her.”

"What if she's not bluffing?”

"She's bluffing.”

"Baby, if you or Camila had anything to do with her getting shot or the attempt on her life at the hospital, I'd say to pay her."

"Amor, don't be so stupid."

I sat up. "I'm not stupid, Olga." I clutched her arm. "I'm worried about you. You're not ten feet tall and bullet-proof."

She shook me off, and sat up, centered on the huge bed. I sat up. There we were, facing each other, illuminated by candles, a foot from each other, yet miles apart.

"I hate that word stupid," Olga said.

I let it pass as she was the first one to use it.

"I don't need to know the truth. I'm just saying that if Camila ordered what happened, let's pay her. If not a million, an amount she settles for."

Camila didn't answer right away. She lay down and beckoned me to do the same.

"I know how this works. You pay a blackmailer once, they come back for more."

I felt a sense of confirmation. My suspicions were right. One of them had had something to do with the attempts on Lola's life. I could feel Olga caving. She was on the verge of agreeing that Lola should be paid something.

"Make love to me like you were a little while ago, and we talk about this in the morning, si?"

I embraced her, kissed her hard on the lips.

"Si," I said. I don't know why I remembered in that moment that Olga had killed every man aboard the plane. Olga was entirely capable of ordering a hit on Lola. Camila might have a reputation as a badass, but I'd seen Olga's true colors. It could have been either of them.

It was nearly six when breakfast was served on the table in my bedroom. We'd ordered over the intercom. Caro delivered it on a rolling cart which she left outside my door after she'd set the table. A savory steak and vegetable hash for me, Colombian pastries—Arepas de Huevo and Arepas con Quesito[32]—for Olga.

Olga took one sip of her black coffee, set it down, and said carefully, "I'll give you five hundred thousand. We can never tell Camila."

"I think Camila should be in on it, and it's a million she wants."

"Amor, she'll never go for it."

"When will you see her again?"

"Amsterdam in about a week."

"Have a talk with her. Tell her I think she should agree to pay up."

"Why do you feel that way all of a sudden?"

I wasn't going to beat about the bush. I looked her straight in the eye. "Either you or Camila had something to do with what happened. I don't care who, and I'm not interested in the details. All I know is that I'd tell Lola to get fucked if you were both innocent."

"Amor, you know nothing. Don't think that way."

Olga's tone was unconvincing.

"Baby, pay the cop."

"What if it's a trick?" Olga asked.

"Mason says there's nothing there for entrapping us. We're paying her so she doesn't carry out her murder threat."

Olga nodded in agreement. "I'll talk to Camila." She put her hand over mine and looked at me earnestly. "Amor, I had nothing to do with it."

I smiled. "I know," I said. I was lying. I had not forgotten the dead flight crew.

Minutes after Olga, Riana, and the guards left for the airport, my cell phone rang. It was totally Olga to call me right after leaving.

"Olga, miss me already?"

"This is not Olga."

---

[32] Corn cakes with eggs and corn cakes with cheese

It was Lola.

"Way too early in the morning for you to start," I said.

"Did you get my compensation?"

I hesitated, unsure I should say anything. "I'll let you know soon."

Silence.

"Are you putting me on?"

"Tell me how you know what is going on, and I'll tell you about the compensation."

"What do you want to know?"

"You call me minutes after Olga leaves my house. Is that a coincidence?"

Silence. Long pause.

"It's a coincidence. Olga was at your house?"

"Lola, call me later. I have to split for the office. I'm working on what you want."

I called Mason from my car. "I want my entire house checked again like you did when you first came on board," I said.

"I assume she doesn't call you on the private line?"

"Nope. Seems like she knows everything that is going on."

"I'll check, but I doubt anything is compromised. Last time it took five days to go through the house."

"That's okay. Whatever it takes." I didn't mean to sound frustrated, but I was.

Pasadena October 5, 1990

My secretary Alicia was off for a week. Letty and Tangles took her place as needed. Alicia's desk was unmanned. The girls worked out of their own office. At eleven AM according to the clock on my desk, Letty walked in, huffing and puffing. I knew she wasn't out of breath. The Boston Marathon wouldn't make my girl break a sweat. She is way too fit to be out of breath.

"Boss, that bitch Lola is at reception. Want me to run her ass out?"

"Easy," I said. "She's a cop. Don't mess with her. Go get her and be extremely polite. Pretend she's still the girl you used to like."

"Are you sure, Boss?"

"Letty, go get her."

She stuck her tongue out at me and saluted.

I couldn't help wondering why she would be here again.

Letty opened my office door, stepped inside, and Lola walked in. Behind her, Tangles was standing there with her hands on her hips, looking belligerent. I got up, walked past Lola to the door, and shooed out the girls. I locked the door. Lola grabbed my arm.

"Have a seat," I said.

"No hand shake, no kiss. You've gotten so cold."

I looked her over without trying to look like I was looking her over. She was dressed the plainest I had ever seen her. She was wearing a slim black pencil skirt, black stockings, black heels. The skirt reached halfway down her calf, but there was a deep slash that showed peeks of her legs when she walked; and when she sat, she took a seat across from my desk, the same seat she'd used during her previous visit, and crossed those exquisite legs. My mouth dried up. The shirt was plain cotton, blindingly white, buttoned down the front. She wore something around her neck, a splash of color, tied like a man's tie. She fixed her eyes on me. No coyness there. She loosened that tie and slid it up over her head the way Letty wore a headband when she was working out. Her fingers went to her top button and opened it. Second button. Third button. The shirt revealed a deep v of her creamy skin. I could see her collar bones, the hollow at her throat, the pulse throbbing in her neck. I won't lie. I was waiting for the next button.

My intercom light flashed. I didn't pick it up, but it was enough to get me out of the trance. I hit the mike and told Letty to hold my calls.

"Lola, I'm busy. Tell me in five words or less why you came here." I must be a hell of an actor. My insides were a volcano, but my words were ice.

"You baited me. That's why I'm here."

"Baited you?"

"You said you were working on my compensation."

I sat down and looked across at her. Lola was beautiful and like no other cop I'd ever imagined, even now with her face bare of makeup, and her long brunette hair pulled up in a pony tail, the knot of the tie over one of her ears, the long ends trailing down almost as long as her hair. She still had that kittenish heart-shaped face that had first attracted me to her; when I saw that face, I re-membered the woman I'd liked, the woman I thought she'd been. I wondered how anyone could look that vulnerable and be a cop. But I was not about to forget that she *was* a cop, she'd been with me under false pretenses, and she was threatening the Camachos who were now my family.

"I *am* working on it. Not sure about the number I can get you."

"The number is still a million. Not a nickel less."

"Like I say, I'm working on it."

"That's chump change for them," she said.

To keep my cool, I pretended that I was on the mat with an opponent.

"Chances are pretty good I will do something about the compensation you are looking for, but there is a catch."

"But—"

I interrupted her, cutting off whatever she was going to say. "Leave me a number where I can always reach you. Do not call me. Do not show up on some street, or at my house, or at this office, unless we agree in advance that you can show up. You do that, and I'll probably get you paid. I know what you want. I don't know I can get that much. At this very moment, I am not sure of any-thing at all. I have a good feeling that you might get lucky."

We talked for about five minutes after that. No argument, no sex, no lunch, no kiss, no seduction, no sarcasm. Not even a handshake. She stopped at the door, her back to me. Fifteen second of buttoning, and adjusting the tie, and she was as cool and unapproachable as when she'd arrived. She was gone. She wanted the so-called compensation in the worst way.

Letty and Tangles appeared the instant she left. I raised both hands to stop them from coming any closer.

"There is nothing new to report. She's gone. I have three leases to go over."

"She's gone for now, Boss," Letty said.

"Babies, scram. I know you have work to do."

I opened the door and walked over to the leases Andrea had left early this morning when we'd met in the conference room. This time it was Tangles that saluted, but without showing me her tongue.

I reached for the stack of leases. I ran my eyes down the first page and realized where I was. Sitting at the conference table. I pictured when Lola had been here before, how we'd made use of the conference table. I must have started that first page over a dozen times. An hour passed, and I had made no headway. It was like the leases were written in pig-Latin. It is true that I regretted not biting the apple that Lola offered. My mind kept drifting to the last session in the conference room, and all the times before. Whatever her profession, Lola and I were sexually compatible.

I found myself oddly sympathetic to Lola. In personal injury cases, the business I had been in for most of my life, a person gets hurt at the hands of another, and they get compensated. A family loses a loved one in a plane crash, they go for compensation. Doesn't bring the loved one back, but compensation is a must.

Lola survived being shot after being with me at the Hilton, and she survived the second attempt on her life when she was in a coma. The dude that Mason's man shot to death had been there to finish Lola off. I had zero evidence, but I knew Olga or Camila—or both—had had a hand in that crime. Lola was entitled to compensation. She was right. She should have money coming.

Lola's threat to kill one or both of the Camachos if compensation wasn't paid was unnecessary. Was the threat pure drama, or was Lola serious?

If she was that pissed off, what was to stop her from following through on her threat after she got her compensation?

Mason's experts finished combing Casa Luna from top to bottom and reported there were no bugs, no compromises of any type, anywhere.

"I'll write you a check. How much do I owe you?"

"It's part of my billing to Olga. Don't worry about it."

"I ordered the extra work, Mason."

"Mario, work it out with Olga, please."

I let it go. Fuck it.

A day did not pass without my talking to Olga. We connected one way or another. In spite of what Lola had said, in spite of what Mason had said, I was very careful on the phone.

"Did you speak to your sister?"

"I discussed the matter, told her about your recommendation. She was not happy about it, but she did agree."

"Can I tell her?"

Silence.

"Olga?"

Silence. I thought the call dropped.

"I'm here," she finally spoke. "Can it wait until I return?"

"I can take care of it, and you can give it back to me when I see you."

Silence.

"Olga?"

"Why this sudden rush?"

"Olga, if you got the green light, let me just do it."

Silence.

"Olga what is it?"

"I hate the fucking bitch," she said in an angry voice.

Pasadena October 15, 1990

I called the number Lola had given me. It had been maybe ten days since I'd seen her. She'd kept her word. She had neither called nor surfaced anywhere.

"I need to see you at Casa Luna," I said.

"When?"

"You tell me," I said.

I had a million in my safe. It had stayed snuggled in there for a very long time. It was there when the safes were taken from the fourth floor and moved to the first level of the house. It had made it through the last fire. It was now going to Lola. I put the hundreds in a duffle bag and carried it up to my office, leaving it next to my desk.

"Letty, Lola is coming over," I said. "I'll get the front door after the gate calls."

"I'll be in my room, Boss."

Tangles had gone home, so it was just Letty and me. The workers had gone to their quarters.

Lola arrived a little after nine that night. We rode the elevator up to the fourth floor. She was again dressed in black. Black slacks, black silk shirt untucked, black shoes and her hair was pulled back.

We rode the elevator in silence and entered my office that was all lit up. I pointed to a chair.

"You're so cold," she said.

"You're the cold one, baby," I said. "I'm going to ask you to remove all of your clothes, and it's not because we're going to have sex."

"You think I'd be wired when I'm here to commit a felony?"

"I don't know what to think, Lola."

I sat back in my chair.

She was out of her clothes in a minute. I was surprised she was wearing panties.

"Is this enough?"

"I'm afraid not. Shoes and underwear."

I picked up her clothes, and felt every inch of fabric to see if there was anything sewn in. I inspected the shoes and had her dump the contents of her purse on my desk.

She was not happy.

Her badge was sitting on my desk. I flipped it over and glanced down. *Nina Caputo.*

"Are you sure you don't want to explore my cavities?" she asked.

"You can get dressed," I said. I lifted the duffle to my desk near her. "Twenty-two pounds of hundreds. One million bucks. Lola, if you double-cross me, you will become my enemy. Don't do it."

"Who is threatening who now?" She turned her back on me and shrugged into her shirt, then the skirt.

"Not a threat, a simple warning. I don't trust you."

"The bitches are copping to attempted murder, or they wouldn't have come up with this bread, right?"

"You asked for a million dollars. You got the million. Tell me this is over."

She turned to face me, stared at me with no challenge in her face. She buttoned her blouse.

"It's over."

"Tell me you will make no attempt to hurt or kill Olga or Camila, not ever."

"Fuck off, Mario."

I put my hand on the duffle bag.

"Are we going to play games, Mario?"

"Promise me."

"Did you really think I was going to kill anybody?" Lola laughed. "I'm not the crook here."

My hand remained on top of the duffle bag. I pulled it toward me. I remained seated as she put everything back in her purse, including the underwear she had not put on.

"Olga, if you want to take this twenty-two pounds of money with you, I want to know your threat is off the table. If you think I'm bluffing, try me."

She reached for the duffle bag. "The threat is off the table. I promise not to harm Olga or Camila in any way, ever." She grabbed my hand. "That will change if I get even the slightest inkling that they have sent someone after me again." She let go.

"I don't know what you mean by again," I said.

"Mario, it's you who are playing a game."

She grabbed the bag. "I'm out of here," she said.

I got up and followed her to my office door. When I opened the door, I saw Letty about fifteen feet away, leaning against the banister.

"Boss, I'll see her out."

I nodded.

"Okay, take the stairs."

I figured the stairs were safer than the close quarters of the elevator. I didn't want Letty taking a punch at her or the other way around.

"I'll walk behind you," Lola said and pulled her gun out of her purse. "No games, Letty."

Before she finished the sentence, Letty disarmed her and waved the gun in Lola's face.

"I should pistol whip you, bitch," Letty said.

"Letty, stop that shit," I said. "Get away from her."

I moved to the stairs, grabbed the gun from Letty and handed it back to Lola.

"Put this fucking thing away right now," I said. "Let's go."

I grabbed her arm and that's how we walked down to the second floor. We exited via the front door. I stood on my front steps while she got in her car, cleared the guard house and passed through the front gates. Letty walked behind me back into the house.

"I'm sorry Boss. I couldn't control myself. I don't know what's going on except that I know she did you wrong. I wanted to beat her to a pulp. I thought about throwing her over the banister."

I said nothing.

"I'm sorry." Letty started crying inside the house. I picked her up and carried her up to the fourth floor to my bedroom. I cradled her close to me. Tears became sobs that made her chest convulse. I had never seen her cry like this.

I told Letty the story she had not heard—the payment and the reason. Letty deserved to know that Lola wasn't threatening me directly. The beef was between Lola, Olga and Camila.

"I believe they had something to do with what happened to Lola. A million seems like a lot of money, but when you consider how close Lola was to death, it's a trifling amount." I was remembering what Lola had said, the amount was a pittance. For the Camachos, a million was peanuts.

"You can't jump the gun, ever," I said. "If you had hurt her, she would not have it coming. She lied to us about being a whore, but she had a job to do. Tonight, this was personal. She was here to get paid money she deserved."

"I was ready to kill her. I'm sorry. Please, no more secrets. You know you can trust me. I wouldn't have felt like I needed to defend you if I'd known what it was about. You're my life. Mario, you and me, we're like one. I would never let you down."

I hugged her. My eyes watered and I felt a lump in my throat. "I love you, Letty."

"I love you so much more," she said between tears.

We drank wine sitting up in bed and smoked most of a joint. My cell rang. It was Lola.

"Mario, thank you. I owe you."

"You don't owe me," I said.

"Not tonight, but I have more to tell you. I'll be in touch."

"I heard her," Letty said. "Could be she wants to come through for you."

I took a good swallow of wine.

"I haven't wanted to believe everything she told me about Pepe, but tonight I believe it. I also believe she does know more and will be back to tell me. She said if she got compensated, she wanted to quit her job," I said.

"Do you think she'll really quit?"

"I don't know her well enough to answer that. A million dollars is a whole bunch of money. I know the shooting and the coma, they messed with her head. They made her think about life."

"I don't hate her any more. Am I looney or what, Boss? Is it the pot talking?"

I hugged her close to my chest. I kissed the top of her head. "You're not looney, baby. I think she got a raw deal." I got out of bed. "Come with me," I said.

I walked into my office and switched off the camera. I took the video out of the VCR. Letty followed me as I walked down to my safe and put the recording away for safekeeping.

"Boss, how long has that camera been hidden there?" Letty asked.

"I set it up knowing she was coming to pick up the money. You were asleep."

She nodded sleepily and put her hand in mine.

"Good idea."

Hopefully, I'd never have need of it.

Pasadena October 15, 1990
Letty

Mario believes Olga or Camila tried to kill Lola. He said we're going to tell Tangles the entire story. No more secrets. I can never trust Lola after the undercover shit, but if those Camachos tried to kill me like they did her, I would have demanded more than a million. I don't believe Olga and Camila will let her get away with the money. If she ends up missing or dead, it will be a Camacho move. If she's really been watching them for years, she should know how vindictive they are. Lola has no chance. Cops can get killed too.

If I ever talk to her again, I will tell her to sleep with one eye open and not to quit the agency. It may be the only protection for her. I was ready to throw her off the banister. Thank God I didn't. At least I know what it's about, now. That's a long way to the bottom, and dead is forever. I almost killed her. I gotta get over this. Point is, she's still breathing, and I'm still breathing. I can't believe I'm so shaken up over something that didn't actually happen.

Pasadena October 15, 1990
Tangles

I've always known Olga is a mafia tramp. Lola's a tramp, too, not for the sex, but for being an undercover cop that lied to all of us. Olga though, she sends out to kill the cop and fails, fails twice then Lola flexes and demands a million fucking dollars or else. And she gets it! Fuck, marvelous. Olga and Camila were found out and they had to pay up. Gutsy move for Lola. Problem is, her life expectancy ain't what it used to be. No way the Camachos just let her get away with blackmailing them.

Munich October 16, 1990
Olga

It's cold outside. October in Germany, you can't expect anything else. I'd like to be having breakfast on the patio, but it is too cold out there. Camila and me—our suites are not adjoined but were on the same floor and side by side. I dressed for the day and came over here to breakfast with Camila in her suite. She was still in her robe but would be leaving the hotel in two hours or so. I will be out of the hotel by noon and wheels up an hour later. I am headed to Panama. Camila was going home to Bogota.

"I let you talk me into it." She slammed down her coffee cup. The china clattered but didn't break.

She was still hissing like a wet cat about Lola.

"Hermanita, enough already. Let's move on. I trust Mario's instincts."

"I could have just had her done in and really be done with her," Camila snapped.

We'd polished off half of the croissants from the basket that room service had delivered on a silver platter. Nice platter, and it should be. This is one of our hotels. We finished a couple of decorative pats of butter that were shaped like fruit and served on ice. The jam at the hotel is marvelous. We were only having bread and jam and coffee for breakfast, but the bread was excellent, and the jams and jellies were even better. Nothing's wrong with our appetites.

"Hermanita, I know you love me. On the love you have for me, promise me that you will take no action against the lady cop." I brushed the crumbs off my hands and put my knife aside. I knew this was going to be an important confrontation. Camila was out for blood. It's how her father would have been. It's how her brother was. I wonder if her father had ever taken her aside as mine did to teach her the details of the role no one would have expected Camila to inherit.

Camila tore into a fresh croissant, avoiding my look. She ripped a piece off savagely, and buttered it, tearing into it with her sharp teeth.

"Hermanita, promise me."

Camila focused on me. We stared at each other, frozen, no longer eating.

"You are willing to forego that this whore blackmailed me, us?"

"Yes. I want this to die right here and now. I don't want to mess with cops. I don't want Mario to get any backlash if something happens to her. We are everywhere, but Mario is there in the US, and he is making you millions, Hermanita."

Camila blinked. Her voice was expressionless. "I promise, I will do nothing."

After Camila left for the airport, I sat with Riana while she had breakfast.

"If it wasn't for Mario, I would not have pushed Camila like I did. The cop deserves to die for threatening to kill us."

"In Spain, even the meanest mafioso will not harm a cop. Even I know this."

I laughed at Riana. She seldom looked serious. "How do you know?"

"I watched movies for years. The ones made in Spain."

"You don't want more blood on your hands, Olga. Be nice. I keep thinking of those men that died in your plane."

"Amor, those men would have killed us had I not beat them to it."

"Oh, I know. I was there, and mine was one of the lives you saved. I'm saying that you don't want more blood on your hands. Let this creepy cop be. She will certainly take that money and disappear."

I can only hope that will be true.

"Amor, if she comes back looking for more, she will be dead meat."

Chapter 17
Pasadena October 16, 1990
Mario

Andrea had Letty and Tangles working via phone with Rene Guzman, a small, mostly domestic airline operator headquartered in Guatemala. He had six Boeing 737s. His only international flight was to Mexico City; his other routes were domestic. Three of his planes were upwards of twenty years old. We—GAL—leased newer planes to him. Leases were negotiated in writing and on the phone. Operators rarely came in. Rene wanted to lease more planes than his credit qualified him for.

"He hasn't been with us long enough to expand his credit line," Andrea told Letty and Tangles.

"Then why give him to us?" Letty asked.

"Because we want him happy. You and Tangles can delay him for a year. Break it to him a little at a time. His deal will fly when he has more credit history with us."

"Boss, the owner of LAG in Guatemala wants an appointment," Tangles said. "Letty and I have taken turns telling him we can't expand his credit line for at least another year, but he's not buying it."

"Okay, check in, and make an appointment."

According to the credit application on file, Rene was a year older than me. He walked in with determination, a small, muscular man in a decent suit, but nothing fancy. His hair was black and cut short. His records mentioned he'd been a pilot in the Guatemalan military, and had built his airline career from that, though he rarely flew his commercial flights any more. He spoke good English. I saw sunglasses folded in his coat pocket, and the telltale pale skin they left around his brown eyes.

I switched to Spanish. "I have the reports. But you tell me where you stand. I'm listening."

"We sell out two daily flights to and from Mexico City," he said. "I need another two planes, newer planes. I can make a bundle of money if I have more flights."

Andrea had given me the latest financials that he had faxed to Letty and Tangles. I had never been good at math, but I was getting quite good at reading financials. For years I studied the monthly reports I received for my apartments. It was easy to tell that Rene was in the black, and with his positive cash flow, had some money in the bank.

He hadn't been in my office twenty minutes when he revealed why he had come in person. He had a proposal.

"Lease me three planes and I'll give you ten percent of the company."

"I'm in the leasing business. Don't want to be an operator," I said.

Pepe had started with his own airline company, then sold his routes and leased out all his planes. It must have not been as profitable to own the airline as it was to lease them.

"Take a chance with me," he said, leaning forward. "I don't pay off, pick up the planes, lease them to someone else. 737s, you can dump them easy."

I smiled at Rene. He was determined, I'd grant him that much. "Even if I agree, I have to find three planes for you," I said. "Newer 737s are not easy to get."

"I know an operator in Paraguay that has the planes. You can buy them and lease them to me."

I was surprised that anyone had planes to sell that I didn't know about. Good used planes were something we were always searching for.

"I'm not promising anything. Give me details about the planes, and I'll look into it."

Rene had an outdoorsy face, sun-darkened like he rarely went into his offices. He flashed his white teeth, a big smile cutting deep grooves in his leathery cheeks.

Several months later, instead of the three 737s he asked for, GAL leased him four.

I told Camila and Olga about the ten percent interest in his airline.

"Keep it for yourself, Amor," said Camila.

"Yes," Olga agreed. "It will look messy for GAL to own a piece of an airline it is doing business with."

"As you wish," I said. "But don't come crying later when I am raking in money off my interest in the company. And by the way, I got an option to purchase another ten percent at any time for $500,000 US."

"Amor, wonderful," Olga said. "Our children can use the money."

"What children?" Camila snorted, rolling her eyes.

Olga's lips turned down the tiniest bit, but otherwise, she ignored her.

I had a good feeling about Rene. Since his visit to Los Angeles, we had stayed in touch by phone on a regular basis. He was instrumental in hooking me up with the operator who had the planes and provided a solid package to justify stretching his credit line.

GAL carried the paper on his lease, and no justification was necessary. Andrea was a thorough financier.

"No one can ever criticize you for going overboard," she'd say to me after we closed a deal that was iffy.

The reason we were growing so quickly was the relaxed way we extended credit. Pepe had gotten started by taking chances with marginal operators looking to lease an extra plane for a short term. I wasn't quite the gambler that Pepe was—it was not my company —but just as I had rolled the dice with Rene, I had done it before, and would do it again. I was getting quite wealthy working Pepe's idea of capitalizing on aviation leases. I'd been his friend, but I'd never known him. Now that the secret of his abuse was out, I despised his memory. If he had not died in the plane, I'd have killed him. Just like that.

I was certain that Letty and Tangles had enough of hanging around waiting on plane crashes. It was official. I had them back on payroll plus commission.

"Andrea, I don't want to push them, but if you see potential, go out of your way to teach them."

"Keep them together? One office, shared secretary, partnership desk, same clients?"

"At first, yes. Maybe they work better together. They've always been a team with me. If you see that they will benefit by splitting them up, see how they feel about it, and do it gradually."

Letty had done a good job getting Wong to expand. I had the feeling she wanted to do more. She and Tangles did work well together. They had transitioned from working occasionally and filling in when someone was on vacation to the acquisition of used inventory and finally to full-time leasing. It is possible that a big chunk of what they earned went to clothes. The way they dressed like bankers reminded me of Melina. She used to get all dressed up to work in her market. Letty had picked up Melina's sense of style. Sometimes she acted as an office concierge, putting out food from my private kitchen or the office kitchen during a meeting. She'd picked up a real sense of sophistication and style from all the traveling. She was a quick study and could do anything.

"Andrea, I'm indebted to you for what you've done with my girls."

"No, you are not. Besides, they are our girls. GAL needs people like them."

Pasadena October 16, 1990
Andrea

I want to tell him that the payback I want is for him to fuck me right here and now. Bend me over the desk and slam me from behind. Dan would never know, but I would. We agreed there would be no sex outside of the two of us. Dan was no angel before we met, but he said he would give it up if I did, including giving up Camila. There was not much to worry about Camila, because she hasn't been around since the office opened in Los Angeles. I left my relationship with her back in Milan. Dan and me, we're talking about just saying fuck it to all the tradition and pomp, and just running off to Las Vegas, telling no one until afterwards, just to be done with it. Neither of us wants a big wedding. His family is tiny, and I have no family in the US other than the office staff and Mario and the girls.

When Dan brings up how we should get married, I tell him, "We will. What's the rush?"

"For one thing, I can give up my apartment, or you can give up yours."

"My apartment is a work benefit. I pay nothing."

"Our marriage would settle your immigration situation."

He's right. My attorney is working on getting me a green card based on GAL needing me permanently in Los Angeles. Eventually that will result in my getting legal, but marriage is faster.

Pasadena October 16, 1990
Letty

I am learning the ropes of working with millions of dollars worth of planes. My first day, I didn't even know for sure how to write one million. Such a dumbass. I'd feel bad about it, but at least Tangles didn't know either. We passed up two airline crashes this year. Gonor was mad as hell, but we are busy up the ass at GAL, and I love it. I should say, we love it. Tangles digs it, too. We work for our paychecks, and the bonuses are coming in.

I love working near him. Sometimes I don't see him until it's time to come home, but just knowing he's across the hall makes me feel like everything is all right.

The brat just won't go out for lunch. He orders in. Sometimes I have lunch with him, and sometimes it's Tangles and me both having lunch with him.

Boss is on Tangles to move back in her room at Casa Luna. She's been in and out before, here during a crisis or when she was sick or hurt, but always moved back out. She finally caved but would not get her stuff over here until Boss got Olga's blessing..

Olga said, "I like the idea because without Letty and you, it would be a lonely house for my baby."

I guess Olga doesn't know, the boss doesn't tolerate being lonely. If we're not around, he finds someone to keep him company. He does not like being alone, and maybe that is part of his wanting Tangles around—so I won't be lonely when he's not around. I'm thinking she considers Tangles and me as a pair are less competition than either of us alone. Anyway, Tangles quit going home every night to her apartment. She still has her own place just like I do, but we basically live in our bedrooms at Casa Luna. And why not? You could fit our whole apartment into either one of our bedroom suites. Anyway, we have a routine, and living in the same house, she doesn't have to drive over at five in the morning to work out with me. We are right there. Boss gets up and works out about that time in the same gym, but alone. Tangles and me, we work out together. At about seven, we have breakfast. If Mario hasn't left yet, we eat with him. If not, we have breakfast and get to the office by 8:30 when Andrea wants us to clock in—only we don't have to actually use a clock. Boss likes to leave at three in the afternoon to avoid traffic, but sometimes he doesn't get out until late. Tangles and me, we hang out until he's ready to leave, then follow him home.

Tangles and Boss talk sometimes about going out to eat or go clubbing. Sure, we get out once in a while, but why go anywhere when we got Casa Luna? Casa Luna's got everything.

I don't think Mario would stay home if we were not around. When we were out on plane crashes, he'd get lonely and end up consoling himself at the Whisky, Playboy, and other clubs. That's how he met up with Lola. And the one before her, and the one before that.

Pasadena January 15, 1991 (Tuesday)
Mario

A couple of months went by after I paid off Lola. Christmas came and went, and my birthday. Sometimes I thought a call was going to be Lola, but it never was. I wondered if she was still alive. We were halfway through January, almost noon, and she caught me at my desk in the office.

"It's me," she said. "How you been?"

"What a surprise," I said. I was glad to hear her voice. Glad to know that the Camachos had left her alone.

"Guess what?"

"Tell me so I don't have to guess." I was happy that she wasn't six feet under.

"I got my medical discharge. A week ago, I got my walking papers from my employer. I'm free."

I heard excitement in her voice.

"Is that good?"

As an FBI agent, I figured she'd be safer than as a civilian, although that had not stopped anyone that night she was shot.

"Yes, it's good."

"In that case, I'm happy for you. Should I call you Lola or Nina?"

"Take your pick." She laughed. "Do you feel like seeing me?"

"Not a good idea. Everything seems peaceful. Let's keep it that way."

"Oh, come on. Do I have to beg?"

"Lola, what do you want from me already? You got what you wanted. You seem happy you got your walking papers. Go have fun. Travel. Do something you always wanted to do but couldn't."

"I still have something to tell you," Lola said.

"Lola, don't do this." There she was again, dangling answers I've been needing for a long time.

"Don't be so sure of yourself, Mario Luna. I'm not after you precious body. There's lots of men with big dicks just ready to latch on to a chick like me. I just want to meet up with you, lunch, dinner, hang out together, talk. We don't *have* to fuck."

There is something about what happens in a man when a woman is talking the way Lola was talking to me. I wasn't upset at her any longer.

"When and where?"

"Beverly Wilshire. I'll ring you between two and three."

Fuck it. I had to hear what Lola had to say, and I had to hear it soon. I'd learned my lesson with Bruno Bruno. A few years ago, I put off talking to Bruno. He had something he wanted to tell me. I was pissed off at him and put him off. He was dead the next day. I still don't know what he wanted to tell me. I wasn't waiting around this time.

I flipped my cell phone open and got Olga on the line.

"She called. She wants to meet up. She has things to tell me that I've been trying to figure out for a long time."

Silence.

"Olga, are you there?"

"Why are you telling me this?"

"I'm not asking for permission, if that's what you mean," I said.

"With all the pussy you have hanging around the house, it isn't enough? You still ache for Lola, a bitch that blackmailed your fiancée, threatened to kill your fiancée."

"It was a mistake to call you," I said. "I'll be in touch."

I closed my flip phone, and that disconnected the call. What did I expect Olga to say? At least I told her the truth and got it out of the way.

My cell phone started ringing. It kept ringing. I didn't answer. A few minutes later, Alicia's voice came over my intercom.

"Miss Olga is on the phone for you. Line four."

I took a deep breath and picked up the phone. "I don't want to argue with you," I said.

"Don't hang up on me like that. Mario, it pisses me off."

Before I could respond, the phone went dead. Olga hung up on me.

It wasn't funny. Ironic maybe, but not funny—but I gave a harsh bark of laughter. I was more irritated than amused or angry. And it was no surprise, either. Olga liked to have the last word.

Letty was at her desk deep in conversation with a potential client when I stuck my head in her open doorway. Tangles was somewhere else. I waited a minute or two till the call ended, and she saw me standing there. She started to get up, but I waved her down.

"I have something to do and will be late getting home. Don't want you babies worried about me."

"Sure, Boss. Anything you want to share?"

"Not this minute, but I got nothing to hide. Talk later."

It was two and change when I drove towards Beverly Hills. Minutes before I arrived at the Beverly Wilshire Hotel, I got the expected call from Lola.

"Room 735."

The valet took possession of my Rolls. A few minutes later I rang the doorbell to 735. Lola let me in wearing a silk hotel robe and a big smile. I closed the door, picked her up and raced up the stairs to the bedroom with her in my arms.

I was out of my suit in record time. No conversation, only sighs and breathing. The comforter went flying off the bed and we crash-landed on it. I was on top, balancing so that I didn't crush her. She felt like horsing around and roughhousing, so we rolled, and she was on top, and than I was on top again.

After what had to be a solid hour of sex, we conked out, breathing heavily. I started laughing first.

"I thought we weren't going to fuck," I said.

She was also laughing.

"I never told you to fuck me or not to. You just ran up here with me, and it happened."

The menu is elaborate at this hotel, but we ordered loaded cheeseburgers, steak fries, and a tub of pistachio ice cream.

We ate at the dining room table on the first level of the suite. She was across from me.

"You said you had more to tell me," I said.

"I lied. I told you everything before. Something important like that, I wouldn't hold back."

I was not shocked, nor was I angry to hear this.

"Tell me, what you shared with me is true, right?"

"Absolutely. Pepe was behind everything I told you about."

"I believe you, but every so often I have my doubts."

"Don't doubt it, Pepe was behind it. He was a real scumbag."

"Thanks for telling me," I said. "I told Olga you had called and had to tell me something you hadn't told me before."

"And what did she say?"

"She wasn't happy."

"Why tell her anything?"

"Because I'm stupid," I said.

"You're a lot of things, Mario Luna. Stupid isn't one of them," she said.

I held out my hand. She took it.

"Lola, Nina, you're so hot," I said.

"You say that to all the girls," she laughed. "Do you have any idea how many times I heard that on a bug? I never really thought you'd be saying it to me, but I hoped so." She laughed and changed the subject. "There's a great jacuzzi in the master bathroom. Want to give it a whirl?"

"I'm so full," I said.

"So am I. We can do it later. Are you in a hurry?"

"I'm not in a hurry," I said. I looked at her. "You are so pretty, Lola. Way too pretty to be a cop."

"You know I got my walking papers. I'm out. I'm not a cop anymore."

"Do they let you keep your gun?"

"Better believe it," Lola said.

After another round of sex, the room was thrashed. Lola called housekeeping. I handed the maid a ten spot, then Lola and I got in the jacuzzi. It was way too small for me, but being challenged by suchtight quarters made it fun. A half hour later, we came out to a bed made with fresh linen. The maid hit the bathroom like a white tornado, leaving them looking like they do when you first check in.

Lola said, "I'm spending the night. You should get dressed and go home."

"Just like that?" I chuckled.

"We had fun. Don't get the bitches pissed at you."

"You mean at us."

"They already are pissed at me, but I say fuck them if they can't take a joke."

I smiled at Lola. She was like Olga, in a way. Fearless.

I dressed but rolled up my tie and stashed it in my jacket pocket.

"I want to pay for the room," I said. "So, don't think I'm paying you like the old days."

Lola laughed hard. "I love getting paid to fuck you, but this time, it's my treat."

I put two thousand dollars on the dining room table, hugged her, kissed her.

"Lola, I'm really very sorry that you got shot and almost died. I don't blame you for what followed."

"I got my compensation. I hate them, and at times want to put a bullet in them, but I'll get over it. I know you had nothing to do with it."

I hugged her tight and cupped her ass through the silky robe.

"If you don't stop that, we're going to start it all over again."

When I got home, the girls did not greet me at the door like they used to. They were in their own beds. I went straight to my room and slept like a baby until nine the next morning when I rang Miguel and asked about the girls.

"They left for the office at 7:45. Told me not to disturb you."

I stayed home. At one in the afternoon, I headed down to my gym, stared inside, and went back up to my office. I didn't feel like messing with a workout. I called Olga from my office, worried over the possibility that Olga or Camila or both would do something to Lola. Not that Lola would be an easy mark. She was smart, knew who her enemies were, had extensive training, and no longer had to put herself at risk as she was when she was undercover.

"I should hang up on you," Olga said right off.

"Don't baby."

"Did you fuck her?"

"I didn't even see her," I lied.

"Lying asshole," she said in Spanish.

"I fucked her," I admitted.

The line went dead.

Fuck it.

I had dinner with Letty and Tangles that night in the wine room. I kept my promise about no more secrets. While we were eating, the craziest thing happened.

"Boss, look at the TV!" Letty said. She grabbed the remote and turned the sound on. It was a scene of Lainie sitting in a coffee house, singing some bilingual public service announcement. I didn't get the gist of what she was talking about, but we all laughed our heads off because it was Lainie. I think it was about safe sex.

"First thing in the morning, call the TV station and find out the next time that airs. Let's record it for Pixie."

"Sure thing boss! I wonder if this is remedial publicity after Jason. Anyway, she's right about the condom thing. Boss, if you want to fuck me again, you will need to use a condom, like Lainie says," Letty said. "That Lola, she has you under a spell."

"I don't believe in spells," Tangles said.

"I'm not under a spell," I said, taking a long drink of wine.

"Why tell Olga?" Tangles asked.

"She has Mason's dudes everywhere. How can she not know?" Letty asked.

"Thanks," I said. "Exactly."

"Boss, why cop to it?" Letty said. "Plausible deniability."

"Olga will get over it," I said.

"I'm more worried that she'll do something to Lola," Letty said.

I stopped eating and looked at her. "Do you think she's capable?"

Letty looked right at me. "You think she's capable or you wouldn't have given up a cool million. You want me to say she's not? One or both of them was capable last year. You think they got religion since then?"

Tangles said, "Boss, don't get pissed. We all know your fiancée and her sister are tough cookies. There's no telling how far they will go."

I said, "Babies, I love you with all my heart, but we can't just sit here and discuss this like it's not a crime. I had no evidence and still don't. So, chill."

"Chilled, I am. Just one question."

"Shoot," I said.

"When you gave her the money, she said she had more to tell you."

"I told you that when I asked her about it, she said she had nothing else."

"Boss, could she be holding out?" Tangles asked. "Maybe about that guy in the pickup that shot up the back of your car or the one that rammed you."

"Like it wasn't fishy that he gets bailed out, and taken to Mexico for questioning," Letty said, "We never hear from that guy again."

"What did Mason have to say when that asshole got shot?"

I said, "Stop. Of course, I want to know everything. I don't think those incidents are connected, and it wasn't Pepe, because he was dead when they happened."

"Unless he's not dead," Letty said.

"I've thought about that, too," Tangles said.

"We went to his funeral," I said.

"Boss, all we saw was a casket."

"After that fire, there wouldn't be anything to see," Tangles said.

I started laughing. "I think we're high. Do you hear us? Could we sound more paranoid?"

Letty and Tangles exchanged looks and joined me in laughter.

"I'm buzzed," Letty admitted.

Tangles high-fived her agreement.

Letty giggled. "Our weed supply is Olga. If she's ever pissed enough, she could poison us easy."

"Nothing would surprise me," I heard myself say, not meaning it. It got a laugh.

Later that night, I was in bed alone, almost asleep. The door opened and closed. The glow in the fireplace wasn't enough to show details. Side sleeper that I am, and facing the wrong way, I didn't need to see to know it was Letty. She slid under the covers. I felt her lips on my chest as she coiled herself next to me.

"I wasn't serious about the condom," she whispered.

If she had been looking at my face, she would have seen the smile. I kissed the top of her head.

"You can't believe Olga had anything to do with Lola's shooting," she whispered. "Tell me true, Mario."

"I told you already."

"If you believe she was instrumental in something so horrible, you couldn't possibly still want her. What am I missing?"

Letty's head pressed against my chest. Her left leg wrapped around my legs. I caressed her hair and kissed it again.

"Why you bring that up, baby?"

"Does it bother you I ask?"

"No, it doesn't bother me. How is Camila or Olga being behind a shooting any different from you wanting to toss Lola off the landing?"

"It's different. I wanted to, and maybe I would have, but I didn't. I had nightmares after just thinking about hurting Lola. But Olga—that kind of thing doesn't phase her at all."

I wasn't sure that Olga had anything to do with Lola's shooting. I was pretty certain that Camila did. Olga had said she'd had to talk to Camila about the million. It was Camila who pulled the strings. But even if Olga had something to do with it, I would still love her.

"I love you, Letty," I whispered.

"I know you love me. Thank you," she whispered back.

"Please don't thank me," I said.

"I don't mean thank you like thank you. I mean it like, it's good to hear you love me because I love you so much."

She moved up, her lips touching mine.

"Good night, Boss, sleep tight."

She moved to the edge of the bed and swung her leg over. I could hear her shuffling her foot around, searching for an errant slipper.

"Where do you think you're going?"

I caught her arm and pulled till she was beside me. She smiled up at me and gave a contented sigh. We slept that way through the night. Mostly slept, anyway.

Somewhere over Istanbul January 30, 1991
Olga

The main cabin on my plane is like a living room, only each seat has a seat belt, including the two sofas. Riana and I sat across from each other, a table between us. Our feet were stretched out, and occasionally we played footsies without bothering to look each other. We were both glued to a couple of magazines. We were flying from Istanbul, destination Morocco.

"The bastard hasn't called me in two weeks," I said to Riana.

"I know. It's the fiftieth time today you have said so," Riana said. "So call him."

"I can't call him from up here."

"Call him when we land."

"Are you paying attention?"

Riana laughed a little. "No."

"Puta."

"Yes, I'm a puta," Riana said.

I laughed. Riana is so laid back and easy to be around. I would be lonely flying without her.

"Want some popcorn or something?" I asked.

"Popcorn upsets my stomach."

"Stop reading already."

"Why? You're reading too." Riana looked up from the mag. "Have her make us some nachos with lots of cheese."

"That sounds good."

"Maggie," I said loud enough for the flight attendant to hear. "We're hungry."

We had a luxurious suite in Morocco at a hotel with a casino more lavish than any I had been to in Las Vegas. My Moroccan banker, Ahmed, got twenty-five million dollars delivered in two Louis Vuitton trunks. He simply loved the fancy trunks.

"Olga, you must send the monthly deposits like this, and I keep the beautiful works of art."

"You got it, Ahmed."

Each trunk cost a thousand dollars.[33] No wonder he loved them. I wondered how he intended to use them. They are not practical to travel with unless you are on a cruise, and even then, how many can you take on a cruise? If only the only expense of monthly deposits were the cost of two trunks. Ahmed was making a good chunk of money for allowing me to deposit cash in three accounts for clients. In Morocco, the accounts were numbered like in Switzerland. Moroccan banks were not as sophisticated as the Swiss, but all that mattered was getting the money into a bank account, from which it could be wired or moved or spent.

There is so much for me to keep track of. You can't make mistakes with big money like this. I keep a ledger with my own codes. For every million I deposit for a client, Camila gets between twenty-five and thirty percent. Camila honored the agreement I'd had with Pepe on my cut of each deposit.

After his father died, when Pepe inherited the family business, Pepe used his local connections to clean money for his customers. Ironically, his clients, the five cartel families, had been his father's competition. After I graduated from University, Pepe brought me in, taught me how he deposited cash in banks where he had connections. It had been his idea for me to travel making new connections, engaging friendly bankers everywhere except in the United States. "I am almost totally out of my father's business. I can make more cleaning the money for the competition," Pepe used to say.

He had a flat fee—thirty percent of everything he 'washed' was his. That was the source of the cash that Camila used to acquire assets.

I flew around paying for assets Camila purchased, and the rest of the time searched for bankers friendly to large deposits of green cash. I had to find more and more bankers, because the quantity of money from customers kept

---

[33] $1,000.00 in 1991 is equal to $1,877.68 in 2019.

increasing. I kept track of Pepe's thirty percent from each transaction. Eventually I had to put that money in banks too, because there was too much of it to turn quickly into assets. The benefactor of the excess, after I was paid, was Pepe's LAI company.

Pepe's father had cash stashed in many countries, including the United States. Pepe was against doing anything in the United States. The money in the US — millions of dollars—remained hidden, parked. Pepe feared moving it. He hated the US because of the year he spent in jail fighting a case that belonged to his father, not him.

When Mario came along, he got Mario to start acquiring assets using his father's old cash that was sitting around in storage. With it, Mario acquired a bakery, liquor stores, apartments, real estate, car washes and other finds. Once the assets were purchased, each business became another link in Pepe's money laundering network. Money from his father's stashes in the US was deposited as phony sales in each business thus reducing the US hoard of cash and increasing the banked capital. Taxes were paid on the income, and the money found its way into a bank account for LAI to work with any way it wanted. Of course, LAI was Pepe.

With Pepe gone, Camila became the contact person for the clients. They fed Camila the cash. My plane was loaded. Once I reached the destination where I had a friendly banker lined up, I was taken to a hotel and the cash delivered to the bank. In Amsterdam, the cash was moved to a container. Pepe had once told me that in Amsterdam there were multiple twenty-foot containers for cash. If a client sent ten million to be banked, it could be months before they received a bank deposit receipt for their seven million. Three went into Camila's pocket. My percentage came out of that three million. It's a good thing I'm a mathematical whiz.

Before Pepe presented the idea of money laundering to the competition, huge amounts of cash were lost: buried, lost to mold, flood, decay, etc. There was just more money than could be used without drawing the attention of authorities. Pepe's proposal to bank mob's illicit green cash quickly caught on.

Pepe stopped the drug business cold turkey, and let the competition take it over.

"Eventually the drugs would lead to getting caught. I'm over and out. I don't ever want to see the inside of a jail again. It's a wonder our parents were not locked up."

Once the plan had been to keep our customers happy for three years, and after that, they'd be on their own. Three years had come and gone, and I wasn't sure if it was really going to be over. My own money was growing tremendously. Getting richer is addictive. As far as Camila was concerned, just with the LAI assets, she is a billionaire may times over, but it is never enough. We are two of a kind. I want more and so does Camila.

Normally I would have stayed in Morocco one night and then be off, but on this trip, Ahmed was able to arrange a meeting for me with a banker who had a bigger bank. Just the kind of man I needed to be my friend.

"Make this happen, Ahmed, and I'll fuck you for an entire night."

Ahmed said, "Yes, with one condition."

"Condition?"

"Your friend sitting out in reception is part of the package?"

I pretended to be offended. "I'm not enough for you?"

"No negotiating. Say yes. I promise you will make a deal with my friend."

Here's what happened: I made the deal with his friend, Said. Said was fortyish, and good-looking. He did not get the money in designer trunks; he didn't get as high a percentage as Ahmed. He did get a night with me. It was effortless. I was pissed at Mario anyway. I needed a good fuck and I got it. I rode him hard, and he made me come till all I could do was moan and giggle.

Afterward, we lay around the hotel suite naked on the sheets. Said was smoking, looking tired and satisfied.

"This is a one-time thing, Said," I said.

"I don't buy that line," he said. "What if I waive my fee and take it out in trade once a month?"

"You think I'm worth that much?"

"You are," he said.

I figured he was playing me. He wasn't going to give up a million bucks for a night of sex with me.

"Sure," I said, "It's a date. I'll remind you next month."

The next night Ahmed got his way with Riana and me. Riana, she made it fun and exciting. She kept him occupied. I was rather out of it because of the night before with Said, but Ahmed would never know that. Besides, I could tell he favored Riana. The sex was a one-time thing. Once was enough. AIDS is everywhere.

When we left Morocco, I felt good. I had found a home for fifty million dollars,[34] and in thirty days, another fifty million.   The flight time from Morocco to Amsterdam was less than four hours. We stayed awake, and as soon as we were in the hotel in Amsterdam, we went to bed.

We shared a bed and sat talking in the dark like a couple of schoolgirls.

"We got laid, finally," Riana said as she moved close. "I lost track. Have you called him?"

I kissed her. "Nope. You'll be the first to know if I do."

"Oh, now it's if?"

"Said doesn't know it, but I'd fuck him every month, fee or not."

"Ahmed wasn't bad," Riana said.

"Said is hung like you'd have to see to believe." I used my hands to show how big.

Riana's eyes glinted in the dark. She moved closer. "Tell me more."

---

[34] $50,000,000.00 in 1990 is equal to $99,616,574.15 in 2019.

Pasadena February 17, 1991
Mario

I talked to Rene Guzman often. After all, I own ten percent of his airline, with an option for another ten percent.

"Mario, I have a good friend of mine, Rogelio Maduro, a small operator with two planes with one route from Montevideo to Sao Paulo. He has about a million in the bank, but almost no credit. He pays cash for everything. Can you talk to him?"

I knew what he meant but I asked, "Talk to him about what?"

"About leasing him a couple planes."

"What's in it for you?" I asked.

"Ten percent of the company, maybe."

"What's he going to do with two more planes?"

"Ask him. You will like him."

"How did he get the million?"

"Ticket sales and who knows what else?"

Right away I thought of drugs.

"Have him call me," I said.

When I hung up, I got this itch. Maybe owning a piece of these small airlines would turn into something for me. It was too early to tell if I was making any money on my ten percent with Rene, but I had a good feeling.

I called Letty and Tangles in and told them I would be talking to this new prospect that their customer Rene was referring.

"He's your customer if I do anything with him," I said. That would mean commissions for them.

Chapter 18
Pasadena February 17, 1991
Letty

It was just past eight. Mario had already told us he would be home late and not to wait up for him. Miguel had fixed us chili-lime vegetable soup and salad. Tangles and I sat with Miguel in the kitchen and ate. As savory as it was, none of us were very hungry. My uncle finished, stuck his dishes in the dishwasher, cheerfully told us to clean up after ourselves, and went off to work out—he's still into weightlifting. Tangles and I sat in the kitchen for a while, chattering away, though I don't think Tangles was feeling too good.

"I'm not positive, but I don't think he's talked to Olga for the longest time."

"Not that long. Right away you exaggerate. Maybe two weeks, big deal." Tangles puffed out her cheeks, then made a raspberry noise.

"Fuck, what's wrong, bitch?"

Tangles made a face. "I hate these fucking cramps."

"I'll make you some tea."

"You know I hate tea."

"Ungrateful is what you are."

"Why, because I don't want tea?"

"Want me to make you cookies?" I asked.

"Yeah, cookies and hot chocolate."

"Go to your bedroom. I'll do a delivery."

"I love you, Letty, even if you are a bitch."

I gave her the finger; she stuck her tongue out and left the kitchen.

I went in the pantry for a box of almond Hershey's, fixed a pan of cookies in record time, made a pot of hot chocolate for the two of us, and headed up to her room with a big tray.

We went through the hot chocolate and the cookies, then I tucked her into bed with a heating pad.

"Scream if you need anything," I said with a giggle.

"I don't think I can work out in the morning, so don't wake me at five."

"Sissy," I said.

"Right-on, I'm a sissy, bitch."

I leaned over and kissed my friend again. This time she bit me on the lip.

"Thank you," she said. "You take such good care of me."

The gameroom did not hold my attention. I grabbed a book from the den, and went to my room wondering if Mario was out with Lola again. I hoped not. Anyone else, but not Lola. Olga would be furious on top of already being furious. Olga hasn't called. He's playing hard to get and hasn't called her.

If Olga is what he wants, I hope Mario wises up. Lola is poison to Olga.

Pasadena February 18, 1991
Mario

Lola and I had been together since noon. It was almost ten. This time, I rented the room and called her with the number of the suite. Minutes after her arrival, we tore our clothes off. We devoured each other in endless sex. It was hours before we finally took a break. My lips found the scars. I made a trail of kisses where the surgeons left their mark when they went in for the bullets. The damage wasn't easily visible any more, because Lola had covered up the scars with a tattoo of a beautiful sunset scene.

"Don't fret, Mario. I don't hurt, and I'm alive. I'm going home next week."

"Where is home?"

I remembered she said the team had gone back to Florida.

"Miami. Will you come visit me?"

"If you want me to, I'll be there."

"Are we going to have an affair?"

"I don't know what you call what we're doing with each other," I said.

"It's called fucking."

"You're so hot," I said.

"So are you." She beckoned me close. We ordered food, then made a mess eating it off of each other. We ripped the sheets off and had room service come in and refresh the bed before we used it again. Maybe Letty was right that she had a spell on me. I left the hotel at two thirty AM. Lola stayed the night. Mason had mentioned she had a house in West Los Angeles, but I had never gotten her real LA address. As I drove home, I remembered the hours we'd spent at this same hotel. I was glad she was moving out of my immediate reach. As much as I wanted her, I wanted to get over her. What sense is that?

Pasadena February 19, 1991

I got home at four. I went straight to the gym and worked out, unsure where the energy was coming from. About the time I was finishing up, Letty came in for her workout.

"Where's Tangles?"

"Sleeping late and curled up with a heating pad."

I knew what that meant.

"Boss, I didn't think you made it home," Letty said.

"Of course, I made it home." If she'd gone to my bedroom, she already knew I hadn't sleep there.

"Boss, I think you're fibbing."

I smiled. "I'm fibbing. I got home an hour ago." I wanted to ask if Olga had called, but Letty would have told me right off if she had.

I showered, had breakfast and left for the office alone. I had an appointment with Rene's friend from Montevideo. I was excited at the prospect of owning a slice of another small airline. My meeting with Rogelio Maduro went three hours long, and that included lunch in my conference room. His financials showed how well the small operation was doing.

I agreed to find and lease him three aircraft, possibly 737s, and the newest ones I could find. It wasn't the ten percent offer that convinced me to help him, as much as his financials. After the meeting, the adrenaline wore off. I was tired and planned to leave early. Being sleep-deprived doesn't sit well with me.

My cell phone rang.

Olga.

"Were you testing me?" she asked, right off.

"Not testing you. I miss you," I said in a very calm voice.

"It's been twenty-one days. We haven't talked in twenty-one days," she said.

"Twenty-one long days," I said. "I miss you."

"Are you seeing her?"

"You mean Lola?"

"You know who I mean."

"No," I said.

"Amor, you have me. You have the girls. Why on Earth do you disrespect me by seeing this cop who threatened me?"

"Baby, that's in the past. I'm sorry I hung up on you. I'm sorry I haven't been in touch."

Silence.

"I'm sorry, too, Amor. I was so hurt."

She sounded so sincere that I felt guilty that I had just lied.

"Amor, with Melina, you almost married her a number of times. It was not a fuck and go. She was a threat, relationship-wise. Lola was a hooker, no threat. Then she went from hooker to cop and became a threat—and from cop to blackmailer, a double threat."

"Baby, we're on the phone."

"I don't care. You should know why I have a problem with you seeing Lola. You saw her again yesterday. It has to stop, Amor."

I made no attempt to deny or confirm. I heard her crying.

"I love you, Olga. No matter who I see or what I do, it's you. Come home."

"I can't. I'm stacked with commitments. Maybe you can come see me when I can stop in one place for more than two days."

"Deal," I said.

"Si, Amor. I want to see you. I adore you."

Pasadena February 19, 1991
Lola

It is three in the afternoon when I walk out of the hotel room. I have my overnight bag and purse. I am wearing jeans, a sweater, and a short ski jacket I would never wear in Miami. I take the elevator to the lobby and switch to the parking lot elevator. I dial Mario as I wander through the maze of cars on the second level.

"About to leave the hotel," I say, "if I can just find the damn car."

"I hope you got some sleep."

"I slept," I tell him. "How about you?"

"No sleep. Going home soon as I hang up. Thanks for a lovely time."

"Thank you too."

"You're leaving for Miami next week?"

"I am. I'll call you before I go."

"Be sure to."

"I found the car. Don't hang up. Let me get in. Keep me company for a minute."

"I'm here for as long as you want me."

I open the door to the Plymouth, toss my overnight bag and purse on the passenger side and get in the car. I close the door. "Okay, I'm in my rented wheels."

"Be sure it's your car. Don't want you arrested for getting in someone else's car." He laughs.

I laugh.

"Mario, thanks to you, I feel like the most beautiful woman in the world. That's how you make me feel. I'm sorry we started off with a web of lies from me. It was a job."

"Say no more. That's all in the past."

Holding the cell phone with one hand, I insert the key into the ignition.

"I had a crush on you going way back to the beginning, back when the team and I first started watching you from afar. I guess that goes back to when you first met Pepe. That was after you got back from Venezuela, when you'd been kidnapped back in 1975, like…fifteen years ago. That's a long time to be dreaming up ways of getting up close to you. Eventually my handler came up with the prostitution idea. Now that I've been with you, it's worth the wait. How lucky am I, getting what I've been wanting for so long?" I laugh, turn the key in the ignition.

Pasadena February 19, 1991
Mario

I heard a distorted noise, loud enough I pulled the phone away from my ear. Maybe she had dropped her phone.

"Lola, are you there?" I repeated myself a couple of times. I got up from behind my desk and walked over to the television which was on. I had turned on the TV this morning to see Lainie's spot because it just tickled me—but now that I was worried about Lola, I was not in the mood. I turned the sound off and left the remote on top of the television. There was no sound on Lola's end of the line. I had lost the call.

I went back to the desk, sat down, and dialed Lola's number. No answer.

I had a bad feeling. I could hear my own heartbeat, steady, regular. I quietly put my cell down on my desk. The office was quiet, but active. I could hear the heat being pumped through the vents, the muted voice of someone walking past my door, elevator music being piped in. Everything sounded normal except that unnatural blast I'd heard through the phone. It was like nothing I could compare it to. I grabbed the phone and hit redial again.

Nothing.

"Oh my God," I prayed aloud. "Don't let it be what I think." I was still hitting redial over and over. With my free hand, I dialed Letty on my desk phone.

She and Tangles walked in chattering with each other about some client thing. I was pretty agitated.

"Something happened. I can't get her on the phone."

"Her who?"

"Her—Lola. It's Lola. Something happened. She was in Beverly Hills. She just got in her car, then the phone blew up in my ear. I was talking to her. There was a loud blast. I mean boom! She was just getting in her car and the line went dead. Now she won't pick up." I was anxious, talking away like I was high on something. I hate feeling helpless.

Letty said, "Let's go there, Boss. Why mess with the phone?"

I nodded and grabbed my coat off the coat tree. Letty stood there watching me redial. She didn't say anything. I didn't say anything. She reached out, and put her hand over mine, trying to stop my dialing hand. I shook her off. She looked over my shoulder, pointing at the television. The silent screen was showing a Channel Five helicopter circling above Wilshire Boulevard, smoke pouring out of Lola's hotel.

"It's Lola," I said. "They got to her."

We watched the screen in horror.

"Boss, I don't think we should go there," Letty managed to say. "Not if you think Lola is at the center of what we're watching."

If this was a movie, Lola would have called by now to say some explosion knocked off our conversation, and I would be filled with happiness that she was okay. In a movie, I would be driving like a crazy person from downtown Los Angeles to the hotel where I had left Lola.

This is not a movie. Until I knew for certain, I could hope that Lola was not a victim. So far, the police were not saying it was a car bomb. I knew better. There was nothing I could do for her. Beyond our adventures in bed, I knew almost nothing about her, no hint of her family, nothing beyond her home being Miami.

I refused to let Letty or Tangles drive me home. I drove my Rolls. They followed in Letty's car. On my way, I called Mason.

"As I know you already know, I was with Lola yesterday in Beverly Hills. I have reason to believe that the explosion on the news is connected to her. Got it?"

"I'm not watching the news."

"Mason, effective immediately, call off your guys. I don't want anyone following me around or sitting out in front of my house. Did you get that?"

"Loud and clear."

"Pull them off. I am not kidding. I am sick and tired of every detail of my life being tracked. I can't piss in the bathroom without a herd of your men, and you, and Olga knowing about it."

"You think that Lola was the person hit in the car bombing that I'm watching on television now?"

"Yes. I was talking to her on the phone when it happened. Boom."

"I'll look in to it and confirm. Hopefully you're wrong."

"I'm not fucking wrong!"

I closed my flip phone and disconnected the call. I slammed the phone down so hard it bounced off the door of the passenger side and on to the floor. Maybe it broke. I don't know. I gripped the steering wheel so hard my knuckles were white.

When I walked in, Miguel asked what I wanted to eat. I brushed past him, and I told him to take the night off. I showered downstairs and went straight to the gym to burn off some excess emotion. I didn't really feel any better, but if I managed to exhaust myself, I was hoping I'd be able to fall asleep tonight. After two straight hours of moves followed by some weights, I hit the pool for a dozen laps, showered again, and put on sweats.

The girls were eating in the breakfast room. One of them had fixed an array of vegetables. I didn't feel like eating. I watched the girls do justice to their plates. At least the wine was good. I finished one glass, then another.

Tangles finished off her food and got herself seconds. Letty pushed away from the table early and bussed her plate. She paced the room. It's more of a niche than a room, so the pacing was noticeable.

"Sit down already," Tangles said.

"Keep eating like that, and you'll have to get bigger clothes. On the other hand, you keep on sitting. You're doing enough sitting for both of us."

Tangles ignored Letty's mood, and finished eating. She got up, plate in hand.

"Boss, it's not for me to say," Tangles said, "but you got to figure who did this."

Letty slapped Tangles's shoulder so hard, the plate flew out of her hand and landed on the carpet across the room.

"There's no proof, idiot," Letty sniped. "Don't say that."

"You been a bitch ever since—" Tangles looked my way and switched whatever she was going to say. "—ever since this afternoon," Tangles said. "Today was shit, but I ain't your punching bag." She took a swing at Letty but missed. Letty was too fast.

"Tangles, Letty is right. We have no proof, and even if we did, it does no good to talk about it."

"I'm not afraid of Olga or Camila." Tangles wouldn't let go. "Sorry, Boss, but—"

Letty was about to tear into her. I could see she was itching for a fight.

I raised my hand for Letty not to say anything. She stopped pacing and crossed her arms over her chest. I knew it wasn't Tangles she was mad at. It's just that's how she burns off steam.

"You're entitled to your own opinion," I told Tangles. "The last time I checked, Olga was my fiancée. Nothing has changed."

Letty was still wound up.

"Boss, I'm going to do some laps to cool off." She flounced out of the room; her color high. Usually she and Tangles work out together, but under the circumstances, the pool was a pretty good choice for Letty. I didn't know where Tangles went, but she disappeared for an hour, then returned.

I wanted to mourn. It was too soon. I was too angry.

Letty rejoined us in the living room in a couple of hours later. She'd changed into sweats and seemed in a better mood. Her short hair was still wet and smelled of pool chlorine. Tangles looked like she was about to goad her into a fight, but just then, Olga called.

"I'm in Peru. Mason told me what happened."

"Mason wastes no time," I said, standing up and walking to a window. Looking out put my back to the rest of the room and gave me a sense of privacy, though I wasn't alone. I didn't ask them to leave. I wasn't keeping secrets.

"Mason looks out for you whether you believe it or not."

"He's on notice. I don't want him or his guys around me, not here at the house, not at my office, not anywhere."

"I didn't call to talk about Mason. For what it's worth, I'm sorry."

I wanted to hang up on her, but I had no proof she was involved.

"Did you hear me?"

"I did, thanks, but I'm not her family. I barely knew her. Your condolences are wasted on me."

"Amor, call me when you feel up to it."

She hung up.

I turned around. Letty and Tangles were facing me, making no pretense. Obviously, they'd been listening.

"Let's hit the wine room," I said, already out of my seat. We weren't there long. I'd been without sleep too long. I hit the pillow, and was out like a light, into a night of restless dreams, dreams I did not remember when I woke. It was not a refreshing sleep.

Pasadena February 20, 1991

The next morning, Mason showed up at the house without calling first.

"You're lucky you caught me here. Normally I'm on way to office at this hour."

The fucker was still having me watched. I knew it.

"I took a chance. I didn't want to talk on phone."

I nodded. I didn't feel like arguing.

"My source at homicide told me the car was totally demolished. The serial number shows that it belonged to Nina."

"I didn't realize she had a car," I said. Then it hit me. When we were talking just before the explosion, she had said, 'I'm in my rented wheels.'

Mason was staring. I wasn't about to tell him. For all I know, he planted the bomb.

"Mario, I strongly suggest you find a psychiatrist to talk to. It may help you."

"Why do I need one? You're a psychiatrist. You tell me."

Mason was hesitant. "I believe you were infatuated with Nina. I can't be your doctor."

"So, as a shrink, you're saying I'm in love with Lola, and that's a psychiatric condition."

"Her name is Nina. No, not love, infatuated."

"Lola, Nina, whatever," I said. "Yes, I know her name was Nina Caputo. Mason, one more time. Your contact told you that the car bomb was in a car registered to Nina, is that what I heard?"

"Right, no question."

"Does your contact know she was a federal agent?"

"I told him she was, and that she may have recently quit, retired or whatever. He tried running her, but there are no records for her."

"Just like a movie," I said.

"Yes, only this is not a movie, Mario. This is serious. If the room you met her in was rented to you, we need to get you over to speak with the detectives handling this. Own up to the fact that you spent some hours with her, a fling or something, and that you heard this happened after she left the room. Like I say, this is serious."

"What do I tell them when I'm asked how I know whose car it was?"

"Tell them your private investigator told you so," Mason said. "If I'm asked, I can handle it. Staying silent is not a good idea."

"I'll talk to a lawyer," I said. "Thanks for the advice."

"I'm here for you, Mario. I'm sorry you want to dismiss the boys."

"Mason, I dismissed them yesterday when I called you. I want them gone."

"I hear you." Familiar words.

I wanted Mason to leave. I needed to be alone to think the car thing out. Why would she have told me a rented car? Why would she have her car in the parking garage and a rented car? Did I hear her wrong? Had she been playing me again?

"Mason, did your contact say anything about the remains? Identifiable or burned beyond recognition?

"I didn't ask. My contact stays money-hungry, and he's the man in the know."

"I want to know everything there is to know, Mason."

"I will be back to you. Are you sure you won't reconsider keeping my men?"

"Mason, I want them gone. How many times am I going to say this before it sinks in?"

Mason said, "I got it. On another matter, I believe I have one of your neighbors tied in with the phone number of the Mexico City contact that was killed."

I thought a moment. "I don't understand."

"I told you I was working your neighbors. Let me make sure and I'll lay it out for you."

"This is what Lola would do to me, toy with matters she knew I was at a loss for."

"I'm not Lola," Mason said. "The character of this neighbor fits the pattern of someone that would be a hidden danger, getting even for something. I promise to give you more as soon as I know. At the moment, your plate is full of what just happened in Beverly Hills and you need to get some advice about talking to the police about Lola."

That night, I asked Tangles for a sleeping pill. My dreams were wild, maybe caused by the pill. I found myself lying in the hotel again with Lola, having furious, exhausting, delicious sex. She was mounted on me. I was glad she was alive and said so. I was glad we were back at the hotel. She laughed, and said I wasn't paying attention. We were in the back seat of her rented car.

Pasadena February 21, 1991

I woke two hours later than my normal workout time and had the weird comforting feeling that Lola had told me something. I didn't get up. The room was dark. I was alone with my thoughts. It had to be Olga. Olga was jealous. It could have been Camila, but why would Camila hit her at the hotel where I had been with Lola? Olga was my suspect. I was still thinking about the situation. By the time I showered, it was Olga and Camila. By the time I arrived downstairs to have breakfast, I had figured that Lola had staged her death. She gave me a clue by telling me that she was in her rented car. If Mason knew what she'd said, he would track down car rental companies to learn if Lola had rented a car. But as a Federal agent, she probably had ways to complicate that search, like maybe having a coworker rent the car. I wasn't telling Mason. I didn't tell Letty or Tangles either because it was just a hunch. The thought that this was another play by Lola was comforting to me. One day she would surface.

I got to the office late, but I was not in bad spirits.

"I didn't think you'd come in today," Letty said when she saw me.

I met with detectives handling Lola's case in Beverly Hills.

Pasadena February 28, 1991

A week later, I had a visit from two federal agents with ATF. They weren't interested in my affair with Lola. Their questions were just like the detectives had been: Did I have anything to do with the explosion? No one mentioned anything about her being a federal agent, retired or not.

Pasadena March 11, 1991

In a month, I put together a lease for my new partner in Montevideo. My personal attorney, located in the same building as I was, prepared the new airline's paperwork. I would receive stock equal to ten percent ownership. I did not get an option to purchase additional stock.

I only saw Olga one time in two months. I flew alone to Milan to spend two nights with her. I didn't bring up Lola.

We were having breakfast before both of us would be leaving for the airport.

"I had nothing to do with what happened to her," Olga said. "Not this time or the time before."

"I believe you," I said.

I had heard from Camila no less than a half dozen times during the two months, mostly to chat about how it was going at LAI. At least twice, she casually let it drop that she had nothing to do with what happened in Beverly Hills.

I figured it like this. If I refused to believe them, that would mean that I believed Lola was dead by Camacho orders. That would burst my bubble. I preferred to believe that Lola was out there somewhere. I wondered if her team knew what she'd done, and whose remains were in the car, if any.

"Bottom line, Mason, what happens when there's no ID? What is her family told? Do they assume she died in her car?"

"Right now, the decedent in that car is a Jane Doe."

Neither one of us said anything for several minutes. I think he was waiting for me to say something first and I did.

"Nina died in that explosion," I said, looking at him for confirmation.

"Yes," he said. "That is the consensus of the investigation."

As long as Mason believed she died in the car—which is what I wanted him to believe—then Olga and Camila would believe it.

Pasadena March 11, 1991
Letty

Boss was out somewhere. Letty and I were in the wine room, drinking very little but smoking a joint and getting intensely wasted. There was a box of Sees candy leftover from Christmas, and we were nibbling. We had the munchies.

"Damn good candy," Tangles said.

"That's the pot talking." I said.

For a number of years, I delivered Sees candy boxes to the neighbors for Christmas. I never remember their names without looking them up on my neighborhood list. For the last couple years, Tangles has been with me when we go ringing door bells outside big gates. Sometimes we don't get an answer, and we return and try again. If we don't get an answer after two tries, no candy. After the first fire that totally destroyed Casa Luna, the entire neighborhood was evacuated to the street. They ended up at Melina's house—now Pixie's place. It never developed into friendships. Just on Christmas when we deliver candy, we say hi. Maybe we wave on the street, in passing. On Christmas, the security guards bring baskets dropped off by the neighbors.

Boss said one of the neighbors could be a suspect. He couldn't recall exactly what Mason said. I can't imagine any of the neighbors we met stalking the Boss.

"I see so little of the neighbors I can't even picture them," I told Tangles.

"You're trying to figure out who Mason has pegged?"

"Aren't you?"

"I've been trying. They're all old."

"What's old got to do with it?"

"Well, old doesn't make sense they would hire hit people to go after Boss."

"That stupid Mason drops a bomb like this on Boss then doesn't tell him everything he knows. What an asshole," I said.

"I don't like the prick," Tangles said.

"He probably knows it. He's a shrink," I remind her.

"Fuck him and the degree he rode in on. He's nothing but a spy for her."

"You mean for them."

"Right, for them."

"Don't be a hypocrite," I said. "When Olga and Camila are around, you kiss ass."

"I am a hypocrite," Tangles said, "If they knew how I really feel, they'd have me shot or drawn and quartered, or poisoned or snuffed, for sure."

I hate to admit it, but we both laughed.

"You shouldn't say that." I reminded Tangles that Olga is his fiancée.

"That don't mean nothing to me, girl. I can understand why he wants her. I'm not even a guy, and I'd like to fuck her, too. That don't mean I like her, and I sure as hell don't trust her ass."

"Shh. Stop it already, Miss Ungrateful. You sure like smoking the pot she sends us."

"Okay, okay. But if I knew then what I know now…If I had known Pepe was behind the biker, that weekend I fucked Pepe, I would have done him in. No shit. Mother fucker."

I reminded her about the six-carat pear-cut diamond pear he had given her.

"I'm not stupid. I knew he was a mafia dude. But I gotta hate a guy that had Casa Luna burned down to the gutter. Fuck him for fucking with Mario's head for so long with that fucking biker fucker.

Morocco April 25, 1991
Olga

It was my fourth trip to Morocco, and I had not tired of Said. I didn't make him give up his commission to have sex with me as he had offered on our first time, but it didn't matter. I loved fucking him. It was a win-win for me. He took twenty-five million each trip, depositing to various accounts I was feeding cash into. It's possible it was the unconditional sex that drew me to his bed. I don't remember how long it's been since I had more than a one-night stand with a man other than Mario. I was not in love with Said, nor he with me. He loved the sex and the million I gave him for each twenty-five million he accepted at his bank.

Ahmed never got me in bed after the first time, but Riana was with him overnight whenever I was with Said. Ahmed's bank took a twenty-five million deposit each month, and he got a little over a million as a commission.

That morning, we met back at our hotel as always to shower and get ready to leave for the airport. Riana was racing around to pack and griping that there wasn't time to sit down for breakfast.

"It's a hard life, Toots," I said, teasing her. "Order what you want. We can take it with us."

"Reheated eggs? No thank you," she said.

I got a call on my cell from my plane captain.

"Miss Olga, we have a problem. There are at least twenty police officers on the plane. My crew and I are not allowed to board."

"Have you talked to anyone?"

"I have an Arabic document that I cannot read. The officer in charge said it was a search warrant."

"Have they asked for me?"

"No."

"Find a place nearby to park yourself and let them do their search."

"We are sitting on our luggage outside the plane. We don't plan to move, Miss Olga."

I told Riana the problem.

"Give us time to eat breakfast," Riana said with a shrug. "I'm dialing room service right now."

I couldn't help myself. She made me laugh. "You are a toughie, Amor."

"I wouldn't be as tough if I saw that you were worried," she said.

"I'm not worried. Curious why?"

"This is our fourth trip in four months," Riana said. "Big plane like yours, and you don't know anyone at the airport like in other places."

"Let's eat while we see how this plays out."

If the coppers had been there when I landed the day before, it is highly possible that they would have found the money, but now that was safely deposited.

We ate as if all were well. I called the Captain hourly for the next four hours to get his progress report. They moved inside the executive terminal at the airport.

"I can see the plane from where we are sitting," the captain informed me.

"There is nothing to find."

The captain didn't seem concerned. My crew knew nothing. All I knew was that everywhere I went, it was a little different. A team always moved in after we landed to remove the cash. In Morocco, two team members took the cash and delivered it according to Camila's orders. I was never involved with the teams that did the dirty work, except once in a while, when establishing the account.

Sixteen hours and fifteen minutes after the cops had seized control of my plane, they left empty-handed. We were cleared to go.

"What did they tell you?" I asked the captain.

"The officer in charge found me in the terminal and told me we could board the plane. He apologized for the inconvenience. I did not ask any questions, nor did he ask me anything."

"Did he speak to the rest of the crew?"

"No, Miss Olga. We're on board now."

"We're headed to Bogota," I said. "I'll be there within the hour."

On our way to the airport, Riana said, "If that lady cop was alive, my guess would be that she did this to you."

"I wish you hadn't said that, Amor."

"Why?"

"Because I haven't even thought about that bitch in ages."

"She's dead. Sorry I brought it up."

We arrived at the airport at three in the morning. Our SUV and a station wagon with my guards parked alongside the plane. As soon as I was out of the car, a tall man almost got close to me. He was stopped by one of my guards.

"I'm the airport manager," he said, pointing to the badge on his lapel.

I extended my hand out to him. "Sorry about the shove from my over-zealous security guard."

"I'd like to have a talk with you. Can we go to my office?"

"Riana, go on to the plane. I'll be there in a few minutes."

I followed the manager. Three of my guards walked close behind us.

Once inside his very nice office, I asked, "Do you always work this late?"

"I was waiting for the police to leave. Your senior officer advised me you were on your way here and planning to fly out. I wanted to talk to you."

"Okay, I'm here."

"I was criticized by the police for not having more information about your business and your company. If you plan on returning, I need you to fill out this form and fax it to me before your next trip." He handed me a stapled bunch of pages. "Are you coming back?"

"I'm coming back," I said. "I am looking for investments here in Morocco. We are a global company with assets all over the world." I handed him my LAI card.

"Yes, we have that much on file." He set the card down on his desk.

"Do you have any idea why the police would conduct such a thorough search of your plane?"

"No idea at all. Do you?"

The manager chuckled. "No. I don't think they were happy that they found nothing."

"What's your first name?" I could have looked at his badge.

"Walid."

I got up and extended my hand out to him. His handshake was firmer than when we shook outside.

"When I return, I'll bring you a gift for having you wait all these hours today," I said.

Walid smiled. "That would be very nice of you."

I was going to reach in my purse and hand him some US hundreds, but I'd save it for next time. I knew station managers and terminal managers and airport managers all over the world. I should have made it a point to look up Walid once I realized I would be coming back each month.

Thirty minutes later, we were wheels up. Bogota was more than twenty-five hundred miles away.

"Let's get some sleep," I told Riana.

"What happened to dinner?"

I had to look at my watch to make sure of the time. "We had dinner hours ago at the hotel. It will be breakfast soon."

Once we were in bed, I asked, "Were you worried at all today while we waited at the hotel?"

"I saw no worry in you," she replied. "Why should I worry?"

"Amor, I love you."

We hugged in the dark cabin on the king-sized bed.

"I love you, too, Olga."

We slept, lingered in bed, and when we finally got up, it was well past dinner time. We were both ravenous but decided to wait to eat at home. I purposely did not land at the Army Base.

On our way to my house in Bogota, I got a call from Ahmed.

"I've been trying to call you," he said.

"I've been flying for hours."

"I heard what happened. I think we need to take it slow. Said is in agreement."

I was going to object, but who knows if someone was listening. He seemed quite serious, not at all like his usual cheerful self.

I could explained that nothing was found, so what is the big deal? But I was curious who told them about the search, and that wasn't a topic for the phone.

"I'll be in touch," I said.

I hung up the phone.

Riana did not meddle with my business, but she has eyes and ears. She knew enough.

"There's a bright side. You farmed out two hundred million in four months."

I gave my friend a hug.

We were just minutes from home.

Camila arrived at my doorstep three days later for breakfast, though she'd flown in, and gone straight to her own home to spend the night.

"If that bitch was alive, I would point the finger at her for causing this search," she said.

"Riana said the same thing."

"Someone got suspicious of two young women in a big plane visiting Morocco four times in a row over a period of four months," Camila said.

"I think so, too," I said. "I'll fly from here to Amsterdam, make a quick drop and return for more."

"You are so brave, Hermanita," Camila said.

I smiled at her.

"I want you," Camila said, reaching across the table for my hand.

"Here or your place?" I asked.

"My place. Come over later."

After she left, I called Mario. I didn't tell him what happened.

"When are you coming home?"

"Amor, I have several quick trips to make, then I'll know what my schedule is like."

"Okay. Then let's get back to talking every day. We haven't been doing that."

"I know, Amor, I'm sorry. I've been so busy."

I thought of Said. He was hung like a bull, just the way I like it. Then I thought of how he brushed me off, having Ahmed call me, not bothering to call me himself. The chickenshit bastard.

"We talk tomorrow then," Mario said.

"Si, Amor." I thought for a moment, not sure if I should bring it up. "I know this may sound silly. Do you think Lola died in that explosion?"

"Mason says she did. Why you ask? Did you see her?" He laughed.

I laughed, too.

"No, Amor, I just had a dream."

Of course, there had been no dream. Foolish of me. There were more agents in the world than that one dead cop. I was being afraid of ghosts. Still, I was unsettled. I wondered if this is how Mario had felt about his stalker.

Pasadena April 26, 1991

Mario

Letty and I were in the wine room.

"I sometimes wonder what good it is that Olga and I are engaged," I said to Letty. "Are we looking to get married when we're seniors?"

"I didn't know you were in a hurry to get married, Boss."

"I'm not in a hurry to get through my forties. Not even sure what happened to my thirties."

Letty laughed. "Boss, you look thirty."

I leaned over and kissed her on the lips. "You look twenty," I said. Letty is thirty-seven and does look in her twenties. She's fit, has a knock-out figure and is a karate warrior. Apart from that, she's been the love of my life. She's kind and caring to me, a companion who sticks to me like glue and gives me space when I need it.

"Thanks, Boss. I feel twenty something."

I looked at my watch. "This is the third date with this guy," I said.

"You keeping track of Tangles?" she giggled.

"I'm not," I said, and laughed. "I am."

"She's not going anywhere. Boss, she loves you, loves living here and loves her job."

"I don't own her," I said.

"Funny, Boss. Of course, you don't own her. Tangles owns herself."

"This guy is a doctor. It's a good match for her."

Letty said, "He's not a doctor yet. He's an intern, but close. He has no money and is buried in loans that got him through school. They're just friends."

I wasn't smoking pot, just drinking wine, and feeling a bit tipsy. I rounded the table. Letty hopped up and walked out alongside me.

"I think you and Letty are burning up the best years of your life on me."

She put her arm around my waist. "Boss, hush. We aren't burning anything."

I put my arm around her, my right hand on her shoulder as we walked to the elevator. The alarm chime rang, indicating the front door had just opened.

"It's Tangles, Boss."

"Alarm's on," Tangles yelled out. "Where are you guys?"

"In the elevator headed to the fourth."

As we stepped out, Tangles was just getting to the landing of the fourth floor. She'd clattered up the steps wearing her high heel knee high boots.

"You look hot," I said.

"Thanks, Boss."

"Where's your doctor friend?"

"Headed to the hospital. He's working an eighteen-hour shift."

"Ouch," Letty said.

"I forgot his name," I said.

"Nate Morgan," Tangles said.

"A gringo," Letty said. "But he's a cutie-pie."

"Bring him over whenever you want," I said. It was not the first time I told her.

"Thanks, Boss."

"Boss doesn't mean to bring him so you can fuck him in your room, slut."

"Boss, tell her to radio it, or I'll have no choice but to kick her ass."

I laughed all the way to my bedroom and shut the door behind me.

Letty knocked. "Hey, Boss, what about us?"

I went to bed alone. I kept thinking of Lola, figuring that if I went to sleep with her in mind, I might dream about her again. Mason had said I was infatuated by her. On a scale of one to ten, how much did I love Lola? Five. On a scale of one to ten, how much did I love Tangles? Eight. On a scale of one to ten, how much did I love Letty? Ten. On a scale of one to ten, how much did

I love Olga? Ten. Lola was only a five because I was infatuated by her, nutty and curious about her, hungry for her, couldn't get enough of her, but I didn't love her. She was gone before I could get my fill.

Lola, send me a sign you are still alive?

Lola, can you hear me?

Lola...

I was driving to work. The girls were in the back seat. I looked over to my right, and Lola was sitting in my passenger seat, naked as the day she was born, her fed badge on a chain around her neck.

"What the fuck? Where the fuck did you come from?" A car crossed lanes in front of me, and I had to concentrate on driving to prevent a collision. When I looked to my right, Lola was gone.

"Where the fuck did you go?"

"Nowhere," I heard her say.

She had not gone far. She'd moved to the back seat with Letty and Tangles. All three of them were dressed up like prim secretaries, with huge round glasses, dull matching office suits, saddle oxford shoes, and holding steno pads. They all had GAL office name tags on chains around their necks. Lola was in the middle. The three of them were staring diligently at me with their pencils out, like they were waiting for dictation or something. I've never dictated to a stenographer in my life. I talk over the intercom or into a recorder.

"Don't worry Boss," Tangles said.

"Do worry, Boss," Letty said. "I worry all the time. You do too. Nothing you worry about ever happens. It's always something else. If you can manage to worry about everything that could possibly go wrong, there won't be anything left to not happen."

I broke out laughing. I heard thumping, like someone was banging on my car door trying to get in. I sat up still laughing and found myself in bed. Someone was knocking at the door.

"Come in," I said.

Letty opened the door and glanced around the room. I was on top of the blankets wearing briefs. I hadn't even bothered to shut off the light on my bed stand. She was wearing only an over-sized t-shirt. I must admit, I was relieved she wasn't in big glasses and saddle oxford shoes.

"Sound doesn't travel in this house—how long have you been out there, waiting?"

"Not long," she said. "Ok, ten minutes, tops. Are you ok?"

"She's been out there since you closed the door on us," I heard Tangles yelling, either from the landing, or maybe the office.

"Are you okay?" she asked, looking worried. "I was in the hall, and I heard you."

"I was dreaming," I said, smiling at her. "In the dream, you said something. I don't remember what it was, but apparently it was funny." I patted the spot beside me on the bed, and she turned off the light and jumped in.

Chapter 19
Leaving Amsterdam for Bogota, Late April 1991
Olga

The entire shipment of money was deposited by the secret team into a twenty-foot container. The money belonged to clients who wanted the cash deposited, but the containers were the Amsterdam holding area when there was a queue to get the cash accepted somewhere. I knew that there were three containers and the total amount of money sitting there. What I didn't know is if the containers were together, miles apart, nor where they were.

"Is this going to be another fast one?"

"We'll be in Bogota three days at the most, then we return to Amsterdam for ten hours, and then, guess what?"

Riana opened her eyes wide. "Tell me."

"We can go anywhere you want for four days. In Amsterdam overnight and we're gone. Where do you want to go?"

"Paris, definitely. No. I think you should head to Pasadena. You haven't seen him."

"We might do that," I said, unsure.

"What's going on with you two?"

We fastened our seat belts. It was getting a little bumpy. I looked out of the window. Nothing to see out there but clouds. I took my time getting around to an answer.

"He went poking around with that bitch cop Lola after she threatened me and Camila. The wound is still bleeding."

"Olga, you fucked Said and did Ahmed once to boot. Not like you're an angel."

I could never get pissed at Riana.

"You don't get it, Amor. It's not the fucking. It's the who. Fucking a cop who blackmailed us into paying a million dollars. She makes death threats against us, and then he gives her the money, and then he goes to her, at least twice, like nothing had happened."

Riana lifted her stockinged feet on the table and pressed hers against mine, sole to sole. I managed not to knock over the toast points and caviar.

"If you're that serious, give this back to him. Let him fly off free as a bird, and you do the same."

I held my hand out, admiring the ring.

"Did I ever tell you what I did to keep this ring? It was almost repossessed by Sami's step-mother."

"Tell me. I love your stories."

"I never tell you stories."

"That's why I'm going to love this one."

"You runt," I said straightening my legs, which pushed her feet across the table, putting her knees around her ears. It made her laugh.

"Okay, I'm a runt. Now tell me."

"Sami gave this ring to Mario on her deathbed. Mario kept the ring in his safe until he gave it to me. When Sami's father died, Sami's step-mother inquired about Sami's estate. Turns out, the assets were all mishandled. In going through the inventory of assets, this ring comes up. When Sami gave this ring to Mario on her death bed, Jason was there—but he's the screwed-up executor who committed suicide when he got caught—and Sami's father was there—

but he's dead too. There are no surviving witnesses, since Jason never did the paperwork."

"I didn't know all this," Riana said. "Let me light up. This is getting good."

"Amor, wait, listen."

Riana nodded, cigarette case in hand. With her free hand, she dipped a toast point into the caviar and took a nibble. She made a face, shook off the caviar, and polished off the toast.

"The step-mother's London lawyers filed against Mario to produce this rock. I told him to give it to them. He could have bought me another stone or use one I have. I have a box full."

Riana laughed. "You sure do."

"Mario was taking this ring situation personally. I called upon one of our contacts, a reliable Colombian who was tight with my dad. He came out of retirement to fly to New York, find Sami's ex-wife, break into her apartment, and get her on the phone with me. I should mention, he carries a knife." I held my hands apart to show how big the knife was, then moved my hands apart farther. It was a big knife. "Of course, she didn't know it's me. I told her that if she doesn't drop the case to recover the ring, the man in her bedroom that is holding that big knife will return to finish what he started."

Riana laughed. "It's like the Godfather movie."

"No, there were no scenes like that in the Godfather, dummy."

"You know what I mean." Riana lit up.

"Anyway, the step-mother quit pursuing the ring. The case was dismissed. To this day, Mario doesn't know why the case was dropped. The estate attorney issued Mario a bill of sale or whatever it was to prove provenance that he owns the ring. He had to pay a tax or something in London. So you see, I'm wearing this ring, but I wouldn't have it had I not taken the steps I did to keep it."

Riana took a deep toke. "In that case, don't give the ring back to him,"

Riana said, smiling and exhaling a cloud of smoke. She handed the joint to me.

"I love him. I'm not going to break up with him." I took a hit of the joint. "I need time to get over what he did. He admitted going to that bitch, admitted he fucked her, not caring a fuck at all about what she threatened to do to me."

"Get over it, Olga. It's not the end of the world. You are making a big deal out of this. Maybe you are looking for a way out."

I took another hit and leveled my eyes on hers. I'd taken my feet off the table, and Riana's knees were no longer around her ears.

Was Riana right? Did I want a way out?

The turbulence had stopped. The flight attendant, Margarita, took away the caviar and toast, and replaced it with a big platter of Riana's favorite nachos. They weren't my favorite, but these were fixed the way I like best, with lots of melted cheese and the chips so well done, they are almost burned. We made short work of the nachos.

"Let's get in bed and get wild," I said, eyes still leveled on hers. We both love sex with men, but this, this was about us.

Riana blushed. She wasn't shy. It was the weed.

"Yeah, I'd dig that very much, Olga. Should we start right here in the main cabin and work our way back?"

I unbuckled my seat belt and got up.

"Right on," I said. I started unbuttoning my top.

Riana mirrored what I was doing.

I know we were high, laughing as we took everything off and tossed it around the cabin. I walked around the table between us and hugged her.

"If you were a man, I'd marry you," I said to her, my lips on her.

"I thought we were already married," Riana said, her breath hot into my mouth.

"All we have is now," I said, hugging her tight. "From one split second to the next, we could be extinguished, just like that," I snapped my fingers.

When I was at home in Bogota, once in a while, my personal maid would put my ring in an ultrasonic cleaner that was in my bathroom. The magic machine leaves diamonds looking as gorgeous as when they were first cut and buffed. Other than that one exception, I swam, took baths, showers, never took the ring off. I put lotion on my hands. Ring stayed on. I fucked Said recently and others before him. Ring stayed on. Riana and I, we were on the bed, and it was the first time I could remember taking Mario's ring off. I placed it on an anchored onyx ashtray next to the night stand. Riana was so engrossed that I doubt she even noticed.

Montevideo May 1, 1991
Camila

I was in Montevideo for five hours from the time I landed until I got out of my hired limousine parked beside my plane. Three of my guards climbed the plane stairs, and three were poised around me as I got out of the car. Just as I put my foot on the first step, a whistle buzzed beside my left ear. I looked back and saw Miguel Angel drop to the ground. My other two guards pushed me forward on the stairs. I cut my mouth on something. They covered me with their bodies.

The guards who had gone up first rushed down to me, guns drawn.

"It came from the rooftop of that terminal behind us," Lupe Daniel said.

"Stay down," Miguel said.

I could feel my heart racing. Tense moments passed as we waited for more gunfire. Too many moments. I felt claustrophobic.

"Let me up," I demanded, tasting blood. "Whoever did this is long gone."

My plane was a distance from the main terminal. Airport personnel were busy fueling planes and driving around in trucks and at passenger terminals unloading and loading luggage on airliners. No one had noticed.

Lupe Daniel, probably the strongest man on my security team, swooped me up, and ran up the stairs into the plane. He cradled me like a baby, and when he let me down in the cabin, he mentioned the trail of blood, blood on my face, and from a gash on my right knee. A flight attendant gave me a handful of napkins. I dabbed up the mess on my face and knee. They brought Miguel ice packs and towels.

I sat up. "Who's got my purse?"

Miguel handed it over.

"Nothing fell out, Senorita Camila," he said. He looked pale and was holding an ice pack over his shoulder wound.

"You need to lie down. You need a doctor," I said.

"Not here, please," he said. "I'll wait till we get home. If I die on the way, you can fire me." He gave a little laugh.

I got my mirror out. My lip looked terrible, but my teeth were intact.

My entire cockpit crew clustered around me in the main cabin.

"We need to call a doctor," the captain said.

Like Miguel, I didn't want a doctor. I didn't want to spend another minute in Montevideo. Twenty minutes later we were airborne. I was eight hours from Bogota. I sent the security team to their space on the plane. My two flight attendants took care of me, applying ice packs even when I dozed off in my cabin. Due to their care, my cuts stopped bleeding, and my swollen knee looked much better by the time we landed in Colombia. We had never taken precautions for a sniper attack, and even now, I didn't plan on going to that extreme. But I would find out who was behind this and terminate them. When the mutiny occurred on Olga's plane, I saw to it that the families of everyone involved died. Someone had been missed, and that resulted in the attack on Olga in Milan. That's why you have to kill everyone in a family. I thought it had been done. It was the first time I have ever been shot at. You do not know how it feels unless you are a victim of a shooting like I had been that day. On my way home, I called Olga in Paris.

"I'm on my way to Bogota," Olga said as soon as she heard what happened.

"No," I told her. "Finish what you have to do. I'm going to be fine. I have a doctor meeting me at the house, just to be sure my knee is okay."

"You need to X-ray the knee," Olga said.

"I'm sure the doctor will know what to do, Amor," I told the worrier.

"I don't think it's a family member of my mutinous flight crew," Olga said. "They could do the same in Colombia. Why Montevideo?"

"Amor, two men went after you in Milan."

"Yes, you're right. I think those two were the end of that revenge."

"I'm going to get to the bottom of this," I said.

"Amor, thank God the shooter missed, assuming you were the target."

"How can I not be the target? Why one of my guards?"

"You're right. How is he?"

"He's going to be fine."

May 1991
Olga

I called Mario and told him about Camila.

"What can I do," he asked. "Should I go to Bogota?"

"No, she's got it under control. I offered to go. She told me to stay put."

"It's going to be difficult defending against a sniper," Mario said.

"She's determined to find out who did it. What is puzzling to me, why Uruguay? We have little going in Montevideo."

I picked up the phone. Camila again.

"Some bastard called and said he missed me on purpose."

"What?"

"He spoke in a loud voice, a voice I never heard before. When he hung up, he was laughing."

"What?"

"Are you hard of hearing or what!" Camila was pissed, now at me.

"Hermanita, I'm in shock, sorry."

"I'll have his balls delivered to his mother, and his head to his wife and children."

It took a good ten minutes to calm Camila down.

Riana took a long drag of a joint and exhaled before she spoke. "Guards will have to start looking above and not just around."

"I think this is on Camila, not me."

"Be serious, Olga. This is a wakeup call."

"Give me a hit of that," I said reaching for it.

"You'll feel better, I promise," Riana said.

The lady cop had threatened to kill Camila, and me. I wondered how she had figured on getting to us through the security around us all the time. I was deep in thought, thoughts racing. I took a deep drag of the weed.

Riana said. "It can't be Lola. She's dead. Is that who you're thinking about?"

I looked at my friend and nodded, yes. "But the caller was the man who called Camila."

I called Mario again, buzzed but not as buzzed. "Camila called me back. Some loud-mouthed guy called her cell and told her he had missed on purpose."

"What?"

"You sound like me, Amor. That's what I said to Camila."

"You need to take extra precautions," Mario said.

"Don't worry, Amor. We will start looking at roof tops and places we never looked before."

"Maybe it's time to retire."

Silence.

"Olga, did you hear me?"

"I heard you, Amor."

"What if something had happened to Camila?"

"Amor, nothing happened to Camila, so we don't go there."

"I'm sorry," he said. "I worry about you."

"Something to talk about in person," I tell him.

"Yes. When?"

"Soon, Amor. I have some things to take care of."

In the morning, we checked out of the George V Hotel. My lead security man suggested I put together a bigger team.

"No need. If someone wants to take a shot from afar, hiring more men won't make it safe."

If he was after me, it wouldn't be near the George V, where thousands of people were either walking or driving. An attack wouldn't be in such a public space. At the airports, we just had to be more careful.

Riana scooted close to me in the back seat of the car taking us to the airport. She spoke in a low whisper so only I could hear.

"Maybe Camila got one of the customers mad. The owners of the money you handle have to be scum. When something goes wrong, anything is possible."

There was wisdom in what she said, but I didn't want her to worry. I glanced at the closed partition behind the driver. I never trusted how private it really was, so I whispered my response.

"My father was part of that scum you are referring to, Amor. There is a code of respect and mutual integrity among those people. As long as Camila does everything she promised, they will never be her enemy. Scum, maybe, but scum with integrity and mutual respect. Now they have tens of millions of dollars in banks just like reputable business people. They would be hurting themselves if they took out Camila. It's none of them, Amor."

Pasadena May 1991
Mario

Mason appeared at my office.

"Tell me about the neighbor. Which one is it?"

"What I have are calls to the number in Mexico City. The number matches a number Perez gave us. Remember Perez, the guy who rammed your car, got arrested and was bailed out."

"Yes, I know, I know who that guy is. None of the detectives told me Perez got kidnapped right after he got out on bail, that he was taken to Colombia, that he copped to being paid by the dude in Mexico City, and that your friendly bounty hunter took him back into custody. We were supposed to do something for him. Get him out of jail, or something. We just let him sit there."

"I fixed it so your subpoenas to appear never got to you. That resulted in a dismissal of his case."

"I figured this guy was sitting in jail. Thanks for telling me. Why is everything a secret, Mason?"

"No, he's not in jail. He's in Mexico with his family. He's been warned if he ever goes after you again, he will never be found."

I laughed. "I never heard you talk like that Mason. Bravo."

"We're alone," Mason reminded me.

"I'm still waiting for you to say which neighbor it is?"

"The seventh neighbor east of your house."

"I don't know the neighbors. They're all behind gates."

"So, you aren't ready to accuse my neighbor."

"Normally I wouldn't have told you until everything was certain."

"I'm surprised you didn't keep it secret."

"What's the verdict?" Letty asked. "I could hardly wait till he left."

"Seventh neighbor to the east, but the evidence is weak."

"The candy we give out we doesn't go that far," Tangles said. "Maybe they're butthurt about that."

"Yeah," Letty said sarcastically. "That must be it. Neighbor went postal because he didn't get Christmas candy. I'll put them on the list. That will for sure put the stalker to rest."

"Only if it is rat poison candy," Tangles said. "There's an idea. Does Sees make any of that?"

Seventy-two hours later
Amsterdam May 31, 1991
Olga

We landed in Amsterdam at one fifteen in the morning. When we flew from Paris to Bogota, we landed at the Army Base. Seventy-two hours later, we left my house for the base, and in an hour later, we were wheels up headed to Amsterdam. This flight, I knew exactly how much money was on the plane. It was delivered to the container. I made that entry into my log. At a glance, I knew how much money was in Amsterdam in containers. As I only had two bankers in Amsterdam that accepted money on deposit once a month, it would take a long time to clear the containers. More bankers there was not a possibility. I had surveyed most Dutch banks. The owners of the money considered anywhere safer than Colombia. They wanted their money out of Colombia.

Riana and I arrived at the hotel before three and went right to bed. We planned to take off for Pasadena by noon. Riana had pushed me over the fence. Now I was excited we were going to see Mario and surprise him. At seven in the morning, Joe Medina, my plane captain called—not the same one as when they searched the aircraft in Morocco.

"Yes, I am here, Captain." I said. I was dressing and put my phone on speaker so I could talk hands free. I put my top over my head and pulled it down.

"Miss Olga, I just arrived here. The plane is swarming with police."

"What did you say?" I was hoping I had heard him wrong.

Riana heard too. She said, "Not again?"

I nodded and whispered, "Again."

I knew that by now, the plane was totally clean. I had not been angry in Morocco when I heard about the police. But this was Amsterdam where I had been flying in and out for years. I was so furious my teeth chattered.

Riana grabbed the phone and told the captain to keep us informed. She handed the phone back to me. I put it to my ear, but he had hung up. I threw it at the couch.

"Olga, easy does it. You can't change what's going on. Let me get room service up here with juice and something hot."

Just before noon the captain called. The head police officer wanted to see the owner of the plane. I wasn't the registered owner of the plane, but I'm the person they would want to see. When we arrived, it was still a cop circus. I ignored the swarm of them like cockroaches. No one stopped me. I left Riana in the terminal and boarded my plane along with my security detail. The head police officer found me there.

"Who are all these men?" the officer asked. Her name badge said Katy Jansen. She was probably in her forties, tall, and slim and colorless. Her brows and lashes were white, her hair scraped back flat to her head, probably in a bun under her hat, and she wore glasses.

"My security."

"Why do you need so many men?"

"You can wait outside. I am sure I am safe here with Officer Jansen." I told my security guys. They tromped out reluctantly. I knew they wanted to argue, but they didn't want to argue in front of a cop.

"Officer Jansen, you didn't call me over here to discuss my security team."

"Correct. I have some questions."

"Please have a seat," I said. We were in the main parlor of my plane. I knew the rest of the cops were somewhere aboard, like the roaches they are, searching, but not in view.

"What exactly brings you to Amsterdam?"

"I come here often. My employer LAI owns a number of commercial buildings. I'm always on the prowl to buy something else."

"Which buildings does LAI own?"

"I can provide you a list, asset value exceeds twenty million dollars."

Katy Jansen raised her white brows. She also eyed my engagement ring.

Around this time, Riana ambled in carrying something in a little brown bag that smelled like a bakery.

"I brought you some Dutch waffles from the airport restaurant," Riana said, stopping when she saw the police woman. "They said these are okay, they're duty free. I didn't do anything wrong, did I?"

I was still angry, but almost laughed. Riana can really put on stupid. The woman glanced in the bag Riana was holding open.

"Not waffles. Stroopwafels," she corrected. "Stroopwafels are legal."

Riana heaved a huge sigh, like she was very relieved, and flopped down by me. She was wearing a huge sun hat, and sun glasses, and occupied herself with untying the bow at her throat.

"Why are you searching my plane and what is it you expect to find?" I interrupted.

"The search stopped fifteen minutes before you got here. I gave a copy of the search warrant to Joe Medina, your flight crew's senior officer."

I held my gaze on Katy Jansen. Riana, by now, had removed the ridiculous hat and placed it on the table. She was sitting next to me, also staring at the plain clothes cop. The bulge at the cop's hip was no doubt where she had her gun in a holster of some kind.

"What else you want to know, Miss Jansen?"

"If your company has that much property here in Amsterdam, I don't need to know much at all today. Can you give me a list of the properties?"

I wanted her gone.

"Yes, I can give you a list." I left her. Riana and I went in to a small study right outside the bedroom. I took a file from the desk. It had eleven addresses just on the first page. I removed the page and returned to hand to Katy Jansen.

"I don't have a copy machine aboard, but you can have this. This is only a summary. Details of the purchases are public record. I suppose you can get that yourself if there is a particular reason you want to get into the affairs of the company. Here is my card."

"We were looking for drugs," Katy Jansen said as she got up.

Riana said, "Drugs like from a pharmacy?"

I looked over to my looney friend.

"No," Katy Jansen said. "I mean drugs like cocaine."

"Never," I said with a ha-ha smile.

She nodded her head at me first, and then Riana, and then she was gone. I looked out a window and saw her get into an unmarked car. Behind her, I saw a caravan of cars jam-packed with cops. I guess they were cops. I went to the door of the plane and signaled for my flight crew and security team to come aboard.

"Let's get the hell out of Dodge, cowboy," Riana said.

The way she said it made me laugh. She reminded me of Pixie, but I knew Riana's first experience with English had been spaghetti westerns.

"Don't call anyone from here," Riana said.

"I'm not."

As soon as Liz walked into the plane, I asked her for a bottle of wine.

"White or red, Miss Olga?"

"Anything," Riana said, "As long as it is fast."

I elbowed Riana. "We'd like red," I said. "Merlot."

The wine hadn't even been poured when my cell phone buzzed.

"Hello?" I said.

"Thank me that search was after the cargo was off the plane. Just like Morocco." I heard a loud male voice just as Camila had described it. I heard mad laughter, and then he hung up.

I looked at Riana and repeated what he'd said.

"Who was it?"

"The guy behind the attack on Camila," I said.

The plane began moving away from the terminal.

Riana had plenty of questions, but I held up a finger for Riana to wait and went to the cockpit.

"Change in plans, Captain. New flight plan. Bogota."

"Yes, Miss Olga."

He radioed the tower and moved the plane to where they told him to park it. The Captain deplaned to do the paperwork. In under an hour, we were airborne.

"I can't go to Pasadena. Who the fuck knows if we are being tailed? I'm not leading them to Mario."

She looked out the window toward the back of the plane. "Nobody's out there," she said. "Olga, what do you mean by tailing us? Who do you think is out there? Mad Max?"

"I'm glad you have a sense of humor," I snapped.

"Olga, don't be mad at me. I'm trying to make this disaster bearable."

I nodded. I raised my glass and clicked with hers in acknowledgement.

"I know, Amor."

"Somebody is fucking with us."

"The same person who took a shot at Camila," I said. "The shooter, or the shooter's boss. He said 'like Morocco.' This guy must be responsible for what happened there."

"But how can one person do that?"

"Easy as making a call to the cops or customs probably."

Riana said. "They had warrants."

A judge had to sign warrants, at least in the US.

"I am so pissed I can't see straight," I said.

"Whoever is fucking with you, they could just be fishing."

"He said cargo. That doesn't mean he knows what the cargo is."

"Exactly," said Riana.

"How does the fucker have our cell phone numbers? How is it possible for someone to have our phone numbers?"

"Somebody on the inside," Riana said. "Or maybe your private numbers got out somehow. Time to change them."

"Light up," I said, surprising myself. Normally Riana would be making the suggestion. "It's a long way to Bogota."

"If they are tailing us, you are taking them to the lion's den."

"We have nothing to hide anywhere, Riana. By now, cops all over the world must know that the Camachos are not in the cocaine business. LAI is not a secret. It's a global enterprise soon to be launched in Switzerland as a public company. The company has been vetted and passed every possible scrutiny."

"Then don't worry. Like you say, it's a long way to Bogota."

Thank goodness Riana is so easy going. The feeling is catching. She smiled that smile of hers and I could not take my eyes off her. We smoked the entire joint, which gave us cotton mouth. That called for more wine. We giggled away our cares, and sipped wine. The feeling that there were insurmountable problems ahead of us slowly faded away.

Bogota, June 3 1991
Olga

It was a good thing I had not told Mario I was coming to Pasadena. We did talk daily while I was in Bogota. He offered to fly down to see me for a few days. I didn't take him up on it. Camila had commitments in other parts of South America and took her time getting there. I didn't tell her what had happened in Amsterdam. I was done with phones. No more taking chances.

On the fourth, Camila came home.

"You should have told me. I would have dropped everything to be here for you," Camila said, annoyed.

"I needed to think this out," I said. "Someone is on to us. It doesn't seem like they want me arrested or you shot dead. What do they want?"

"I agree that we are dealing with the same person or group," Camila said.

I had my journal on my lap. "Hermanita, we have four hundred eight million parked that doesn't belong to us. Four clients own this money."

"I know, Amor," Camila said impatiently. "I'm the one who deals with them."

"Let me wire the money to their accounts and let them know we can't operate for a while. When things cool off, I will deliver the cash to LAI accounts. Your credibility is on the line."

I had hit a nerve. "That's a lot of money to let go of," she whispered.

"You won't even feel it, Amor," I said. "They will be happy there is nothing on hold."

"But they will want us to keep taking cash," Camila countered.

"Can't do that. They will understand we need to find who's behind this. Tell them you're fronting this money out of your pocket. The three year arrangement has run out, anyway."

"They will think that we are closing up shop. Who knows how they take that?"

"We are not closing up shop. But what if the cops had found the cash?"

"I would have paid the clients the money. You know the deal. Once the money is in Camacho possession, the client is protected unconditionally to the tune of seventy percent. They give us a million, we guarantee that seven hundred thousand will eventually be deposited in their bank account. If something happens along the way, a bust, a confiscation, Camacho pays the seventy percent and then Camacho has the option to stop doing business for self-protection."

I nodded.

Camila said, "Amor, is there any other way?"

"I don't think so. We'd be stupid not to put business on pause until we get to the bottom of this. Put Mason on this or put the families on it. We need to find who is fucking with us."

"Are you sure your numbers are correct?"

I smiled at Camila. "I don't make mistakes with money."

After a glass of champagne, Camila capitulated.

"Make the deposits," she said. "I'll visit the clients one by one and explain. You are right. They can help find the dead man who is doing this to us."

"You say man because a man called you and me. We don't know if the caller is responsible. We don't know for sure it's a male."

"Are you suggesting that Lola is alive?" Camila asked.

"Not at all. She's dead. But there could be another one like her."

Mason said that Lola was dead. She died hating Camila and me for almost taking her life. If she were alive, that hatred would be alive too. Only Camila and I knew that I had nothing to do with Lola getting shot. Even Mario had thought I was part of it. When she'd been undercover, she never did anything like this to us. The searches, phones calls, none of it was her style. But I wasn't going to get into that with Camila.

Two days later, I was in Geneva with written wire instructions. At the bank, I had wires sent out to the five clients, ending their ties with the cash that was stashed. It now belonged to Camila. When I got back to the hotel, Riana looked a little gloomy.

"Does this mean you're going to drop me off at home?" For her, home was Spain.

"Only if you want me to."

"No, I don't want that."

I hugged her. "We got some time off," I said.

"Mario will be thrilled," Riana said.

Primarily because of the phone thing, I hadn't mentioned any of this to Mario. If I had a leak it could simply be the phone.

"I don't know if I want to go to Pasadena. Let's go to Rome."

"Olga, are you sure?"

"I'm sure. If he wants to come and see me in Rome, no problem." I hugged her tighter. "Let's go have fun in Rome, Amor."

"Yes," Riana said. "That big plane costs a bundle to be flying around in it. Won't Camila mind?"

"The plane is mine until I stop working for Camila. When I retire, I get a brand-new plane, smaller but new, with all expenses covered for ten years."

"You're so smart, Olga. Did you make that deal?"

My stomach churned when I thought of when I'd made that deal with Pepe. "Yes, I made that deal, long ago. Amor, I have enough money for ten or more lifetimes. Don't worry."

"That makes two of us," Riana reminded me. "I haven't drawn on the trust my dad set up, not one time since I've been flying around with you. And the old ex ball and chain hasn't been able to touch my trust since I dumped him along with his name. It's thanks to you that I am back to being Riana Carrera, not Mrs. Piece of Shit."

I patted her hand, and remembered when I had seduced her father, Felipe Carrera into our using his bank in Barcelona. He was an old dog, to be sure, but he had a hot penthouse in Portugal, and I have to admit he knew his way around a bedroom. Riana had showed up at the bank during one of my early drops, and after her father introduced us, we really hit it off. I first brought Riana to meet Mario in July of 1985. From the very beginning, she had been cool about my interlude with her father. She knew what he was like. My friendship with Riana had gone much farther than I'd expected. We had weathered her break-up with her husband, and her first love—cocaine. But I don't know if that's entirely fair. Enrique Vas had brought drugs into her life, and when he was gone, she'd kicked her habit pretty easily. Except for a couple of times getting wasted when we'd partied during our first months together, she'd been drug free.

I called the captain.

"We're leaving for Rome at eight in the morning."

Riana was all smiles, and pantomimed clapping so that the pilot didn't hear her.

Before we boarded the plane, I called the main number at the Rome house.

The chief of staff, Leonardo, answered the phone.

"We will be there tomorrow afternoon," I told him, "Security will call you to let you know when to have cars waiting for us. Get me two male masseuses for late afternoon. Experienced therapists. No older than thirty."

We boarded the plane as expected, and once we were in the air, Riana's conversation took a turn for the serious.

"I think Mario deserves to know that you are down for a while," Riana said, "And that you choose to be alone to sort things out, not necessarily things about you and him, maybe just business."

"I agree, but I am not going to do it on the phone."

"We could have flown there, stayed a little while and then come to Rome."

"I thought you wanted to come to Rome," I said.

"I do, of course I do. I'm soaking wet thinking of the heavies Leonardo will have there for us." Riana was all giggles.

"You like Mario, don't you?" I knew the answer.

"With all my heart, yes."

We arrived in Rome, had a late lunch, and settled in two bedrooms. We got massaged for the longest time in the roomy spa. It was not as glamorous as Casa Luna, but it was bigger, and the massage tables were in private rooms within the spa. The lighting was candles throughout, and incense was burning. Each room had wet steam, shower, rest room and a steaming stone tub floating with red rose petals. Below the headrest of each table was an arrangement of red roses to see and smell when lying face down.

Five minutes into the massage, I told the masseuse to dump the sheet.

"Don't be shy, Cristobal. I expect a full body massage," I said in Italian, though he spoke English. "Drop the shorts and shirt," I added with a little laugh.

The massage stopped for just a minute while he did it. My right hand wandered to his upper thigh and beyond. When I called a time out, it must have been more than two hours later. I lost track of how many times, but my orgasms shook my entire body. Riana was still at it when I went up to my room, but later she came up to see me.

"It was fantastic," she said, finding me lying in bed watching television.

"Come here, Amor," I patted a place beside me on the bed.

"How about you?" she asked.

"Fantastic, yes."

"Did you do it?' Riana asked.

"You mean did I fuck him?"

"Of course, what else?"

"No reason to fuck him. He took good care of me. Got to have him back tomorrow. And you?"

"I fucked him. He had a problem keeping it hard, but he's a beast when it's erect. Anyway, it was good. No, it was fantastic."

I put my arm around Riana and made room for her on the pillows.

"Aren't you hungry?" Riana asked.

"I was waiting for you."

Riana was a food junkie, but she hadn't a trace of fat. Her metabolism is impossible to understand. If we'd been in Pasadena, maybe we would have raided Miguel's kitchen. The contents of his refrigerators are to die for, and that does include Letty's cookies which are in cookie jars if you know where to look. We went down and ordered pot luck from the kitchens. In Rome, that means lots of pasta and bread, tiramisu, choux à la crème, cannoli, gelato, crème caramel.

Two days later, we landed at the Ontario Airport in California. In the back seat of the car as we left the airport, Riana said, "I'm so glad you decided to come see him."

"Amor, it was the only way to get you to stop bugging me." I hugged her. "I love you, Riana."

I dialed him from the car. Mario picked up.

"Amor, are you home or at theoffice?"

"Office. Where are you?"

"Leaving Ontario Airport. I was going to surprise you, but I'm giving you a heads-up in case Letty and you are baking cookies in the kitchen."

I laughed. Mario joined in.

"I'm leaving right now for the house."

Pasadena, June 7 1991
Mario

I stopped by Letty's office to let her know I was on my way home and why. She followed me into Tangles's office. They were still working as a team but now had separate offices.

"Leave here early," I told them.

"Boss, go make some quality time with her. Long time since she's been around," Letty said.

"We'll get home at our regular time," Tangles said. "We have some loose ends to finish up here. You know how it is on Friday."

I kissed Letty who was beside me and blew a kiss to Tangles at her desk. She lifted her hand to catch it, then put her palm to her lips.

I beat Olga and Riana by thirty minutes. The guard called when the caravan reached the gates. I high-tailed it to the second floor. I made it down in time to open the back door, and there was my gorgeous fiancée.

As usual I had her in my arms, up off her feet, amd was smothering her in kisses and hugs. I leaned to the side and kissed Riana when she made it out of the car.

"Too long gone," I said to Olga as I carried her inside. "Too long, baby."

Pasadena, June 7 1991
Riana

I simply love this house. I took the same room as always. It's like my home away from home in California. Mario and Olga went right to the bedroom, of course. When they get enough of each other they probably will let me get in on the action. They always do. That's okay. I have plans of my own. The tub had my name on it. I prepared a bath and used way too much bubble soap, just the way I like it.

When I was drying off, Letty and Tangles got home. Their rooms were on the third floor, like mine. They were all dressed up, and looked professional, reminding me of the executives that work for my father at his bank. We ended up in a big huddle of hugs, then Letty took a fresh towel to my wet hair. Tangles got a towel and started helping her. We were all laughing. They kicked off their tall office shoes and got into shorts and t-shirts. Olga and Mario didn't come up for air, so the three of us ate dinner in the wine room. On the intercom, Miguel told us the lovebirds were going to eat in the bedroom, so we could have whatever we wanted.

"I want American. Is it okay if I have a hamburger and a hot dog, oh, and French fries?"

Letty and Tangles squealed in delight.

"And onion rings," Letty said. "If you haven't had them yet, you've got to try 'em. You haven't lived till you've had Miguel's onion rings. He does them like that restaurant, whole, but his are way better."

Letty conferred with Miguel. In short order, we were presented with all the goodies I had been craving. Miguel surprised us with milk shakes. Letty said they were made with ice cream. I don't know how they were made, but they were delicious.

Chapter 20
Pasadena, June 7 1991
Olga

He was on top of me, his hands under me, fondling, probing. I always go wild with him, always have. Everything was perfect. It was perfect until Lola popped up in my mind. I only knew what she looked like because Mason provided pictures. I've never seen her live and in person. I had wanted her out of Mario's bed, and now I wanted her out of my head. From the beginning when Mason told him about his suspicions that Lola was a cop, Mario should have pulled away from her. Stupid pussy-enamored fool. He continued to see her until she died. Camila got her shot, but it wasn't Camila or me who blew up her car. For the millionth time, I wondered, who did it. I needed to be alone with Mario, but there were the three of us in that bed.

One of Mario's servants brought up dinner and parked it on the table out on the balcony. I went outside and looked over the back yard. The night was perfect, with the scent of summer. Someone had cut the lawn, and the smell of grass was flavored with some kind of blooming flower, some native species I do not recognize. The koi pond below the balcony has a filter that keeps the water trickling constantly, so if I got very quiet, it sounded like a bubbling brook. When the servant left, and we seated ourselves side by side looking out toward the fence line, with the doors open behind us. It was a typical Mario meal. Shrimp on ice with red dipping sauce, steak, baked potatoes, ice cream sundaes with hot fudge and crumbles of peanut brittle. We started on the shrimp.

"Amor, let me bring you up to date with what is happening." That's how I started the conversation. I reminded him of Morocco, which he already knew about, and Amsterdam that he didn't know about. I told him about the phone call from the laughing bastard, and our solution for it.

"Until Camila and I can get to the bottom of this," I said, "I'm out of business."

"That's great news," he said.

I looked at him in silence, looked down at my plate and forked the baked potato.

"Isn't it great news, baby?"

I did not think it was great news. "What are you thinking?" I asked.

"I'm thinking that you can be home for a change."

"And you'll be at the office while I'm home?"

Mario looked at me like he didn't know how to answer. He took a bite of steak.

"I can take time off. Sure, I can do that."

"Amor, I need to know who is doing this. Camila just dished out 408 million, just to keep her credibility."

He looked at me puzzled, no doubt trying to figure out why Camila dished out that much money and to whom. I could have answered his questions, but he didn't ask them. As I expected, he said, "I don't want to know," like he always did. "I'm just looking forward to your being here."

"Amor," I said, reaching for his hand, we were sitting beside each other. "I adore you, truly I do, but I need to tell you that I don't want to be your fiancée anymore." I was almost surprised as I heard myself say this. I suddenly felt sad, but relieved.

Pasadena, June 7 1991
Mario

My years of karate and judo training include countless tournaments and competitions. I have learned to be on guard. I have been that way since my formative years growing up in ELA. In my real life, I am always on guard. I am always ready for the unexpected, for that blow that could take me down or give an opponent the advantage over me.

Olga told me she no longer wanted to be my fiancée. I heard it. I felt it like that unexpected physical blow. The words hit my ears, melted into my consciousness, and the armor went up. I went into protective mode. I didn't react as she may have expected me to react. I didn't react at all. I didn't grip her hand tight or turn to look at her. I was saved by years of training. I was calm.

"You love someone else?"

"Amor, no. I've been thinking this over. This is how I want it to be. I'm sorry, Amor. I can't do this anymore."

Do what anymore? I wondered. "You know best," I said.

She was quiet for a while. I could hear her breathing.

"Amor, that's all you have to say?"

"Olga, what do you want me to say?"

"Look at me." Her voice was soft. We were holding hands.

I turned to face her, poker-faced. As my opponent, she would not be able to read my expression.

"Do you love me?" she asked.

"You know I love you. What difference does that make now?"

At least a minute of silence.

"The Lola thing. It wounded me. I need time to heal."

"I'm sorry, Olga. I never intended to hurt you." I released her hand. "The road to hell is paved with good intentions. I'm sorry if that's what brought this on."

"I had nothing to do with her shooting, the attempt at the hospital or the car bomb that took her life."

I could have said what I'd said before, that I believed her. "Good to hear," I said.

After her announcement, she went to a guest room and made the arrangements to leave that night.

"What's the hurry?" I asked at one point, though it was good she was leaving. It would be awkward to spend the night with her after her surprise proclamation.

"I'm going to Rome. The sooner I get there, the better. I need to get myself together. Amor, don't hate me."

"Does Camila know?"

"No, she doesn't know. I didn't know till I said the words."

"I'm asking because of LAI. What's the plan moving forward?"

"Amor, Camila would have me killed if my actions resulted in your leaving the company. You have a stake in GAL. Eventually you can own a piece of the company. GAL is by far the most profitable asset that Camila owns. GAL needs you. Camila needs you."

I considered her words. I nodded. Working with Olga in the future could be problematic. Only time would tell.

"I'm happy doing what I'm doing, but I don't have to be there, and neither do Letty and Tangles."

Olga hugged me, her face on my chest. I looked down at her. I knew so much about her. I knew, for example, that she tended to dress formally for the airport though she would change into whatever suited her mood once she'd jumped through any necessary hoops at customs. She looked like she was going to a very exclusive office; she was dressed to leave my house—what I have been calling our house—maybe for the last time.

"Who knows? Maybe we'll be together again one day." She gave a little laugh that had some emotion other than humor in it. "Amor, it's not like we are not going to talk. Our personal affairs have nothing to do with GAL. Run the company as you see fit. That's what Camila will want when she learns about this."

Olga took the ring off, kissed it, and handed it to me.

At two in the morning, Olga, Riana, and her six guards drove out the Casa Luna gates on their way to the airport.

Pasadena, June 7 1991
Riana

Olga came down to find me with Letty and Tangles in the wine room.

"Go pack," she said. "We're leaving for Rome tonight."

"You just got here," Letty said. "Is everything okay?"

Tangles hopped to her feet and walked over to Olga. She touched her hand. "What's wrong?" "I have to leave right away. Forgive the drama. It's a personal matter. Mario will tell you," she said, stopping in the doorway to the wine room, and looking past me to Letty and Tangles. "I'm sorry." Then she left.

I didn't have to pack because I never really unpacked. I wanted to have a conversation with Olga on the way to the airport, but I was messed up from the wine and the weed. I fell asleep with my head resting on her shoulder. Once we were on the plane, we had thirty minutes before wheels up. The cat nap in the car and the hot black coffee on the plane snapped me back to life. We sat in the main parlor, across each other in big comfortable seats, the shiny coffee table between us. Her hand looked naked to me.

"Olga, I'm dying to hear what happened. I don't see the ring."

Olga smiled as she lifted her hand. Her tan line showed where the ring had been. "I wore it so long that I have a white ring on my finger."

"What did you say to him?"

"That I didn't want to be his fiancée anymore. That the way he handled everything hurt me badly."

"You mean, Lola?"

"Of course. Who else?"

"And what did he say?"

"Practically nothing," Olga said. A tear welled up in her eye and trailed its way down her cheek.

"If you have second thoughts, just call and tell him. We're still here. You can do it."

"I don't have second thoughts. This is what I want." Olga shook her head, blotting her eyes with a tissue.

"I don't believe it," I said. "I thought maybe you had an argument and decided to leave right away to prove a point."

"I'm sorry, Riana. That's not what happened. I didn't plan it. It just came out. When it did, I was relieved like you wouldn't believe."

I remembered how I had felt when I'd told my husband to fuck off. It had taken a long time to get around to it. I felt great relief after I did. But Mario was not the creep that my husband was, and she didn't plan her confrontation the way I had. I nodded to let her know I understood.

"I'm glad we have this downtime. Riana, we're going to have fun. At the same time, I'm going to come up with a plan to find out who is doing this to Camila and me. Maybe use someone other than Mason."

My eyes always blink rapidly when I'm stumped. Olga knew this and didn't remark on it.

"Miss Olga, with your permission we are pulling back." The pilot came on speaker. All her pilots said that, but never actually waited for the permission.

"Hello Rome, here we come," I said with as much glee as I thought was appropriate.

Olga smiled. Her eyes were a little red, but the tears were gone. She yelled back, though they wouldn't hear her in the cockpit, "Permission granted. Rome, here we come!"

"I don't know if I should be this happy," I said to Olga.

"Be happy, Amor. It makes me happy when you're happy. I love you."

"I love you too, Olga. I'm not sure I should tell you whether I'm sorry you broke up or not."

"Amor, I'm not sorry. Don't be sorry. I adore Mario, and I won't let him forget it."

I wasn't sure what that meant, but I didn't blink. I sent her a flying kiss. The plane started to move. The cabin lights dimmed in preparation for taxi and takeoff.

Pasadena, June 8 1991 (early)
Mario

For the first time, I didn't see Olga and Riana to their car. I turned off the lights in my bedroom and got back in bed. A few minutes later, Letty and Tangles walked in. Letty was in one of my old t shirts. Tangles was in a short gown. Both of them were wearing huge animal slippers.

"Want to be alone, Boss?" Letty asked.

"We can bug off in a flash," Tangles said.

"Come on in. The bed's a mess." I didn't need to look at the rumple of sheets and blankets to know it was a shambles. Olga and I had gone at it for hours before dinner and the break-up. Even with the balcony doors open, the room reeked of sex and Olga's perfume.

"Boss, go sleep downstairs. I'll be there in a minute after I get someone up here to freshen up."

Tangles followed me down to the third floor. I went in a guest room that had not been used that night. "In here," I said.

"Hey, Boss, my bed doesn't have any cooties," Tangles joked. By then, Letty must have finished talking to the staff, because she came running in, standing across from Tangles to turn down the bed.

"My bed doesn't have cooties either," Letty said.

I laughed. "I know, Babies. Let's get some use out of this room. No one ever stays here."

Nothing would compare to my huge bed, but this bed was mine too. The girls kicked off their shoes, and the three of us got cozy under the sheets.

"Tangles, do me a favor. Get me a sleeper. I need to knock-out."

"I'll be right back, Boss."

"Boss, I can give you head until you go to sleep," Letty said, her face up close to mine.

"Baby, I love you," I said. "I'd never go to sleep if you did that."

Letty is very good at not asking questions I knew she wants to ask. Tomorrow would be soon enough to give her details. I planned to stay home and take it easy. My beautiful home was all mine again. I had to get that straight in my head and sort out as much as I could. I did not want to worry about the future. Coping with right now is more than enough.

I slept straight through my work-out hour and I didn't wake up until nine thirty. I kissed Letty on the lips, and she stirred.

"Am I chopped liver, Boss?" On my other side, Tangles piped up.

I cupped her face with my hand and kissed her lips.

"Oh my. Listerine, get over here to Tangles."

Tangles sat up, hand up to her mouth, blowing, trying to smell her own breath. "Boss, so mean."

I laughed and kissed her again.

Letty sat up. "You owe me one," she said. "You gave her a second kiss." She kissed me on my nearest body part which happened to be my elbow and climbed out of bed. She put on her slippers. "In case you want to go up now, your room was cleaned up last night. I checked while you and Tangles were sleeping."

"I've never showered in a guest room," I said, then laughed. "Maybe I did the first day I moved in. I don't remember, exactly."

"Oh Boss, in that case, you need to try out all the guest bathrooms," Tangles said with her own laugh.

Tangles joined me in the shower.

"Get off the throne and get in here," she said to Letty.

"I was just brushing my teeth, Bitch."

I am just glad that neither asked me to explain what happened with Olga.

London, June 8, 1991
Camila

Olga called to tell me about giving Mario back the engagement ring yesterday but would not say anything else except that she wanted to wait until she saw me in person. I am going to Bogota to spend the down time. I arranged for everyone who needs me for business to see me there. I'm taking LAI public soon. The Swiss firm I hired put over ten accountants on the project. Instead of heading straight for home, I surprised Olga and Riana in Rome.

"I'm out of here tomorrow," I said. "London is so close that I couldn't resist a little reunion."

I trust Riana. Her father is doing business with us not only as head of the bank consortium financing part of the aviation leases we give them, but also because his bank accepts cash deposits on client accounts. Still, I have always been a little uneasy about Riana knowing so much about Olga's business because Olga's business is my business, too.

The three of us sat down for a two o'clock lunch on the deck overlooking the swimming pool. At this time of year, the manicured lawn was forest green. The landscape was punctuated with statuary, flower gardens, grape arbors, terra cotta fountains, and a marble pergola held up by a dozen vestal virgins. A person could spend the rest of their life here and never have to leave the house. It was as complete as the Milan villa.

"Hermanita, it's not like we need any more money, especially you," Olga said. "When you go public, you will be in Fortune Magazine."

Riana said nothing, concentrating on rolling the perfect forkful of pasta.

"I don't want to be in any magazines, especially ones that circulate in the United States."

"You have nothing to hide, Amorcito," Olga said with assurance.

"Is he going to stay with us?"

Olga did not pretend not to know exactly who I was talking about.

"Amor, he loves leasing planes. He's still planning to buy in for at least ten percent, probably as much as you will let him in for. He goes to the office every day, spends hours there."

"I know, Amor, that's why I'm worried. I don't want this personal thing to get him on edge, and he springs on me." I took a sip of wine and toyed with my salad.

"He's not going to spring. He's making serious money with you," Olga said.

I know Mario. He doesn't play around when it comes to business. He committed to GAL and he'll honor that commitment. He's principled that way.

"What are you thinking?" Olga asked.

"I think you're right. Besides, he wouldn't just abandon me."

"He's not going anywhere, Amor, though he knows that Andrea is there and could run the company for you."

"Andrea is good. She taught Mario what he knows of this business. Andrea doesn't want the kind of pressure that Mario thrives on. We're lucky to have Mario. He's one of a kind. You know that better than anyone," I reminded Olga.

If we weren't running scared from a bastard with a loud voice, we'd be discussing strategies to move the cash from Amsterdam to somewhere like Riana's father's bank in Barcelona. I was reluctant to discuss the crazy guy in front of Riana. It was bad enough to be talking business in front of her at all. "Amor, let's leave the money where it is. I don't trust…" I looked over at Riana, still engrossed in her pasta. I knew she was listening. She's not that stupid. "…what is going on."

"You work the clients to investigate," Olga said. "I'm thinking of hiring someone other than Mason to work on this. Mason has billed you tens of thousands of dollars and never came up with who is after Mario."

"Don't blame Mason," I said. "He's been good with us. It just takes him a long time. He's careful."

"I can find someone," Olga insisted.

"I already spoke with the families. They don't want to be sitting on their cash for long. They are investigating. They kill each other over competition, but on this, they agreed to work together. They have a common cause."

I don't now how Riana felt about it, but Olga and I slept together that night. What happened between her and Mario did not come between us at all, though I had feared it might. Between bouts of sex, we talked.

"Are you going to make up with him?"

"I want him as a friend. I want to fuck him when I want. I want to spend time with him. But I don't want to talk about getting married. First, there's how he handled the Lola situation. That was dirty. Second, he wants me out of the money business. He's happy that we're down right now. He should be concerned that someone is doing us wrong. He should understand if..." she looked at me earnestly, and took my hand across the table, "...if we decide not to step down."

The next day I was on my plane, destination: Bogota. Mario and I had been close when we first met. The sex was remarkable. I knew he was a womanizer, but I'm a realist. All men who are not gay are womanizers, especially a hunk like him. At the time I thought if I was going to marry someone, it would be Mario. When Olga came in the picture, I knew he favored her. I gave up my claim on him. Now that Olga no longer wears his ring, I can admit that none of us are the marrying kind, not really. Who needs to be in their forties raising babies, anyway? How he handled the lady cop was dirty. I don't know if she is at the root of the break-up. I don't know how I would have handled it. His blindness to how this woman hurt us all will stain how I see him in the future, but I need his acumen at the leasing company. I wish the damn cop had asked me directly. I'd have told her to her face that I sent the assassin after her. Olga had nothing to do with it. I wish I'd ordered the bomb that exploded her car.

I'm not surprised she pissed off someone enough to blow her up. She must have had more than her share of enemies.

Bogota, June 12, 1991

After a few days in Bogota, a lawyer, Noah Witzer, and three Swiss certified public accountants came to see me. They spent three days with me going over their findings on the assets of the company. After their departure, I called Mario.

"I'm sorry about what happened, Amor. If it's meant to be, it will come back."

"Yes, I suppose."

"I had accountants here for days going over the public offering of the company. There are some things I need to do, but I need your help. There is nothing illegal about what I want to discuss, but we should do it in person."

"Fine," he said. "Glad to be of service, but I will need to get back to Pasadena as soon as possible."

Bogota, June 14, 1991

Forty-eight hours later, Mario was picked up at the airport in Bogota and driven to my house. The kisses and hugs were enough to get me steamy, but that was not happening on this trip. In our strange new reality, it didn't come up. It was going to be a fast trip.

"Amor, this is about the bakery, tortilla company, liquor stores and donut shops we own in the US. These businesses don't match up with our other assets. At the time, they were the solution for handling cash we needed to get into a bank account. Over the years, they have done that. These businesses don't measure up to my current needs. In short, I need to get rid of them.

Bogota, June 14, 1991
Mario

Unbeknownst to Camila, Letty and Tangles were waiting in the plane—that's how short this visit was going to be. She assured me that all she needed was a couple of hours to explain her dilemma. Camila has always appealed to me. But after what had happened with Olga and me, I didn't have those feelings any more for Olga's adopted sister.

Olga no longer needs these companies. Without green cash in Los Angeles needing to be moved and cleaned, they were just businesses. Each had taken in huge amounts of cash that showed up as sales. But they were actual working businesses.

"The liquor stores and donut shops are not just the business. You own the real property for each store," I pointed out.

"The accountants would like to just wipe the slate clean, and not show these assets as ongoing businesses."

"Did you call me over to see if I want to buy these?"

"That's a good idea, but no. I wanted to pick your brain on how to rapidly dispose of these."

"Did your accountants tell you what you need to get for these assets?"

"As close as we can get to what we have them on the books for. That should be less than market value. You would know best."

"I don't know anyone that would step in and buy the whole lot. It would be a big bite. I wouldn't know where to begin to run it all, and a management company like you have would cost an arm and a leg. For your purposes, whatever they charged you was worth it because they had a lot of work to do to keep the books in order."

Camila didn't even blink at my suggestion that with all the crooked stuff going on, the management company had had their hands full and had probably been paid accordingly.

"Amor, you can have it all on a promissory note. No cash out of your pocket. Name the terms."

"Tempting," I said. "Have the accountants send me the reports on each company. Let me see if there is any actual income to make the note payments to you."

"Amor, talk to the management company. No one is saying the businesses are no good. It's just too many small businesses under the umbrella of a management company they never heard of."

My mind was racing. I remembered the deals I had made. The bakery was a gold mine, the biggest in ELA, maybe the biggest in Los Angeles for Mexican breads. The tortilla company been around over fifty years, a brand staple in every supermarket in Los Angeles. The liquor store's sideline of cashing paychecks made more profit than the liquor.

The timer on my watch went off. Two hours on the dot.

"Maybe we can work all this out on the phone. There's nothing we can't discuss." I said. We weren't going to talk about cash being laundered, or anything that someone listening could run and get an indictment over.

"Amor, stay for lunch at least. Why are you running back so soon?"

"I have lots of work to do for you back in Los Angeles. Seven new lease deals. And a breakfast meeting Saturday with another potential buyer."

I kissed her. It was passionate because that's the way we always kissed. I didn't feel it that way, though, not down to my bones the way I used to feel with her.

"I should be mad at you, too," she said as I started for the door.

"Why?"

"I don't think you did it on purpose."

"You mean Lola?"

"Yes, but that is a story for another day. Safe travels, Amor. I love you. We're family, no matter what. Remember that."

I was at the door, but the tone of her voice made me pause. I went back a few steps, hugged her again, kissed her again, and I looked at her straight in the eyes.

"Camila, I love you."

This elicited the hint of a smile from her.

"I felt bad for Lola. I have no evidence, but my heart tells me that you—with or without Olga—ordered the kill."

Camila instantly turned beet red.

I raised my hand because she was ready to object or explode. "Wait, Camila, let me finish. If that's true, in the end, you did the right thing. You gave her the exact compensation she demanded. To use Lola's exact words, the payment ended the beef she had with you and Olga, period. I felt bad for her. She was just doing her job. You should see the scars on her body that the bullets and the doctors left behind."

"Mario, leave before I say something that I won't be able to take back."

I gave her a peck on the lips, and this time I left.

As soon as the car door was closed behind me, before the driver and guard got in the front seat, I said aloud, "Lola, I hope you are alive and listening. I hope your beef with them really is over."

On my drive to the plane, I felt relief that I'd said what I did to Camila. I'd been wanting to say it for a while. I had absolutely no regret. Fuck Camila, and fuck Olga.

I gave a whistle as I boarded the plane, and headed for the parlor, the room I lived in on this plane. Letty and Tangles came running from the bedroom. Their shorts were so short that, well, if I was looking, I would be able to see anything I wanted to.

"That was fast," Letty said.

"Are you hungry, Boss?" Tangles asked.

"Starving, but let's get going." I picked up the phone next to one of the seats and pushed the button for the cockpit. "Paulo, a bit earlier than I expected, but see if you can get us out of here, pronto."

As soon as the AirFone was available for planes, Andrea had them installed. It performed with as many annoying drops as a cell phone, but we kept using it.

When we were airborne, I called Andrea.

"I'm headed back," I said. She would know by now anyway. Everything on board this plane went through her somehow. Andrea was a master with heavy planes like mine.

"Safe travels, Mario."

"I have a meeting Saturday, and I'll be in the office Monday, but I'm planning to take a couple weeks off as soon as I can do it."

"I'll get everything ready that needs your okay in a couple days, Boss."

Unlike the girls, Andrea switched from Mario to Boss on a dime.

Tangles said, "Where you headed, Boss?"

"I'd like to know that myself," Letty said.

"We three are going to figure that out on our way home," I said. "First we eat."

If I was supposed to get married in this life and I couldn't have Melina, as it turned out, then I should be married to Letty and Tangles. For certain, Letty. I was not a stupid kid, but I was thinking like a kid. I couldn't marry both of them, but I was going to take them on a honeymoon.

Tokyo June 28, 1991

Two weeks later, we were in Tokyo. I finished going over the financial reports of the businesses that Camila wanted me to relieve her of. My conservative CPA told me I didn't need it, but the real property appreciation was going to be substantial in the coming years.

I called Camila from the hotel we were in. Letty and Tangles were nearby, listening, watching.

"Can we discuss selling the businesses?"

"You sound so serious, Amor. You blasted me before you left. I should be upset, not you."

"Camila, I'm not upset. Are you still interested in selling me the businesses?"

"Yes, I have to rid myself of those companies."

"Okay, here's what I'm willing to do," I said.

I offered twenty-five million for everything. No money down. A note payment at interest only of three percent per annum with a balloon payment due in five years.

"Amor, you just threw me on the bed and raped me. The real property alone is worth twice that much on the worst day."

"You are absolutely correct. I think you should tell me to piss off and go away," I said.

The girls were frowning, wondering where I was going with this.

Camila was silent. After a few minutes, she hung up. An hour later, maybe a little more, Camila called me back. She accepted thirty million under the same terms, the low rate of interest and I would get clear title in exchange for the promissory note. The promissory note was unsecured. It took an hour because Camila had to call the accounting firm for input. When she called me back, I agreed to boost the price by five million. It was true, it was worth much more. Even with the extra five million, it was a steal.[35]

"No hard feelings about what I said before I left?" I asked.

"Are you apologizing?" Camila asked.

I loved her enough to say yes.

"I don't believe you," she said, apparently in pretty good spirits. "But at least you apologized."

On the phone, I wouldn't say more.

"Have fun on your vacation," she said before we disconnected.

After we hung up, I told the girls, "I was going to say, not a vacation, it's a honeymoon. But I thought she might not react kindly to that."

From Tokyo, we flew to Singapore, went across to Indonesia on a barge to a beautiful resort where we spent five days surrounded by the jungle, the ocean, and monkeys who kept stealing anything and everything they could grab from the house we were in.

On our return to Singapore, we took my plane to our next stop, Jakarta, Indonesia. We didn't care for too much for that big city. We explored for two days and took a short flight to Bali. The beach there was like no other. Our hotel suite was fit for the royal family. The locals were wonderful hosts, no mat-

---

[35] $35,000,000.00 in 1991 is equal to $65,718,647.23 in 2019.

ter where we went, and we went everywhere. While we were there, there was a four plus earthquake. Everyone in the hotel ran out but us. We were from Los Angeles. Nothing new about an earthquake. Besides, we were lying around naked in bed.

On July fourteenth, I got a call from Olga on my cell.

"Amor, Andrea says you've been away almost two weeks. You never took me away that long."

It wasn't true. I'd disappeared with her for longer than that, but I wasn't going to quibble over details. She did not appear angry. Her laugh was genuine. I could tell, none the less, it was a message.

"Baby, it's good to hear your voice," I said. "I hope you are well. Are you in Rome?"

"Yes, Amor, still in Rome. I love it here."

"What's there not to love?" I said.

"So true. Anyway, I wanted to check in with you. Safe travels, Amor. Kisses to Letty and Tangles."

Either Andrea told her the girls were on the manifest or she guessed.

"Stay in touch, Olga."

I heard her quick intake of breath. "How I love it when you call me by my name, Amor."

"If it bothers you I won't," I said.

After she hung up, Tangles said. "She'll want you back soon enough."

Letty was quiet.

"There's no going back," I said.

A fragile smile appeared on Letty's face. Tangles was looking at Letty and wearing a smile of her own.

We flew from Bali to Hong Kong.

"Reminds me of London," Letty said.

Tangles said, "I think it's rented or something to the Brits."

"Know it all, Bitch," Letty said.

"Boss, tell her to cool it," Tangles said. "I don't want to end up in jail here in Hong Kong for kicking her ass."

"Behave, Letty," I said. "Argue if you must, but after I finish reading this." She came over and stood over my shoulder to see the thirty-two page fax outlining the purchase from LAI.

"When we get home, ladies, remind me to call Jo and Niley. I wonder if they might be interested in absorbing the management company that LAI was using for my new properties." We could all get together and work out what businesses were worth keeping, which were worth selling, and what was worth hanging on to just for the property value.

"Great idea," Letty said. "Don't think they can handle it. They have enough to do just managing your apartments for them to handle anything else, but it would be nice to get together with them. They work and live so close, but we never see them."

"I know," I said. "Time has a way of separating even those we love."

Letty looked thoughtful. "Maybe Jo wants to grow. Liquor stores and donut shops would be a change. It would be a challenge."

"Don't forget tortillas and pan dulce," Tangles added with a giggle.

"I'm going to have a sit down with the existing management company."

"If the financials you reviewed are the result of their management, cut a deal with them."

I nodded. "I'm going to look into selling off some of the businesses and keeping the real property to rent back to the buyers."

Tangles said, "Boss, you're so smart."

"Kiss ass," Letty said.

"Oh, you don't think Boss is smart?"

Letty looked at me and smiled. "Of course, he's brilliant."

"Now who is the kiss ass, bitch?"

If I was hard of hearing and had hearing aids, I could just turn off the power and let them go at it while my brain worked on something else.

Somewhere in the world, some time in July
Tangles

I dig being with Mario and Letty so damn much, but I feel guilty for not being at my desk back at the leasing company. I dig that job. The challenge of working these high dollar plane leases is enough to get me soaked. I'm so nasty when I'm thinking. Nah—I'm nasty all the time. I dig the bucks, and I dig the authority Andrea gives me.

We flew from Hong Kong to Cairo, Egypt where we rode horse-drawn buggies across the sand to check out the pyramids. After we got to know the friendly camels, their attendants let us ride alone, and they walked behind. The Nile was beautiful. The excitement of being there and being together offset the sweltering heat of the day.

The two days in Rome, Boss never called Olga though we knew she was at the house with Riana. We stayed in a swanky hotel at the Spanish Steps, then flew to Paris for three nights, London for two nights, then to Washington D.C. for two days. One day was spent in incredible luxury in bed at a fabulous hotel, and the next we played tourist, toured the White House and then shopped all day. We went from store to store weighted down with bags and boxes, filled up the car and would have called it a day.

"Done so soon?" Boss challenged us. "We have the entire cargo bay to fill up. There's room down there for the luggage of a hundred fifty passengers."

It's ridiculous. Once I was getting a ten spot for a massage and a hand job and barely making it. Now I am running around with Mario Luna in a plane worth millions of dollars, shopping like Malibu Barbie.

We had left in June, screwed around all over the Far East, Europe and the Middle East all through July. When we got home, it was August. The three of us were fat, sleek, and bronze. Egypt was heavily responsible for our healthy color.

It was good to be home, and I wasn't thinking about my apartment.

"I don't think I can have sex for a month," Boss said as we walked into the front foyer of Casa Luna.

"No sex? Oh, Boss, how could you," Letty said, and gave the kind of little shimmy Boss can never resist, then caught sight of herself in a floor to ceiling mirror. I'm not saying she was fat, precisely, but what she saw, she didn't like.

"We got to start working out," Letty said like a pissed-off drill sergeant.

"I'm afraid to get on the scale," I said.

Boss said, "Don't remind me of how much weight I gained."

"All of us, Boss," Letty said.

Pasadena August 24, 1991
Mario

It took longer to get over the jet lag because we were gone longer than usual. The longer you stay away, the longer you suffer when you return. The three of us were terrible about eating junk food, and the only thing that normally saved us from showing it was the religious daily workouts. It was harder than usual getting back into the workout routine. The first day back we whined like Jack Lemmon in the Odd Couple but hit it like gangbusters. The second and third days, our bodies were protesting. Even after three weeks, we were not up to our usual speed, but at least we had stopped complaining about the weight.

It was late August and still sweltering hot. The kitchen counter was one of our favorite spots to sit and eat ice cream. It was not unusual for us to have three or four containers sitting there in front of us to spoon directly to our mouth. When we did this, Letty usually banned wine the rest of the day. Ditto for weed and munchies. Drill Sergeant Letty (as Tangles was calling her), was kicking us out of bed at five to work out every morning, even on weekends.

"It's been six weeks since Olga called you," Letty said while we hit the pistachio ice cream.

"He should know," Tangles said in my defense.

Letty's dates were off. "She called me on July 14 just before we left Bali. I'm not expecting her to call. I talk to Camila once a week or so," I said. Our conversations were always about the leasing business.

"Are you going to ever marry, Boss?" Tangles asked.

"I'm married to you and Letty," I joked, switching gallons and eating away at the fudge peanut-butter ripple.

"Boss, seriously, are you?"

"I don't have a crystal ball." I said. "Let me switch the question. Are you and Letty going to get married?"

The girls looked at each other and laughed. Not just a little giggle, either, but rollicking, falling-off-the-stool rolling-on-the-ground, bona fide belly-shaking horse laughter from both of them.

"I think if Letty was marrying a girl, it would be Pixie, but Pixie would never give up men," Tangles said.

The gatekeeper announced that Betty and Storm were driving up.

"That Storm is so hot," I said, going over to the sink and rinsing off my ice cream hands and face.

"She's hot," Letty agreed, gathering up the cartons and tossing them in the trash. She opened the door of the pantry and scribbled something into the little book Miguel used for his grocery list. "I'm making a note here, Boss. How was the fudge peanut butter ripple?"

"Tolerable," I said. "Too much fudge, not enough peanut."

She laughed and kept writing.

"We need a third therapist so the three of us get a massage at the same time," I said.

"Eventually," Letty said. "Betty is looking around. Don't want to bring just anyone here, right?"

"Right, baby."

She shut the pantry door, came over to wash off, and I kissed her.

Tangles was still at the stool at the counter, scrubbing at her face with a washcloth that had emerged miraculously from her pocket. At least she hadn't been wearing plastic gloves when diving into the ice cream. "I pass on the massage tonight," Tangles said, laughing at us. "You two go ahead." She put her hand up, and Letty tossed her a sponge from the sink. Tangles swiped at the counter, and tossed the sponge at Letty's head, which Letty dodged, snatched out of the air and ran under the faucet.

"You can get one after," Letty said, "or go first. I can wait."

Tangles said, "Nate is picking me up at seven. It's Saturday night, and he's got three hours off. We're going to a show or something."

I said the same thing I always said. "Bring him over whenever you want." Nate Morgan the intern never came in. At least I never seen him in the house. I had never met him.

"Thanks, Boss," Tangles said.

Pasadena August 24, 1991
Tangles

Nate never drives to the front of the house when he picks me up. He waits behind the guardhouse where a person would make a u-turn to go back out to the street. He never gets out of his car. It was a hot night, but it wasn't dark yet. Dark in August in Pasadena is at about eight thirty, and it was only a little past seven. I got in his Camaro. The console between the two seats prevented me from slipping across to kiss him. Good thing I'm limber. I half stood, put my right hand on his face and kissed his lips.

"I get turned on when you touch my face like that," he said.

I felt his hand on my breast.

"Nate, you're horny. And here I was thinking we were going to a show."

"We have time to go to a show," he said.

"You want to go to my apartment, first?" I asked.

As the car came to life, he leaned over and took my face in his hand and kissed me. "Only if you want to," he said.

Nate worked hard to get his doctor chops. He was on the naïve side, two years younger than me, and he'd spent all his life in school. At first, I figured studying to be a doctor, he should know everything there was to know about the female body, about a woman getting off, about the clitoris, about how a woman doesn't just have an orgasm because she has a dick in her pussy. I found out the hard way that he didn't know that much about sex, but he is eager to learn. He is easy to like. I know he likes me. I like him, and I respect him for working so hard to become a doctor.

He always told me he loved me after he had finished inside a condom inside me.

"Nate, don't tell me you love me. It's not necessary. You tell it to me like it's payback for the fuck."

"I say I love you because I love you, Tangles."

"Why didn't you tell me that before you fucked me?"

"I'll tell you all you want," he said. "But my father would have washed my mouth out with soap if I talked like that. Tangles, the way you talk. It's not all fucking, and fuck this and fuck that." When he uses language like that his face gets all red. It's so sweet.

There were a lot of dates like that, but everything between us is cool. He has no time to see me often, and that's okay by me. He is buried at General Hospital in ELA serving out his internship.

I haven't slept in my apartment in ages. Like Letty, for ten bucks a week, I have a lady who comes over to dust, vacuum and change the linens on the bed. She washes and dries the linens before she goes home. The only thing I keep in the refrigerator since I moved over to Casa Luna is a six pack of Coca Cola. I have more in the pantry, but I only keep one in the fridge.

That night, Nate could barely hold a conversation. As soon as we walked in my apartment, he started tugging me toward the bedroom.

"Nate, wait. Let me give you a treat."

I took a Trojan out of the dresser drawer and tapped the sealed condom against my lips playfully. I didn't say it aloud, but it was a signal saying I'd go down on you like you like and bang, you'll feel better.

Nate was a good-looking stud, about five foot nine. Sometimes he said he wished he had abs like mine and that his body was more toned, but what can I say? He spends his free time studying. I spend mine working out. He took off his clothes and got on top of the comforter. I kicked off my sandals and crawled up from the foot of the bed to his waist and kept on my shorts and shirt. I put the condom on his erect penis and went down on him. It was maybe about five minutes before he exploded. Before AIDS, a blow job was raw, no condom. If I was fast enough, I got nothing in my mouth when the guy got off.

"I wanted you to cum," he said.

"Next time," I said.

Twenty minutes, tops, after we came into the apartment, I turned off the lights, locked the door and—each of us carrying a coke—we walked to his car. We went to a movie theater in Pasadena that had a choice between Backdraft, City Slickers, and Terminator 2: Judgment Day. I never turn down a chance to see Billy Crystal, even though they said the movie had started ten minutes before.

I bought us buttered popcorn. They didn't sell cokes. We ended up with Pepsi. All we missed was the *Let's All Go to the Lobby* promo. As for the movie, I loved the three guys who went on the cattle drive. They reminded me of Letty, me and Boss, but of course I didn't tell Nate that. Nate drove me to Casa Luna, all the way to the entry to the house. His eyes got big looking at the house up close and personal like that.

"What did you say he does for a living?"

"Long story," I said. I got out of the car and walked around to the rolled-down window on the driver's side. I stuck my head inside the car and kissed him.

He pulled my head gently toward him and he kissed me again.

"Stay in touch, Nate," I said. "Thank you."

Nate always wanted to pay for whatever we did, dinner, show, whatever, but I knew he was short of cash and I always paid. It was fine.

As soon as I walked inside, I ran up to the fourth floor where I knew they would be. The door to Boss's bedroom was open, and it smelled of candles, massage oil and incense, all the way down the hall. There were tons of candles going.

A comforter that wasn't Mario's was draped over the bed linens. Being a masseuse myself, I know it was there to keep the oil and sweat away from where they would sleep after. The spoiled brats were getting massaged on Mario's giant bed.

"Hey," I said to everyone. "Why no tables?"

Nobody answered.

Letty said, "What did you see?"

"Billy Crystal. City Slickers. Boss, can we all go on a cattle drive? I promise, it'll be a hoot!"

"We'll see," Boss said.

Betty and Storm lost their chance to explain about the tables. I didn't ask twice. I figured on the bed was just where Boss wanted it.

"Come get in bed," Boss said. "Storm can do you."

"Nah, thanks, Boss," I said, slipping into bed. He was face up, so I kissed him.

"Boss says you're hot." I smiled at Storm.

"Boss is too kind," Storm said.

"Betty, do you hear your polite assistant?" Letty asked, giggling.

Betty laughed. "Storm knows she's hot."

Storm was on her knees between Mario's legs working on his chest.

I looked at his dick, but it was placid. If I was in that position with him, he'd be hard as a bat. After a month of traveling around with Letty and me, his dick never got a rest.

I got out of bed, undressed down to my bra and panties, and slipped back on the bed. Letty was face down, so her voice was muffled.

"Did you douche, Bitch?"

"I'm going to slap you silly," I said.

Betty and Storm weren't laughing, but in the candlelight, I could see they were smiling.

"I didn't fuck him," I said. "Want to smell, Bitch?"

I love arguing with Letty. To say I love her is not strong enough. I think she feels the same about me. We don't talk about our feelings, but we make love and I can feel it. A man would never understand, except Boss. He knows us too well. Even if he didn't know us, he could figure it out. He's got radar or something that makes him get what makes others tick, feel and think.

On the trip, we did it all. I didn't want that trip to end.

I read an article about testosterone in men, what it does and how there's less of it after they hit fifty or something. Mario must ooze with the stuff. That article said that women's testosterone doesn't do the same for libido, but where Letty and me are concerned, those scientists don't know shit. Letty and me are sex-starved every single minute. If Olga ever saw or guessed what went on with all of us and witnessed it for as long as it went on (and on) with us, she would have blown us up out of pure jealousy. Hell, she'd have flat out exploded with jealousy. Kaboom. I'm glad she's gone. I know I might say otherwise to Mario, but I'm a hypocrite, and I'm not ashamed to admit it.

When Letty turned over, I was between her and Boss. Betty was doing her legs. I put some oil on her stomach and began to massage her. She opened her eyes, smiled at me, closed her eyes again. I massaged her breasts. Her eyes opened again. She was all smiles. By then, Boss had rolled over on his stomach. Storm was working his back with mighty energy. If Betty and Storm had not been here, I'd have poked Boss to get his attention, because he likes to watch.

A massage table is good for a massage, but the bed thing is sexier.

If not for Betty, I would not be here. Her introduction to Mario and

Letty changed my life. I would do anything for her. I've told her this countless times.

I got turned on massaging Letty and watching Betty massage her below the waist. I guess Nate not touching me had left me wanting, but I didn't want the five-minute rabbit fuck that Nate would have given me.

A three-tier brass rolling cart near the bed was stocked with wine and ice, but nothing to eat. Probably Letty's doing, still watching our calories like a damn drill sergeant. I wasn't hungry for food, anyway.

Letty's eyes were closed. She took my oily hand and moved it close to where Betty's hands were. Letty smiled when I touched where she wanted. The only one not getting handled was Boss who was still on his stomach, groaning as Storm worked his legs now.

"It's ok, Boss," I whispered. "Your moment will come."

He heard me. I heard a little chuckle from Boss and Letty at the unintended play on words.

We never have another man with us. I know that in my head, but fantasy can be anything. I thought of Nate with us, watching me, watching all of us.

Chapter 21
19 weeks after business freeze
Rio, October 15, 1991
Olga

We had been out of business for nineteen weeks. Riana and I flew to Rio to my new house that was finally completed. It had taken more than four years to build the damn thing. It was grand. Huge, of course. The workers were slow, and their boss was the worst of all. The contractor was an idiot who kept soaking me for money and delaying the completion date, over and over again. Pepe had gifted the construction of this house to me, so the money I paid this stupid contractor was not my money. He was still a thief, and I had wanted my house completed. It was only finished now because six months ago, I had a Camacho soldier from Bogota pay the contractor a personal visit. Idiot learned that he had seven months to finish the project, or he'd be buried where no one would find him. I must have sent the right soldier to do the job because he never asked for another dime and finished a month ahead of the final deadline.

The elaborate stainless-steel hoods in the kitchen and outdoor kitchen were made locally, but all electrical and gas appliances were bought in America. A month before the target date, I took the house plans to a store in Los Angeles. Two weeks later, crated Sub-Zero refrigerators, Wolfe stoves and ovens, food warmers, microwaves, beverage refrigerators and assorted appliances were loaded into the cargo bin of my plane. Before I flew in, these items, plus furnishings I ordered manufactured from scratch and furniture and accessories that I collected during my travels were arranged in the house by a decorator who knew my specifications. Four years is a long time. Everything had been stored in a warehouse, waiting for the house's completion.

Riana and I spent the first night in my suite, breaking it in. The next morning, Camila was flying in.

"Don't worry about me," Riana said. "You and Camila won't even know I'm here."

I made sure the housekeeper knew to have all Riana's needs met.

Rio, October 16, 1991

Camila flew in from Bogota to inform me—without benefit of phone—that two men had engineered the rooftop shooting that missed Camila and hit a guard instead. Both were relatives of a family that had been eliminated on Camila's orders.

"How can you be sure?"

"They called the authorities in Morocco and Amsterdam. The calls were made from one of their cell phones."

"And how would you know that?"

"Mason checked. The authorities had been called from that phone, in both places. The same phone made the call to my cell phone, and yours after the search in Morocco and after the search of the plane in Amsterdam."

"Mason cracked the case? Finally doing the job you pay him for."

"Amorcito, I rarely use Mason. It is you with the Mario thing that uses him. No matter, he's the best there is. But no, it wasn't Mason. The lead came from the Lopez family. Who knows how many people they put down to get to these two? The problem is solved."

"What was their intention? I mean, what did they think they were going to accomplish?"

"They planned to kill me, eventually," Camila said. "The lead came from a cartel and Mason verified the technical stuff like phones. The Lopez extracted the information."

"Chilling," I said. "Good thing I don't frighten easy."

Camila snapped, "Hopefully a sniper won't ever take a shot at you like one did at me."

"Amoricito," I moved close. "I didn't mean anything. You have the heart of a lion. Your strength has always been my strength."

That was not true. Ever since we were kids, I protected her.

Camila was suddenly very angry. "After me, they were going for you."

Camila and I had walked the property many times. This was the first time she'd seen it finished. I took great joy in walking her through all ten thousand square feet of it. In many ways, it was like the Camacho beach house built on a bluff with a walkway down to the sand.

Camila's house was twice as big, but my house was brand new, totally modern, built exactly to my specifications. The entire ocean side of the house had a twenty-five-foot-tall wall of tempered wind-resistant glass. In spite of the contractor screwing around, the finished house was close to perfect.

Camila and I walked through every room in the house except for Riana's suite where she was holed up. After the tour, Camila and I ended up on a sofa facing the ocean in a room off of the living room. The glass provided a panoramic view I don't think I could ever get accustomed to.

"Do you miss him? Do you call him? You always talked about sharing this house with him."

I knew what 'him' she was talking about.

"I'm getting over it. He doesn't call me. Why should I call him?" I said. I miss him, but I didn't want to say it aloud. Saying it makes it more true.

Camila shrugged. "Amor, you know best. The leasing company can't keep up with the demand for new leases. He's right on it."

"I'm up to date with that. I speak to Andrea, but I tell her not to say anything to him."

"I know. Andrea tells me, Amor." Camila laughed.

I poked her lightly in the stomach. "You know everything, Hermanita. I wouldn't ask her not to tell you."

"Are you ready to get back to business?"

I said, "I'm ready but only because you believe we're safe now."

"We're safe, Amor."

"Si, Amor, I'm ready." I nodded.

"I'm out four hundred million on the six hundred million sitting in Amsterdam," Camila said.

"I'll get rid of that first, Amor," I said. "I'll deposit the entire amount to your accounts."

"I'm not worried, Amor. It was smart to return the clients their money. When I went to tell them we were shutting down temporarily, they were appreciative that I had a receipt for the deposit you had made on their behalf."

My commission on the six hundred million would go directly to my own account.

Rio, October 18, 1991

Riana stayed secluded in her room with her telenovelas. Camila and I slept together that night, then she flew out to Mexico City early in the morning. After she was gone, Riana joined me in what was quickly becoming my favorite place, a small sitting room with a huge chandelier above an extra wide suede sofa facing the glass separating us from the ever-changing ocean vista. Today the wind was high, and green waves were crashing wildly on the beach, trailing foam that disappeared into the sand.

"I'm calling this the sunrise room," I said.

"I like it," Riana said, "but they're all sunrise rooms. The house is spectacular. You believe they got the bad guys?" Riana asked.

"I do, Amor."

"Okay, let's hit the road," Riana said. "When we leave?"

I was about to answer but paused when a servant brought us coffee and pastries. She was a girl, pretty, a local.

"Thank you, Caskata," Riana said. "You took very good care of me yesterday."

Caskata blushed at the compliment. I looked at her more closely, noticed how young she was, and how her face was free of makeup. I would guess she was sixteen or seventeen. She had long thick hair in a braid going down her back.

"Thank you Caskata," I said. "I would like for you always to take such wonderful care of my Riana. She's very special to me. Would you like to be her maid when she is here?"

"Yes ma'am," Caskata said in careful English, looking pleased and shy and very young.

"You can speak Portuguese. It's okay," I said.

Riana said, "She probably wants to practice her English. She's really very good. I told her I can understand Portuguese, but she has to speak very slowly."

Caskata went back to wherever she had come from.

"Where was I?" Riana said. "When are we leaving?"

"Tomorrow or the next day. We're going to Amsterdam."

Riana and I went down to the beach and played like a couple of kids. We got hot and sandy, and then showered outside, and let the ocean winds dry us. I met with the staff, just as I've always done at Camacho homes. For this house, I'd personally hired a husband and wife, a seasoned couple who had worked for two decades in a big home in Rio. Their employers had sold the house, and rather than staying to work for the new owner, they showed up for an interview and I hired them. I put them in charge of hiring four locals for general work. I would decide later if I wanted a chef. Caskata was one of their hires. When I was done with the staff, Riana and I retired to her bedroom.

"I love this bedroom so much. Thank you, Olga."

"Oh please, it's nothing. We'll probably sleep in my room more often than we do here."

"This is better than what I had at home, and twice better than my parent's house. Do you want to watch a novela or an American movie?"

"Novela," I replied because I know she loves them, and likes me to watch with her. She pointed the remote, and the television turned on.

My cell rang. It was Andrea. I put my finger to my lips. Riana, smiling, hit the pause button, and sat down. I was still standing.

"Olga, I heard from Camila's chief of security, Marcos."

My heart stopped. "What's wrong?"

Riana stood beside me, practically cheek to cheek to listen in. I clutched her hand.

"Camila was shot exiting her plane in Mexico City forty minutes ago."

"What's her condition?"

"I will have a hookup in a few minutes at the hospital and will connect you."

My knees melted out from under me. Riana's face went pale. She put her balled up fist in front of her mouth and bit one of her fingers, as she does sometimes when she's upset.

"She's alive. Tell me she's alive!"

"She was alive when our helicopter delivered her to the hospital. No time was wasted at all."

"I don't know what to do. I need to get on a plane, and I need to wait for you to call back."

Andrea said, "Olga, stay put. I'm all over this."

"Does Mario know?"

"No one knows," Andrea said. "It's not my place to say anything. Do you want me to tell him?"

"No, say nothing," I said.

Andrea hung up.

"Riana, I have to keep my phone free. Get Mason on your phone. Look in my phone book. It's in my purse."

I felt sweat on my forehead and a chill go through my entire body. I got up from the sofa and felt dizzy. I sat back down. I had to be calm. Couldn't cave now. Must stay focused.

"Camila, hang in there," I said aloud. "Don't die on me, please."

I stared at my phone next to me on the couch, willing it to ring and for Camila to tell me she was all right. Riana handed me her phone. I looked up, confused. She pushed it into my hand.

"Mason," she said, reminding me.

"Mason, I have bad news. Here's what I know…" I rattled off what Andrea had told me. I yelled at him for not keeping Camila safe. I think I hung up on him. I'm not sure. He has nothing to do with keeping Camila safe. I was losing it. I'd have to call back later and apologize. Riana took her phone back and handed me mine. Andrea had one of Camila's guards, Ponce, on the phone with us. He was at the hospital.

"Miss Olga, Miss Camila is alive. I'm going to pay my way into the room where the doctors are working on her. I will give you updates as they happen."

"Yes, Amor, I will not forget this. If you need cash, get it from Camila's purse. Whatever it takes."

"Yes, Miss Olga. Do not worry."

"Ponce, tell me what happened?" I needed to know.

"We were coming down the stairs. Halfway down, three shots came from a terminal roof east of where we were. I think two bullets hit her. No one else was hit."

"The shooter got away?"

"No sign of the shooter, Miss Olga. Must be a professional sniper for that kind of distance."

"Are the authorities aware? Did they send police?"

"I saw no police, Miss Olga, but they might have come after we left. It was like the last shooting. The terminal is far from main terminal. No one noticed. The helicopter that was going to deliver her to your house was there. That's how me and the other security people got her quickly to the hospital."

"What hospital?"

"Guadalupe on Reforma. They have a helipad."

"Okay, I don't know the place. I hope it's the best. Ponce, go wherever they have her. And keep me informed."

"Yes, Miss Olga." I heard his end of the line click.

"I'm still here," Andrea said.

Across the room, I saw Riana open the double doors to her walk-in closet. Two suitcases were on the luggage benches built into the closets. She opened one suitcase and started tossing clothes into it. She hesitated and looked in my direction. I nodded, and she kept packing.

"Andrea, round up my crew. Wheels up soon as you can assemble everyone."

"I'll fix it," Andrea said.

"Be sure Ponce knows how to reach me. I'll stay available."

It took two hours for us to get on the plane. Ponce called back.

"Miss Olga I am in surgery where Miss Camila is."

"Good. How is she? Did you speak with her? Is she conscious?"

"She's under anesthesia and being operated on by two doctors. I never saw her awake."

"Ponce, are the doctors saying anything?"

"I'm too far away to hear what they are saying, Miss Olga. They are working on her. She's alive."

As great as having a radiophone like AirFone is, it is impossible to stay connected. I had to start over mid-conversation and reconnect with Ponce.

The flight took thirteen hours with a fuel stop. In spite of Riana's best efforts, I was white-knuckled the whole time. I could not stop thinking about

Camila.

Riana and I sat in the parlor across from each other like we usually do. No wine this trip, just cokes to start off with, then coffee, then sandwiches with more coffee. Riana said nothing about my being so wired. I avoided talking about what was going on with Camila, though she never left my thoughts. I urged Riana to go to the bedroom and relax, watch movies or something, but she did not leave my side. I normally would have felt claustrophobic from all her mothering, but this time around, I was glad she was close by.

I called Mario on his cell.

"Sorry to bother you, but I thought you'd want to know what happened to Camila," I said. I told him everything.

He listened quietly.

"This is devastating," he said. He had more to say, but I didn't want to talk to him. The sound of his voice ripped my heart in pieces. "No, no. I need to call Ponce for an update," I said, interrupting him, and hanging up.

"What did he say?" Riana asked.

"He was devastated by the news."

"I thought I heard him say that he'd fly to Mexico, and you told him no?" Riana said.

"He can't do anything for Camila. I'm not turning to him just because there's an emergency."

I didn't have to call Ponce. He called me.

"Miss Olga," Ponce said, "I got one of Camila's doctors here with me. He can talk to you. His name is Dr. Aquiles Portillo."

The next voice I heard was the doctor repeating his name.

"I'm Olga, your patient's sister," I said in Spanish. Will she be okay?"

"It's too early to tell. Two bullets in her upper torso did not cause any major damage. We got them out. The third bullet went through her liver. We can't suture the liver. However, she's had a number of blood transfusions, and the bleeding appears to have subsided."

"I didn't know there was a third bullet," I said. What was the difference what I thought? I should be asking about the bleeding.

"Yes, there was a third bullet. It went straight through."

"Doctor, I need you to keep my sister alive. Do you understand?"

"My colleagues and I will do everything we can."

I wanted to believe that it was the AirFone that made the doctor sound so morbid.Riana and I were silent.

Camila had been so sure that the stalker was handled and done, just two people related to a family killed on Camila's orders. The men admitted to the shots fired at Camila and to making the calls to the authorities. Had they been lying? Were others involved? How did Mason verify their identities without showing the calls to the authorities? Who had known that Camila was flying to Mexico City? Who knew her schedule so well they could time an ambush for the right time and place?

"Olga come back from wherever you are," Riana said.

I blinked and focused on my friend. "I'm sorry, Amor. I've never been so confused. The doctor sounded more like a mortician than a healer."

"Don't talk like that," Riana said.

Camila bled out before my plane landed in Mexico City.

Rio, October 19, 1991

Ponce arranged for her body to be moved to a private room. When Riana and I arrived, Camila looked like she was sleeping. There were no tubes, no needles. Her face was pale, but she often looked that way without makeup. I kissed her on the lips and clasped her right hand. It was cold like her lips were cold. Riana's arm was around my shoulder all the time. It was just us and Camila, the three of us in that mustard ugly hospital room. I had no tears left.

Pasadena, October 19, 1991

Mario

Getting the news that Camila passed away was like a nightmare. I can't say what it was to the others who gathered at Casa Luna. Letty, Tangles, Betty, Pixie, Lainie, Jo, Niley and even Storm—who didn't know Camila—were there with me less than twenty-four hours after I got the news of her passing. Pixie flew in from the Bahamas where she was vacationing with a new boyfriend, a famous Mexican singer twice her age. Lainie flew in from Miami where she had just finished a single appearance at a stadium there. Everyone but Storm had talked to Olga since the announcement, and all were personally invited to Bogota, Colombia to attend the service and funeral for Camila. She would be put to rest where her parents and Pepe had been laid to rest in the cemetery on the family estate.

Mexico, October 20, 1991
Olga

When Camila took over for Pepe, she became the contact with the cartel families. She was the contact person for the team leader in every city where I landed with cash to deposit or store. As far as I knew, Amsterdam was the only place with shipping containers holding cash waiting to be banked. I'd never seen them, but I know we didn't need three containers for six hundred million dollars. The weight of the money was a little over thirteen thousand pounds. Knowing Pepe and his relationship with the truth, there weren't three containers. It could be one, none or something else entirely. What I knew for sure is that there was six hundred million sitting somewhere in Amsterdam.

I knew the face of the team leader in Amsterdam, but only in passing, as I happened to be at the bank when money was first delivered. The secrecy went back to the days when Pepe was handling everything.

Camila's point of contact with the security teams moving the money was Jeronimo Valencia, the man I call the voice. He was in his seventies, lived in Bogota, had been employed by her father most of his life, and after that, Pepe. Rumor had it that Valencia was fluent in six languages. In his younger days, he had done some kind of drug-related work for her father, and now he worked for her from his home. He arranged when my plane was loaded with cash, who loaded and unloaded the cash. Valencia arranged how much money was to be delivered at what bank and when. He got this from Camila, and Camila got it from me. I provided the list of banks to Camila. I'm the one with relationships with the bankers. Camila was the one with the relationships with the cartel families. It wasn't difficult because we only did business with five cartel families and not always simultaneously.

The night before, not even an hour after I left Camila's body at the hospital, I called Valencia to advise him of her death. He offered his condolences and seemed very sad to hear the news. I called Valencia a day later from Mexico City, ready to make some changes.

"I need to speak with you in person. Get on a plane right away and come see me," I said.

"I work at home," he said.

I couldn't understand his attitude. I needed to see him.

"You know who you're talking to, Valencia?"

"Olga, I know. I don't work for you."

I could not understand his macho stance. He had to know that the mantle of command had fallen to me. I could not let it pass. In two hours, my guards, four pilots, three stewardesses, Riana and I were on our way to Bogota, Colombia.

"Why do you need to see him in person?" Riana asked.

"Amor, he's like the gatekeeper of all movement. I don't *want* to see him. I've always stayed away from him, never wanted any connection to him. He was Pepe's gatekeeper, then Camila's after Pepe died."

"Can't you wait until after the funeral?"

"There is something I must do in Amsterdam."

"It's okay, Olga. Sorry for asking all these stupid questions."

"No questions are stupid, Amor."

We landed at the Army Base where I broke the news to General Durazo.

"I loved Camila very much," he said. "I am sorry for your loss."

I kissed the tall uniformed man that my father had known for many years, and who had been part of Camila's and my childhood.

"I may have trouble with Valencia. He would not come to see me in Mexico," I told the general. "My men are going with me, but I don't have time for his games."

Estevan was the Camacho enforcer, but I wasn't sure what his reaction was going to be now that Camila was gone. I would deal with him later.

I left the crew on the plane with orders to sleep.

"Amorcito," I told Riana, "I would die if something happened to you. I don't know what will happen at Valencia's."

"I want to go, Olga. We've been through worse."

I sweet-talked Riana to cozying up in the bedroom with her movies until I got back.

I left the army base in a caravan of three SUVs: two guards with me in one of the SUVs that I kept at the base, followed by four more of my guards, and eight uniformed soldiers. My men were wearing bullet-proof vests.

I had never been to Valencia's, but I knew he lived forty-five miles outside of Bogota. I did not know what to expect other than his attitude had been confrontational and combative.

An armed guard at Valencia's gate made a call, then opened for my three SUVs to make the five-minute drive from the gate to the residence. Valencia's traditional hacienda was beautiful: red tiled roof, white stucco colonnaded porches stacked several stories high symmetrically on either side of a pair of massive painted wooden doors a few shades redder than the roof tile. As we got closer, I saw more details. Statuary, plants, outdoor seating areas, stone patios, a fountain. It looked better and better the closer we got; and everything on the route was green and manicured. Valencia had done well for himself working for the Camachos.

I got out of the car, my guards behind me, soldiers bearing automatic weapons behind my men.

"What is this?" asked a guard standing outside the door.

"I'm here to see Valencia. Tell him Olga is here," I said in Spanish.

"He's busy," said the guard.

"Wrong answer," Ponce said, pointing a gun at him. Valencia's man reached for his pistol, but never pulled it. Too slow. Ponce shot him and he went down.

"Let's go in," I said. "I need Valencia alive."

Ponce nodded. "I understand."

The front doors were even more massive than they had appeared from a distance. The sound of gunfire did not bring anyone out.

Ponce turned the big doorknob on one door, and it swung inward. He stepped inside and shots began. One of the soldiers behind me pushed me out of the way. From a vantage point on the ground, I peeked out from behind a stucco wall. Through the open door, I saw Ponce drop to the floor inside the house. The soldiers and my guards inched their way in, their method like an armed ballet.

My men killed eight of his inside guards before I finally got to see Valencia. Ponce was my only casualty. I felt terrible, but the time to feel it was later.

Looking like a librarian, Valencia was seated behind a huge desk piled with books.

"I want the names and contact information for all the teams we use everywhere," I said. "You will contact Amsterdam immediately to tell them I am headed there to pick up all of the money from the so-called containers. As usual, after I land, I will leave the plane. Get them to load the cash on board."

"I don't take orders from you," Valencia said boldly. He was putting up a front. I saw the beads of sweat on his forehead.

"Bring me everyone in this house," I said to my men. I might not be a Camacho by blood, but I am my father's daughter. "Valencia, Camila is dead. What is it that you don't understand?"

"I'm not taking orders from you," Valencia said again.

One of the soldiers brought in a woman in her late sixties. I saw him poke her in the back to encourage her to walk faster, and she glanced back at him, offended and terrified. Her hair was gray, pulled into a bun. Her casual clothing and jeweled hands told me she was family. Another soldier came in with two women in maid uniforms.

"You are his wife?" I asked the older woman.

She nodded, glancing piteously at Valencia and avoiding my eyes.

"Tell this fool husband of yours to do as I say, and not be stupid."

Valencia got on his feet. "Keep her out of this."

I reached in my purse, pulled out a forty-five, and moved up close to the woman. I pushed the pistol to the side of her face. She inched away.

"Hold her," I said to one of the soldiers.

"Stop," Valencia said. "You are the beast your father was."

"You haven't seen anything," I said. "I am first my father's daughter; and I grew up in the house of Camacho."

When the guard grabbed both of her forearms, the woman went into panic mode. She was crying and screaming, struggling to get free. The soldier held tightly as she fought his grip.

I cocked the pistol to the side of her face, ready to fire.

"Valencia, if I depart without what I came for, I will leave you and your wife on the floor, dead like your guards. I will hunt down your entire family. I will kill all of them, every last one."

Valencia flopped down in his chair. "I'll give you what you want. Put your gun away. Tell that bastard to let my wife go."

"Do what I said. Not another word from you."

He gathered up a typewritten list of names and locations. He had a copier and used it. He gave me the originals. He did not use a cell phone as I expected but communicated via a computer to Amsterdam.

As I accepted the papers, his servants were led from the room.

"I don't know what you were thinking," I said softly. "You know who I am."

Valencia broke down into a pathetic mess, babbling excuses and whining. Even after I encouraged him to straighten himself up, it still took him an hour to explain what he did and how he did it. He had begun using private computer networks to communicate. Before that, it was cell phones; and before that, he had used faxes, telegrams, ham radio, ticker tape.

"Valencia, if you cross me, a caravan of army soldiers will come here and burn everything you own and kill everyone you love."

He made a small, terrified noise.

"You asked for this confrontation," I said.

Senora Valencia was now sitting, gasping for air. I did not know if her trouble breathing was from fright, stress, or illness. Her husband did not reply, but she did. "He will do everything you tell him to do. He knows Camila would have wanted him to cooperate with you. There is no one else left."

I sat down across from him, my men and the soldiers at my back.

"Did you hear that, stupid?" I said.

"I was in shock," Valencia said. "You told me what happened to Camila. I thought you had her killed to take over."

"Fucking fool. She was my sister."

"I'm sorry, Olga. I'm sorry," Valencia's hysteria had returned. He started weeping, no doubt certain that now I had everything, he and his wife were facing immediate extermination.

"You will continue making whatever Camila was paying you," I said. "Just remember my words. Cross me, get smart with me on the phone as you did yesterday, and it's over. If you run, I'll find you."

"No," his wife said. "We will be here. He will do for you what he did for Camila and before her, Pepe."

I didn't know what Valencia had done for Pepe's father. In those days, they had not been in the money laundering business. Back then, they'd been in the drug business. No telling what job Valencia had filled. For sure, he had been with the Camachos for decades.

"Do you need help with the bodies out there?" I asked as I got up.

His wife calmly said, "We will take care of it. Thank you, Olga. I haven't seen you since you were a little girl." She started crying.

I walked over to where she was sitting, leaned over and kissed the gray bun on top of her head.

"I'm sorry it came to this," I said. "Blame him for it." Then I added. "If your husband crosses me, you will not be spared. I'm sorry."

I had the soldiers collect Ponce's body and bring him with them. I would ask the General to contact his family.

I told my second-in-command, Ramirez, "Call Estevan. Tell him what happened. I need a replacement for Ponce."

I felt like a gangster. Everyone always talks like only men kill. I just came from a home where I left nine men dead, not counting Ponce. I am my father's daughter, as I said.

Valencia had given me no choice. The five cartel families we did business with were vulnerable if Valencia flaked out on me as he had on the phone. I felt bad for Ponce. I felt bad for the guards who were killed. They had only been doing their jobs. So had I.

On the way back, Ramirez rode in the front passenger seat of the SUV. Minutes after Ramirez spoke with Estevan, he called me on my cell.

"I could have handled Valencia," Estevan told me. "You cannot take chances like that. You are the Camacho now."

"It's done, Estevan."

"We will find out who did this to Camila and personally take care of him," he said.

"Estevan, yes we will," I agreed. Estevan was a mean one, but like Valencia, he was old now, and someone else did the killing for him.

"Come meet me at the army base before I leave." I wanted an eye to eye with him.

Ramirez and I went directly up the plane stairs. The crew and stewardesses were asleep.

"Amores, wake up. The general will show you where you can shower and change. I want to leave in two hours." I told Ramirez who was right behind me, the same thing. "Have your men shower and change like the crew. I don't need you guys right now. You know when wheels up will be."

He nodded.

"Just so you know, I'm giving the general a hundred thousand for Ponce's family."

"Thank you, Miss Olga," he said.

I found Riana lying at the foot of the bed, feet in the air like a teenager, watching a movie.

"Kisses," I said. Riana got up and I hugged her.

"What happened?"

"I'll tell you later, Amor."

I opened my safe and took out two bundles, each of them a hundred thousand dollars. That almost wiped out what was in there.

"I'll be right back," I said, grabbing a Neiman Marcus shopping bag from some long-forgotten trip to a store.

I met up with the General in his office. "Your men did an excellent job for me. Thank you, my friend," I kissed him. "Here's a little something for you. You may want to give your soldiers who went with me a touch of this."

He looked at the ten ten thousand dollar bundles wrapped with thick rubber bands and hugged me.

"Olga you have always been so generous with me. I love you."

"I love you too," I said. I reached in the paper shopping bag and came up with the other bundle. "This is for my guard Ponce's family. Please see to it that his wife gets this."

"I will personally handle this, Olga. May I treat you to dinner?"

I kissed him again. "I'm going to the plane to shower, then we can refill the water tanks."

I went back up the plane stairs alone. It was strange to have no guards. They were always around these days. No one was aboard the plane but Riana and me.

"Let's shower, Amor," I said. "We can use up all the water just as if we were home."

Riana pulled off the white lantern sleeve smock dress she was wearing and tossed it on the bed. The embroidery on the sleeves and around the corset-style lacing was lovely and intricate. It must have taken someone a long time. There was nothing underneath but her white panties, which were a startling contrast with her tawny skin—tawnier after our time at the Rio Beach house.

"Which home?" she asked. Her panties joined the dress on the bed.

I pinched her ass. "You are so goofy," I said. "I love you so much."

"I was worried about you," Riana said.

"Mission accomplished," I said. "The worry part is over. Come on. Let's get in the shower."

It was a decent size shower for being on a plane, and it was bright and spotless. Nothing was powered down. The lights and air-conditioning were running on power from the base.

Sexually, I was turned on beyond belief. Mario and I had had sex right after he killed the attackers at the Milan house. I got excited after I put down Alonso and his crew. As I stepped in, I realized how turned on I was. My body was ripe and primed to erupt without any effort from Riana. The orgasm made me scream, lasted for ever, ended with me hugging her tightly as it went on and on, as the water rained down on our bodies.

Estevan arrived before the crew was back on board, and he brought a man with him that he introduced as Gabriel, a tall, fit guard to replace Ponce if I approved. He had dark brown hair cut short, a muscular physique, and an old scar that crossed the side of his face and cut into his hair. Other than the scar, his features were regular, his lips thin, jawline square, and I think he had a dimple in his left cheek. I knew that he had shooting skills. Estevan would not have brought a security candidate without those skills. He was good with knives too.

"You speak English?"

"Yes, Miss Olga, I do. I also have a passport and visa to travel to the United States."

"Go find Ramirez. If he's okay with you, you can come along with us," I said.

His leaving left me alone in the main cabin with Estevan.

"I need to know you will give me the loyalty that Camila had. If you have any reservations at all, you can retire a happy man and as my friend."

"Olga, I do not want to retire. You have my complete loyalty. There is nothing I will not do for you."

Once in Amsterdam, I arranged for my banks to accept one hundred million dollars to be deposited to my own personal accounts. By computer, I sent Valencia the coded message of how much went to what bank. The money was delivered in plane packages to the manager of each bank as always before.

The balance of what was left in Amsterdam was challenging. I could not forget the search of my plane and my meeting with Officer Jenson. I wasn't worried about it happening again, but I was worried. On my Compaq laptop, I connected with Valencia as before, using a modem and a file transfer application telling him all the 'coffee' in stock was needed. While Riana and I were asleep at our hotel, team Valencia loaded the cash. It was risky. Valencia and the team knew what had happened before; they knew of the search the morning after the cash had been unloaded from my plane. Time would tell, time being the hours between the cash being on board and me flying away from Amsterdam to Spain where I planned to deposit the money. Had Camila been right that those responsible for the searches of my planes were eliminated? If they had been responsible for the first attempt on Camila, and they had been eliminated before Camila was shot, who killed Camila?

"Riana, let me charter a plane for you to take to Barcelona. It's too risky for you to fly with me. What if the police surprise us with a search this time when the plane is loaded with cash?"

"Why don't we both fly in the charter and let your crew fly to Barcelona without us?"

I had thought of that, but I needed to know that even without Camila, without the buffer of secrecy around Valencia, with all the recent disruptions in my life, at least I could keep doing what I had always done without the fear of getting busted. I could lie and say I wouldn't make my crew take a chance that I was afraid to take for myself, but it wasn't that. It was like I needed to take the chance. Stupid? Yes, it was. Riana and I boarded the plane in the morning and were wheels up at 10:10 AM without a hitch.

"I am elated," I said. I guess it's late in my life to discover I'm an adrenaline junkie. Doing my job is a rush not unlike getting away with murder.

Riana unbuckled her seatbelt, walked around the table between us and sat by me. We hugged and held on as the plane climbed to 30,000 feet.

I don't know how Felipe Carrera planned to do it, but without hesitation, Riana's father agreed to his end of the deal. He had agreed to accept the money at his bank. He knew only that I had been caught off guard when Camila was killed, and I was stuck with this cash with no place to store it or deposit it on short notice. We communicated as I had with Valencia, a first for me. I blocked thinking of the possibility that the security of our communication could be breached. For now, at least, it was better than talking phone or fax. Valencia said it was safe. Of course, Valencia was in Colombia where if he got arrested, he'd be immediately released by a friendly judge. For me, away from our friendly connections in Colombia, it was indeed risky, especially if cops were reading our barely disguised messages.

The team in Barcelona followed instructions from Valencia to take the cash to Carrera's bank at nine in the evening.

"Your father is a gutsy man," I said. "How will he manage to move that money around? Is he alone? Is someone with him at this hour?"

"Daddy loves the commission you've been paying him for accepting deposits. This is a big one for him. He will manage somehow."

"Amor, I'm so lucky to have him."

"Daddy is thrilled with the leasing company business, too. He told me himself that he and the consortium partners love the investment return. He finds profit to be very stimulating." Her sidelong look was amused and a little sly. "I'm surprised he didn't ask you to his penthouse."

Her words surprised a laugh out of me. She knows her father well. He had made the occasional veiled reference now and then about my returning to the penthouse for another friendly visit.

I knew everything about everything to do with the finances of LAI and GAL. Only I had total knowledge of each bank account. Every account I opened, I arranged. Pepe and Camila granted me power of attorney that empowered me the same as if I owned the accounts. The older accounts that I knew of, Pepe had granted me power over back when he had trained me to do this job. It's true that Pepe was a secretive man, and he might have held back knowledge of something.

What I didn't know is if Camila had a will. Pepe had no will but that had not stopped Camila from taking over. She was on all bank accounts and had possession of the stock certificates that represented the shares issued for LAI and more recently from GAL so there was nothing to do.

I had spread out my personal earnings to many banks. My total savings from the years of working for Pepe and Camila was humongous by any standard. With six hundred million added to my coffers, I could give a damn about LAI and GAL. Or was it that simple? The company was going public.

Camila had estimated getting as much as three billion dollars or more from going public. Should I let LAI and GAL slip through my fingers because Camila has no relatives left?

Pasadena, November 1, 1991
Mario

Miguel and Pixie's chef had prepared a buffet fit for royalty, and we were in the dining room to eat it. The buffet started at one end, with a crab salad, a dozen vegetable side dishes, roast beef sliced to order, a grilled tuna, roasted chicken, a wide selection of breads, then a cluster of desserts at a separate table. The linens and dishes were black, which, I suppose, Miguel felt was appropriate for a death in the family, though it could have been because his food looks spectacular on black dishes. There was no background music piped in on my speakers. The conversation was sedate. It was easy to hear each other when we spoke.

"The funeral is in three days," Pixie said, "It's fourteen days since Camila died. It still hasn't sunk in she's dead."

"Passed away sound better," Lainie said.

Pixie ignored her daughter. "Where has Olga been?"

"No idea. She's keeping to herself," I said. "Our phone conversations are brief and formal. She delivers her message, then says she has to go."

"She hasn't been long-winded with me," Pixie said. "And that's unusual."

"She's uptight," Letty said. "I talked to her right after it happened, gave her my condolences and we were off the phone fast. The next time we talked, she stayed on just long enough to invite me to the funeral. She said I was special to Camila."

"She told me the same," Tangles said. "I didn't even know that Camila had taken notice of me, but it was nice to be personally invited."

"I was surprised to get the call," Betty said. "Olga took the time to call and invite me personally, and that moved me. She also said that Camila loved me very much."

Letty said, "If this was not a sad time, I'd tell you why she was in love with you." She smiled a Mona Lisa smile, barely a curve of the lips.

"I don't think Camila would want us to sit around and mope about her," I said.

"Camila wouldn't want us happy she was killed, for sure," Tangles said.

"Excuse me," Letty said to everyone, then stood up, and whacked Tangles on the back of the head with her rolled up napkin. There was a bout of furious whispering between the two of them, then Tangles apologized for her comment. "No one is happy about her passing," she said. "I'm sorry if I seemed disrespectful to her memory."

"I hadn't seen her in a long time. Olga's call surprised me," Jo said.

"And me," Niley added. "Still, it was nice to get the call."

Andrea arrived while we were eating. I noticed her eyes were red as she went around the table to kiss and hug everyone. As she was serving herself from the buffet, she said, "There are flatbed seats for everyone on Mario's plane. I'm having linens delivered so that everyone is comfy. Four stewardesses will be seeing to your needs, and Miguel worked with the catering company about what foods to have on board."

"Thank you, Andrea," I said. "Forgive me if I seem inappreciative. I just don't have the energy to see to things like this. I know you always handle the planes, but I especially appreciate it now. Camila's passing has exhausted me."

"Boss, this is what I do. I just wish it wasn't for this occasion."

She took a seat at the table and blotted her eyes with the linen napkin.

She had been very close to Camila, not only working together, but they'd been bed partners in Milan. Andrea was married now, but feelings like that don't just disappear.

"Is your husband coming along?" I asked.

"No, he's busy with his job. He'd met her, but he didn't really know Camila. Olga understands the situation."

Pixie asked who was going to occupy the bedroom on board and didn't wait for an answer.

She looked in my direction and saluted me with her glass. "As if I didn't know," she giggled, a more mellow giggle than we were accustomed to hearing from her.

I said, "I have plenty of room on the bed for anyone who wants to forego the flat bed seats."

"I'm on your right side," Letty said.

Tangles said, "Mmm, left side."

"There's plenty of room for all of us, right Boss?" Pixie said.

"We're going to a funeral," I reminded them.

Tangles said, "Camila was a sex-hog. If she was here, she'd encourage an orgy in her honor on the way to her funeral."

"Bitch, don't talk like that. If Olga heard, who the fuck knows what she'd do to you," Letty said sharply.

Silence. Everyone in the room sat staring at their plates.

Andrea broke the silence. "Tangles is right. Camila was no angel. We don't have to sit here and pretend exaggerated grief."

"Camila was my friend. I am in pain for her loss," I said.

"I didn't mean it the way it came out," Andrea said. Andrea was a private person, and now she was maybe too transparent.

"Who would want to kill Camila?" Pixie asked.

"That's the million-dollar question," Jo said.

After we ate, everyone went to the den to talk in small groups. I went up to my office and called Jack Fino. It had been a long while since I'd spoken to him regularly. At one time, we'd met every Wednesday for lunch at the Pacific Dining Car. That seemed a very long time ago.

"You're welcome to join us on the plane. We have room, Jack."

"Thank you, Mario. Taking my own plane. I'm coming right back after the funeral."

"I figured," I said. "Just wanted you to know you are welcome to come with us. I know you knew Camila for a long time before I met her. I don't want you to feel like you must grieve alone."

Bogota, November 1, 1991
Olga

By the time Riana and I arrived in Bogota, Camila's body had already arrived from Mexico. The Camacho mansion where Pepe's life had been celebrated is where I decided Camila's celebration should be. I was at the family mansion, in the midst of preparations to mourn my sister when I received a call on my cell from Noah Witzer, a name I did not recognize. He introduced himself.

"I'm in Switzerland. I am the attorney handling taking LAI public. I extend my deepest condolences to you. I visited Bogota not long ago to meet with Camila along with three accountants and spent a number of days with her. Camila named you as her successor."

"I didn't know this."

"It's a good thing I got her to tie up loose ends. This was not the only loose end she had."

"Noah, this is very unusual to have such an important conversation like this on the phone."

"Yes, it is."

"What does successor mean exactly?

"It means you have control," he said.

I was more than shocked. I'd thought I would bury Camila, then poke around to learn what my options were. I had not thought Camila had left a will. I had a feeling she had not. She and Pepe had believed they would live forever. I'm no better. I have no will either.

"I felt I needed to reach out to you," Noah said. "When is the service and where?"

I gave him the details and invited him. I told no one about the call.

I had wasted no time securing that six hundred million plus, depositing it to my accounts in case everything else was out of reach. So, if I'm her successor, then I didn't steal that money.

I couldn't wait to meet Noah, to talk to him, to have him guide me through the hurdles of taking LAI public if that was the course I should follow. Camila had left me out of the plans going public, no doubt figuring that I was busy enough parking cash in banks. I'd only known of a meeting in Bogota she'd had with the Swiss people. She never told me she had a personal lawyer in Switzerland. She had never been under any obligation to tell me anything. I guess I don't know everything, after all.

Somewhere over the Pacific, November 2, 1991
Mario

I've always loved Camila. Although I never judged her, I wouldn't be surprised if her killer had been out for revenge for an execution or other terrible atrocity she'd committed against her own people. All I knew is that Camila had been good to me from the day we met. We'd been lovers from the beginning. Even after I became engaged to Olga, we had remained good friends.

Here I was with a plane full of people I love, and we were headed to a funeral instead of some kind of vacation. I remember when I used to fly commercially, taking a much longer route through Miami. We were taking a seven- or eight-hour route straight down the Pacific coast. I planned to eat a midnight dinner soon, hit the bed, and try to get some sleep before sunup in Bogota. By the time we reached our cruising altitude, food was laid out on a long table, a catered buffet that was piping hot and delicious. It was late, and we may have been somber in mood, some more than others, but our appetites got the best of us. We ate like a bunch of bears getting plumped up to hibernate through the winter, but that would be Miguel's doing, for advising the caterers too well.

The seats went flat. I tried one, and it was just a few inches too short for me.

"Marvelous invention," I said. The seats were plush, beautiful leather.

Like in Olga's plane, the crew's sleeping area had been equipped with the sleepers. Just for this trip, Andrea had had all the seats on my plane changed to sleepers.

Jo got up close and personal to where I was sitting. She climbed on my lap, her arms around me. I don't recall the name of the perfume she was using, but it took me back to those early days working with her. She still smelled delicious.

"Boss, I'm so proud of you, not because you're rich, but the way you handle it. You haven't changed at all. Just look at this plane. Flying everyone to Camila's funeral. It's very generous of you."

I kissed my friend. "This plane belongs to Camila's leasing company. It's not mine."

"It may be registered to the company, but it's his plane, right Andrea?" Letty asked.

Andrea nodded, loading her fork with avocado. She waved the full fork around, and said, "It's Mario's plane, yes."

She dipped a tortilla chip into a batch of guac. "Have you tried the guacamole? It's unreal."

The girls finished eating first and went to bed. I chased my steak and thrice baked potato with a massive sundae before I headed to bed. I said goodnight to everyone I passed as I walked back. Most of my friends were already asleep.

As I made my way back, I wondered what would happen to everything now that Camila was gone. Olga was playing with me. Phone calls cut short. No words about the future and the business. There was so much uncertainty. I could understand if she wanted to bury Camila first. I wondered what was in Camila's will, and who she left everything to. I wondered what LAI would do without Camila. Who would finance our share of a lease? Would GAL be sold or closed out? I wasn't facing ruin by any means, because I had more than enough money sacked away to live in luxury the rest of my days. But I wanted to keep working. I wondered how Olga was handling everything. The stress for her must be unbearable.

I can understand you are grieving Olga, but why shut me out? Fuck it,

Olga, you're a snob. I am grieving too. I need to know who killed my friend. Lola, if you are alive and you did this, keep running.

The stewardesses had already passed out linens, pillows and sweats to everyone.

I stopped in the open door to the bedroom. It took a few moments for my eyes to adjust. It looked, at first glance, like a trim little hotel room with an oversized bed, except the shades were up, with the dark endless sky visible. The king-sized bed looked huge here, but less huge with four bodies already crowded on it. I found Letty, Tangles, Pixie and Lainie curled up like sardines in a can, with a body pillow beside Letty showing me where I could squeeze in. When she saw me, Pixie ran Lainie out, playfully, but out. We lay down in our sweats, cuddled, and eventually slept. Some time later, I felt other bodies join us. Jo and Niley. I turned on my side to face Letty, and our lips met. The turbulence we encountered was only on the inside of the plane. We clung to each other. The belts on the bed were for three, but we managed without a sound.

Niley

If this is a dream, I don't want to wake up. He's close. I raise my arm, reach over Jo and I touch his shoulder. I don't see him, but he doesn't move. I leave my hand there, like I used to do in the old days. I remember a case when it was just Boss and me at the hotel. We took a tub bath that all but destroyed the bathroom. Bubbles everywhere, water everywhere. We laughed so much. We rolled around in bed all night and were up in the morning to go visit with the family, with no sign of how tired we should have been. I'm so tired now. It feels like a hundred years ago. But I'm so glad I'm here. There's no place I'd rather be.

Tangles

I thought it would only be Letty and me on the bed with him though I'm not surprised that Pixie would put her claim in. I hoped she might not get so personal since she has that famous singing boyfriend of hers. Her picture and his on magazines and posters and gossip columns and papers all over the country—how lucky is that? What does she need Boss for? Why can't she just leave Boss for us? There isn't a woman on this plane that Boss hasn't fucked, even the stewardesses, at one time or another, I bet. I can tell by how they eye him, thinking they are sly. I'm so wet. Too many of us on this bed. I should take a sleeper so I can actually sleep.

Letty

Why do I think he loves me more now that Olga is gone? Am I fantasizing like a fucking dumb ass teenager? He just kissed me. Pixie is on this bed with us, and he kissed me. Fuck, what would I do if he wanted me for keeps? No, he doesn't want anyone for keeps. He made so little fuss when Olga gave him back the ring. That was a surprise. If he felt bad, he hid it well. I looked for the hurt for weeks, and I am sure I haven't seen it. I could be wrong. It could be wishful thinking. I want to devour him right here and now, but the others may attack me. A pillow fight on the way to a funeral. What's funnier, a pillow fight or an orgy on the way to Camila's funeral?

Pixie

None of these bitches know him like I do. No one has been as tight with him as long as me. No one has shared as many secrets as him and me. I taught him how to jack off when I was a corner girl, a street kid anybody could have for the price of cup of coffee. He was tall and handsome. He was in school and I was a drop out, and one day I made him show me his dick. He was embarrassed as all fuck when he got hard. He didn't have a clue what to do with it. He had seen too many dirty magazines and thought the only thing he could hope for was to put his dick in a pussy. And then what? Fucking young pup. It was so funny. I love him. He's my soul mate. Always has been. That bitch Olga is a chump for cutting him off. I hope he's taking it the way he shows it, like it don't mean nothing. If I wasn't under contract with her, I'd kick her ass. Or maybe not. Isn't it better that he's not tied up with her? She better not get him in trouble with the law.

Jo

The first job I ever had with him was getting accident cases, rear-enders, left had turn cases, pedestrian cases. We started getting bigger cases, passenger buses that turned over, people were killed. Once we got a big train crash. Boss knew exactly what to do with the victims' families. If he couldn't get a signature on the retainer, he was still friendly and helpful, a class act. After we got into aviation cases, a lawyer handed him a check for a million bucks—we had signed so many families of victims on that plane. We did it one family at a time, day after day, week after week, sometimes months after the tragedy. I was there when he purchased his first apartment building. Thanks to him, Niley and I own a company that manages his apartment units, always a growing number. He was there for me when my husband died, and when I got remarried to a man Mario put back on his feet after he went bust in the construction business. I love you, Mario Luna. I close my eyes and can still feel your warmth, and the way our bodies used to meld together, perfectly.

Captain Largo

We were over the Pacific Ocean parallel to Mexico when the port engine jolted the plane, then shut down.

"Try to restart," I said.

I picked up the phone that rings to the galley. Myrna answered.

"Get Mr. Luna or Andrea to come to the cockpit immediately. Emergency."

Andrea came running through the open cockpit door.

"Port engine shut down, and we can't get it to restart."

"How bad is this?"

"I am about to declare emergency. Mexico is right over there." Though she wouldn't be able to see the coastline, I pointed east in the night sky. We were flying south over the Pacific ocean.

"I'll tell Mario. Broadcast instructions on the P.A. in two minutes. That way I'll have time to tell him before he hears it from you. Captain, how bad is this?" Andrea asked, again.

I did not turn around to look at her. I had enough to deal with.

"We can fly with one engine. Do not worry."

Counting myself, I had sixteen lives to preserve. This plane can carry a hundred passengers, their luggage and cargo. We are light as can be.

I gave Andrea her two minutes and spoke into the microphone to everyone aboard.

"Our left engine has shut down. The cabin lights will go on now. Please bring your seats to a sitting position and buckle your seat belts. Mr. Luna, please have anyone in the bedroom return to their seats in the main cabin and buckle up. Flight attendants will show you where the life jackets are on this plane and how to use the oxygen masks if it becomes necessary. This plane is flying fine with one engine. We have declared an emergency and will be landing in Mexico. We are awaiting coordinates."

Mario

Andrea woke me from a sound sleep. I squinted up at her as I tried to figure out what was going on. She was shaking me by the shoulder and had turned on the cabin light. I was blinded by the glare and couldn't make out her face or her words. My body wanted to keep sleeping. In her panic, she was pounding my shoulder like a slab of beef she was trying to tenderize.

"Boss, we lost an engine. We gotta get everybody into seat belts."

Everyone on the bed roused with her words.

"Move along, babies. Stay calm." I herded them in front of me while they were still adjusting their sweats, walking us all into the main cabin where everyone was scrambling to get seated upright and with their belts on. "I'm not going to tell you not to worry, but I am asking you to stay positive."

I kissed Jo and Niley. They hugged me, both on the verge of crying.

"Hang in there. I love you," I said.

They nodded. Betty's smile was a little forced. I helped her adjust her seat belt.

"I could be doing massages," she said, grabbing my arm while I was tightening her belt.

"I promise, you will, as soon as we get through this." I kissed her on the lips.

"I love you, Boss."

"Ditto," I said.

Storm was sitting next to Betty, saying nothing. Storm's hair was tinted lilac, and in a poof that reminded me of the sixties. I think I remember someone saying this was her first time on an airplane. She wasn't handling the flight very well.

"Storm, you could have stayed home," Betty said. "I'm sorry I asked you to come along and take care of us with your great hands."

Storm's eyes were tearing, and she was shaking so hard I could see it. I don't think she could talk.

"It's okay," I said. "Have faith. Pilots can get us to a nearby airport. A DC-9 can fly on one engine."

The sofa Andrea, Pixie, and Letty were on could open and make into a bed. The table could push down so that the sofas could come together. I hoped they were well anchored in position, if the worst-case scenario happened, whatever that might be. I moved on to Andrea who was at one end of the sofa, Lainie at the other, and Pixie in the middle. I checked their belts. I kissed each of them.

"Stay positive," I said.

"I'm positive," Andrea said it like she meant it.

I kissed her on both cheeks, then for just a couple seconds, I looked into her eyes, my face right up to hers. "Love you, Andrea."

I did the same withPixie and Lainie.

"Love you, Mario Luna," Andrea said.

"I love you Uncle Boss." Lainie said brightly. I kissed her too. "Tell the pilots to bring it on!" she said.

Lainie and Pixie were clenching each other's hands. Whatever differences they'd had in the past, it seemed they were over them. They'd both changed into the sweats the stewardesses handed out, and they'd both pulled their hair into low ponytails that highlighted their strong cheekbones. "You sure are beautiful," I told Pixie, and turned to Lainie. "Have I ever told you how much you take after your mother? Heart of a lioness, both of you."

Pixie hugged me around the neck for half a second, long enough to whisper in my ear that she loved me, then cuffed me in the shoulder, while her eyes teared up. "Quit sweet-talking me and my kid, and get over there by Letty, you fucking SOB."

Letty and Tangles were also on a three-seat sofa, buckled in. I took the seat between them. I kissed the top of Letty's head, then Tangles. They both looked up at me. For some reason, I thought of Camila, and her air kisses. I kissed them both again. Real kisses. Real hugs. I put my arms over their shoulders.

"I love you, Letty. Love you Tangles."

"I love you so much, Boss," Tangles said.

"Okay, so far so good. Plane seems to be flying fine," I said, buckling myself in.

"We are fifteen minutes from the airport where we will be landing," the captain said over the PA system. "As we descend, I will have to turn off the cabin lights."

"Boss, tell him to leave them on," Tangles said.

I spoke loud enough for the flight attendant in charge to hear me.

"Myrna tell the Captain not to dim or turn off the cabin lights if he can manage it."

"Will do, Mr. Luna."

Pixie said, "This reminds me of when I thought I was going to crash on that stupid plane the studio sent me in to Los Angeles."

"But you didn't crash. You landed at some airbase out in the desert. It took us ages to hear about it, and we were all at the airport for hours, freaking out, and scared you were dead, and the whole time you were flirting with a bunch of fanboys in uniform. Thanks for not being dead, girl. I would have missed you," Letty said.

Storm said, "I never heard that story. And I'm a big fan."

"Me neither," Andrea said. "And I'm a big fan too."

"Mami, do I have to hear that story again?" Lainie said, "We may be dead any minute."

"We're not going to be dead any minute," I said.

"For sure, bebita," Pixie said, her arm going around Lainie.

Letty and Tangles and I were taking this in. Pixie and Lainie had been fighting tooth and nail ever since Jason—may he rest in peace—had come between them. It was good to see they were making up.

Then BANG!

And another BANG!

It sounded like a pipe bomb exploding. Not that I have ever heard a pipe bomb explode, exactly. The closest thing I can compare the sound to is what I heard when IRA terrorists blew up the London pub Sami and I were drinking in.

That explosion had cost Sami her life. I could only hope no more tragedy was coming now.

The plane shuddered. My heart doesn't often race, but it was racing. Tangles was gripping my arm like it was a lifeline. On my other side, Letty was looking at me with such a look in her eyes. All the love in the world was there.

"Oh God, what was that?" Pixie shrieked.

"We just lost our second engine," the captain said on the PA system.

From where she was seated in the forward cabin, Myrna came on the PA System.

"Please put on your life jacket, then buckle right up again. Do NOT inflate the life jacket. Place your feet and knees together. Rest your feet firmly on the floor, then place your head against your upper thighs since you do not have seats in front of you. Cover your head with your hands like this."

Three other stewardesses came rushing through to help with the jackets. They were remarkably efficient, making sure we were belted in and in crash position again once the life jackets were on. I wondered how long momentum could maintain a glide without engines.

"Do not inflate your life jacket until we exit the plane through an emergency exit. We will guide you through this. Do not panic, please," each stewardess said.

"This is the brace position," I said. "Stay positive, all of you. We're going to make it, I promise. I promise."

Letty gave me another look. "Head in your laps, folks, and kiss your ass goodbye," she said, a brave dimple showing in her cheek.

I touched her face. Beside the bright orange of the life jacket, her face looked pale.

"Orange looks good on you," I said softly.

"We have a big landing field on the Pacific Ocean," the captain announced. Except for his voice, the cabin fell into complete silence. "It can't be much worse than landing on an aircraft carrier, which I did more than a thousand times. I have done this many times in a simulator. I will do my job, which is to land this plane. And you do yours, which is to stay calm, and do not move from your brace position, please."

"Tell the Captain to fly the plane," I told a stewardess. "We don't need real time updates."

Myrna ordered the other flight attendants to take their seats then went rushing from passenger to passenger to make sure everyone was braced properly and buckled into their deflated life jackets.

"Mr. Luna, the captain has the relief captain and copilot in the cockpit with him. He's fine."

"We're fine, too. Go take your seat, Myrna," I said.

The plane was descending. I'm no pilot but the engines were dead silent, and I could tell we were gliding. I pictured us falling straight down, but no, we were coasting.

I could not tell the passage of time. It was all happening too fast and felt like hours.

"I'm sorry Mr. Luna," the captain said. "I have to cut the lights."

If I had answered him, he would not have heard me.

The cabin went dark. The darkness made everything so much worse. Tangles and Letty and I were shoulder to shoulder. Tangles released the death grip on my arm and covered her head as she was supposed to. Letty and I covered our heads one-handed. We all held the brace position, heads down. I felt Letty groping for my hand, and we clutched each other. It seemed like we were going extremely fast. When the fuselage hit the water the first time, it felt like we were in a Bugatti going a hundred fifty miles per hour straight into a brick wall. Someone screamed. The impact was hard, and the plane still moving extremely fast as far as I could tell. Maybe we bounced, because we smacked the water again, the impact again, hard. And the noise! It was like a dying animal— cracking, popping, crunching metal, roaring water. It sounded like the plane was falling apart. No, like it was being ripped apart between our momentum and the opposite force of the water. I was waiting for some sign, some sense that it was time to help everyone off the plane. The plane bounced again, and there was another horrific shriek of metal, like giant hands ripping the plane into pieces. It struck me, the irony of dying in a plane crash, considering how I'd made my life. The metal, and the sound of the terrified people around me, the smell of ozone, and plane, and fuel, and fear, the seat bucking wildly beneath me, the sense of Letty at my side sharing this dark terror: everything was intensified by the dark. I was ready to release the seatbelt when—if—water rushed in. No reality existed but Letty's small hand in mine in the dark.

Epilogue

I closed my eyes and pictured the Virgin of Guadalupe.

I prayed. "Please spare everyone else. Virgencita, por favor." I had once prayed for Melina this way. Now I was praying that everyone else survive.

"Please take my life and let them live. Virgencita, they are the world to me."

I pictured how I had crawled up the aisle of the church in Mexico City, giving thanks for Melina's survival. For an instant I could feel the church around me, and the presense of the Virgin. But then I was flying through the darkness and the rolling sea. I felt a sharp pain in my head, and the world went black.

About the Author

George Hatcher is an entrepreneur with a gift for business and storytelling. Whether he's traveling the globe as a consultant/strategist for lawyers in high profile wrongful death cases, running one of his many enterprises, or at home with Molly amid the birds and cats in California, he's always got his eye on the next project. He does a whole lot more than what is mentioned here.

A longer bio is on his website at: www.georgehatcher.com/bio/bio.html

www.ingramcontent.com/pod-product-compliance
Lightning Source LLC
Chambersburg PA
CBHW070729120726
47910CB00001B/27